"You are taking me hostage," he said.

"I'm *not* taking you hostage," Syd replied.

He looked away, started to inch along the ledge with his back pressed up against the house. He had never stood this high up before. The ground seemed to rise and fall with every breath he took. The city shimmered across the horizon. Its heat bent the air. He realized he had no idea how he was going to get away from this silent neighborhood, let alone out of the city.

He hated to admit it, but he needed Knox. If he ran without Knox, he'd be easy to destroy. Having Knox with him gave Syd leverage.

Through the window beside them, they saw a flash as the bedroom door exploded open. Knox couldn't believe they'd gone in, even though, as far as they knew, he was Syd's hostage. Blasting in like that was what you did to end a standoff if you didn't care whether the hostage lived.

Syd was thinking the same thing.

"Fine," said Syd. "You're my hostage. Now, how do we get out of here? I don't think the Guardians are going to fall for an antique pen."

"They don't have to." Knox didn't elaborate. "Follow me."

And then, without warning, Knox leapt from the ledge and windmilled his arms through the air.

OTHER BOOKS YOU MAY ENJOY

PROXY

ALEX LONDON

speak

An Imprint of Penguin Group (USA)

For Tim, who inspired, Robert, who believed,
and Jill, who elevated

SPEAK
Published by the Penguin Group
Penguin Group (USA) LLC
375 Hudson Street
New York, New York 10014

USA * Canada * UK * Ireland * Australia
New Zealand * India * South Africa * China

penguin.com
A Penguin Random House Company

First published in the United States of America by Philomel Books,
an imprint of Penguin Young Readers Group, 2013
Published by Speak, an imprint of Penguin Group (USA) LLC, 2014

THE LIBRARY OF CONGRESS HAS CATALOGED THE PHILOMEL BOOKS EDITION AS FOLLOWS:
London, Alex.
Proxy / Alex London.
pages cm
ISBN 978-0-399-25776-6 (hc)
Summary: "Privileged Syd and his proxy, Knox, are thrown together to
overthrow the system."—Provided by publisher.
[1. Science fiction.] I. Title.
PZ7.L84188Pr 2013 [Fic]—dc23
20120339704

Speak ISBN 978-0-14-751133-1

Printed in the United States of America

1 3 5 7 9 10 8 6 4 2

Both were being denied their childhoods: the prince by a smothering excess of privilege, [the whipping boy] by none at all.

—Sid Fleischman

In the . . . landscape ahead, you will either create the software or you will be the software.

—Douglas Rushkoff

[1]

EVEN A PERFECT MACHINE wasn't built to go this fast.

Knox knew it, but still he pressed harder on the accelerator. Ripples of heat blurred the air around the car, and the girl in the passenger seat squealed.

Terror? Delight? Did it matter?

He took a turn too sharply, felt the stabilizer engine straining. His windshield lit up with warnings: lane markers flashing red, speed indicators blinking. Sweat beaded on his upper lip, but the car held the road.

R U glitched? popped up in his datastream in translucent green letters. He could see through them to the pavement, but they were impossible to ignore.

He glanced at the girl, giggling to cover her nerves.

They curved up the speedway, slicing like heat lightning over the slums of the Lower City, past the blast barriers and security fences, rising higher and higher. There were parts of the Mountain City you just didn't go to if you were lux, parts you didn't even see. The city below them blurred. The city beside them gleamed. Knox accelerated.

srsly?! blinked double sized in front of Knox, each letter wiggling and changing colors. The font was chunky; the y swished like a cat's tail. Very retro. Probably custom-made for her by some trendy for-hire coder. Her hands waved in the air in front of the windshield, swiping out another text. ☺ she added.

Suddenly, her smiley face vanished.

Reduce Speed . . . Reduce Speed . . . Reduce Speed . . . scrolled in front of Knox in an unfriendly industrial font. All the road signs and advertisements now said the same thing: DANGER DANGER DANGER.

Knox waved off the augmented-reality hookup. You weren't supposed to be able to turn it off, but Knox had yet to find a security system he couldn't hack. AR driving was for amateurs and accountants anyway. He gunned the car forward. The speed pressed him against the auto-cooled leather seats.

"You even know how to drive?" the girl cried out loud, her voice shrill and excited.

Knox didn't say a word. He liked to let the growl of the engine do the talking.

He also couldn't remember the girl's name.

Amy? Pam?

Something old-fashioned. He shot her another glance, his emerald eyes flashing mischief. He smirked.

That usually did the trick.

She was new in Mr. Kumar's History of Robotics class, a transfer from homeschooling. She liked the animations Knox hacked onto the public display on top of their teacher's scowling face. Sometimes Knox gave Mr. Kumar devil horns or a top hat or made it look like he was lecturing them from a seedy strip club in the Lower City. The girl had complimented Knox's work on her first day at school.

Mr. Kumar never had any idea his image had been hacked. He just talked away from his wood-paneled office at EduCorp. He couldn't figure out why the kids always laughed so hard at his lectures. Not that he could do anything about it. They were all paying customers and could laugh all they wanted. That was a perk of going to a top-tier patron school. The customer was always right.

Knox had a knack for hacking datastreams, but school wasn't really his thing. He could do the work when he wanted, when he had the right motivation, but grades weren't it. A girl—any girl really—now *that* was good motivation.

Curvy, skinny, smart, dumb, Retroprep or NeoBuddhist, Causegirl or Partygirl, it didn't matter to him. They all had something beautiful in them. He loved finding out what it was. And they loved letting him.

Knox knew his assets. With a few little hacks of a holo projection or two, a green-eyed wink, and a lopsided smirk, he could get most girls to do anything.

Well, almost anything. *Absolutely* anything would take this drive in the borrowed silver CX-30 and an after-hours tour of the patrons' zoo on the edge of the city. Girls loved extinct animals, didn't they?

Scare them with a few hairpin turns, show them a live polar bear and some real penguins, and then, cue the melting into his arms. This wasn't his first time down this road.

"You ready to meet a polar bear?" he asked her.

She giggled again.

"What's so funny? Polar bears were deadly creatures. Carnivorous, fearless, and wild. You have to be careful around them."

"Sounds like someone I know."

"Me?" He feigned innocence. "I'm harmless as a puppy dog."

"Yeah, but are you housebroken?"

Oh yes, Knox liked this one.

Emily? Ann? Sue?

He couldn't ask her now. If they were at one of his father's parties, he could introduce her to people, get her to say her name to the vice president of Birla Nanotech or something. But it was just the two of them in the car and it would be just the two of them at the zoo. What did names matter, anyway? Knox didn't plan to do much talking.

He swiped through his datastream, clutching the wheel with just his palms, and locked on to a holo of a long-faced puppy, its tail wagging and its little pink tongue hanging out. It bounded to her side of the windshield and licked her in 3-D. She laughed. It was an old stock pic; he'd used it a thousand times before, but it never failed him.

She waved her fingers around the glowing projection in the air and tossed a text back to Knox.

CUTE lit up on the windshield in front of him.

She wasn't just talking about the puppy. Knox half smiled and bit down on his lower lip.

She noticed. He was watching the road, but he knew that she noticed.

Alice? Debbie?

Her mother was on one of those Benevolent Society volunteer committees. Saving the orphans or matching organ donors or something. Maybe both. They'd go well together. Her father was a mining executive for one of the big firms, data not dirtware. The real value was in data. He was a client of Knox's father's company, but that didn't narrow it down much. Everyone was a client of Knox's father's company.

Her father was bald, right? Knox thought he remembered a shiny bald head when he'd met the man. Must be nostalgia, like her old-fashioned name. No one with money needed to go bald. He was probably a history buff. Or was that the last girl's father? It was hard to keep these fathers and their hobbies straight. Charming fathers was so much more work than charming their daughters, with so much less reward.

The girl's family must have some cred. You couldn't get into their high school without paying for it, no outside sponsors allowed. And you couldn't get eyes like hers without some serious biotech. They practically glowed purple. Her dark hair also had a hint of purple, probably designed to match. The DNA install for that kind of work must have been a nightmare for the coders who wrote it. Very lux.

Knox eased on the straightaway. He was way above the suggested maximum speed, and he was way below the suggested minimum age. He'd stolen company property from his father's private lot; he'd violated the restricted speedway, violated driving regulations. He planned to do some more violating before the night was over. In the end, someone would have to pay for it.

Everything costs.

But really, who would set the access code to a brand-new CX-30 Roadster as 1-2-3-4-5 and not expect his son to take it for spin? If anyone was to blame, it was his father. Knox was sixteen. He was just doing what came naturally.

Like the polar bears.

And look where that got them.

"What's so funny?" the girl asked, seeing Knox chuckle.

"Just thinking about polar bears," he said and he reached over to squeeze her thigh.

That was his first mistake.

The next two came in quick succession.

The car swerved slightly toward the guardrail when he took his right hand off the wheel. At that speed, on manual drive, it took both hands to keep the vehicle straight. He'd have known that if he had ever taken a manual driving class.

He hadn't.

He overcompensated for the swerve, jerking the wheel toward the center lane. That was his second mistake.

His heart skipped a beat as he felt himself losing control. If he hadn't shut off the augmented reality driving, it would have taken over right then. These cars drove themselves if you let them.

Instead, he tried to brake.

Mistake number three.

An alarm sounded. The car jackknifed, spun sideways, and flipped over at 162 mph.

Airborne.

The stabilizer engine screeched helplessly at the sky.

Or maybe that was the girl.

He felt the car hit the ground and roll. The entire universe shattered into blinking lights and screaming metal. He heard a crunch, a snap of bone. He felt like he'd been punched in the throat.

There was heat, an intense heat, and an invisible fist pulled the air out of his lungs and ripped the sound from his ears. He couldn't hear anything now, no screaming, no screeching, just the blood rushing to his head. He thought he was upside down. Twisted metal pinned his arms to his sides. He felt the urge to laugh. There was a warm wetness on his face and he tasted something metallic.

And then darkness.

[2]

DARKNESS.

Nothing but darkness.

What could be wrong?

Syd swiped and twisted; he dragged and dropped.

Still nothing.

He tried resetting the power source, rebooting the software. When that failed, he tried the oldest repair trick he knew: whacking the thing with his palm.

Nothing.

He couldn't get a holo to project. There was just a void hanging midair in the hallway.

Syd shook his head and handed the kid back the beat-up piece of plastic he used as his datastream projector. "There's no connection between the projector and your biofeed. No input. Broken beyond repair."

The boy didn't deign to take the small device back, even though it belonged to him. "So, like, what? You're saying you can't fix it?"

"I'm saying no one can fix it. It's not picking up your signal anymore. Could be the receiver, could be that you aren't transmitting anything to receive." Syd looked down at the kid, some snot-nosed first-year, zit pocked and sneering, trying to look tough because he figured he was being scammed. Probably not a bad assumption to make, but Syd wasn't scamming him. Life in the Valve was hard enough without everyone trying to get one over on everybody else all the time. Even in high school.

EduCorp scammed the teachers, the teachers scammed the students, and the students scammed one another. Maybe somebody learned something along the way, maybe not. But everybody paid.

Syd was just trying to get his certificate and get out without owing anybody else anything.

The kid's lip quivered.

Exams were coming up for the first-years, the kid whined. How was he supposed to get through them with no datastream access? He couldn't afford a new biofeed install. He already had eighteen years of debt, he said, and he'd just started high school. Blood work cost, what, another three years at least?

"What am I supposed to do?" he pleaded. "I've already been volunteered for two weeks of swamp drainage because of a stupid prank my patron pulled."

He went on whining. He needed new malaria meds and sunblocker patches. Probably another six months of debt right there. He couldn't pay for new software in his blood on top of all that. He'd have to repeat the whole year at full price if he didn't make the tests.

"Bribe the test proctor?" Syd suggested. Half the kids did that. Some of them didn't even show up at all, just paid for their grades. Easy to do if you didn't mind borrowing the credit. Credit was easy. Studying was hard.

The kid made a face like he'd been hit in the stomach. No go on the bribe.

Syd felt for the kid. He couldn't afford to bribe the teachers either. Not without borrowing himself into oblivion or starving himself to death.

The floodgates broke; the kid wept, standing in the green tiled hallways of Vocation High School IV. His shoulders shook and he buried his face in his hands.

Syd stared at the wet armpit circles on the kid's shirt. The climate control was out again. Nothing smelled worse than three thousand sweating teenagers trapped in a concrete bunker of a building made for half that number. The Valve was at the lowest point in the Mountain City, where the wet heat lingered, unmoved by the breezes that kept the peaks of the Upper City comfortable. Breezes were for people who could afford them. All the Lower City kids got was the heat of nature's indifference.

Other kids stared at Syd as they passed, shaking their heads, rolling their eyes, whispering to one another. Shoulder bump after shoulder bump.

Syd ran his hand through his short hair and his fingers tapped absently on the birthmark behind his ear. The mark was changing. He'd had it as long as he could remember, but in the last few month, it had been growing, little black dot by little black dot, like pixels. The dots had formed shapes, four of them, darkening day by day. He worried that maybe it wasn't a birthmark. Maybe it was cancer. Or plague blemishes.

Were those a thing?

He didn't know. But he couldn't afford to have a cancer patch installed to correct it. Talk about debt. Medical installs cost a fortune; at least, medical installs that wouldn't make you sicker than you already were.

Syd had more to worry about than this crying first-year and his broken datastream.

Advos based on the kid's purchase profile flashed on the walls around them. Some off-brand acne care called Pus-Popper and three flavors of Fiberizer Diet Supplements from EpiCure Incorporated.

"Hey, your advos are still working." Syd pointed at the wall where the advertisements were displayed. "At least your biofeed is still broadcasting."

"Those aren't mine." The kid denied it. Of course he denied it.

This was not helping Syd with his image. The advos were linked to your biofeed, read off the scanners that picked up everyone's background radiation. If you had a biofeed installed in your blood—and everyone in the Mountain City did—then your advos belonged to you and you alone; your body was networked. If those advos weren't the kid's, that'd mean that they were Syd's. Syd did not want everyone thinking he needed PusPoppers or Fiberizer Diet Supplements.

These advos were so not his.

Syd kept his purchase profile boring. Most of the sales pitches he saw were for dehydrated noodles. Original sodium flavor. He didn't like to make it easy on the predictive marketing software. He bought as little as possible and used the black market whenever he could. Of course, the black market sold its data upstream to the legit companies too, but they didn't care if the data was accurate or not. They got the same price for a lie as they did for the truth.

Everything costs.

"You could just drop out." Syd tried to stop the kid's crying. "Go to the recycling yards, work as a runner? Or join the Rebooters to fight the system." Syd held up his fist in mock solidarity. "Bring on the Jubilee."

The kid shook his head.

"Guess you're not a Causehead," said Syd, lowering his fist. He couldn't blame the kid. Syd didn't believe in all that Jubilee stuff either. Universal debt forgiveness was a pipe dream and the Rebooters were a bunch of losers living out in the wastelands, eating rats and waiting for their debtor messiah or something. Even their corporate terrorism was laughable. When they blew up a datacenter, three more went online in its place. When they trashed a protein depot, the price of food went up for everyone and EpiCure hit record profits. Rebooter anti-market actions had been integrated into the market. There was no changing the system. Best you could do was get yourself clear of it any way possible.

"You could sell an eye for hard cash?" Syd suggested. "Sell a kidney? One of the dupe organs anyway."

That suggestion only made things worse. The kid blew a loud blast of tear snot and wiped it on his sleeve. Charming.

"Calm down," Syd groaned, a trickle of sweat running down between his shoulder blades. The small of his back felt like a swamp. "I was kidding." He put his hand on the kid's shoulder, because what else was he supposed to do? The boy lowered his hands from his face. Syd stooped to look the kid right in the eyes. "What's your name?" he asked.

"Tom," the kid sniffed. "Tom Sawyer."

Tom Sawyer.

Of course. The name said it all: a refugee and an orphan, renamed from a database. Probably a West Coaster by the sound of his accent.

No wonder he had all that debt. It came with the name. The Benevolent Society charged ten years for a "rescue" from the desert and another three for installing the datastream into your blood. Three more years got tacked on for foster care, and two more just to get into school. That made eighteen altogether. Syd knew that eighteen years of debt well.

He had it himself.

Syd sighed.

Why was he such a sucker for these charity cases? *He* was

a charity case. Sixteen years old and eighteen years in debt to the Xelon Corporation. Once you got so deep into debt, it was almost impossible to get out. Civilization wasn't free.

But it was better than the alternative. Better than life in the swamps or the desert or the ruins of some squatter city out in the badlands. Better than going freelance, out of the system, scrounging in the dumps for recycling, working a corner for the syntholene gangs or in a hacker pharm, going blind writing cut-rate codes for the Maes gang. It sure beat getting rolled for your organs, used as meatware.

Some would consider Syd lucky. He had access to credit. He got to be in school. He got to be out of the hustle, if he chose, if he wanted to take on the debt.

His problem was, he didn't want to.

Egan, his best friend, the one guy he trusted in the whole damned city, had like thirty or forty years of debt by now—he was always buying the newest biopatch, up-dating himself with new eye colors or hair colors or skin colors, buying data-enabled contact lenses from the Upper City, tiny projectors that slid under his fingernails, crazy climate-control clothing. He went out all the time too, got girls presents, and did whatever designer patch was popular with the patron kids up above.

Egan didn't care. His patron was a saint, never got in trouble. Egan never had to do hard labor. He never got hit with an EMD stick. He never had to teach his patron a lesson about responsibility.

Syd wasn't so lucky.

He'd missed more nonrefundable school days for "volunteer work"—Xelon corporate code for forced labor—than anybody else in his class. He felt like he'd hauled every ton of cement in the Hayek Memorial Dam up the mountain by himself and single-handedly ripped all the copper wire from all of Old Denver. He figured his was the worst patron anyone had ever had in all of history.

But that was the system. Patrons owned the debt and proxies took their punishments. A simple contract, a free market. Debts had to be paid.

The work built Syd's muscles up so that he didn't have to worry so much about Maes gang thugs giving him a beating, but it was murder on his knees. He'd been hit with an EMD stick more times than he could count. Electro-muscular disruption fried your nerves, but you could endure anything once you got used to it. By now, Syd was very used to it.

Still, just two more years of debt and Syd would be no one's proxy, his own man. The thought pulled him through. Soon he'd never have to owe anybody anything ever again.

He worked in the back of an illegal repair shop in the Valve, and he studied hard and he avoided the corners and the dumps and whatever new schemes Egan cooked up. He put in his time with his head down. For friends he had Egan and dating wasn't even a remote possibility. Not for him, not in the Valve. Easier to keep to himself.

And yet, Syd knew, he wasn't going to let Tom Sawyer drop out because of a busted biofeed. He never could say no to someone desperate.

Syd was a sucker.

"All right, Tom." He sighed. "Just get through the day, okay?" He dropped the projector into the boy's shaking hands. His fingertips left sweaty smudges on the cheap plastic. "You know Mr. Baram's shop? Down by the runoff?"

Tom shook his head. Syd rolled his eyes, but brought up his datastream again.

"UtiliBoots! Give your other boots the boot," an advo squawked. "Now with burn retardant dura—"

He swiped the advo away and brought up a holo of the entire Mountain City, with the swirling roads and private communities of the Upper City blurred out—wouldn't want undesirables learning their way around. The chaotic jumble of the Lower City appeared in perfect detail. He zoomed in on the shop near the dried-up river in the heart of the Valve.

"Meet me there after school," he said. "Maybe I can rig something to get you back on the datastream for a while."

Tom smiled and for a second Syd was afraid the boy was going to give him a hug, but he ran off to class instead, and Syd stood alone in the middle of the emptying hall, sweating by himself. Advos for hair product and the newest holo games flashed at the edge of his vision. He watched through the glowing map floating in the middle of the hallway as Tom disappeared around the corner.

And then, without him doing a thing, the map vanished and a message appeared:

Report immediately to the school aid station.

Syd stared at the words.

The aid station.

Maybe he really was sick. His fingers went to the birthmark behind his ear again. It sat on that lump of bone where his ear met his skull and he found the thumping sound calming.

He didn't feel sick. He felt fine. Other than the fear of slow, painful death from some undiagnosed disease, he felt fine.

Report immediately to the school aid station flashed again in front of him. This time he noticed the logo of the Xelon Corporation in the hologram. He reached up and swiped the projection out of the air.

This wasn't about his health. This was about his patron. What had the brat done this time?

[3]

"YOU'RE LATE, MR. CARTON." Mr. Thompson's face glowered from the holo projected on top of the bot at the front of the classroom.

"I . . . uh . . ." Syd stared up at it as it rolled toward him. He swayed on his feet and rubbed his arm where the bot at the aid station had shoved a needle in. He shuddered at the memory. He really hated needles.

"*I, uh* is hardly an excuse," Mr. Thompson snapped. "Do you expect the entire district to wait for you?"

"No, sir," Syd muttered, knowing that his words were being broadcast to four other classrooms across the Lower City at the same time. There were about fifty kids in each one, which meant he was being called out in front of two hundred people. So much for keeping his head down.

"I was at the aid station. I had to give blood."

"So we are all to be punished for *your* obligations?" Mr. Thompson demanded.

"No, sir." Syd wobbled. He worried he was going to pass out. He was having trouble focusing. They'd taken a lot of blood.

The aid station bot hadn't explained *why* he had to give blood, just that he did or he would be in violation of his debt contract. The blood was *required* of him.

That was the only answer he could get, but it was from an official Xelon datastream, so he had to obey. The aid station bot also had EMD capabilities. He'd prefer a simple blood donation to an EMD blast any day.

So he'd closed his eyes, looked away as the needle went in, as his blood flowed through a tube into the medical bot. He'd heard the term "blood debt," but he'd never had to donate blood to his patron before. He always thought blood debt was some sort of historical thing. Why should his blood pay a debt?

Then again, why shouldn't it? Value is in the eye of the creditor, as they say.

The debt paid, the bot let him stagger his way to class. Now that he was there, he just wanted to sit down and be left alone.

"It won't happen again," he mumbled and rushed to take his seat.

"See that it doesn't, or it'll be a fine on your account." The holo of Mr. Thompson's face followed him as he crossed the room. The bot was an old teaching model, but their school didn't get lux equipment for anything. Mr. Thompson was probably in an office somewhere in the Upper City in front of a bank of monitors, enjoying the climate control and the fact that he would never have to meet his students in person.

The bot was seven feet tall and sat on a large swivel ball that made it maneuverable in any direction and impossible to tip over. It had multiple channels of video and sound to pick up the whole room, though half of them were jammed with simple jabber apps. There was also a transmitter for uploading and downloading from the students' datastreams, and that was a lot harder to jam. EduCorp proprietary software. Interference with biodata transmission was punishable by hard labor and six additional months of debt for each count. No one bothered with those hacks. The crime was not worth the punishment.

Once Syd sat, the bot went back to pacing, rolling over the tile with a mechanical purr and a disconcerting click where the tiles weren't level. It would be pacing the same way in all the classrooms where Mr. Thompson taught. He probably had it on an auto-pacing program designed for "dynamic instruction to meet the developmental needs of the modern vocational student."

Educational jargon. Syd had read the manual.

Syd had read all the manuals.

His boss at the shop where he worked bought them off the black market so Syd would know how to repair or modify anything that came in. It wasn't technically legal, but the Valve security companies looked the other way. Every business in the Valve broke some regulation or another. It was the only way to survive. As long as only small rules were being broken, no one cared. If you lived in the Valve, lawlessness wasn't a vice, it was a life skill.

Syd's transmitter vibrated the moment he sat down. He tapped it and brought up a tiny projection on the palm of his hand, small enough that only he could see it.

Blud? Egan's text popped up in his cupped hand. They messed with their spelling so the EduCorp wordworm didn't pick up on their conversation.

Syd looked up at Egan and shrugged.

Egan fired another text off and Syd looked down at it.

Yr pAtrOn = a$$. Egan shook his head, sympathetic.

Syd didn't disagree. Egan changed the subject.

wHt's w/the sndRat? Sawyer . . . nw b/f?

Sandrat. That's what they called the West Coasters and anyone from the lowlands around the Mountain City. There was no civilization left out there, just desert sand and festering refugee camps. To the east were the pestilential swamps and the radioactive cities. They couldn't even support refugee camps. If you came from the east, you were a swampcat. Like Syd.

y? u jeLus? Syd texted back. He ignored Egan's sandrat comment. They'd been friends forever, though lately it seemed like they had a lot more history than current events. Egan was always tweaked on something.

u Wsh. Egan's eyes flickered. He didn't use a projection.

He got his datastream from contact lenses, right against the eye. Very lux. Private projectors did not come cheap and with these lenses, you couldn't even tell Egan was getting data, except that he blinked more than usual and his eyes didn't seem to focus on anything. Although Egan's eyes never seemed to focus on anything anyway, lenses or no. A side effect of syntholene. Or maybe its intended effect.

yr nt my Typ, Syd replied. 2 sKnny.

stLL crShing on Atticus Finch?

Sht up. Syd swiped.

oo la la he so hndsme . . . u wunt 2 kiss kiss w/him . . .

Atticus Finch, a sandrat who was going places, a skilled gamer with sponsors and everything. He wouldn't be living in the Valve for long and it didn't hurt that he was easy on the eyes.

imd, Syd replied.

mega tmi.

Unauthorized text flashed across the palm of Syd's hand and suddenly he was staring at Mr. Thompson's face hovering in front of his fingers. Egan flinched. He'd just gotten an eyeful of the old coot. Thompson could multitask, that was true. He'd hacked them without stopping his lesson for a second.

Syd looked up from the teacher's face in his palm and saw that he was staring down at them from the holo on his bot too, double faces glowering at Syd and Egan.

"There is an old saying, gentlemen," Mr. Thompson declared. "It goes: Secrets, Secrets Are No Fun. Secrets, Secrets Come Undone."

Suddenly, their brief conversation went public, projected into every datastream in the class, in all five classrooms across the city.

Kid's he'd never meet, never would meet, were reading Syd's texts with his best friend. Years of keeping his head down, gone in a flash of data, just like that. Instantaneous.

Egan shrugged it off, but Syd turned rust red. Kids glanced back at him, muttering, their own unauthorized texts pouring out in torrents. He saw a dozen hands drop down, colors in their palms as covert holo projections exploded with the new info, a handheld light show of Syd's humiliation.

"Projections on desks please," Mr. Thompson barked, and the palm-sized glows rose and flattened onto the tables in front of each kid.

A few rows up, Atticus Finch raised his projection straight over his head. He glanced back at Syd and his perfect lips sneered. On the holo above him a message popped up in bright red, clear to Syd from across the room, clear to everyone. It was fully spelled, wordworm be damned: Don't look at me, You Chapter 11 Punk.

Atticus put his index fingers up and banged them together in Syd's direction.

"To you too!" Egan grunted and did the same right back, but Atticus had already turned away.

Syd pressed his hands into his eyes, shutting out the world.

Chapter 11.

Slang for guys like him. A bankrupt 1 and 1, a binary

insult. Two of the same thing pressed together. The old way of saying it was homo.

So much for a private life.

Everyone probably suspected it already—he'd never had a girlfriend—but now they knew, right there in undeniable digital. Syd had a thing for Atticus Finch, or at least for the *idea* of Atticus Finch, just like all the Fangirls did.

He sank into his chair.

Class continued. Something about the emancipation of the working class through open credit markets, but it was boring stuff. Ancient history. Syd stewed where he sat.

"Hey," Egan whispered, not daring another text message. "Don't worry about it. Thompson's a knockoff of a man. Don't let him get to you."

"I'm not worried about Thompson," Syd whispered back.

"You could do better than Atticus Finch."

"Shut up, okay?"

"I guess you like 'em dumb, huh?"

"Just. Shut. Up."

"How about the sandrat with the busted projector? He . . . uh . . . open for your sort of business?"

"You aren't helping."

"Relax. If anyone messes with you, you tell me. They'll regret it."

"*You're* messing with me."

"Other than me."

Syd sighed. He knew Egan was as good as his word. He was ruthless and always had been, but he valued loyalty above all else. He didn't care that Syd was a Chapter 11, as long as he was loyal.

Egan had come to the orphanage around the same time Syd did, though Egan was local. Not a refugee, just unwanted. When they first arrived at the orphanage, they were assigned to share a sleeping compartment. It was an accident of fate, but it worked.

Egan called Syd "swampcat" until they were eight years old. Then Syd hit a growth spurt first and punched Egan in the face. He called Syd "Syd" from then on. Syd had only ever called Egan by his name.

They stuck together. They looked after each other and fought with each other and fought for each other. They told each other their plans and their dreams and their secrets. Some of them were even true. They were, in short, best friends.

After Syd took up working and living in the shop, Egan kept freelancing for the security firms. He trashed stores that competitors were supposed to protect, stole from other people's clients, and looked out for anyone who'd come into some success and might want a little peace of mind. Syd never had a talent for that kind of commerce and he had no interest in salvage picking or selling himself to leering old has-beens. Egan, however, didn't mind getting dirty. Blood washed off easier than poverty.

Blood. Syd couldn't tell if he was lightheaded from giving away half his blood or if he was lightheaded from shame, but he definitely needed to lie down.

Instead, he stared at the public projection of the day's lesson in front of him. Thompson had moved on to the Nigerian Trade Embargo.

"Hey, Syd," Egan whispered again. "Syd!" He was not about to let Syd just tune out and pass the time in peace.

"Why are you even here today?" Syd whispered back at him. "I thought you paid Thompson off every week?"

"It's not all about grades," Egan said, wrinkling his eyebrows at Syd's tone. "And don't get snippy with me, princess. I came to school for *you*."

"To ruin my life?"

"To make your day," Egan smiled. "Tonight. Upper City party. Mega lux. Patrons only. Supposed to be insane. Party of the year."

"Right."

"I'm serious. It's exclusive."

"So how are you going to get in?"

Egan glanced up at the robot pacing in the front of the class. He leaned closer to Syd. "You mean *we*. How are *we* going to get in?" He smiled a fiend's smile. "I know a patron. Guy can get me inside and he's got a hookup for two ID patches that'll get us past the scanners. My treat."

"I've got to work."

"It doesn't even start until midnight. I know you're not working at midnight."

"You know dancing's not really my thing," Syd tried, but Egan was relentless when he got an idea in his head.

"Not your thing? You ever been to a patron's party

before? Everyone's beautiful, Syd. Everyone. And they don't have hangups like in the Valve. They're Upper City. They're all, like, NeoHumanists or something. You can be as eleven as you wanna be. No one'll judge the lust of your loins."

Syd's face flushed. "You're disgusting."

"I'm desperate," said Egan. "You gotta come with me."

"Why do you care so much if I'm there?"

"Because girls love a Chapter 11 guy," he said, as if it were obvious. "I need you to be my sidekick."

"Pass."

"Oh, you cannot leave me hanging. You. Can. Not." Egan looked serious. Furious. This was a matter of principle. Not going would be an unforgivable breach of Egan's unwritten contract for their friendship, signed in so much blood over so many years.

"Fine." Syd caved, sighing.

"Good," said Egan and turned back toward the front of the classroom, acting as if he were looking at the graph that Mr. Thompson had displayed on a public projection. "Come by my place at ten," he whispered. "I'll give you clothes. You can't wear those run-down Valve rags. People expect a certain standard from a homosexual."

"How do you know so much about it?" Syd smirked.

"Like I said: You wish." Egan smirked back. "Just don't be late. I don't want all the girls taken by the time we get there."

Syd shut his eyes. The day just kept getting longer. Now,

in addition to helping pathetic Tom Sawyer fix his broken transmitter and figuring out how to avoid Atticus Finch for the rest of his life, he had to get ready for some lux happening in the Upper City that, like all of Egan's schemes, was sure to be more trouble than it was worth.

How was it not even noon?

[4]

MR. BARAM'S SHOP WAS on the left bank of what used to be the South Platte River. It'd been dammed for a few years now. People in the Valve couldn't draw their drinking water from it for free anymore, nor could they bathe or wash their clothes for free. Which was kind of the point: basic economics. Scarcity creates value.

Syd's workroom/bedroom was a windowless closet in the back. Not pretty, but it did have its own entrance from the alley, which he often left propped open. Mr. Baram spent a fortune on wasted coolant, but Syd liked the fresh air, even when it was hot and humid. He liked the *idea* of fresh air.

The early evening had cooled off a bit and a tiny, putrid breeze whipped up the garbage in the alley. Syd watched the trash dance by the open door while he put his feet up on the workbench and leaned back on the high stool.

He heard the Changs arguing across the alley, shouting about the latest recycling numbers. Mrs. Chang did most of the shouting. Mr. Chang did most of the apologizing. There wasn't enough scrap metal in the world to satisfy Mrs. Chang. She had plans for her children and not a bit of debt and she aimed to keep it that way.

"It's all I found," Mr. Chang said. "I tried."

"You can buy a ticket to Lagos with *trying* now?" Mrs. Chang groaned. "The Nigerians open their border up again just for *trying*? No money, sir, but we tried! Ha! And ask my mother if *trying* will treat her melanoma, eh? You want bad blood for her? You *trying* to kill my mother? Is that your kind of *trying*? I'll tell you, you are trying my patience is what you're trying!"

Syd peered out the door and made eye contact with Mr. Chang, who smiled meekly. Mrs. Chang spat and shut their door, yelling all the while.

Syd closed his eyes. His fingers ran back to the birthmark again. He rubbed it, but felt nothing. It was smooth and flat. He tapped on it, doing his own trying. He was trying not to worry about what the mark might mean, what kind of blood work he might have to buy to treat it. He was trying to make the thumping of his finger match his heartbeat. Deep breaths. Put the horrible day at school behind him.

He couldn't believe the perverted hacks that his classmates had blasted into his datastream all day. Whenever his projector came on, some filthy image would appear, complete with hi-fi sound, and he'd have to debug and delete before the EduCorp PicturePeeper software noticed. Porno on the holos in school? That would mean fines for sure, and maybe a bribe to avoid getting expelled.

Egan would probably be happy getting expelled. Syd, however, did not want to find himself at the mercy of the streets or Egan's neophyte criminal enterprises. He knew exactly what became of guys like him outside the system.

The advos had caught on too, trying to sell him new things to match his public humiliation. Suddenly he was seeing hair products and eyelash extenders and colognes. The advos were as insulting as they were pointless. He didn't intend to buy any of it.

He spent most of the day at school ignoring the holos and trying not to pass out from blood loss. It'd been a relief to get to work. Mr. Baram gave him a juice—real fruit juice from who knows where—and his body felt better almost instantly. As for his anxious mind, there was plenty of work to keep that occupied.

When the South Platte got dammed up, there had been unintended consequences. Toxic sludge pooled where the water once flowed and pestilent mosquitoes flourished in the pools; there had been a brief outbreak of malaria, followed by a longer problem with cholera and some unidentified brain fever. Health deteriorated and debts increased. Thousands died. The squatter settlements on the banks disappeared.

The consequences probably weren't unintended at all.

The squatters had to go somewhere. Housing blocks—giant concrete cruciplexes—were built. The squatters were rounded up and resettled. Some formed new settlements and tried to stay one step ahead of the private security companies paid to shut them down. The threat of eviction hung over everyone below.

The security companies also enforced minor contracts, coerced new customers for whatever enterprise had hired them, and retrieved payment for unredeemed debts. All of these companies needed cheap parts and repairs and that's where Mr. Baram and Syd came in.

The shop wasn't licensed, so Syd never got to fix any of the high-end stuff. He didn't really even fix anything new. But Mr. Baram's shop was the place to go to get junk working again, whether it was spider-sized scanner bots or mechanized holding cells the size of garbage bins. They'd refurbish, repair, and rebuild with no questions asked. They bought and sold parts too, also no questions asked. Syd took care of most of the repairing while Mr. Baram took care of the buying and selling and not asking questions.

Mr. Baram also had a room off to the side where local kids who didn't go to school gamed on his old holo sets in the cool of his climate-controlled shop. Some of the kids might have even been his. No one knew for sure. He didn't charge the young ones for the hours they spent playing games. He took his payment from them in other ways. There were feral kids running around all over the Valve and no one paid them any attention.

That made them useful to Mr. Baram.

He used them to gather information and to run messages, to warn him if any of the private security thugs were coming around. Everyone paid somebody for protection, and the security companies targeted one another's clients as a matter of policy. Businesses often paid three or four different gangs at the same time, but Mr. Baram paid none. He did business with everyone and everyone needed his skills. He also had a concrete storefront with heavy bars on the windows and a military-grade fracture cannon behind the counter. You'd need an army to lay siege to his store. As far as places to live went, it wasn't so bad at all.

If it weren't for the nightmares, Syd could have slept easy inside Baram's.

"Tell me something, Sydney." Mr. Baram surprised Syd, appearing in the open door to the back alley. Syd dropped his finger from behind his ear. He didn't like revealing his personal tics. Mr. Baram raised his eyebrows for a quick instant, then took a drag on one of the expensive Upper City cigarettes he always seemed to have a carton of.

"Yes, sir?" Syd took his feet off the workbench and sat up straight.

"Is it true you are giving away more repairs to the needy urchins of this forsaken city?" Mr. Baram chuckled to himself because he already knew the answer. He always already knew the answer.

"I'll keep track of anything I use," said Syd. "You can take it out of my pay."

"Ah, who would I be to punish a boy for his charity?" He stubbed his cigarette out with his toe just outside the doorway. He stepped inside. "But you should keep your kindness in a harder place. You wear it in your hair and every *schnorrer* from here to the Upper City can smell it."

"They can smell it in my hair?" Syd ribbed him. "Is that some kind of saying?"

Mr. Baram was always making up little turns of phrase as if everyone said them. Half the time they made no sense. He claimed his great-grandfather Amichai was a chief rabbi in the Holy Land, before the wars. He claimed he had the blood of sages in his veins. And he figured if he threw some of his old language into it, it made the saying authentic.

"It could be a saying," Mr. Baram declared. "I just said it, didn't I? And what do you know about proverbs? Your people were goat herders in the Holy Land."

"Who says my people were ever in the Holy Land? You don't know who my people were. I don't know who my people were. No one knows who my people were."

"I can tell these things."

"Because I'm brown?"

"Because, my ignorant young friend, we are kindred spirits. Somewhere, long ago, I think your people were in the Holy Land. Backwards, goat-herding idol worshippers, but there in the mix, certainly. Why else do you think I hired you?"

"Because I have small hands and I don't steal."

"These things are all true," Mr. Baram answered. "But that doesn't make them my reasons. Perhaps not even I know my reasons."

"I'm sure your reasons are as noble as your visage," Syd joked.

"My visage, eh?" Mr. Baram chuckled. "You've been reading through my library."

"You should password protect it if you don't want readers."

"Oh, I want readers, my boy." Mr. Baram sighed. "A world of readers I want, and yet, all I have is you. You want information, mere data, just like everyone else. That's not reading. Wisdom? Inspiration? Phfft! Their time has passed, eh?" He waved his hand in the air. "You cannot nourish the soul with data!"

"You're worried about something, huh?" Syd asked. Mr. Baram only got philosophical when he was nervous.

"The world being what it is, only a fool is not worried about something."

"Yeah, but you're not worried about earthquakes or solar flares or Sino-Nigerian arms pacts," said Syd. "You've got a new worry."

"And how do you know?" Mr. Baram leaned on the table. He'd taught Syd how to cold-read people and now he was testing him.

"Well, first off, you were spouting deep nonsense about the Holy Land and goat herders and nourishing the soul, which you only do when you're nervous. Second, you put your cigarette out outside, which you only do when you don't want the store to smell like smoke, which you only want when someone important is coming by. Third, you're wearing a new shirt. And fourth, you stood totally still when I said you were worried about something, and every muscle in your face froze, which was you trying not to give anything away, and which gave everything away."

Mr. Baram looked at him for a long minute. His nostrils flared and his eyes blazed. Syd thought he might get hit. It wouldn't be the first time. Mr. Baram could be moody, especially when he was nervous.

But he broke out in a wide smile and put his hand on Syd's shoulder. "You've learned very well," he said, laughing. "I knew you weren't a hopeless case. Ever since you were a little boy, I knew! You see? Kindred spirits, Syd! My *mishpucha*! Well done!"

"So what's the worry? A big deal? Something good or bad?"

"Good or bad, who can say until Messiah comes and all our debts are forgiven?" Mr. Baram cleaned his glasses with his shirt.

"You sound like a Rebooter," said Syd. "Praying for the forgiveness of debts."

"There are worse things than forgiveness, no?" Mr. Baram shrugged. "We should all get a little forgiveness—without it, there can be no kindness."

"Kindness is expensive," Syd said.

"And yet, you are going to help out this sewer boy."

"Sawyer," said Syd. "Tom Sawyer."

"These orphan names, I'll never understand."

"They get them from old books," said Syd.

"I wonder if they read any of them."

"Doubt it. It's just a database."

Mr. Baram rolled his eyes. "So, Sydney, I gather that you are helping this Tom Sawyer with no compensation in return?"

Syd shrugged. "Like I said. Kindness is expensive."

Mr. Baram smiled. "So shines a good deed in a naughty world."

"That another of your sayings?" Syd asked.

"Ach!" Mr. Baram threw his hands up in the air, muttering to himself. "You don't know Shakespeare?" He shook his head. "They teach you nothing in that school you pay so much for. Next time you use my library, read something beyond the dictionary. My visage? Phfft."

"So what's your worry? Anything I can do to help?"

"Now, Syd, I don't go prying into your personal business, do I?" His tone was friendly, but he wasn't joking.

"No, sir."

Mr. Baram nodded and went toward the inner door that led back to the rest of the shop. "Use what you need with this charity case of yours . . . with my blessings." His eyes lingered on Syd for a moment, then he left the room and shut the door.

Syd watched one of the holos on the wall. It showed Mr. Baram walking into the front of the shop and sitting on his usual stool with his hands resting on his belly. He looked like a lazy old man taking a nap, but he was certainly looking at his datastream on his glasses, getting feeds from informants all over the city about parts to sell and parts to buy. He could broker entire deals through his glasses without ever appearing to do a thing except blink and wiggle his fingers.

Syd watched him for a while, trying to get a clue about what could have Mr. Baram on edge, when he saw Tom come in the front door and linger nervously, looking around for Syd.

"Come in, *bubeleh*, come in." Syd heard Mr. Baram's muffled voice through the door. He used his old language much more whenever a new customer came in. He called it Yiddish, and said it was a language of great history, texture, and richness and a shame that nobody bothered with it anymore. "*Nu*, you must be Tom?"

Tom nodded and said something, but it was too quiet for Syd to hear.

"Welcome, welcome. You can go right through the shop back there." Mr. Baram pointed. "You'll find Syd. You're a lucky young man. He's quite a *mensch*. Not a lot of those left in the world."

Tom looked as confused as a fish off the farm (another of Mr. Baram's sayings), but he went to the door and Syd opened it for him, letting Tom into the workroom.

"Leave the door cracked open a bit," Mr. Baram called in a forced casual tone. That was his way of saying he knew

about the Atticus Finch disaster at school today and he
didn't want anything untoward happening under his roof,
but he'd never embarrass Syd by bringing that sort of thing
up directly. Or maybe he'd known about Syd for years.
Sometimes an open door was just an open door.

[5]

"I BROUGHT THE . . . UH . . . projector," Tom said, keeping his distance from Syd, as if he were contagious.

"Well? You gonna give it to me?"

"Right, yeah," Tom said and pulled the small device from his tattered canvas bag. Syd took it from him and went back to his bench. The kid didn't move.

The projector was smooth gray plastic, about an inch thick and three inches long. It had a small slot for the battery and another for the lens. The receiver in the middle picked up its owner's datastream and transmitted to the lens. This model had all kinds of problems with interference from background radiation. Even new, it hadn't been very high quality, and it was very far from new.

Syd set it in a cradle and fired a laser into it. The specs popped up in a holo in the air and he grabbed his micro tools and set to work. He removed the cover and the sensor inlay. He pulled apart the processor and looked at the power supply. He studied the parts under different beams and magnifications. He tested the signal strength one more time, and set the whole mess down and started to rummage for something to repair it with that might at least get Tom through exams.

Tom watched him carefully, stepping up on tiptoes to see what Syd was doing, as if he'd understand.

It amazed Syd how much people relied on these little devices for their datastreams, without having the slightest idea how they worked. The biodata everyone had installed when they were born (or in the case of the refugees, when they were rescued) linked everybody to the network so that creditors and advertisers could track you, but if you wanted to use the datastream yourself, you needed your own projector. Knowing how they worked, Syd felt more like a shaman than a repairman, a keeper of wisdom and mystery. He liked the feeling. It was good to be admired for something. Everyone should feel that way sometimes, he thought. He wondered if Tom ever had.

He doubted it.

The kid's device was glitched beyond belief. It looked like he'd dropped it into sewage more than a few times. "I gotta look in the storage for a second, okay?" Syd stood. "I'll be right back. Don't . . . touch anything."

Tom nodded and Syd went down the concrete stairs next to his bench. They kept most of the parts in the basement storage room. When the hatch was closed over the stairs you could barely see it was there, which kept things difficult for thieves or anyone else who felt like looking around. When they were in the shop, they left it open. Syd almost tumbled down it by accident every other day.

Once he was down the stairs, motion sensors flicked on the LEDs, so the room didn't feel like a creepy, cluttered cellar. It was a mess, but a brightly lit mess. There were holos on the wall where he could watch the shop from down there. He saw Mr. Baram back on his stool again, although he was slightly tilted toward the door to the workshop, keeping his eye on Syd and Tom.

As if.

Tom stood where Syd had left him, shoving his hands into his pockets and pulling them out again. He didn't know what to do with his limbs. He picked his nose. He clearly had no idea anyone could see him.

"Glitched." Syd shook his head.

He rummaged through bins of glass fronts and outdated monitors, antique keyboards, some of them going back two hundred years or more, before the melt, before the storms, before the resource wars. They were probably worth a lot to collectors in Upper City. Baram should have an expert do an inventory sometime. Syd found robot wheel treads and cracked motherboards and leaking jars of who-knew-what. He found all kinds of drives and discs and cords for mismatched machines.

He knew that he wouldn't find anything to save Tom's

projector. It was burned out. He could probably get it to project again, but it wouldn't pick up Tom's interface very clearly. It'd never get him through testing. Syd could always give the kid a new one, something cobbled together from all these parts.

A gift, an act of kindness.

What did Tom Sawyer do to deserve a gift?

Syd stood in front of one bin of half-assembled transmitters and exhaled slowly, wondering how he always got himself into this kind of mess. Why did he wear his kindness in his hair where any *schnorrer* could smell it?

And what the hell was a *schnorrer* supposed to be?

He laughed at himself for thinking about Mr. Baram's weird saying and picked up an ancient plastic pen that had rolled out of one of the bins. He mindlessly clicked the back of it to make the little tip go in and out with a satisfying sound. Why did they even have this antique? Who knew how to write by hand anymore?

He dropped the pen into his pocket out of solidarity with the total pointlessness of its survival and he rubbed his eyes. He couldn't believe he'd agreed to go to an all-night Upper City party tonight. He just wanted to sleep and forget that today had ever happened.

He lowered his hands from his face, let out a long breath.

And then he froze.

On the monitors, he saw Mr. Baram talking with two of the most beautiful people in the world. Their features were perfect. The woman's hair was blond and pulled back into a tight ponytail. The man had a neat wisp of brown hair. Both had bright blue eyes like pieces of a perfect sky. They were dressed in simple custom-made gray suits. They projected authority and inspired longing at the same time, which is exactly what they were designed to do.

They were Guardians.

And they had come for Syd.

[6]

SOUNDS OF SUCTION AND electronic pulses, beeping, blipping, clicking. Lights danced. He tried to push himself up, but thick straps pressed him to a cushioned table. His knees itched, but he couldn't scratch them. His side ached, but he couldn't touch it. He heard a screech, metal scraping metal.

"Stabilize the head," a voice said, the sound muffled.

"We have some bleeding," another said.

He felt a pinch in his stomach, a wave of nausea. Suddenly, a face loomed over his, a face in a holo projection, wavering in the air, translucent.

"Knox? Knox?" the face said. Giant teeth. The voice bubbled, like it was underwater.

Knox remembered seeing a giant fish tank once when he was little. Every few minutes a column of bubbles would roar up and rise to the surface, smashing on the water's underside. He had pressed his ear to the tank to hear the bubbles roar. Prehistoric sharks, massive toothy creatures swam by his head, inches from his face. Just the glass between them, a tiny bit of plexi between life and death. He remembered his heart racing in his tiny chest.

He could have stayed there for hours, listening to the bubbles, pressing his face near the shark faces swimming by, but his mother took his hand, led him to the children's area. It was a party. He remembered laughter and the chatter of grown-ups; his mother's warm hand on his back, sharks swimming around the room. The roar of bubbles echoing in his ears.

"Knox? Can you hear me?" The toothy face on-screen was tiny next to a shark's. Time was collapsing. The shark swam in front of the face. There was no shark. Just the face.

Knox drifted into aching silence.

Awake again.

Staring straight up. He was lying on his back on that same soft table, still restrained. He was in a tube. Plexi all around him, just like the shark from his dream. Sharks can't stop swimming or they'll die. Knox couldn't move, but he felt movement inside him. He wasn't the shark, he was the bubbles crashing on the surface.

He heard muffled voices on the other side of the plexi, his father's voice.

"Will he survive?"

"He's through the worst of it," said that screen voice.

Knox tried to turn his head to see, but his head wouldn't turn. He was locked into some sort of brace. "We've closed the punctured lung; the ribs are mending. Some ligaments need to be reattached and muscles rebuilt. He lost a piece of intestine and one ear. We had the cells on file, so we could reattach most from his own. The liver was in sorry shape, causes beyond the accident I think. We had a healthy one from a donor. Replaced his, gratis."

"There was no need," said his father. "We could have paid for the liver."

"You've been so generous with our institution. It's the least we could do."

"I appreciate your assistance with this."

"Boys need a firm hand. He is lucky to have a father who cares so much."

Knox's father grunted.

"He should be stable to transfer in a few hours," the other voice said. "We're just waiting on a blood transfusion to arrive from the Lower City. That should get his strength up."

"Good," his father replied. "Message me when he's awake."

"Of course, sir."

Knox managed to twist his head, to see his father, blurry through the plexi tube. Their eyes met and his father shook his head, just once, and put on his dark glasses. He turned his back and left the room without a word. Did he know Knox could see him, could hear him?

Of course he knew.

Knox closed his eyes, wishing he could press his face against the shark tank one more time. He saw himself, so young, on the other side of the plexi tube, his ear pressed against it, his mother's hand on his back. His missed his mother.

He tried to speak to himself, to ask himself what was happening. Where was he? Why was he in this tube, re-strained? Why was his father so disgusted with him? Why did everything hurt?

But his voice gurgled like a column of bubbles. He saw himself run off, felt his mother's warm hand on his back as she led him through the grown-up party. Sharks swam around him, but she kept him safe with her touch.

Knox slept and dreamed he was still awake.

Then he woke.

[7]

KNOX WAS LOOKING AT a room someplace. It hovered in a holo at the end of his hospital bed, like a window hanging in thin air, a window into a dump.

There was junk everywhere. Pieces of robots and computer parts, strange tools, bits of grime in the corners. There was an old guy, hairy. Talking. The volume wasn't on yet. No sound. It didn't matter. Knox didn't want to hear what he was saying.

He tried to focus past the holo projection at the wood-paneled wall behind it, but the double focus made his head spin. He rolled his eyes to the ceiling. Everything ached. He felt himself drifting off to sleep again when a rush hit him.

The nurse had her own holo projection up, off to the side. She tapped it and the patch on his arm glowed as it installed whatever biodata they were using to keep him awake. The patch made everything sharper, brighter. His veins tingled with the signal shift. It would have been fun if it didn't also make his pain more vivid, like a thin knife blade stuck into his belly button. He groaned, mostly for effect. They'd hacked his biofeed and could keep him awake as long as they wanted. They could have made the pain go away too, but they didn't. He groaned again.

"This is for your own good," Knox's father said with that same tone he probably used to fire people.

Knox looked over at him. His father sat in a mod chair next to the hospital bed. He wore a dark suit and hid his eyes behind dark glasses so no one could tell if he was looking at them or at his datastream or both. Even out of the office, he was never away from the office. Knox felt ridiculous wearing a hospital gown while his father was in a suit and dark glasses.

It struck Knox that he wasn't in a tube anymore. He was in some kind of lux hospital room. He didn't recall being moved. Everything was hazy. A hose stretched from his arm to some sort of bag. Bright blood flowed into him from the bag. A transfusion. Why did he need a transfusion? And why were they keeping him awake to look at a holo of some dumpy room filled with junk?

Knox gritted his teeth and looked around. Wood panels and brass fixtures. A 3-D holo on the wall looked like a window over snowy mountain peaks. Maybe the Rockies or Everest before the melt. What were those old European ones? The Alps. Hadn't they been vaporized in the war?

Knox never was good at history. Whatever. The projection was lux, whatever it was. He could smell the snow.

Knox didn't know why he was in this hospital room. Something about a car? A girl named Pam? Was that it? Emily? He couldn't remember. Why was he in so much pain? He'd been having a dream about his mother and a shark tank.

The nurse patted him sympathetically. She'd be pretty out of that uniform . . . nice legs and good curves just above them. He winked at her. His eyelids hurt. He didn't dare try a smirk. Better to wince and get sympathy. He couldn't pull off rakish from a hospital bed, especially when he didn't know why he was there.

"Watch the projection," his father commanded without even turning to look at him. "This is all pointless if you don't watch the projection."

So that's what this was: proxy business. What a hassle.

Knox wanted to be left alone to heal. He needed his rest. He was injured. He was in pain. His punishment could wait, couldn't it? Not like his proxy was going anywhere.

On the holo, two Guardians stepped closer to the old man and then one of them noticed a door cracked open in the back. They walked to it without asking permission and shoved it wide. Knox couldn't take his eyes off them.

Why Guardians?

He'd done a lot crazy stuff over the years and his proxy never got picked up by Guardians. They usually just outsourced this sort of thing to a local security outfit. What had he done that called for Guardians? Guardians were barely even human; they'd had so much code written into their DNA, their bodies were basically hardware, networked and programmed, and they were the exclusive property of SecuriTech. They were developed to preserve the market from terrorists, to prevent the chaos of strife and anarchy from ever returning. They were never used for picking up a proxy. It wasn't worth it. The program each one of them had installed when they were culled as children cost more than the entire economic output of the Lower City.

"Kind of over the top, huh, Dad?" Knox glanced at his father.

"Pay attention," his father grumbled in reply.

Knox felt his breath quicken as the Guardians stepped into the next room.

There was his proxy now, sniveling and frightened in front of the Guardians. Knox didn't remember the boy like this. The proxy he remembered was broad shouldered, wore his hair short, and had skin the color of a dark beer. Maybe that kid was gone. Maybe this was a replacement. Knox had no idea if that happened. Could they just replace a proxy without notifying you? He'd sort of grown used to that other kid. Not that it mattered. The proxy would never know Knox. Patron confidentiality was, like, a law.

But this new kid, he almost demanded punishment. That kind of defeated the purpose, no? Even without the volume on, you could tell he was whining. Knox was grateful there was no sound. His head couldn't take it. He imagined the kid's voice like a squawking penguin.

Why was he thinking about penguins? Did he steal a penguin? Was that what this was about? He remembered something about the zoo. He tried to remember flapping wings, those tuxedo birds, anything at all, but there was just blankness, a hole in time.

Suddenly, another figure was in the room on the screen, a boy he recognized. He rose right out of the floor. That was the boy, Knox's proxy. The kid must have a rough time of it living in the Valve, if this was his house. Had he come out of a basement? Was that where the old man kept him?

"Can we get some sound, please?" Knox's father snapped at the nurse. "This is hardly a useful exercise without sound."

"Yes, sir," said the nurse. She brought the sound on with a swipe of her finger. She'd been sparing Knox the volume up to that point. He'd have to get her ID before he checked out. Her hair had this amazing copper shine against her pale neck. It wasn't the fanciest gene-job he'd ever seen—the color profile was just a little off—but that made it even more endearing. Of course, she worked for his father, which was a point against her.

"I'm Sydney Carton," the boy on the screen said. "You're looking for me." The female Guardian checked a projection to get a match on his biofeed. She nodded at her partner. They had the right kid.

"What is it this time?" Sydney asked.

"Please come with us," the female Guardian said. Talk about nice curves. The Guardian was amazing.

The theory was that people followed the orders of an

attractive person more readily than an ugly person, so all the Guardians were hot; they were chosen for their attractiveness. "Genetically sourced" was the official line. Everything else could be programmed in. Biomanipulation was a booming business, especially in the security sector. There was no shortage of threats to guard against—smugglers, hackers, Nigerian-backed saboteurs, debt-crazed Rebooters trying to overthrow the system. Some people didn't want to pay their fair share. Some people hated the prosperity of others.

Knox tried to pay attention to the holo, but his mind kept wandering. He found himself thinking about a polar bear. What did that have to do with anything?

"I already gave him my blood today. What else do you want?" Sydney sighed. He didn't look alarmed. He looked bored.

Knox glanced at the bag of blood pouring into him and the scruffy dark-skinned kid on the holo. He felt suddenly itchy, like the poverty of that boy was flowing through his veins now. His stomach turned.

"Is that hygienic?" he asked his father.

"We test the blood, Knox." His father sounded bored too.

"Aren't you supposed to tell me what I'm being punished for?" Sydney on the holo said. Knox pushed himself up to lean his lower back against the headboard.

"Did my patron hack another diet supplement pill? Make the steak taste like sewage? Foot-sweat crème brûlée?" the proxy grumbled.

The sniveling kid stared at the Guardians, unblinking. Knox wondered what sketchy scene they'd wandered in on. Codesnappers? IP thieves? Cut-rate gene rippers? Anything goes in the Valve. You get the laws you can pay for, and no more. The Guardians weren't there to enforce some petty Valve crimes. The sniveling kid looked like he had never even seen Guardians before. Probably hadn't, if he was lucky.

The old man was suddenly back in the room, coming toward them, wagging his finger in the air.

"Sydney is a good kid," he was saying. "He follows the rules. You have to tell him what this is about."

The Guardians turned to the old man and stared him down, stopping him in his tracks with their eyes.

"These are *your* rules," the old man added, much more quietly, almost to himself. "I have a terms of proxy agreement statement here somewhere." His eyes twitched as he scanned the datastream in his glasses, projections flashing in the air in front of him, but the female Guardian grabbed his wrist and bent his arm back like a mischievous child with someone else's doll. The projections vanished. The old man's eyes focused.

"Sir," the Guardian spoke calmly, but with a tone that left no doubt as to who was in charge. Knox leaned forward. At least now he'd find out what he'd done. Stealing a penguin wouldn't land him in this hospital. Stealing a penguin wouldn't hurt this much. Although he'd never actually stolen a penguin that he remembered. Maybe it could.

Or maybe a polar bear? Had he been that tweaked? What kind of punishment did stealing extinct animals from the zoo require of his proxy?

"The proxy owes his patron a debt accrued for theft, trespassing, destruction of property," the Guardian said.

"What an idiot," Sydney muttered.

"And homicide," the Guardian added.

"Wait, what?" blurted Sydney.

"Wait, what?" Knox blurted with him. "Homicide . . ." He looked at his dad. Machines started beeping; holo projections of his vital signs appeared all over the room.

"Yes, Knox, and I hope this will teach you a lesson," his father answered, peering over his glasses. "Marie died."

"Who?" was all Knox could muster before the world went black again.

[8]

IT WAS SOME TIME later, Knox couldn't tell how long, when that familiar drug rush of clarity and pain woke him. His father and the nurse were on either side of him and he was staring once more at Sydney, his proxy, on the holo at the end of his bed.

Knox hadn't moved, but Sydney had. He was in a tiled room, brightly lit. The proxy's skin looked almost gray under the harsh lights, and he didn't look bored anymore.

He looked frightened.

The picture zoomed in close on his face, probably for dramatic effect now that Knox was awake. He hated those cheap tricks. The punishments should really speak for themselves. But some case agent in some office somewhere probably had his own ideas about cinematography.

The image widened to reveal that Sydney was tied up by

the wrists and suspended by some sort of chain overhead. He'd been stripped down to his boxer shorts. He had a large scar on his upper arm, probably from the cheap biofeed install when he was a child. He had two more scars along one side of his rib cage and another along his collarbone that looked like it had been sewn shut with concertina wire. Knox wondered why he didn't get the scars fixed. There were patches that could do the repair work and they weren't even that expensive. Maybe the kid took pride in looking like a thug. Maybe that was fashionable in the Valve.

The Guardians were with the proxy, flanking him, maybe the same ones, maybe different ones. It was impossible to tell.

Sydney's clothes were piled on a table in front of him, just a shirt and cargo pants. His plastic holo projector sat beside them on the table, smashed, useless. That seemed excessive to Knox, adding inconvenience to injury. What lesson could breaking the kid's datastream access possibly teach Knox?

"Sound again, please," Knox's father commanded and the nurse brought up the volume. All they could hear was Syd's deep breathing.

No one spoke.

Knox had seen his proxy punished in all sorts of ways over the years: zapped with the EMD sticks, forced to work under the blazing sun out on the dam construction above the river, even just held alone in the dark for days. That was how the system worked. Knox's father purchased the boy's debt and when Knox broke the rules, the boy was punished.

It was a transaction, plain and simple, the cornerstone of civilization. The free market.

But this—tied up, nearly naked. It was too raw. Too physical. Knox wanted it to stop.

Calm down, Knox, he reminded himself. Think clearly. It's not like anyone forced this Sydney kid to go into debt, right? Was it Knox's fault the boy had bad luck? The proxies were randomly assigned by age group. Xelon purchased huge blocks of debt in bulk, sold and resold them automatically. Nothing personal at all.

Some other kid in the Valve was probably racking up debt with some patron kid who never broke the rules. Like that kiss-ass in his Intro to Financialization class, Duross Wen. He never did anything wrong. He'd probably never even seen his proxy and never would. His family paid and paid and the proxy got credit for nothing. It was a gamble. Duross's proxy had won. Sydney had lost. It was that simple.

But this time a girl had died.

A girl named Marie.

She died because of him.

Knox still couldn't exactly remember how or why, but he'd find out. That was the deal. When his proxy was punished, Knox was forced to watch it happen. Even now, even in his hospital bed. His father sat in judgment beside him.

Knox had known Sydney since they were both four years old, even though Sydney would never know him. The first time he saw Sydney Carton was because Knox had broken one of the ancient tablets his great-grandmother rescued from the ruined museums of the East Coast when the floodwaters rose, a stone slab with little dents and shapes in it, some contract from some long-forgotten civilization. Messoposomething. Knox had tried to ride it down the stairs. It shattered halfway to the landing.

Sydney was pulled right out of his bed in a part of the city Knox hadn't known existed. He was skinny and brown and his hair was wild and kinky and he didn't look anything like the other children Knox knew. Just seeing him made Knox frightened.

When he was brought into the room, Knox remembered Sydney laughing. He stopped laughing when he saw the EMD stick. Sydney got five low-power zaps and he obviously didn't understand why, even when the matronly head of the orphanage explained it to him. He just cried and cried and screamed and cried some more. Knox cried right along with him.

Then Knox apologized to the holo and to his father and even to the little vacuum robot he'd tried to blame for breaking the tablet. He vowed to be better, promised he'd never be a disappointment again, but that lasted about six weeks, until he tried to see if the vacuubot could fly by throwing it off the roof.

It couldn't.

For that, Syd got ten zaps.

Within a year, Sydney had stopped crying and Knox had stopped wincing when he watched. They varied the punishments as the boys aged, but it never affected Knox as it did the first time. And Sydney seemed to take it in stride. All part of the system.

But now Knox felt that old pang, that feeling he hadn't really known since that old clay tablet. He was watching the screen and he was afraid. He felt like he was in the room with Sydney, like he *was* Sydney.

"Your patron has committed serious crimes," the female Guardian said. "Per the terms of your contract, you will be administered the full punishment unless he files a waiver to appear in your place, is that understood?"

Sydney didn't answer. He just looked around the room.

"Where is he?" Sydney asked, eyes darting. No way he'd even see the cameras, but still, his glances made Knox wrap his hospital gown tighter. He hugged himself.

"His whereabouts are not your concern," the Guardian said. "Do you understand why you are being punished?"

"Because my patron is a waste of meat," Sydney said.

The female Guardian smiled in an imitation of sympathy. She nodded and the male Guardian stepped forward with an EMD stick and put it against Sydney's side.

The proxy squirmed and writhed; his feet left the floor and his toes curled. When the stick was pulled away his head slumped forward and he gasped. He looked up again. The view zoomed in on his face. Knox wanted to close his eyes, but he wouldn't give his father the satisfaction. He wasn't in that room. He wasn't Sydney. Nothing like someone else's pain to put you back in your own body. He was here, in this room with his own pain and he wouldn't blink.

"Do you understand?" the female Guardian asked again. Sydney nodded.

"Good. You currently have two remaining years of debt to repay. We are required to give you the option to repay in full now. The current rate of exchange is four thousand eight hundred and sixty-two credits per month outstanding, for a total of one hundred sixteen thousand six hundred eighty-eight, plus processing fees. Would you prefer to repay in full now and defer punishment?"

This was the standard script. The rates changed based on a formula only the top executives could see, but the choice was the same every time. It's either you or me. Someone's got to pay.

It was pretty absurd when they were little kids. Knox didn't know what any of those words meant, and it didn't look like Sydney did either. But it was like the old religions: Repeat the prayers over and over for years and years and only later come to understand them.

Knox got worried as they got older that Sydney would say yes one of these days, and buy his way out of the system. Would this be the time? He held his breath, not sure what he was hoping.

"Repay with what?" Sydney sneered.

The Guardian nodded and a holo appeared in front of her. She tapped it a few times to enter the response, then vanished it with a wave of her hand. She met Sydney's eyes.

"We will administer the punishment as follows—" Knox held his breath. He was going to hear the full list of what he'd done. "For your patron's crime of larceny of corporate property you will receive twenty pulses at level eight-point-seven. For the crime of trespassing and destruction of property, you will receive forty pulses at level twelve-point-five"—Sydney slumped where he was hanging—"and for the crime of negligent homicide, your flesh be branded with the name of the deceased, one Marie Louise Alvarez, and you will be sent to Old Sterling Work Colony for the period of sixteen years, eighteen days and nine hours."

Sydney's head snapped up. His face showed a new expression, the lips turned down, the eyebrows collapsing toward each other. "You can't . . . I only have two years left . . ."

"Per the terms of the agreement, all policies are based on penal recommendations as defined in the current actuarial tables available through the Xelon Corporation Information System at the time of contract. The compensation for the life of a patron is the equal number of years from the offender's proxy as replacement for lost productivity, as your contract clearly states."

"But, I never . . . I was a baby when the contract was made."

"The Benevolent Society enrolled you *in loco parentis* to repay your debts. You should have filed a formal objection at the time."

"I was a baby!"

"Unless your patron would care to waive his exemption, we will begin immediately."

"You can't do this . . . Sterling . . . sixteen years . . ."

The silence hung heavy around the hospital room. The nurse looked at her feet. Knox could feel his father's attention shift from his datastream to his son, even without seeing his eyes.

He frowned. Whatever he saw on Knox's face was more disgusting to him than the torture Sydney was enduring.

"We will begin." The Guardian nodded at her colleague, who stepped forward with the EMD stick emitting a low hum that seemed to shake the image in the air. Knox winced as it got near his proxy.

"Why shock me if you're just going to send me to Sterling?" Sydney squirmed where he hung, pulling his waist away from the tip of the EMD stick.

"The punishments are not for you," the Guardian said without the slightest hint of emotion in her voice. "They are for your patron."

"Who is he? What's his name?" Sydney yelled. "Coward! I know you're watching! You knockoff patron coward!"

The first shock sent Sydney's whole body rigid. Every muscle tensed. Knox could see the veins in Sydney's forehead and arms pop up. The stick was removed from his side and he slumped again where he hung. The holos from the proxy's biofeed that hovered around the tiled room flickered. The EMD pulse disrupted his signal. It fried every nerve in his body.

"One," said the female Guardian.

Sydney gasped. The stick touched his side again. He

flailed. His legs danced freely in the air; his neck thrashed from side to side. The holos around him flickered again.

"Two," she said.

More flickers.

"Three."

Knox closed his eyes. He had to. He couldn't witness this. In the oblivion, Knox saw an image of the girl. Her purple wink, her dark hair, her nervous laugh. He'd taken a car. He'd convinced her to come. Her name was Marie. Marie Alvarez.

"Open your eyes, Knox," his father barked at him. A rush passed through his limbs and his eyes shot open on their own.

"Do you realize how much this is costing me?" His father leaned forward. "My rates are going to go sky high because of this. I'll have to pay for a new proxy for you on top of this one while he's at Sterling. And you can be sure that Xiao and Grace Alvarez will not let my board of directors forget about this. They are very important clients and they lost their daughter because of you. Do you understand me? This reflects on me. *You* reflect on me. You need to start thinking about consequences, about other people. You aren't some piece of Valve trash who can act without affecting others. You are supposed to be a leader! How will the shareholders react when they hear what my son has done, huh? You hear me? You are hurting your legacy with your foolishness. Our share price is going to plummet and it will be blamed on my reckless son, so you will watch every second of this and think about what you've done. You will not waste my time and money closing your eyes. This is your wake-up call, Knox. It is time to grow up. I will not humor you any longer."

Knox clenched his jaw. He wanted to scream out. He wanted to shut his father up. He wanted to stop the Guardians and set Sydney free. But he stayed silent. He stared forward, watching the holo and breathing loudly through his nose.

Knox watched as the Guardians fried his proxy's nerves over and over and over again. By number nine Sydney had thrown up; by eleven he was glassy eyed, his head lolling about like a zombie in a classic movie; by the last zap he was hanging limp. His wrists were red and raw from where they rubbed against the chain that held him. A tear ran down Knox's cheek, even as he held his head stone still. For the first time since he was four years old and he had been told that this boy was named Sydney and that this boy would be his proxy, and that this boy would be punished because of the old piece of clay he'd broken, Knox cried.

"You are responsible for him," his father had told him after that first punishment, so many years ago. "Whatever happens to him, that is your responsibility. Do you understand?" At the time he had nodded through his tears. He had broken the tablet. He was responsible.

When it was done, his father let him fall asleep. As he drifted off, the holo zoomed in on Sydney's head, hanging limp against his chest.

"Hold that image," Knox's father said, suddenly standing. He stepped forward and poked his finger right into the image.

What was he doing?

Knox tried to focus. His father used his fingers to zoom in on Sydney's head. He put his finger up to some weird birthmark behind the proxy's ear. He leaned in close.

"Get me the proxy's blood test results immediately," he ordered the nurse. She began working in her own projection.

"I have it right here," she said, studying the data she'd brought up. "What is it you're looking for?"

"Dad, what's wrong?" Knox asked, although it came out slurred and hazy. His father turned around, looking surprised to see him there. As if Knox could be anywhere else. "Is something wrong with the blood?"

His father ignored the question. Asked his own. "Have you noticed that birthmark before? Has it always looked like that?"

"I . . . uh . . ." Knox couldn't remember. He never paid that much attention. Who looks at some other guy's birthmarks, especially some proxy's?

Knox was so tired, but he was suddenly scared. What if he'd gotten some weird disease from that proxy's blood, loaded with parasites and pollutants? Rat flu, dengue fever, brain worms . . . who knew what kind of diseases lived down in the Valve? They ate wild animals down there, didn't they?

"Is something wrong with—" Knox tried again, but his

father brought up a holo, tapped around and suddenly, the patch on Knox's arm lit up again. His pain vanished and he felt a glowing, cloudy peace blossom inside him.

"Don't you worry about a thing," his father said. "It will be taken care of."

"But I—" Knox started, but he couldn't hold his eyes open, couldn't even remember what he'd wanted to ask. Even with his eyes closed, he saw Sydney's face. He saw Marie's face. Their faces hung there in the void and then the void engulfed him and he slept.

This time, he did not dream.

[9]

SYD SHIVERED HIMSELF AWAKE, every nerve raw and prickling. The echo of a nightmare shot adrenaline up his spine. He reached back to the mark behind his ear. He could never be a gambler. His finger always went right to that spot when he was nervous.

It hurt to open his eyes, but it hurt to keep them closed. Slowly, his vision came into focus. A steel table leg. White tiles. Bright light. A vague electric hum. The pain and the cold told him he was alive.

He was still in his boxer shorts, lying on the floor of the room where they had shocked him. His pants and his shirt were bunched under his head, as if someone had wanted him to be comfortable but didn't want to spare a pillow. He felt his heart racing in his chest. He tried to slow his breathing, to calm down. He lowered his hands and pressed his palms against the cold tile.

He could hear shouts and screams through the walls. He guessed these were the sounds of other proxies in other rooms enduring other punishments for other patrons.

He'd never been in a prison like this before. Usually, the punishments were given wherever the bounty hunters happened to find the proxy. If hard labor had been ordered, some local security goons would just issue the summons. Failure to show up at the appointed time was a breach of contract, punishable by additional months and years of debt, and, of course, a few hits with an EMD pulse.

The security firms were always liberal with those. They made the whole thing much more vengeful than these Guardians had, taunting and turning the settings higher than required. Competition was fierce to get more patron business, so firms would often interrupt one another to serve the same punishment. Fights broke out. Sometimes, they'd reach a settlement and the punishment got issued twice for the same debt. Double payday. And if the proxy complained . . . well, proxies were replaceable.

Using the poor to control the poor kept everyone in the Valve at one another's throats and kept them from looking too far up in the direction of the skyscrapers and the private communities. The Guardians rarely showed up to haul anyone off. The market preferred to keep its enforcers more invisible than that.

But a girl had died. Syd couldn't believe it. His patron had actually killed someone. Syd never imagined a crime like that or a punishment like this. He never imagined he'd find himself here.

It had to be one of those intelligence centers that Securi-Tech ran. "Enemies of the market" disappeared inside them and never came out.

Last year, after the Rebooters hacked an insurance datastream, two or three dozen guys were pulled out of the Valve in night raids, accused of anti-market terrorism and supporting the debt revolutionaries hiding in Old Detroit. The Rebooters, as they called themselves, were always trying to hack corporate systems to erase data, but they never managed to inflict much damage. The network was resilient.

The men who'd been rounded up in night raids disappeared into a place like this one. Their bodies started showing up in the gutters of the Valve a few days later, dumped out with the rest of the Upper City trash. It was an effective reminder not to upset the status quo.

Syd remembered Egan laughing at one of the headless bodies lying arms akimbo on a heap of discarded processors.

"That's Doolaine," he said. "The butcher who used to pay us to hunt rats and then rip us off when we brought 'em in."

"How do you know?" Syd had asked.

"The neck tattoo. I'll never forget that big knockoff's neck tattoo." Egan spat on the body and the bead of saliva rolled across the purple skin of his chest. "You don't remember the beatings he used to give us?"

Syd had shrugged. He remembered, but he'd developed the philosophy that it was better to forget old beatings. A grudge was just another debt owed.

"No way he was a Rebooter," Syd said. "He wasn't political. He didn't care about debt reform."

"Who cares what he was or what he believed?" Egan shrugged. "Someone must have informed on him for some reason. It's not our problem."

They had walked on, but the idea stuck with Syd. Someone didn't like Doolaine and had made an accusation. It didn't matter if it was true. Truth was a commodity no one down in the Valve could afford. Protection mattered a lot more than truth and Doolaine didn't have any. Too many enemies.

Syd remembered feeling glad he didn't know anyone well enough to have enemies like Doolaine had. He'd kept to himself, private. But now, lying on the floor listening to the tortured screams of whoever it was in those other rooms, he couldn't help but consider the coincidence. The same day he agreed to help Tom, the same day his crush on Atticus Finch came to light, was the day he was taken by the Guardians. Had he formed too many connections, reached out just far enough to get cut off? Did he have more enemies than he'd thought? Or maybe, the wrong friends?

No.

This wasn't about him. It was his patron. It had nothing to do with Syd. That was his weakness. When he got to thinking, it always turned back on himself, his failings, his mistakes.

But he didn't matter in this. He was just a body for the rich to use and to discard when it suited them. That was his place, his market niche, as they called it. He was a proxy and his life was on loan.

His forearm ached. Or rather, it ached in a different way than the rest of him. He looked at it and saw the angry red welt of skin with silver metallic letters embedded in it. They'd done it. They had actually branded him.

MARIE LOUISE ALVAREZ, 16. His arm glistened at him. The metal letters implanted in his skin were hard and surprisingly warm to the touch. They were slick with antibacterial gel.

Syd pressed the base of his hands into his eyes. Another mark on his body. The birthmark, the scars from fights and cheap vaccines, now this, another reminder he had as much control of his skin as he did over the weather. None.

Rage boiled inside him, pushing the pain in his body down. Sixteen more years, added just like that, and in Sterling Work Colony. It wasn't right. It wasn't fair.

He had played by the rules, mostly, for his whole life. He didn't turn squatter or scavenger or freelance. He didn't hook up with the revolutionaries. He didn't care about all the Rebooter stuff, deleting the debts, restoring equality to a corrupt blah blah blah . . . the sermons got tiresome. The debts were tied to the data; the data was in the blood. There was no deleting it, and the people who thought otherwise were no better than mystics, praying for a hopeless deliverance.

Syd could never afford idealism and he never wanted to. He'd rather do his work and get ahead without any stupid games. The debt he had, the debt that had been forced on him for the rescue he never asked for and the upbringing he barely got, he paid. He endured the beatings and the volunteer work and the cruelties inflicted on behalf of his Upper City patron because that's how it worked. He was almost free.

And then they changed the terms.

They changed their policy, just like that.

Sterling Work Colony was a hell. Everyone knew it. Survivors told stories of brutal guards, relentless disease, and ruthless inmates. There was no escape because there was nowhere to go. The Mountain City was the only civilization on the continent. The rest was swamp and desert and ruins. Sterling was the end, a place without compassion, without even the false kindness of the free market. There was only work and death.

And soon, Sydney Carton would be sent there. Sixteen years old and off to Sterling with the unredeemable.

No.

He refused. It was that simple.

He was not unredeemable and he was not a terrorist and he was not just a body they could discard and replace to teach some patron a lesson.

He was Sydney Carton—or whatever his name had been before—and he was a human being and he wasn't just going to lie down and take this. He had to do . . . something. He had to escape before they came to take him away.

He pushed himself up and pulled on his clothes.

He didn't know how, but he had to get out of the city, find some other place to live. He'd never make Lagos. Even if he could get to a coast, stow away on some kind of global shipping hovercraft, the border at Lagos was closed. The Nigerians kept their prosperity by executing illegal immigrants on sight. There wasn't room for newcomers and, like here, there was nothing but desert around their city. Here or there, civilization wasn't an option for a fugitive.

So it was the wilderness. They said no one could survive out there; drought, earthquakes, and storms had wrecked what the wars didn't, and all the old cities had been abandoned or destroyed. The world was like a feral dog. It tore out its hair to get rid of its fleas, but a few clung on, digging in where the paws couldn't scratch. You step out too far, the dog will shake you off.

But there had to be someone who adapted. It wouldn't be civilization like Syd knew, but it'd be something. Maybe he could hook up with some desert nomads, learn to find water in the rocks and suck nutrients from the sand. There were worse lives, he guessed. At least he'd be free. Or he could go east, try to find where he'd come from. But the thought of hurricane winds and tropical disease gave him pause. There was a reason everyone had retreated to the Mountain City long ago. There was a reason refugees clambered to get in.

There were the displacement camps, of course, to the east and the west, but the Benevolent Society knew everything that went on in them. If he tried to hide out there, he'd just get caught again.

Other options? He could join up with the Rebooters. They were supposed to be in Old Detroit, living in the jungle ruins. They'd probably sell Syd to the organ harvesters as soon as look at him. What good was he to a cause he wanted no part of?

Syd didn't plan to live at the mercy of anyone else's institutions ever again, not the patrons or the Benevolent Society and not the revolutionaries. He'd had enough of institutions. They were like fire that way. Useful, but if you played with them for too long, burns were inevitable. He'd choose the nomads, if he could find them, if they existed.

He'd need to get an ID clone first, something to mask his biofeed from the scanners. The system of transmitters and aerial drones could track him, just as advertisers did, unless he could outwit them. With the right hacks, he could overwrite the code in his bloodstream for long enough to get away, but for that he'd need Egan. Egan always knew where to get fake ID.

First he had to get out of this room. And for that, he needed to use the old journeyman lie, low-tech but time-tested.

He threw himself to the floor.

[10]

"UGGGHHH," SYD GROANED. "OOOOOO." He rolled across the tiles. He writhed.

The door slid open and a six-legged black metal bot entered the room. It looked like a cross between a dog and spider. It had two barrels mounted on a swivel where the dog ears should be, and a series of cameras around its body, like spider eyes. The Arak9 Model 6. Top of the line. Their parts were only just starting to show up on the black market. Mr. Baram spoke of them with awe.

"Please tell me the nature of your difficulty," the robot asked in an oddly gentle female voice. Syd was thrown off for an instant.

"I . . . ," he started. "My stomach . . . it hurts!" He groaned. "I think something ruptured. I need medical assistance."

"I am fully equipped to evaluate prisoner medical emergencies. Please stand," the bot requested.

"I can't!" he groaned.

The bot approached. Syd's biodata appeared in holos in the air around it, monitoring his heart, his blood pressure, his brainwaves. For a moment, he was afraid the machine could read his mind, but, like Mr. Baram said, data was not the same as reading.

Once the Arak9 was in front of him, he reached his hand underneath its armor-plated base and found the emergency reset exactly where it was supposed to be. He pressed his palm against it and mumbled a thank-you to Mr. Baram and the blessings of an informal education. They'd had the manual for the Arak9 Model 6 for months. His biodata vanished.

"Now," Syd told the bot when its active light came on again. "Program override. Recognize speech pattern alpha. Accept voice commands from this pattern only. Confirm."

"Pattern confirmed," the bot replied in its metallic default voice.

"Take me to the nearest exit," Syd told it. "Disable any resistance with nonlethal means. Confirm."

"Nonlethal. Confirmed," the bot said and walked into the hallway. Syd followed close enough to keep a hand on its back.

The hallway was empty. They clattered toward a corner with a panel projecting a 3-D image of a white sand beach. It was meant to be soothing. Syd was not soothed.

As they neared it, the image changed to a drone's-eye view of Syd and the Arak9 moving down the hall. A silent alarm had been triggered. The lights in the hallway went out. Guardians could see in the dark. Syd couldn't. He grabbed on to the bot with both hands.

"Don't lose me," he told it.

"Confirmed."

They moved quickly through the dark hallway. Syd's body ached and he struggled to keep up. He was totally blind and going on faith that the Arak9 hadn't been linked back to the network to lead him right into a trap. That's what he would do if he were trying to catch himself right now.

The Guardians' plan, however, was much simpler.

"Stop!" a female Guardian commanded from up ahead. A panel behind her lit up brightly, framing her in silhouette. A half-dozen more identical silhouettes appeared next to her. All of them armed.

"You are in breach of contract," the Guardian said. "And you have vandalized company property."

Syd heard the hum of EMD sticks charging up. The silhouettes raised their weapons. Syd braced for the painful convulsions. They never came.

The Arak9 fired thick foam from its cannons, which flooded the hallway and surrounded the Guardians. The foam hardened instantly and absorbed the charge from their EMD blasts. The robot moved past the mountain of foam and headed toward the exit.

Within minutes they were outside. It was night and the neon glow of the Upper City shone just beyond the high walls of the compound. The upper offices would have a clear view down into the center. Syd shuddered to think of the things those offices' workers could see, the things they learned to ignore.

Syd's bot fired sonic blasts up to the guard towers that stood silhouetted against the neon lights. He heard the screams of Guardians as they were hit with a wall of concentrated vibrations, enough to shatter their perfectly designed eardrums. Male and female Guardians rolled on the ground in anguish ahead of him. His new toy had disabled every living thing in their path. He didn't even hear so much as a ringing. This thing knew how to aim.

He liked having his own bot. Maybe he could bring it with him into his new life, like a pet and a bodyguard all in one, the way people used to keep dogs. He'd need some company, anyway. He wasn't about to ask Egan to go on the run with him. He wouldn't want to make his friend turn him down.

"Let's go," he told the bot. "Exit."

"Confirmed."

The robot charged across a clearing toward a concrete blast barrier with a steel gate. He hoped this bot had a way to get through. The gate was designed to withstand mechanized assault.

Half a dozen combat robots raced after them, firing their own blasts at Syd. As the dirt kicked up around him and the shock waves nearly knocked him off his feet, he realized that they were not using nonlethal weapons. They weren't shooting to incapacitate him. They were shooting to kill.

"Focus," he told himself. No time to think about dying. This was a time to think about living, about staying alive.

At least five of the other Arak9's were closing in. He would never make it to the gate in time, let alone through it. He jumped onto his bot's back. He was going way beyond the instruction manual now, but it was his only hope.

"Leap over the obstruction!" he yelled.

"Leap confirmed," the bot responded, bent its six legs and sprang into the air. The ground beneath them exploded with blasts from the other bots. He shut his eyes as they flew over the wall. He didn't know how well this model would handle impact on the other side. He braced himself.

They hit the ground with a jarring crunch that jolted Syd off the bot's back and knocked the wind out of him. His bot seemed undamaged. Syd stood to get back on, but he saw the others bots leaping over the wall after them.

"Damn," he said, panting, and glanced to the tall buildings around him. He hoped the lower floors were empty, given what he was about to do. "Confirm full core destruct. Five second delay."

"Full core destruct confirmed," the bot said, as the others landed around them in a circle. "Meltdown with five second delay."

They didn't teach this in Mr. Thompson's Robotics class.

"Sorry, pal," Syd muttered, patting the machine on the

back. Then he crawled under it and curled into a ball. He hoped he was right that the epicenter of the blast from the core meltdown would be safe, like the eye of the storm in a hurricane. The other bots tightened in around him. Surrounded.

"Five. Four."

He covered his head with his hands. He squeezed his eyes shut. The whole system worked on background radiation, so the explosion from a combat bot's meltdown should vaporize every machine in a fifty-yard radius and temporarily disable every network in five hundred yards. He'd get a head start and he'd inflict some serious damage on the way out. He just hoped the explosion wouldn't kill him in the process. He'd never even had his first kiss.

"Three. Two. One."

[11]

THE MOUNTAINS WERE DARK against an impossibly star-studded sky. The Milky Way made a smudge over the horizon.

So it was supposed to be night.

Knox hit a button on the bed, and the 3-D mountain scene was replaced with a large digital display: 11:43 p.m. 64° Fahrenheit. Air Quality Index: 97.

Funny, he thought, it wasn't even midnight. It felt later. He took a deep breath. His ribs didn't hurt anymore. His head didn't ache. The biotech they'd been pumping into him must be top-notch to work so quickly. He looked under his hospital gown, relieved to see that he was still all there. He wasn't even bruised. To tell the truth, felt pretty good. Energized, revitalized.

But bored.

He tapped his projector on the table beside the bed, brought up a holo for "entertainment." He swiped through the menus. Sports and movies and short comedy and long comedy and reality drama and reality comedy and reality classics and news.

Boring. Boring. Boring. And boring.

He chewed his nails and spat the little flakes onto the sheets.

An image popped into his head, uninvited, of Sydney, hanging on that chain. Screaming. He had looked up, right into the hospital room it seemed, right into Knox, except it wasn't Sydney's face. It was Knox's. His own green eyes sliced into him.

"Marie," his own face said.

He bit down through his cuticle and the pain cleared his head. He flipped the holo again to a different menu to see what his friends were up to.

Grayden: grnded. @home w/ fam

Simeonie: killr party @Arcadia vry retro

Nine: @Arcadia w. Simi & Cheyenne. D-troit chic=tyght!

Cheyenne: crazy tryp!#$^%!!!

So everyone was at Arcadia, and Cheyenne was tweaked on something. Knox sighed. That party was supposed to be lux.

Someone had found all these retro cars that ran on gas and parked them all in a giant warehouse end to end, so they were like the floor of the place, with all the roofs and hoods and open-top convertibles forming a crazy desert of dunes and craters. A few of the cars actually ran so that the whole place smelled like classic fumes. It must have cost a fortune to get the antique gas from scavengers.

Everyone wanted in to this party, and Knox's friend Nine could make it happen for a price. Nine's father was some big piracy consultant, so he knew everyone in the entertainment business. Nine and Knox had spent a month making fake ID patches to sell to kids from all over the city, Upper, Lower, whatever, even the Valve, if they could pay.

They'd been making some serious credit, although Nine claimed that wasn't why he did it. He said he was "curating" the party, making sure it wasn't just the same old Upper City bores. Knox couldn't believe he was missing this scene.

He swiped the holo to a bright beach, impossibly white sand, no sludge or washed-up flotsam, the sun burning white hot in a clear blue sky. He lay back on his pillow. He wasn't tired. He didn't want to lie here thinking all night.

Thinking was the worst thing he could do.

His door slid open and a tall medibot came rolling in, its white porcelain body glowing delicately in the dim room.

"You are awake, Mr. Brindle," the robot's sweet female voice said. "You have one message from your father. Would you like me to play it?"

"Where's that nurse?" Knox asked. If he was stuck here, he might as well have some fun.

"Nurse Bovary is no longer in the building."

Bovary, Knox snorted. An orphan. He wished she'd

stuck around. He could have shown her what it was like to live like a patron, at least for an hour.

"When does she come back?" Knox hoped it would be soon.

"Nurse Bovary has resigned her position," the bot informed him.

Knox sighed. The workers just came and went like breezes.

"Would you like to play the message from your father?"

"He's not here either?" Knox asked.

"Your father left the hospital at eight forty-two p.m.," the bot said.

Of course. That must have been minutes after Knox fell asleep. Seconds. What did his father care? He was an "important man" with "real responsibilities." Knox would "never understand the pressures his business entailed." It was time for him to "grow up."

How many times had he heard that speech? His father didn't need to work so much. Security was the perfect business. No one could ever have enough of it. He just liked working, liked avoiding Knox. Knox had his mother's smirk and his mother's laugh. All his happy expressions came from his mother. His father didn't like the reminder.

"Right back at ya, Dad," Knox said aloud.

Screw it, he thought. If my father doesn't need to stick around for his only son, then his only son doesn't need to stick around for him.

"Delete message," Knox told the machine.

"You have not listened to the message. Please confirm."

"Confirmed. Delete the message. And bring my clothes."

"Your clothes were burned in the accident."

Knox rolled his eyes. The textbooks could ramble about the "benefits to efficiency" brought by robotics, and the "emancipation of the proletariat from menial labor," but there was something irreplaceable about employees you could flirt with.

"Access my profile and bring me some *other* clothes that I'd like," he groaned. "Something for going out. Retro blue collar."

"I am unsure of the nature of this request," the robot said.

"Like Old Detroit." Knox sighed. "Just scan my profile pics or something, okay? And bring me a some datastream glasses."

"Confirmed, Mr. Brindle."

The robot rolled back out of the room.

"Retro glasses!" he called out after the bot. He didn't want to show up to the party of the year accessing his datastream on glasses that didn't fit the theme. He hoped the bot understood his needs.

Knox put his hands behind his head and looked up at the false sun on his holo.

Arcadia was just what he needed. Collect his cut from Nine, get some of whatever Cheyenne was holding. Clear his head out. Dance. Maybe find a Lower City chick to get crazy with. Or two. In a few hours he'd be normal again and he wouldn't have to think about his proxy or that girl, whatever her name was.

He let out a slow breath. He knew perfectly well what her name was.

Marie.

He saw her black hair, the purple shine of her eyes, the insouciant laugh. The scream as she died. He remembered it all.

Tonight, he'd do his best to forget.

[12]

RRRREEEEEEEEEEEEEEEEEEEEEEEEE . . .

The sound rang in Syd's ears. The blast had worked. Cold hunks of metal littered the ground around him, still smoking. He lay in a small crater beneath the Arak9's sizzling heat shield. It was all that remained of his machine. He checked himself for wounds. His shirt was slightly singed, but otherwise, he was unharmed.

He'd probably exposed himself to all kinds of unhealthy waves and ions and whatever, but he didn't have to worry about that for now. The whole Valve was a cancer cluster anyway, and Syd's life expectancy was less than an hour if he didn't find a way to get lost. And soon.

Every lower window of every building around him was shattered. The Rebooters would no doubt take credit for this attack as soon as they found out about it. It'd give

SecuriTech the perfect excuse for another roundup of undesirables. The farther he could get from the City before that happened, the better.

He jumped to his feet and stumbled through the sanitized streets of commercial office towers, trying to stay close to the tall buildings and hoping their electrical output would hide his signal. Hulking broom trucks zipped past, programmed to clean away any evidence of human filth. He ducked behind the concrete blast barriers, just in case he fit that category.

Syd crossed out of the commercial district and slid under a gap in the fence at the edge of the Valve. Glass and metal gave way to broken concrete strewn with garbage. The streets were narrow and twisting. Everything that could be used had been taken up, turned into a structure or a product. Wires crisscrossed over the lanes in huge jumbles, with hundreds of unlicensed branches tapping off the main lines. Shacks had been fashioned out of old packaging, heaps of projector parts, and solidified industrial runoff. It was a neighborhood where nothing was wasted.

Starved kids rummaged through piles of refuse. They eyed Syd greedily as he passed by. Nothing wasted except the people, Syd thought.

Puddles of postindustrial gel burned on the corners, turning to bricks. Syntholene dealers gestured back and forth to one another, passing patches hand to hand. Tweaked-out junkies sprawled on trash heaps, the code running through their blood, rattling their DNA. Hair fell out, tattoos appeared and vanished, all kinds of havoc wrought from the lowest-grade biopatches you could find. The sight was sickening. Willful mutation. The advertisements hovering around them quivered. Syd's system was so messed up from the blast, every ad he passed was for gum. He'd never actually chewed gum in his life.

Farther on, old gamers sat on piles of junk playing ancient handhelds across from one another, their networks so dodgy that their knees had to touch just to multiplayer like they did when they were kids.

Tattoo-covered thugs from the Maes gang radiated threat from the doorways to the speakeasy bars and members-only clubs. They too eyed Syd as he passed. Rumor had it that to be part of the Maes gang, you had to kill a patron. No way that could be true. If patrons started getting murdered, they'd bulldoze the whole Valve, but still, Maes guys had a reputation for brutality and Syd picked up his pace, avoided eye contact.

Double-wides with shades drawn and electropop blaring. Half-dressed women and outdated personal pleasure bots called out to Syd. Their lips moved but to him it was all pantomime. He couldn't hear a word.

RRRREEEEEEEEEEEEEEEEEEEEEEE . . .

He staggered up to the cruciplex where Egan lived—a 150-story bunker of a building with four wings, like a giant plus sign. There were patches of concrete tucked into ground level at each corner, which the architects originally meant to be communal gathering places for the thousands of low-rent units, but people started throwing their trash down there and no one ever paid to have it picked up.

Only the garbage pickers waded in to battle the sludge-hardened vermin that lived and died in the mountains of waste. Sometimes a picker caught one of the rodents and ate well that night. Sometimes it went the other way. The smell was awful.

Egan had an abnormal pride in his basement unit, even though it was no bigger than Syd's workroom off the back of Mr. Baram's shop and didn't have any way to get fresh air. It always smelled like feet.

When Syd opened the door, Egan pulled a knife on him.

It was a soldier's antique blade that Egan had stolen from Mr. Baram's when they were little kids. He'd learned to throw it and to spin it on his palm so that he could impress girls and older boys. He kept the blade sharp and shining and Syd really wished its tip wasn't touching his throat.

He made eye contact with Egan, who asked a question that Syd couldn't make out through the ringing in his ears. Syd blinked. Egan smirked and pulled the knife away, looked up and down the hallway, and then yanked Syd inside.

The narrow room had tin walls that Egan had covered with 3-D projections showing music holos, violent retro nature shows, and weird abstract images on a 24-7 loop. He said it calmed him. It didn't hurt that the combination of signals and metal walls made low-end electronic surveillance difficult. Any private security firm that was after Egan for whatever his latest offense was would have to go door-to-door the old-fashioned way, and Egan knew that he wasn't worth it. He was an expert at staying on the right side of a cost-benefit analysis.

Syd threw himself down on the black synthetic fur couch that Egan said he won playing dominoes. He rubbed his eyes. Was it still Friday?

The Guardians were after him, and aerial drones were no doubt cruising above the Valve with all kinds of sensors. Their equipment was designed to find people no matter where they were hiding, even in the massive cruciplexes below. They couldn't have a proxy breaking contract. Others might get ideas. And if contracts couldn't be enforced, the system would collapse. Contractual agreements, they all learned from the first day of school, were all that stood between civilization and a return to the age of chaos. Trying to delete a debt was like trying to destroy the world.

Syd was screwed.

"What the hell happened to you?" Syd finally made out Egan's voice through the buzz in his head. Egan handed him a bottle of water. "You look like a truck ran over you. And you're late. I went to all the trouble of making this awesome retro outfit for you, and what thanks do I get? None. Punctuality. Punctuality, my friend, is the hallmark of civilization!" He gestured too broadly for the small space, laughing. He was tweaked on something. "What do you think?"

He pointed to the shiny black jumpsuit with all kinds of straps and buckles hanging off it. It had a patch glued on to it that said, "Ed's Auto Repair." The name kept changing colors through the entire rainbow.

"I thought the rainbow was a nice touch. Took me an hour to get it right," he added.

"It's fine, listen, E, I need—" Syd started.

"Fine? Fine!" Egan leaned down on the couch towering over Syd. "*Fine?* I am an artist! There are three different kinds of synthetic pheromones in that outfit! Hell, I'm almost turned on! And you didn't even see the vintage baseball cap to go with it!" He held up a black baseball cap with a white D on it. It looked like it had been rolled over by an armored assault vehicle.

"That's an authentic hat! The Detroit Tigers. They're more extinct than real tigers. Don't ask how I got it. And all you've got is 'it's fine'? Unacceptable! Unbelievable! Un . . . um . . . whateverable! You are a terrible sidekick!" Egan started laughing again. His mood was swinging under the drug and Syd had to try to keep up. Between swells of laughter, Egan moved Syd over so he could sit on the couch next to him.

"Seriously, okay." His friend cleared his throat. "What the hell is going on?"

Syd told him everything that had happened from the moment he was arrested at Mr. Baram's. Egan nodded and smirked a bit when Syd described blowing up the combat robot to make his getaway. Egan's eyes darted from holo to holo behind Syd's head, but otherwise he was still.

"So," Syd finished. "I need something to fake out the scanners. New ID. And I need it, like, now."

"Intense," Egan whispered. "I mean, like, they really branded you?"

Syd showed him the metal letters embedded in his forearm. The swelling had gone down and his skin was healing over the edges. Egan swallowed. He reached out to touch the girl's name. Syd pulled his arm away and rolled his sleeve back down.

"So," he asked. "Can you help or what?"

Egan put his fingers on his lips. "Hush. Uncle E will make it all better." He laughed again.

Syd sighed. It would be an epic effort to get Egan focused enough to help him, but what choice did he have? He couldn't go back to Mr. Baram's. He didn't want to involve the old man, put his whole business in danger. No way. He'd always been good to Syd. He didn't deserve that. Syd's tweaked friend with the sketchy connections was his only hope.

"I can get you anything you need," Egan told him.

"Okay . . . ," Syd urged him. "So let's have it."

"Oh, my brother, my foolish, dumb brother." Egan patted Syd on the back, still laughing. "The party. We *have* to go to the party."

"Look, E, I really don't have time for this. I need to get the hell out of this city as fast as I can. Did you not hear me? I'm marked. Sterling Work Colony. I have to get away."

"I heard you, princess." Egan's voice changed. All the tweaked humor drained out of it. "And I am trying to tell you. I can't help you here. My friend at the party, he's the hookup. Well, his friend. Upper City kid, his father is some SecuriTech executive. He'll take care of you."

"I can't go to some Upper City party right now. My patron killed a girl and I just assaulted like a dozen Guardians."

"Oh, Sydney, you childish Chapter Eleven chicklet"—the crazy was back in Egan's voice—"would your old partner in crime ever let you go down without a fight? The Arctic will freeze over first." He chuckled, then suddenly stood from the couch with a leap. "Now, put on your outfit and let's go play with the rich kids. I swear, my guy there will hook you up. To quote the ancient prophet of your people: A DJ's gonna save your life tonight."

[13]

ARCADIA WAS MADNESS. THE young and the beautiful and the wish-they-were young and the medically beautiful writhed and slithered all over one another, bathed in the fume-pixilated light of the old warehouse. Images of the ruins of Old Detroit flashed on the walls all around, a jungle of steel overgrown with actual jungle.

Et in Arcadia Ego glowed in neon letters on an antique sign suspended from the ceiling. Knox wondered if it was in some lost language of Detroit.

Nine and Simi rushed over to him.

"I got a WhosWho alert on you and I couldn't believe it!" Nine shouted over the rumbling engines, the drum of feet stomping on metal, and the auto-tuned warble of some remixed tween pop star from a century and a half ago. "I can't believe you're here!"

"Very lux." Simi nodded, tapping Knox's glasses. They

were heavy black plastic, meant to look like something from the days of Moon Travel, before people stopped wasting money on that kind of thing. Mission Control, the style was. Knox liked the sound of that. He was in control, on a mission. "We're so happy you have the use of your higher faculties again," Simi blathered on. "They say there is no greater capacity in man than that of reason and liberty and property as its birthright."

Knox raised his eyebrows at Nine, who just shrugged. Simi wasn't dressed in the right era for the party. He was doing this whole yellow-vest-and-breeches thing, with a powdered wig and a riding crop. He thought historical re-enactment was going to be the next big thing and he wanted to be on the cutting edge of it. The white powder on his wig shimmered radioactive under the party's effect lighting. It dusted his shoulders like fallout.

"Whatever, Simi," Knox said. "So, Niner, how we rolling?"

"Oh, it's tight, my friend. We've got this place frozen! Half the kids here paid us to get in one way or another. Those codes you hacked from your dad . . . unreal."

"Yeah, well, let's hope they hold out long enough. They'll cycle out of the bloodstream eventually. Tell our customers to avoid peeing too much."

"Peeing?"

Knox just shrugged. "Where's Cheyenne?"

"Oh, she is tweaking beyond the beyond," Simi chirped. "I left her in a red convertible carriage somewhere. A Mustang! I believe that was a kind of horse! The cart has become the horse and the natural order has been mastered by the craft of man! Verily!"

The craft of man? Verily?

Simi was seriously glitched. He used to be captain of their lax team. Now he thought the sport was below his "station in life." He called it "savage." Knox couldn't wait until his whole NeoColonial fad passed.

"I'm gonna go find Chey," Knox said. "I need some of what she's holding."

"I hear you." Nine smirked. "Be free, young man! Fly like a whatever!"

"Master the intellect! When in the course of human events!" Simi called.

Knox tapped his glasses and accessed his friend menu. He scanned the list for Cheyenne, tapped his fingers over it in the air, and the augmented reality display lit up with a bright arrow over where Cheyenne was sitting. Knox climbed up onto the hood of the first car and started weaving his way through the party toward the arrow. Text holos flashed in the air around him like a light show as people without lenses communicated over the noise of the party.

It was tacky. Knox believed you shouldn't text at a party unless you had private feed. He didn't want to see all these cut-rate fonts crowding his view.

"Chey, what're you holding?" Knox flopped down next to his friend in the cracked leather seats of the ancient Mustang. The arrow vanished.

You've Arrived appeared in front of his eyes briefly, as if he didn't know it. He swiped the image away.

Cheyenne had shaved her head and hacked her biofeed so undulating tattoos rolled around her scalp all night, old logos from long-vanished corporations sliding and slithering from her neck to her forehead. It was dizzying. Her eyes were wide as galaxies.

"Hey . . . Knox . . . Knox . . . you're . . . Knox." Cheyenne smiled and burst into tears. "You're alive!"

"Okay, Chey, calm down. Help me out here."

Cheyenne leaned over the weird stick between the seats that people used to use to control cars and she hugged Knox. "I heard about Marie. I'm sorry. You should know, though, she's fine. She's free. She's on a journey into a new incarnation, you know?"

Cheyenne's parents ran a chain of NeoBuddhism centers all over the Upper City, so she was always talking like some kind of mystic sage. Knox thought all that superstition was ridiculous—he'd been raised a strict Objectivist—but it helped Cheyenne get through and made Chey's family rich. Two generations ago they'd been nobody.

"Whatever," Knox said. "Just hook me up."

Cheyenne slapped a thin plastic patch onto the back of Knox's hand. It stuck there and lit up. Silver veins glowed on its surface, changing to pink, then to green, then yellow and then the patch dissolved into his skin, leaving nothing but a slight itchy feeling.

"Very lux." Cheyenne smirked and leaned back on her seat. "The universe at your command."

Knox felt lighter within seconds.

A swell of energy ran through his body. His knees started to move back and forth with the music. He couldn't keep his hands still. A smile almost tore open his face, and he felt like his heart might explode. He looked over to Cheyenne to make sure this was normal, but Cheyenne was gone.

Maybe it had been longer than a few seconds.

He looked up at the partiers above him, dancing on the hood of the car, on the trunk, stepping over the seats clutching all kinds of weirdly colored drinks. The projections of their holos flashed and mingled in the air, passing through one another, squawking and beeping and dinging. Why couldn't everyone keep their holos to themselves? The gas smell made his stomach turn. The music felt threatening. He was only smiling because he couldn't stop. He flinched. He feared a spilled drink might wash his face clean off.

"Nice ride." A girl above him laughed and squatted down on the other side of the windshield and it was like she was speaking directly into his mind.

"You going my way?"

She cackled, and though her mouth was open and her teeth were shining at him, it was like she was silent and the laughter was in his head. She stopped cackling and looked at him. She had shining purple eyes and dark, gleaming hair.

Marie. It was Marie.

Knox shot up out of the seat to grab her, but the girl jumped back from him and he hit his head on the transparent windshield. He hit so hard, his glasses went crooked on his face, but he didn't feel any pain. The patch prevented pain. He straightened his glasses.

The girl didn't have purple eyes and her hair was brown, not black, pure Anglo. She didn't look like Marie at all. What the hell did Marie look like, anyway? Knox couldn't remember. His heart skipped every other beat. He felt like he had to remember.

"Freak." The girl who wasn't Marie walked away, vanishing in the fumes and lights and dancing bodies. Her voice was still in his head. Echoing. *Freak, freak, freak, freak.*

Was that a suggestion?

He looked down at his feet. He was standing on the seat of the car. Suddenly he felt like he was moving, like the car was racing, racing down that restricted speedway. He heard a sound like crunching metal. Felt his body fly through the air. Heard a scream, a girl screaming.

"Knox! Knox!" A hand grabbed his shoulder. He spun around, startled to find himself standing exactly where he'd been standing before. He fell onto the steering wheel. Time was unraveling. How long had he been standing up on the seat? How long had it taken him to fall?

He was half wedged under the steering wheel now, and wriggling to free himself.

"Chill, bro!" Nine yelled at him. Where had he come from? The words still sounded like they weren't coming out of the mouth that spoke them. Knox looked up into his friend's face. He looked worried. Confused. Probably reflecting Knox back at himself. Simi was next to Nine, his

powdered wig cocked to the side. He turned and talked to some other kids behind him. Nine squatted down.

"You all right?" he asked.

"YEAH." Knox shook himself and straightened his glasses. His own voice sounded too loud. He whispered, which felt better, "Just, Chey's umm . . ."

"Oh, that stuff's heavy. Drink this." Nine shoved some bright green liquid into Knox's hand. Knox shot it back in one gulp.

"Electrolytes." Nine smiled. *"And some other stuff. Anyway, we've got customers."* Nine pulled Knox up to his feet and onto the trunk of the car. *"These boys could use some ID. Top of the line, they're asking for. I told them you're the man."* Knox shook his head again, tried to get clear. *"He's a little tweaked right now, but he's cool,"* Nine yelled over the music at his customers, lost somewhere in the disintegrating universe behind him. Knox rubbed his eyes. Nine and Simi were still there. So was the universe.

Nine pulled two kids forward and Knox thought the drug was kicking in again, hard. One of them looked like every other retro wannabe in the room. But the other one, dressed incongruously in some queercore jumpsuit, had that proxy's face. Sydney's face.

Impossible.

[14]

THE PARTY RAGED. THAT was the only word for what it was. Raging. Like the pain behind Syd's eyes. Egan's head whipped around at every Upper City girl who walked past.

"He's a little tweaked right now," the kid called Nine yelled over the music at Syd and Egan. "But he's cool." Nine pulled Egan and Syd forward to meet this mysterious savior they'd been promised.

To Syd, at first, he looked like your average Upper City pretty boy. Light brown hair that hung over his ears and fell into his eyes. They were green, as far as Syd could tell, but they were also about as wide and crazed as Egan's, and the lights of the party flashed and shifted on the lenses of some serious designer glasses he was wearing. Behind the lenses, though, the eyes looked pained, and not just because of the drugs. It made the guy kind of beautiful. Exquisite suffering and maybe a little dim.

Totally Syd's type. Under different circumstances, he'd have been too nervous to even talk to a guy like this.

Nine tried to introduce them, but he didn't know their names, so Egan stepped up.

Maybe he thought they had a drug-addled kinship or something, but it didn't work. The guy kept staring right at Syd.

Nine said something offensive about his name. Why had Egan even told him that? Syd hated his stupid name, like another kind of scar, and he hated that Egan wasn't ashamed of anything. He shared too freely. If it was annoying before today, it was dangerous now that Syd was a fugitive from his debt.

He glared at Nine and at Egan to show them he was not amused. Then he put his hand out, tried to reach through the druggy haze and get this rich kid to speak, to help him get his ID and get out of this hellish club, but the guy didn't move. The ruins of Old Detroit flashed behind them.

Syd dropped his hand and looked closer at the rich kid. He was pale, the kind of pale that could only come from expensive sunscreens, and his skin was smooth and clear, although there was some sort of puffiness around the eyes, like a bruise that wasn't quite done healing. He was dressed in a pair of old-fashioned jeans and a perfectly tailored blue "work shirt" that looked like it had been custom-made for this party. He had on some lux AR glasses instead of a projector so that he could keep his datastream private. He obviously took care of himself and had the means to do so.

Syd felt his heartbeat quicken. He studied the boy,

looking for details the way Mr. Baram had taught him to read a person.

He'd been injured recently—maybe a fight? He didn't look much like a fighter. Too delicate. No scars. Although high-priced medicine could make sure there were never any scars. But still. So, an accident.

His fingernails were chewed and rough. It didn't match the rest of him, and any kid with skin that nice and hair that perfect would have kept his nails neat. So the chewing had to be recent. Why would a rich druggy kid chew his nails? Anxiety? Guilt? There was terror in his eyes too, in the way he was looking at Syd. Like he saw a ghost.

The Guardian's words came back to Syd: destruction of property. Reckless endangerment. Homicide.

Syd followed a hunch. He swallowed hard. If he was wrong, he could always play it off as something else, but if he was right . . .

"It's you, isn't it?" he asked.

The reaction told him he was right.

"This is Knox," Nine said. "Dude, Knox, what's up? You hanging in there?"

Syd watched Knox crumple in front of him. Amazing after all these years that this boy—his patron—had a name. Knox.

All those petty crimes. All those brutal punishments he took for a boy named Knox with hazy green eyes and professionally protected skin.

He remembered an ancient clay tablet. When he was

little—about four years old maybe—he remembered being dragged out of bed at the orphanage in nothing but his underpants, almost like today, and made to stand in a bright room off Mrs. Prabu's office.

A light appeared on a wall panel and shone right into his eyes. Mrs. Prabu spoke toward the wall, like she was introducing Syd to the light. He now knew she had been speaking to his patron and whoever else was watching, but at the time he thought it was kind of funny, and he laughed.

He'd stopped laughing when Mrs. Prabu took out the long silver EMD stick. She asked him some question he didn't understand about credits and debt and that was the first time he heard the words "proxy" and "patron"; all he remembered clearly after that was the pain of the shocks she gave him, one, two, three, four, five, like his skin was being burned off from the inside and he cried and cried.

It took him about a year to stop crying when he was punished, and another year to understand that he wasn't being punished for anything that he did. He came to believe he was being punished simply for being born.

When he was about twelve and started to realize he had feelings that weren't like other boys' feelings, when he'd stare too long at Egan while he slept, or watch some of the older boys wrestling in the muddy riverbed too intensely, he started to believe that his patron's misdeeds were a reflection of his own dark thoughts. He went back to the childish belief that he deserved every punishment he received. For a few years, alone with his secret, he convinced himself that this patron of his was cosmic punishment for his desires. Part of him still believed it.

And now Syd stood face-to-face with the author of his punishment, his lifelong creditor, and he was beautiful, and he was tweaked, and he had killed a girl, and only he could save Syd's life.

Knox stared back at the boy he'd only ever seen on-screen, the boy he'd watched get tortured in his place just a few hours ago. The boy who, right now, was supposed to go to Sterling Work Colony in his place for sixteen years.

He felt his hands go numb, his mouth tingle. It didn't make sense. He couldn't be here. Patron confidentiality. He wasn't real. His eyes shone through the haze like polished black diamonds.

What the hell was a black diamond?

Knox shook himself and vowed never to take anything Chey gave him ever again.

He backed away, turned from his proxy, and tried to vanish into the mass of dancing bodies, blurred by the lights and the projections and the fumes.

Syd was not going to let him get away so easily.

"Where are you going?" Nine called, as Syd raced into the crowd after Knox.

Knox didn't look back. He weaved through the bodies, stumbled over hood ornaments, knocked people out of the way.

Syd was right behind him.

"Hey, Ed." A girl with shining silver hair grabbed Syd's

arm and pulled him toward her. Or was it him? Androgyny was a privilege of the wealthy. "You wanna fix my car?"

Syd felt a hand on his chest, another reaching around his back, which was still tender from the shocks he'd been given. He winced and pulled away.

"Where you going, Ed?" his silver-haired pursuer called out. "I need some auto repair! My engine's running hot!"

Syd wished Egan hadn't put that rainbow label on the coveralls. He'd lost time; Knox had slipped away.

Syd climbed up onto the cab of a truck to get a better view of the space.

Knox pushed dancers out of the way, slammed into their shoulders, stumbled. He was too tweaked, moving too fast. Texts popped up in his glasses.

You party?

Hey Foxy Knoxy, where you runnin'?

Knox ignored them. He couldn't stop. He rushed for the door.

Syd jumped off the truck to follow him, when he saw a strikingly beautiful woman weaving through the crowd in the opposite direction. There were two more by the entrance. He whipped around and saw the same beautiful face scattered through the crowd, dressed to blend in, but still far too perfect to be natural.

The Guardians had found him.

[15]

"PATRON CONFIDENTIALITY," KNOX REPEATED to himself over and over, willing it to be true, willing it far too late for his will to matter. His proxy simply could not have found him. And yet he had.

Knox's steps reverberated off the hoods of the cars as he ran, thumping along with the beat of the music. Every face he saw looked like Marie's. Every body that touched his as he passed felt like a threat. He was losing it and he knew he was losing it and there was nothing he could do but run.

Except he didn't know which way to go. He couldn't tell where the door was. His vision was a kaleidoscope of light and skin and impossible faces and he knew he was now just turning in place, spinning, panicked, but his feet wouldn't push him forward. He stood beneath the old neon sign with the cryptic words in the weird language and he just spun.

As the faces around him swirled, one face stood out, like it wouldn't blur no matter how fast he turned. It was beautiful. Striking.

A Guardian. And she was heading right for him.

His father must have sent them. His dad probably knew that Knox had checked out of the hospital and sent the Guardians to drag him home. Watching Sydney's punishment wouldn't have been enough. He probably wanted to keep Knox sealed away to avoid any more "embarrassment." Or maybe he knew Sydney had escaped and sent them to protect Knox. Which one was it? Protection or punishment? Who could Knox trust?

Nobody, he decided, or maybe the patch racing through his blood decided for him. He spun away from the Guardian and tried to head in the opposite direction. The faces around him were laughing. They didn't look like Marie anymore; they didn't even look human, just teeth, just laughing teeth, mocking him as he spun and stumbled and spun some more.

He tried to text Chey or Simi or Nine to get help, but he couldn't get his lenses to work right. He just blinked uselessly and waved his arms, flapping his hands like a dying plague victim. The glasses suddenly felt slick on his face, like they were covered in blood, thick, black, oily blood.

He couldn't see. He pulled them off and wiped at them furiously, snapping out one of the lenses. It clattered between his feet and vanished down a crack between two cars. He dropped the frames and stomped on them, kicked the fragments away. He didn't need any augmented reality. He had the patch for that and it had turned on him. He needed obliterated reality, anti-reality.

Knox looked up. Everything was a little duller, a little grayer, a little more blurry. Still way too real.

"You're coming with me." A voice broke through the noise in his brain, froze his blood, stopped him spinning.

Sydney stood in front of him. He'd grabbed Knox by the shoulder and gripped him tightly. He stared into Knox's eyes.

"You hear me? You're coming with me right now. We're getting out of here. You will not steal my life." His words matched his mouth movements. They weren't in Knox's head anymore. This was a good sign

"I . . . ," Knox started.

One of Sydney's hands went to his pocket. He pulled out a small plastic tube and pressed it against Knox's side. Knox heard a click. This was not a good sign.

Some kind of weapon? Was he being kidnapped?

Knox Brindle, scion of SecuriTech, kidnapped?

Should he cry out for help? Scream for his father's beautiful goons to come to the rescue?

Which was worse, the Guardians and his father or this orphan from the Valve who was probably bent on some horrifying revenge?

He nodded at his proxy.

He didn't need his father to rescue him. He'd do it himself.

"This way." He felt Sydney pulling him forward, knocking dancers out of the way, weaving toward the door as he dug the tube harder into Knox's ribs.

Suddenly, they stopped. He followed Sydney's line of sight to two Guardians coming straight toward them. Sydney spun around so his back was to the Guardians, blocking their view. He looked Knox right in the eyes. Knox wished there was still a holo projection between them.

"Sorry about this," Sydney said and put one hand behind Knox's head and pulled him close, kissing him deeply on the mouth, wrapping himself around Knox, pressing their bodies tight against each other. He felt a little stubble from Sydney's chin. The proxy's lips were chapped and he smelled like sweat and fumes and metal. Terrible breath.

Knox had never kissed anyone with stubble before. He'd never kissed anyone with chapped lips or bad breath either. He had standards.

He tried to pull away but the more he struggled, the tighter Syd held him. Knox went rigid, didn't move a muscle. He thought about biting Sydney, but the Guardians walked right past them and Knox felt Sydney let him go. His face moved away. It betrayed no emotion. It had actually been some pretty quick thinking on the proxy's part. Knox might have appreciated it more if he wasn't being kidnapped.

He didn't hesitate. He took a swing at Sydney, but he was still sloppy from Chey's patch, and he swung wide. Sydney grabbed his arm as it flew past and twisted it around his back and pressed the plastic tube against Knox's ribs again.

"Come on," he said, and they were moving through the crowd.

The music was thumping and the dancers in heavy boots

jumped up and down on the cars. The sound of crunching metal ripped right through Knox and he felt himself going backward in his mind, going back to the accident. He saw Marie next to him in the car, laughing with delight, then screaming. He felt his body fly through the air.

The next thing Knox knew he and Sydney were standing outside, off to the side of the building. Sydney pulled him behind a large generator in the alley.

"The generator will hide our signal from drones," Sydney said. Knox just looked at him. He was insane.

"My father wouldn't have sent drones looking for me," Knox said.

"What?" Sydney snapped. "Your father? What are you talking about? The drones are looking for me. And it's your fault."

Knox didn't answer. He had to remember his training. Every SecuriTech executive's family received training about what to do in a kidnapping. His instructor was some meathead from the special forces of the Benevolent Society. He told them horror stories about his years on the East Coast running rescue operations. He told them about all the violent groups that wanted to see them and their way of life destroyed: foreign competitors, unlicensed scavengers, Sinoid crime syndicates, Rebooters and flesh peddlers, fanatic pastoralists and old-fashioned warlords.

Knox remembered being bored. At the end they'd taken a quiz. Knox hadn't passed and his father refused to speak to him for days.

When Knox objected to the silent treatment, his father told him, "It'll be a lot worse when you're in captivity in some swampy bog, riding out hurricanes and being sold back to me in pieces."

He'd made Knox retake the class with a private security tutor. She was gorgeous. He remembered that much. Natural redhead. Retired combat operations consultant for one of the big software companies. He remembered the curve of her neck, the small piece of her ear that was missing from a firefight with one of the IP piracy gangs. The way she let him flirt and then twisted his neck with one hand when he tried to kiss her. He was thirteen and it was the first time an adult had ever inflicted any pain on him.

He screamed out, begged her to stop. She ignored him. She kept twisting.

"No proxy here for you now," she said. "It's just you and me."

And then he'd remembered her first rule: Make yourself human to your abductor. Tell them about yourself. Become real. Through his tears, he told the instructor how his mother died, how it was his fault. She was the only person he'd ever told.

The instructor let his neck go.

"It's the debts you can't repay that matter," she said. Knox stormed out of the room crying and the instructor never said a word to his father. He passed the course.

He had to make himself human to this boy, Sydney. It was his only chance.

"Listen, Sydney," he said.

"Just Syd," the kid growled.

"What?"

"Just Syd," he repeated. "Not Sydney."

"Oh . . . right, Syd. Well, listen, Syd, I'm sorry about . . ." He couldn't think what. It wasn't like *he* owned Syd's debt. That was his father. "Everything," he said, which he figured was broad enough. You could never repay "everything," right?

"Don't read anything into that kiss back there," Syd said. "I don't like you and I don't want to know you. I don't care what you think about anything or what you're sorry for. The only thing you can do for me now is help me get out of this city. Egan and your friend told me you can do that. Can you do that?"

"I . . ." Knox stumbled. "You don't want to, like, torture me?"

Syd stared at him, breathing loudly through his nose. "You have no idea how much I want to," he said after a minute. Knox swallowed hard. "But that's not gonna happen. I just want to get away from all this and I can't do it without your help. You owe me that."

"I owe you?" Knox couldn't believe what he was hearing. The debt was Syd's, not Knox's. Knox didn't have any debt. He was a patron. He had more money than he could spend in a lifetime.

"Yes," said Syd.

"I don't owe you anything," Knox answered. "Get that? Nothing. You're just the one with the weapon."

Syd clenched his jaw. "Then I guess you owe me obedience, right? I mean, if I've got the weapon?"

Knox seethed quietly, but he nodded. "How did you even find me?"

"I didn't," said Syd. He didn't elaborate and he didn't explain. Knox was suspicious. As the patch's effects throbbed their way out of his system, he started to think more clearly.

He and Nine had been selling fake biofeed patches for a while now. Nine knew all kinds of sleazy characters and Knox knew how to hack his father's company's system to make the IDs.

What if SecuriTech was on to it and they'd given Syd a choice: You can go to Sterling Work Colony for sixteen years or you can help us plug a security leak? Oh, and by the way you'll also get revenge for everything your patron has put you through.

Knox knew what he would do in that situation. It wasn't a choice at all.

The only question was whether or not his father knew what was going on. And his father always knew what was going on. He must have sent Syd after Knox the moment he heard that Knox had left the hospital.

The whole thing had to be a setup. It had to be. Or were the drugs just making him paranoid?

No matter what, Knox knew now that he couldn't trust a word this Syd kid said. He had to get away as soon as possible.

[16]

SYD HAD IMAGINED MEETING his patron so many times over the years in so many different ways. He'd imagined beating him senseless with his fists; he'd imagined hitting him with the EMD at the highest settings; he'd imagined his patron begging for forgiveness and he'd imagined all the things he'd say to this person who'd made his life a living hell since he was four years old.

None of his fantasies went like this.

He'd also imagined his first kiss. He'd imagined it thousands of times, maybe millions, with Atticus Finch, with that one security guard trainee at the dispensary, with some imagined patron who appeared in the shop one day needing an emergency repair on his CX-30 who would sweep Syd away to Upper City to live in love and light and luxury. He'd even thought about a kiss with Egan, though he'd never admit it to his best friend's face.

None of those fantasies went like this either.

He was squatting behind a greasy generator, dressed like some sort of zonked-out club kid, while drones prowled the sky. The Guardians would be here any second. He gripped Knox's arm to keep him down, squeezing it tighter than he probably needed to, and he was holding an antique pen against his patron's rib cage. He was in deep breach of contract now.

Attacking your patron? What happened to the butcher Doolaine would seem like a kindness in comparison to what they'd do to him.

Knox shifted his weight, like he was about to run. His eyes darting around the alley looking for the best escape route. He was probably paranoid from whatever drug he was on. Syd had seen it a million times with Egan. If things got weird, the drug made them weirder. If things got scary, the drug made them scarier. Tonight qualified as both weird and scary, and Knox was probably losing it.

Knox would be useless to Syd if he freaked out again, spinning in circles and muttering, and if he tried to run, Syd couldn't stop him out in the open without the drones or the Guardians seeing him. In truth, he had no idea how he was going to get out of here without Knox cooperating.

He had to convince this guy that he was telling the truth, he hadn't come looking for him. He had to make Knox want to help.

"I didn't mean to find you," Syd explained. "I was just trying to get away and I heard you could hook me up with ID. I didn't know you would also be *you* . . ." He wasn't making much sense. He was probably freaking Knox out even more. "Look, I get it; this is crazy. Impossible, even. But it's happening."

He pulled the pen away from Knox's side and showed it to him, clicked a few times as Knox's eyes went wide and then Syd put it back in his pocket. He let go of Knox's arm.

"You kidnapped me with an antique pen?" Knox asked. The stupidity of it seemed to clear his head, focus his eyes.

Syd shrugged. "Listen: Guys like me don't survive long in Sterling Work Colony. If you don't help me out here, you'll be responsible for two deaths, not just the one. I don't know you and I don't know if that means anything to you, but there it is."

Knox looked at the entrance to the alley. If he was going to run, this was the moment. He looked up at the sky, scanning for drones. After a long silence, he turned back to Syd. His body slackened.

"I didn't mean to kill her," he said. His eyes met Syd's. This was the moment. He opened up. "I swear it was an accident. I swear it."

"That doesn't matter," Syd said. "They're after me because of you."

"I-I . . . ," Knox stammered. Syd had rattled him.

Good. Syd needed to rattle him. He had to get through that arrogant, pampered shell of a patron and try to find a person underneath, someone who might care just a little that he had ruined another human being's life. Syd stepped closer to Knox.

"It's okay," he said. "You can help now."

"I just . . . ," Knox said. Then his expression hardened, and he sprang onto Syd like heat lightning, slamming Syd against the generator and pinning him to the ground with a knee in his stomach. The hat with the D toppled off his head. Knox's forearm was pressed across Syd's throat and all his weight was pressing down, squeezing the air out of him.

Of course. The rich kids must learn self-defense for moments just like this, Syd thought. He'd been stupid to let his guard down.

"Who sent you?" Knox demanded, his emerald eyes flashing rage. Flecks of spittle splattered on Syd's face. "My father? Did my father send you?"

"I . . ." It was Syd's turn to choke out words. He couldn't breathe, let alone speak. He tried to pull Knox's arm away, but he had no leverage, and beneath his pretty boy exterior, Knox was clearly stronger than Syd, better fed and better trained. He squirmed but couldn't get free. "Not lying . . . ," he croaked. He used the side of the Dumpster to edge his sleeve down his arm, revealing the shining metal branding. "Not lying," he said again.

Knox's eyes darted over to Marie's name. He saw the glistening of the metal letters in the raw skin. The pressure of his arm slackened a tiny bit.

That was all Syd needed. He twisted so that Knox lost balance and then bucked with all his might to toss Knox off him. As soon as he was clear, he rolled away and jumped to his feet.

Knox was on his feet too. He charged and swung. Syd

sidestepped and just missed a punch to the throat. He tried to land a kick to the groin—they don't fight pretty in the Valve—but Knox blocked it. He'd been trained by someone who knew how to brawl, or at least, knew how Valve kids would brawl.

They circled each other.

Syd knew he couldn't stay out here much longer, especially not standing up. He'd be found.

Knox knew he couldn't beat this kid easily. He didn't know how long he could keep fighting like this. He hoped Syd hadn't noticed he was already tiring.

"Look, Knox," Syd said, panting. "Just help me and I'll never bother you again. I know you saw me with the Guardians today. I know that's how this works. You've always seen it. And I know your father pays for it. If I hate anyone, it's him. I would never work for him. That's why I never cried when they punished me. I didn't want to let your father use my tears. They belong to me. So why, after all those years that I didn't do his work for him—punishing you—would I start doing it now?"

"Because you're afraid," Knox said.

"No," Syd said, and he thought, maybe he really meant it. "That's you. You're afraid. I'm just angry."

They circled each other, breathing heavily. Syd's eyes kept darting from Knox to the warehouse door and to the alley entrance. Some of the ferocity had left Knox's face. He didn't let his guard down, but Syd could tell he was making progress. He just had to hold out a little longer.

"You don't even have to trust me," he told Knox. "Just help me get away."

He decided to take another chance. He dropped his fists. He stood still.

Knox hesitated, flexed, and then let arms fall to his side. He didn't take his eyes off Syd and time squeezed hours into seconds as they passed. He needed to be rid of this boy. Knox had already killed a girl. He had to deal with that. He couldn't deal with his proxy's issues too. But the easiest way to get rid of him would be to get him the fake ID. Syd couldn't exactly go back to being Knox's proxy anymore. Not after they'd met. It just wouldn't work. The system had to be impartial.

There was an added benefit, Knox realized. Helping Syd get away would drive his father crazy.

"I'll get you the ID," Knox told him. "And then you'll disappear? Never find me again."

"Definitely."

"And if you're lying, I'll kill you. No one will be able to protect you. I have the cred to end you wherever you hide."

Syd nodded.

"All right." Knox scratched the back of his neck as he thought. "I need a datastream to do this."

"Where are your glasses?"

"I lost them inside."

"You don't carry extras?" Syd figured every rich kid had a few projectors to spare.

Knox shook his head. "At home. I can do it at my place."

"How are we going to get there?" Syd asked. He bent down and picked up the old cap. He brushed it off and put it back on, pulling the brim down low over his face. "Even like this, I can't exactly go strolling through the streets of the Upper City."

Knox rummaged in his work shirt and pulled out a little patch. He tossed it to Syd.

"Just put that on, okay? It'll trick the basic scanners for at least another hour."

"You just carry these patches around?" Syd had his doubts. He worried that Knox was going to drug him, that he'd wake up half tweaked out of his mind in a transport to Sterling.

"Just tonight," said Knox. "Selling them to kids at the party. Your friend was about to pay for two of those . . . and now you're getting one at no cost."

"Everything costs," grunted Syd. "So if I put this on, what happens then?"

"It'll overwrite your biofeed for a bit," Knox said.

"I mean, after that."

"You Valve kids have no imagination." Knox shook his head. "There's not much I can't get with this smile." He grinned. Now that there was mischief to get into, it all felt a little less overwhelming. The world started to feel familiar again. He walked toward the entrance to the alley. "Wait here, okay?"

"You're not going to run, are you?" Syd asked.

"It's your turn to trust me."

"I don't," said Syd. "Not even a little bit."

"Not even after our kiss?" Knox laughed. Syd didn't. The proxy had no sense of humor. "Lighten up, swampcat."

Syd glared at him. He was now very certain that even if Knox wasn't his patron, he would hate him.

"You did cry, by the way," Knox called back as he walked away.

"What?"

"That whole first year, when we were kids. You cried from day one."

"When you broke that clay tablet." Syd nodded. "You remember?"

"I remember."

"That makes two of us."

"All right." Knox pursed his lips. "BRB." He turned and left the alley.

You better be, thought Syd, as he put the patch on skin and watched it light up and dissolve. He leaned against the Dumpster, trying to focus, to see if he felt any different as his ID changed.

He didn't feel a thing.

[17]

BRB? KNOX WONDERED IF Syd would even know what that meant. He couldn't believe he was helping this kid. He shouldn't even *know* him.

It wasn't like he meant to kill the girl. It was an accident. Why should he have to go through all this just because of an accident? It didn't seem fair. He never wanted anyone to get hurt. He just wanted to have some fun. He wondered: If he got Syd a new ID, would it cancel out Marie's death? Would his balance be back to zero?

He started to feel better now that the patch was mostly out of his system and he had a sense of purpose, a goal. The right motivation. Clear his conscience and drive his father crazy.

He smirked. The CEO's son's proxy escaping. That would send consumer confidence into the toilet. The stock price would plummet. *Ha-ha, Dad. Who's learning their lesson now?*

Knox found a group of younger girls he thought he recognized from the halls at school standing near the back of the line to get into Arcadia. There was a Guardian up by the door next to the SecuriTech GateMaster Pro X Club Model, a sleek black robot built with a keen eye for celebrity and style. Its algorithm was one of the most closely guarded secrets in the entertainment business. Of course, Knox and Nine had hacked it to get into clubs back when they were thirteen.

He stayed at a distance from the entrance and approached the girls, keeping his head turned away from the club entrance.

"Hey." He sidled up to them. They stared at him, speechless. He had never spoken to these girls before and normally wouldn't, which they certainly knew. He was at the top of the social order. They were not. But maybe they were gaping for another reason. He ran his hand through his hair to make sure it was okay. Finally one of them spoke. The words poured out of her.

"OMG. We heard about the accident? Are you okay? I mean, like, that must have been so . . . well . . . you know . . ." She was a brunette. A little horse-faced, but with a high-end makeup job. Her concern was touching. One of her friends shushed her.

"Thank you." Knox reached out and touched her arm, nodding with appreciation. Her friends all dropped their jaws. Knox let the brunette stare into his eyes for a while. He made them look a little sad, a little pained. It wasn't hard at the moment. No one moved. Knox knew he had them.

On the wall behind the girls, advertising holos flashed from their profiles, gene mods and diet patches, passion scents and romantic restaurants. A sports drink. A horror movie. On any other night he might have been intrigued, might have wanted to get to know these girls, at least for a few hours.

"What's your name?" he whispered.

"Galafrain," the girl answered. "Or just Gala."

"Like a celebration," Knox said. She nodded. Her friends looked back and forth between them. "Listen, Gala, you know my car got wrecked in the accident, and my friend and I need a ride home . . . you think you could help us out?"

"I don't have . . . ," she started, and looked mortified.

"Or just call us a ride, huh? I'd do it, but . . ." He looked meekly at his shoes, rubbed the back of his neck, gave an embarrassed smile, and let the unfinished sentence fade without explanation. Let them fill in their own reasons.

"I can call my mom's transpo service," one of the other girls piped in. Knox looked at her and let his smile blossom. He hugged her.

"You guys are my heroes," he said to the girls as he started to back away. "All of you. For real."

When Knox came back into the alley, Syd stood from behind the generator.

"You're back," he said.

Knox smirked. "You thought I'd ditch you, just like that?"

Syd didn't answer. He'd had exactly that thought.

Knox had seen that look Syd was giving him a thousand times on holos over the years, like Syd thought he was better than everyone else just because he suffered. His arrogance was probably hiding some deeper issue, like he wet the bed or something.

Whatever, thought Knox. He didn't need to analyze his proxy. He just needed to get him away from the city. He wondered what his father would do when the proxy vanished. What would he do when he heard Knox helped? He'd have to take notice, anyway. Maybe he'd want to negotiate for Syd, give Knox something in return.

Knox snorted to himself. It was a dumb idea. His father didn't negotiate with terrorists. SecuriTech rule number one.

The transport pulled up to the mouth of the alley, and Knox motioned for Syd to get in.

"Is it safe?" Syd wanted to know. He didn't like the idea of hopping into some Upper City vehicle.

Knox rolled his eyes and got in. Let Syd make his own choices. Syd didn't know that these private transpo services were paid for their discretion. They ran on autodrive. There was no one to betray them and the program stored no data. Anonymity was a privilege worth paying for.

Syd got in, but he didn't even look at Knox once they were on the way. Didn't even compliment his brilliance at using those girls to get an untraceable ride home. Ungrateful proxy.

Knox leaned back on the cool leather seat and rested his head on the window, watching the glistening skyscrapers pass and thin out, revealing parks with trees and artificial lakes and the private mansions built on the old landfill bluffs. Knox had heard they didn't have green space in the Valve.

It looked like an alien landscape to Syd. He'd never seen so much open space, so much green. He'd heard about it, and seen it in movies, but to drive through it on the restricted roads . . . it was not something he'd ever imagined doing. His senses were on high alert. He didn't like being up here. At least in the Valve, he knew the rules, knew the dangers. Up here, he had no idea what to expect. But they drove without seeing so much as a security checkpoint.

The landscape was far from alien to Knox. There was the corner where Bao Lin's Candies used to be, the park where he first kissed Cheyenne and she punched him, the trail by the lake where he and Nine first tried syntholene and ran around all afternoon singing at the Carebots with their strollers and pink, whining babies.

There was the intersection where his mother's body was dumped.

There was the route to the restricted speedway where Marie died.

Amazing how those places looked just like other places.

They skirted Xelon Park along the side where the weeping willows grew. The trees were already dying, like they did every year. They were expensive, but the park's subscribers insisted on them. New ones were generated and planted every summer, only to die by the next spring.

Knox looked over at Syd, who was looking out the window. He studied the strange mark behind the proxy's ear, four discolored shapes visible even on his dark skin. They looked almost like a word, like a tattoo, but in no language he recognized.

Syd caught him looking and brought his fingers up to the spot, covering the mark and turning his head so Knox couldn't see.

"Just a birthmark," he said.

Knox shrugged and looked back out the window.

When they pulled through the gate into the driveway of Knox's house and drove up, Syd gaped at the view over the park.

Knox hopped out of the car to get inside quickly, but Syd stood gazing out over the driveway to the city below, his mouth hanging open. The transport pulled off to go back to its owner and they were alone. Syd listened to the night. He'd never heard such quiet before. The Valve was always loud with advos and holos and coughing and cursing and shouting and screaming and the everyday noises of living. The residential part of Upper City sounded to him like a paradise. Or a graveyard.

"We need to get inside," Knox said.

"This is your house?" Syd asked in disbelief.

"Yeah." Knox had never seen it through anyone else's eyes before. The staff was robotic, and low-level employees of his father's company never came over. Knox's friends all went to his school. All their houses looked like this.

Seeing Syd see his house made Knox notice things he'd forgotten about, like the way the lights lit the long glass wall on the side or how the infinity pool reflected the image of the house back at itself upside down.

He remembered when he was a kid standing out here looking at the pool and imagining that it was a gateway to a duplicate world, a world almost exactly like this one, except in that world it was his father who had died and he and his mother who lived in the big house.

"Get inside before some drone picks up your signal."

"What about your parents?" Syd asked.

"It's just me and my dad," Knox told him. "And my dad won't be home." Knox didn't elaborate. Syd didn't need to know his life story, how his father rarely came home during the week, how he slept in his office, how he rarely came home at all.

They made their way up the steps to the heavy steel front door and slipped inside. Lights came on automatically.

"Welcome, Knox," the house said. "Please identify your friend."

"Disengage activity assistant," Knox said. "Delete entry file."

"Deletion confirmed. Good-bye," the house said cheerfully.

"We'll be okay now." He led Syd through the living room with its vintage furniture and contemporary art that some consultant picked for his dad. Antiques from his great-grandmother's collection sat in cases around the room. He noticed Syd looking at every clay tablet with more than casual interest.

"Those are, like, two thousand years old," Knox explained, but Syd didn't respond. He didn't care how old they were. He was curious to see the one that had cracked when he was a kid.

"It's that one." Knox pointed. He understood what Syd wanted. "They restored it. I barely left a mark."

"On the tablet," Syd added.

They passed by a case of old books. One of them was displayed open, filled with detailed illustration and tiny writing in some weird ancient language. Knox didn't remember which one.

"Looks kind of like your birthmark," he said, thinking maybe he'd find something to talk to this swampcat about.

Syd didn't say anything. Knox guessed his proxy wasn't much for small talk. He brushed some hair out of his face, just to have something to do with his hands, and he led Syd upstairs to his room.

The lights came on dimly as Syd followed him in. There were at least a dozen projectors and a few pairs of networked glasses and a half-dozen little cases for biofeed-enabled contact lenses lying around. Knox had a momentary pang of embarrassment, like he was showing off.

Syd was not impressed.

Ayn Rand glowered at them from a projection on the wall. The Dying Fish with their original drummer glowered from a projection opposite. There was another of the supermodel Nadia holding an egret at the zoo. Hers was the only image not glowering. Her projection blew a kiss over and over.

Syd raised his eyebrows at the decorations.

Knox waved his hand and brought up a control holo, hovering in front of him. Another tap on it and his decorations disappeared. His proxy didn't need to critique his taste in interior design.

Knox opened a drawer filled with tiny patches for installing biotech through the skin.

"We can do this two ways," he told Syd. "We can trick you out with some biodes that will fool most any machine looking at you and will scan manually as somebody else. There's always a chance it'll fail, though, if they can see through it. It's basically just sending a stronger signal, like a layer of fog to mess with their ID coding. It works against most systems, except the really high-end stuff."

"Knox, look around." Syd waved his hand around the room. "I belong to your father. As far as anyone in that club knows, I kidnapped you. And you have no idea what I did to escape from the Guardians to get to that club. I think they're looking for me with some 'really high-end stuff.'"

"Okay," Knox agreed. "So the other option is we go into the SecuriTech biometric files and change who it is they're looking for. Then we have to do the same thing with the Xelon Insurance Division and any subcontractors we can find. It'll take a few hours."

"Will your dad be home?"

"Maybe."

"You don't seem worried."

"He won't even know we're here on this end of the house."

"What if he comes looking?"

"He won't come looking."

"Seriously?"

"You don't know a lot about fathers, huh?"

"No."

They stood in uncomfortable silence for a while. It was strange seeing Syd in his room. He'd seen him in holos so many times, but to have him here in the flesh . . .

"Look," he said. "I do this better with some music on, so I can focus. Why don't you take a shower and a nap or something? You can borrow some of my clothes to change out of that . . . outfit."

"Thanks," Syd said. He wasn't saying much. He didn't seem exactly comfortable in Knox's house either. On that they were in sync.

"Oh," Knox added, handing him a silver skin patch. "Put this on in the shower. It'll lighten your skin a little. We don't want to go through all this just to have you eyeballed by some low-rent security guard."

Syd grabbed the patch. Knox got him a towel and some

normal clothes and he disappeared into the bathroom, locking the door with a loud click.

Knox heard the shower start up and he turned on his randomizer. Tragic Harpie Bingo came on. He'd seen them live last winter. He actually hadn't had tickets and he'd had to sneak in to the show. It was a blast.

When he got caught, Syd got four hours of volunteer work at the recycling plant. Knox changed the music. Wagner. Old Eurozone. That'd clear his head. He blasted it and got to work on his hack.

If he believed in any of the old religions, or any of the new ones, he might start to think he was helping Syd out of some kind of guilt. But he wasn't. He was helping Syd because it suited him to. It was that simple. He'd made a mistake, a huge, tragic mistake, and in order to settle it, he'd help Syd. The balance would be settled, no debt outstanding.

He turned the music up.

[18]

SYD HAD NEVER HAD a shower like this. The water came from six different showerheads from six different directions and he could control the temperature just by waving his hand. It changed instantly.

No filling up tanks and lighting flames. No timers for water usage or haggling with the shower monitors. No keeping a knife on you while you washed and going half blind from the toxic soap because you couldn't close your eyes even for a second. Knox's shower had a seal that trapped in the steam.

Finally relaxing, Syd felt all the pain coming back, from the EMD pulses, from the punches Knox rained on him, from the dull ache of fear. It reminded him of all the other beatings he'd ever taken, his memory filled with the echo of wounds.

He ran his fingers along the scar on his collarbone.

After they left the orphanage, he and Egan took up with a gang of other street kids, standing lookout while they raided Upper City construction sites. They crouched behind blast barriers and watched the traffic of Upper City transports racing along the restricted roads.

"I'm gonna live up there one day," Egan had declared, pointing at the tallest skyscraper. "All the way on top. You'll see."

"That's the Oosha Panang Chemical Supply Company HQ." Syd laughed. "See the logo? You can't live there! No one lives there!"

"I didn't mean that building." Egan blushed. "I meant . . . the other one."

"What other one?" Syd cackled. "You want to be an office cleaner? You can sleep there when everyone else goes home? Clean the patrons' toilets? Then you'll live there! Toilet King of Upper City!" Syd was giggling uncontrollably.

"Shut up, swampcat," Egan'd yelled. Syd stopped laughing and he punched Egan right in the chin. Egan went down and Syd jumped on him. Egan rolled him over and punched him in the nose. Blood gushed out and tears welled in his eyes. He tried to claw at Egan's face.

Neither of them was strong enough to do any real damage to the other and the fight wound itself down into panting and half-hearted punches. By the end, they were lying on the ground, side by side, laughing about the patrons' toilets.

"You think they shit like we do?" Egan wondered.

"Of course." Syd laughed. "It all rolls right down into the Valve."

"I guess they want us to pay them that back too." Egan laughed.

"We should it bring it back to them!" Syd guffawed. "Dump it right on the top floor of the Oosha Panang Chemical Supply Company HQ."

"Hey!" Egan got serious. "That's my new house you're shitting on!"

They both exploded in laughter.

While they laughed and joked on the ground, they didn't notice the security bots raiding the site and nabbing all the other kids. They only heard the last of the shouting and they ran off. A few days later, when the others tracked them down, they had bruises and cuts and they brought broken glass and heavy old chains to share their wounds with their young lookouts.

At first, Egan and Syd fought them off, but there were too many and they were too angry. Egan lost a kidney and Syd got sliced straight across his collarbone. Mr. Baram had sewed him up in the back of his shop using old fiber-optic threads.

If Syd was being honest with himself, he had to admit that he took more beatings from other swampcats in the Valve than he ever did because of Knox's Upper City shenanigans.

Shenanigans. Mr. Baram's word.

He wondered if Mr. Baram was looking for him right now, pulling strings, worrying. Was he wrong not to go to Mr. Baram for help first?

No. He couldn't drag his boss into his mess. Mr. Baram was the closest thing Syd had ever known to a father. Best to keep him out of it. He had enough worries running his business and feeding his kids. This mess was Knox's doing and Knox would fix it.

Syd wished he could find out what had happened to Egan at the club. He hoped his friend was all right. He hoped the Guardians hadn't picked him up.

As he washed, he wondered what happened after he disappeared. Would Knox just get a replacement proxy, some other kid to take the abuse for his mistakes? Was it right for Syd to inflict Knox on someone else just to avoid the work camp?

It was amazing how little Syd knew about the system, which he'd been a part of for as long as he could remember. No one in the Valve knew much about how it worked, not even the sales agents who worked for the credit companies. Information was too valuable to share with a bunch of slum-dwelling debtors. Information always flowed up. Only one thing flowed down into the Valve. Syd and Egan had pointed that out when they were just kids that night at the construction site.

After he showered, Syd dried off with the impossibly soft microfiber towel. He couldn't believe these things really existed. Even the most lux people down in the Valve, the white collars, the scavenger bosses, the syntholene dealers, Maes's top lieutenants—none of them had anything that could compare to these towels.

He held one up over his face, so the light was filtered through it and so all he could smell was its clean dampness. He stood there for a while with the towel against his face, just breathing with it. He could imagine that he was Knox and Knox was in his place, and that every day he got to ride in autotransports with leather seats or private cars with manual drive on restricted roads and come home to this house with these towels and wear these clothes that were soft and tough at the same time, that didn't itch or chafe or fall apart after the first wash.

A trick of fate.

He got to have Knox's perfect skin, protected from sun and heat and rash, where scars healed and vanished, where pain could be medicated and dissipated and erased. Where the future was his to make.

He looked at himself in the mirror. His face, his skin, his scars. He dropped the patch Knox had given him onto the marble counter unused. He wasn't going to change his skin, even if it was a risk. He was done giving that away. It was his and his alone, from now on.

He dressed in the shiny pants and the undershirt Knox had given him—no more retro queercore, sorry, Egan— and looked at himself in the mirror. He looked almost like an Upper City kid, the heir to some data mining fortune. Except for the metal writing on his arm. He grabbed the gray pullover, covered his arms, and opened the bathroom door.

A wall of sound slammed into him. At first he thought it was a massive engine roaring to life, and then a swell of thunder, a storm rising, a sonic hurricane. The music rose and fell, searching out harmony and then sweeping it away almost as soon as it had been found. What instruments could make these noises? There was nothing electronic about it, nothing processed. The only organic music he knew came from the fiddlers and drummers around the Valve, cheap music, unlicensed, so always short-lived. But this . . . he'd never heard anything like it. It was alive, and, at the same time, seemed to steal the life out of him, absorb him, consume him. He couldn't tell where the music was even coming from. It was everywhere; it had become the world.

Knox had four different holos up and was moving them around, sweeping and spinning, pulling out lines of code and dropping them into each other, or tossing them aside to vanish in flashes of light. His motions almost matched the music. His body swayed and his hips rocked over the chair that he was perched slightly above, not quite sitting, not quite standing. Syd never would have thought the kid he saw at the party was capable of this intensity or grace. Syd couldn't tear his eyes away.

Where the Nadia projection had been on the wall, there was now a holo of some man in a black-and-white outfit with long tails and bow tie standing on a platform in front of a field of musicians. He was waving his arms around in the air and it was like he was controlling the music. His motions on the projection almost matched Knox's motions as he worked on hacking the datastreams.

Knox appeared to sense the shift in the mood of the room. He shot a glance at Syd, then turned back to his screen. Syd looked at the floor, hoping Knox hadn't noticed him staring. The volume of the music went down and Syd felt a little diminished for the lack of it.

"This thing is glitched," Knox said. "But I'm glitching it right back." He laughed and spun one of the projections before shoving it away and bringing up a new one. "You're going to be Frobisher Wick in about five minutes."

"Frobisher Wick?"

"What, the name not to your liking?" Knox twisted another projection around. "You want another orphan name? I can make you Jane Eyre, if you'd be happier, but I just don't think you have the breasts for it." He laughed and kept working.

Did he know about Syd? Was that some kind of Chapter 11 insult? Or was Knox just crazy?

"Laugh a little, Syd," Knox said. "Life is too short for perpetual misery."

"You would know," Syd replied, "about short life expectancies."

Knox stopped working. The muscles in his jaw flared and he clenched his teeth. He closed his eyes. "I'm trying to help you. You don't have to be such a knockoff."

Syd seethed quietly. He needed Knox for his escape and that meant he had to put up with the insults and the sarcasm in silence. For now.

"We aren't done yet." Knox changed the subject. "I still have to get into the SecuriTech router files and find someone else to tag with Mr. Sydney Carton."

"Wait?" Syd came up behind him. "You mean the system is going to think someone else is me, and . . ."

"Go looking for them," Knox said. "Yeah. That's how this works. You have to feed the beast. Data doesn't just vanish. It flows. You can't stop it, but you can . . . uh . . . redirect the flow. Like that river that ran through the Valve." He looked back at Syd and saw the horror on his face.

He spun around all the way to look Syd right in the eyes. "Look, I can tell you've got some kind of moral thing going on right now, but it'll be fine. The company will track this new you down, run them through a few hoops, and straighten everything out. They'll realize they have the wrong guy and cut him loose."

"How do you know?"

"That's the system," Knox said, not unkindly. More like someone who had never been on the wrong side of it.

"But how do you *know*?" Syd repeated. "What's the difference to them? One Valve kid's life isn't worth spit. They'll send him off to Sterling in my place before they admit to a mistake."

Knox didn't have an answer, so he asked his own question. "Do you want to get away or not? I could just as easily message SecuriTech that you're right here, in our house, and you'd be at that work colony before sunrise. No one else. Just you. Your call."

Syd's nostrils flared and his eyes blazed, but he just nodded.

"Good." Knox spun around and turned the music back up and got to work again.

Syd sat down on the bed and listened to the rise and fall of the music. He felt his eyes closing, pressed down by the weight of the day. He couldn't believe that the Atticus Finch incident had only been that morning, that he'd been in Mr. Baram's shop that afternoon, and that this life he was in was separated from that one by the tiniest bridge of time, although he could never cross back over it. He knew he was falling asleep in Knox's house and that he could easily wake up in Sterling, but he didn't care.

He just needed to close his eyes for a minute.

Over the music, Knox could hear the occasional grunt and groan from the sleeping figure on his bed. His proxy turned and thrashed in his sleep, but Knox didn't wake him. His dreams, like everyone else's, were his own.

So were his nightmares.

[19]

SYD HAD THE NIGHTMARE he always had.

He was on a steel table, strapped down, but also, in the impossible metaphysics of dreaming, watching himself on the table from a metal balcony above. The table was on a factory floor. Rusted machines littered the space, some toppled on their sides, their ancient robotic grasper arms forever gaping open. The floor shimmered with bits of broken glass. Outside the factory he heard screaming.

On the table, he squirmed.

Figures rushed in. They wore white suits with hoods, goggles, and rubber boots. Their hands were covered with blue latex gloves. They wheeled in a new machine, shimmering with polished metal. There was a small plexi tube coming off it and the figures lifted him from the table and shoved him in. He was a baby. Just a baby.

Outside, the screams grew louder. He heard explosions.

He tried to reach out from the balcony, reach down to rescue himself, but he was too far away. As he leaned over the railing, as he stretched out his arm to save himself from the tube, he began to fall. He fell and he fell and he fell.

And he was inside the tube. The air was close and hot. He cried and wailed like a baby. He was the baby. He wanted to explain that he did not like it in the tube. He wanted to explain that he was afraid, but he had no words. Only wailing.

Bright lights shone down on him. Their heat burned.

"This is the way," a voice said. "The only way."

"We'll lose him," another voice said.

"We need to lose him," the first voice responded.

"Not forever."

"One way or another."

That's when he saw the needles. Three of them, two on his left, one on his right. They moved in from the sides, sharp points like a monster's teeth. They touched his skin. He screamed. They pierced him. They went in deep and then blood flowed out from one of them. His blood.

He felt the blood leaving him. He cried out. Inside his plexi tube, he could still hear explosions. His blood came back to him from the other side, two needles pumping it back in. When it entered, it burned.

"No," he said. "It burns me." But still his words came out as the wails of a child.

Suddenly, the men around him fell. First one, writhing on the ground, shaking and spitting. Then another. Shrieks and explosions everywhere. The dead soon outnumbered the living.

And then Syd was back on the balcony again, watching from above, but the bright lights had blinded him. His vision was spotty. A man took the baby from the tube, stepped carefully over the bodies.

Suddenly, the man was beside Syd on the metal walkway. His face was hidden beneath a white hood, his eyes behind goggles.

"One more," the man said. Then he tossed the baby over the railing.

When Syd reached for it, the man grabbed Syd with his blue-gloved hands and bent Syd's ear back. He pulled out a needle and jabbed it behind Syd's ear, punching it through the birthmark, through the bone. The needle pierced his brain. Syd screamed.

The man whispered to the needle: *"Yovel."*

Then, he jumped over the railing. The man fell beside the baby, and Syd felt it in his own bones as only one small body hit the factory floor.

He woke with a start. His finger went to the spot behind his ear, touching it to be sure no needle was there, no hole. He exhaled. He was in the dark. It took him a moment to remember where he was.

He was in Knox's room in an Upper City mansion. The music had stopped. A display said the time was 4:02 a.m. The lights were off.

And Knox was gone.

[20]

SYD FOUND KNOX CROUCHED in the hallway on the other side of the door.

"What's going on?" Syd whispered.

"Shhhhhh," Knox hissed. "Someone's just pulled up to the house."

"Guardians?" Syd's heart raced.

"Probably just my father. No one's inside yet." He looked back at Syd. "Don't make another sound. I have to turn the activity assistant back on."

"Did you . . . ," Syd started.

"Yeah, I finished. The house won't recognize you. But if my father sees you, he won't need a datastream to know who you are. So just shut up."

Syd moved to the door and stood behind Knox, listening. They couldn't see anything in the hallway, but they could hear the front door open and the sound of footsteps.

"Welcome, Mr. Brindle, Dr. Elavarthi, Guardian Eighteen Seventy-four A," the house said. "Welcome, Mr. Alvar—"

"Disengage activity assistant." Knox's father cut the program off.

Knox's whole body tensed.

"Did they just say a Guardian is here?" Syd whispered.

"Shut up," Knox said again. "My father never turns the assistant off. I have to get a closer look."

"What? Why?"

Knox slipped down the hall. Syd cursed to himself and followed him. He was still barefoot and his feet sank deep into the cool plush carpet. They crept along the hallway until they were crouched above the grand double-height living room.

Syd just wanted to get out of there. It'd been a mistake to run off with Knox. He should have found Egan or gone back to Mr. Baram. Now he was caught up here and getting away was getting complicated.

A tall man strolled into the center of the room below. Knox's father. He wore a tailored tan suit and had the same square jaw as his son. His hair was perfectly combed and flecked with gray, like the smelter ash from a scrap yard. His eyes were hidden behind dark glasses.

There were two men standing with him, both of them in suits, and one woman with her back to the room, looking out of the window. Even from behind, she seemed to command the eye's attention. A Guardian.

"What is he doing here?" Knox whispered to himself.

"Your father doesn't live here?" Syd didn't know what to make of Knox's statement.

"Shh. Not him." Knox grabbed Syd's arm and squeezed it, hard, to get his point across. He pointed to the bald man next to his father. "That's Xiao Alvarez."

"Who is—" Syd started, but Knox raised an eyebrow and glanced at Syd's arm, and he knew. He rubbed the spot where they'd branded him.

Alvarez. Marie Louise Alvarez. That was her father.

The boys listened to their conversation below.

"My son and his proxy are missing," Knox's father said. "It appears they were seen together at a party just a few hours ago. And now, nothing."

"Your son will turn up eventually," Marie's father said with a dismissive wave of his hand. "He always does."

"We're in trouble here" said Knox's father. "That proxy . . ."

"Carton," said the third man, who must have been Dr. Elavarthi. "Sydney Carton."

"Right, Carton," said Knox's father. "He was never supposed to find my son. There's no way."

"Your son's kidnapping doesn't change anything," said Marie's father.

"For me it changes everything. How did this proxy with no social capital locate and abduct my son? He's a swampcat who knows no one and whom no one knows."

Knox's eyebrows wrinkled as he listened. At least now

he knew that Syd hadn't lied. He wasn't working for Knox's dad.

"My concern is not for your son, Brindle," Marie's father said. "We had a deal, you and I. I expect you to honor it."

"We have bigger problems than your stock options."

"That's no excuse to back out of our agreement, not after what my family has been through. You wanted to teach Knox a lesson, and you have. Maybe even more than you expected. I imagine if being kidnapped doesn't straighten him out, nothing will."

"Don't get sarcastic with me!" Knox's father pulled off his dark glasses and got right in the bald man's face. His eyes were green, like Knox's but a crueler green. Storm green, like the sky before the monsoon came in. They made Syd uneasy.

"I did what was best for my son," he said. "Knox needed a wake-up call and I arranged one. I thank you for your cooperation and you will be compensated for your troubles."

"Arranged?" Knox whispered. His father had arranged what? The accident?

Knox felt a chill. Of course. His father was a security expert. He wouldn't have left the CX-30 access code as 1-2-3-4-5 unless he wanted Knox to take it. And the only reason he'd want Knox to take it would be to teach him a lesson. Could his father really have done something that extreme? How would he have gotten this guy to give up his daughter? It couldn't have just been a bribe. Although, if the bribe were big enough . . .

"What have you done now, Dad?" Knox whispered.

Syd glanced over at him. He didn't feel exactly sympathetic, but he was following the conversation below well enough to know that as far as fathers went, Knox's wasn't one to envy.

"Hey, maybe you'll get lucky and the swampcat will just kill him," Marie's father said with enough acid in his voice to melt steel. "You won't have to negotiate."

Knox winced. His father looked as if he was about to hit the bald man. He clenched his fists and his chest swelled inside his suit. Syd would not have wanted to bet against Knox's father in a fistfight against anyone, let alone the little bald executive in front of him.

"You will never speak to me like that again," Knox's father commanded. "Or your family will go through far worse than you have these last few days. Do not forget to whom you are talking. If I'm willing to arrange a car crash to teach a lesson to my only son, imagine what I could do to you, about whom I do not a give a damn."

"Apologies." Xiao Alvarez held his hands up with his palms out, surrendering. He even took a step back. "I went too far. The strain of the last few days has been hard. Of course I want you to get your son back safely. And we cannot have this proxy running off. Of course. Apologies."

Knox's father exhaled loudly. He didn't break eye contact with Marie's father until the bald man had to look at his feet, just to escape the withering stare. Knox knew that stare well.

"The proxy will be located." The Guardian stepped up to Knox's father, diverting his attention. She did not flinch at his gaze. "We have teams conducting a thorough investigation."

"Yeah, real thorough," Knox whispered under his breath. Syd couldn't believe his patron. He'd just learned that the whole accident had been a setup. A girl had died to try to teach Knox to behave himself, and still, he made sarcastic comments. Syd knew that the sooner he got away from this kid and his family, the safer he would be.

Knox's father slid his glasses into his jacket pocket and he sighed. He hitched his pants and sat, gesturing for the others to join him. Marie's father and Dr. Elavarthi sat. The Guardian remained standing.

"What about the friend?" Knox's father asked. "Egan something or other."

"We haven't been able to locate him yet," the Guardian said.

Syd exhaled with relief. At least Egan was safe. For now.

"You think the boy will make contact? Were they lovers?"

Knox shot Syd a questioning glance. What did his father mean, lovers?

Syd looked away.

Oh. *That*. At least it explained the kiss back in the club.

"We don't think they were," Dr. Elavarthi said. He brought up a holo of Egan's face. He poked around, displaying all kinds of data. "Although we don't have a lot of information on their childhoods, the proxy appears to have been interested in another East Coast orphan, Atticus Finch, a fellow student at Vocational High School IV." He swiped his hand along the projection, zoomed in on an image of Atticus.

Syd looked down at the image and felt his shame double. It wasn't a good picture. Atticus was much better looking in real life.

"We've questioned him," said Dr. Elavarthi. "But the feelings were not mutual, to put it generously."

"We are monitoring known meeting points for homosexual activity," the Guardian added.

Blood rushed to Syd's ears. His personal life, everyone he knew and everything he felt, was being discussed by these executives in an Upper City living room, like they had the right to know everything about him.

"And the Jew?" Knox's father asked.

"He knows nothing."

"I'd feel better if he were neutralized," replied Knox's father.

Neutralized. Had Syd's escape put Mr. Baram in danger? He couldn't live with himself if anything happened to Mr. Baram. How would all his children survive? Syd had to get back to the Valve. He had to warn him.

"They talking about that old man I saw in the shop?" Knox whispered.

It felt weird to know that Knox had seen inside the shop, had seen his workroom and Mr. Baram, even though they had only just met a few hours ago. The whole thing felt so lopsided. Syd hated knowing less than everyone else.

"Yeah," he said, and didn't elaborate.

"He will be neutralized," the Guardian confirmed.

"I have to go warn him." Syd started to stand, to back away toward Knox's room to get his shoes, when he heard Knox's father burst out yelling.

"I cannot believe this is all you have! Some Chapter Eleven swampcat from a Valve sinkhole disables a whole platoon of Arak9 sentries, locates my son, abducts him, and you have nothing?" He pointed an accusing finger at Dr. Elavarthi. "You did not see any of this coming? Not a clue?"

"Our predictive behavior model is not a perfect program," Dr. Elavarthi explained. "We know his brand of shoes, how he takes his noodles, but our predictions are inaccurate with a profile as erratic as this proxy's. He took great efforts to buy as little as possible and to reveal even less. We have had only a few hours to analyze it, but none of our data suggest that he is any kind of threat. He's not a killer. He does not appear to be political."

"The explosion at our facility?" Knox's father asked.

"A crime of opportunity," said the Guardian. "The Rebooters have, however, already claimed responsibility."

"But the proxy has no connection to them," Dr. Elavarthi was quick to add.

"And yet you have seen the blood tests," Knox's father snapped. "You have seen the mark behind his ear."

Syd's fingers went to the mark. What could that have to

do with anything? What could his blood tests have shown them? He slunk back down again to see. It's not like he could get out to warn Mr. Baram right now anyway. The old man could take care of himself. He had spies everywhere in the Valve. And that big fracture cannon. He'd get away. Surely, he'd get away.

Syd needed to know about his blood. What was wrong with his blood?

The doctor brought up a new holo, an image of Syd hanging by his wrists just after his punishment, his chin against his chest. He couldn't believe how broken he looked. He'd never seen himself like that. He looked over at Knox. This was what his patron saw.

"The blood is a concern," said Dr. Elavarthi.

"What is wrong with your blood?" Knox whispered, urgency in his voice. At first Syd wondered at his patron's new worry for his well-being, but then he saw Knox rubbing his arm. The transfusion. They had taken Syd's blood to give to Knox. His patron was worried about himself. Of course.

Syd shook his head and didn't answer; he focused down below.

"This is more than a concern," Marie's father said. "I cannot believe you had him as your son's proxy all these years and didn't know."

"We never took his blood before," said Knox's father. "Anyway, the virus takes time to develop."

"Virus?" Knox said. He felt the blood drain from his

face. He'd been infected with some proxy virus. Was it fatal? Was it painful? Was this his punishment for Marie's death?

Syd pressed his fingers into the thick carpet. He felt suddenly itchy and at the same time, numb. A virus. As if his whole life had not been punishment enough, now, just as he was about to escape, he was sick. It wasn't fair.

"Here's what we'll do," Knox's father said with the confidence of a man who was used to giving commands and having them obeyed. "We'll issue an alert for Sydney Carton, offer a reward. They need only know he is an escaped proxy who has kidnapped his patron."

"And the nurse?" Marie's father asked. "She saw the blood results."

"She is taken care of."

Knox shuddered. He wanted to believe that "taken care of" meant "paid off," but he knew better. Nurse Bovary hadn't resigned at all. His father could make people vanish with a snap of his fingers.

"Don't you think the news of an escaped proxy will embolden the Rebooters?" Marie's father asked. "It's just the kind of thing they could rally around. Even if we caught him, even without the knowledge of this virus, they'd make breaking him out of Sterling a priority just to send a message."

"They will not have the chance," said Knox's father. "We cannot have him falling into the Rebooters' hands. We'll make our offer clear. Dead or alive. Most firms will choose dead. Cheaper to haul a body than a prisoner. And if they bring him alive, then we'll kill him ourselves."

"Kill me." The words escaped Syd's lips on their own. They didn't just want to catch him because he was Knox's proxy. They didn't just want to catch him because he'd kidnapped Knox. They wanted him dead before the Rebooters got him.

But why?

He was nobody. Just like Knox's father said, some Chapter 11 swampcat from a Valve sinkhole who knows no one and who no one knows. He couldn't possibly matter enough to kill.

"I agree," said Marie's father. "Better for everyone if he just goes away." He rubbed his chin. "Then no one can blame you for missing the signs to begin with."

"Remember your tone," Knox's father warned. "And you." He turned to the Guardian. "Make the arrangements. I want everyone after this kid. Spare no expense. He must be neutralized."

The Guardian brought up a holo of her own, swiped around in it a moment, and then tossed it aside. She nodded.

Syd shuddered. That was what a death sentence looked like. A few taps on a projection, some data transmits, and he's dead.

He was trembling. He knew he was trembling. Knox looked over at him, biting his lip. Syd looked back, eyes wide. He didn't know what to do. He didn't know anything.

He needed help. He just wanted somebody to help him, to fix things, to make all this go away.

"I'm—" Knox whispered, but he didn't know what to say either. There was too much going on. How could he help anyone else with his life when his own was spinning out of control? His father had set him up to kill a girl, had exposed him to some kind of tainted blood. Now he wanted to kill his proxy. All Knox had ever wanted was a good time. How could it have gone so bad so quickly?

"You will not kill that proxy!" a new voice—a female voice—shouted, bursting into the room below. Knox and Syd snapped their attention back down. The three men jumped to their feet, a reflex from years of conditioning for what to do when a woman entered the room. In spite of their manners, they did not look pleased to see her.

The boys couldn't see who was speaking; she was standing underneath the overhang where they were hiding, but all eyes in the room turned toward her, even the Guardian's.

"You were supposed to wait in the transport," Mr. Alvarez said.

"You'll have to excuse me if cars make me uncomfortable," the voice replied as she stepped all the way into the room.

Syd could only see the back of her head. Long dark hair, black with a hint of color. When she turned to look at Knox's father, Syd saw the radiance of her eyes, a bright movie-star purple. She looked like a teenager. Syd wondered what a rich teenager was doing at a late-night meeting. Who could she be? And why was she trying to save his life?

He got the answer to the first question when Knox slumped backward against the wall, his face pale as smoke.

"No way," Knox whispered. He hung his hands on the back of his neck and drew his knees up to his chest, rocking gently. "No way no way no way," he muttered. He looked up at Syd with childish terror in his eyes. "She's alive. How is Marie alive?"

[21]

KNOX NEEDED A MINUTE to think. The crash was no accident. His father had wanted him to steal the CX-30. They knew he couldn't resist. His father had set him up just to teach him a lesson, even though it could have killed him.

Knox's head felt hot, a pulsing headache starting behind his left eye.

Marie was alive and his father knew it. Her father knew it. Even that quack predictive-marketing analyst from his father's company knew it. Why would they have let him crash like that? Knox thought Marie had *died*. They let him think he was a killer.

If his mother were still alive, she would never have let this happen. Knox would be up in his room right now, listening to music, chilling with Simi and Nine and doing whatever. She'd never have let him take the CX-30 for a joyride. She'd have paid attention.

He felt his lip quivering. Tears. Just like a little snot nose, crying. He bit his lip as hard as he could and fought them back. Self-pity wouldn't help him now. He could feel bad for himself later. Right now, he needed to focus.

Beside him, Syd rubbed his hand over his forearm. He could feel the letters beneath his sleeve, the name embedded in his skin. They'd known the girl wasn't dead, but they'd branded him anyway. They'd known the girl wasn't dead, but they still wanted to kill him. Syd's head spun. He felt sick to his stomach.

"Marie!" The girl's father was lecturing her down below. "Show some respect. You're in Mr. Brindle's home."

"It's all right," Knox's father said, which struck Knox as an added insult. If he ever talked to his father the way she had, Syd would have gotten a few shocks just out of spite. "She's been through a lot," his father added.

"Yes, she has." Her father spoke for her, but without warmth in his tone.

"And it was my choice," Marie interrupted. "So I don't need to be talked down to."

"I am still your father," her father said. "And you owe me some manners."

"I owe you, huh?" Marie laughed. "I think it works the other way around, Dad. I'm the one who died for you."

That tone of hers, that sarcastic tone that didn't quite cover her fear, brought back a memory. The car and her laugh and her thigh. Some banter.

Did she know then what was about to happen? Was she setting up Knox with every nervous laugh? Did she jerk the wheel? How did she know that she'd come through the accident alive?

"Behave yourself," her father scolded. "If not out of respect for me, do it for Beatrice's sake."

The girl's body tensed. She moved her mouth a few times like one of those Japanese fish in the aquarium, but no sound came out. She looked away from her father. He nodded.

"Now you understand? Responsibility. It's not always fun, is it?" He pointed to the door. "Go back to the transport to wait."

"I can't let you kill that proxy," she said.

"You've done your part, Marie," Knox's father said, his voice still gentle in a way that stabbed Knox straight through the heart. He had never heard it before. "I appreciate what you did to help, but now you are done. You should focus your worry on your own proxy."

"No." She crossed her arms. Knox tensed. His father did not abide defiance. He found himself licking his lips, almost eager to see what his dad would do.

"Marie." Her father rested his hand on her shoulder. "You don't understand what's happening here. It's for your own good that Knox's proxy be eliminated. They aren't all poor, suffering innocents. Some of them are dangerous. You have to be realistic."

"I wouldn't let you hurt Beatrice, and I won't let you hurt Knox's proxy either." She sat on the couch and put her feet up on the coffee table.

Knox's father slapped them off, hard, and glared at Marie's father, daring him to object. "You won't *let* us?" He leaned over her. "Listen to me, girl. With one swipe of my hand, I can have Beatrice hauled out of bed in that ratty orphanage and executed before your eyes. If it will protect my clients or my son, I can and I will do it. My loyalties do not lie with some teenage brat or her silly causes. I humored you because you were helpful in a private matter. That matter is complete and no longer concerns you. If you interfere . . . well . . ."

He straightened his jacket. Marie sat frozen to her seat.

"Marie, go wait in the car," her father said. It came out almost as a whisper.

"Please, don't—" she began.

"To the car!" her father yelled.

Marie stood slowly and nodded at him. She trudged from the room looking about as willful as a vacuubot.

Knox wished he could remember more about the girl from school or from parties. Anything that would help him understand what was going on.

"She's a good girl," said her father when Marie had gone. "She means well."

"It's for her own good."

"I wonder if our children will ever forgive us for protecting their futures," Marie's father mused.

Knox's father shrugged. "They're children. We don't need their forgiveness."

"You're not so sentimental, are you, Brindle?"

Knox's father ignored him. "My son's proxy cannot make it to the Rebooters. It's that simple. He never should have been allowed to mature in the first place. For that error, I take full responsibility."

"Marie will be heartbroken, of course." Her father sighed. "She thinks she can change the world. She believes in all that debt forgiveness garbage."

"I'm not sure Knox believes in anything," his father replied. "Which I suppose makes it easier. He won't care one way or another when we kill his proxy."

Beside Knox, Syd sucked in his breath.

"As long as we *do* kill him," Marie's father added. "His escape needs to have a happy ending for SecuriTech and for Xelon. This is a serious problem. If he actually ever does make it to the Rebooters as a result of our little ruse, you and I will be—"

"Stop!" The Guardian cut off Marie's father.

The Guardian's eyes rose upward. Knox could feel her crystalline gaze tear right through him. A tug in his chest, a burning urge to go to her.

Syd pulled Knox back from the edge of the railing. They pressed themselves against the plush carpeting on the floor. Knox held his breath. Maybe he was wrong. Maybe the Guardian hadn't seen them.

Syd's mind still reeled. Something in his blood made him dangerous to these executives. They were more concerned with killing him than they were with their own children. He didn't like mattering that much to men like them. He didn't like mattering at all. He longed for the carefully constructed anonymity, the world of not mattering to anyone that he'd spent a lifetime building and seen crumble in only one day. He wanted it back.

"Override code Gamma-Six-Alpha," the Guardian barked, and the house system confirmed the override.

"What are you—?" Marie's father started to ask.

"Locate Mr. Knox Brindle and Mr. Sydney Carton," the Guardian commanded.

"Mr. Knox Brindle is currently in the upper hallway," the house said. "He is accompanied by Mr. Frobisher Wick. Sydney Carton . . ." The house fell silent for a moment. "Calculating," it said. "Calculating . . . calculating . . ."

"He's here." The Guardian rushed toward the stairs, an EMD stick sliding from her belt.

"Who is Frobisher Wick?" Marie's father wondered.

[22]

SYD WAS ALREADY ON his feet, running down the hall toward Knox's room. Knox nearly fell over trying to catch up.

"Where are you going?" Knox panted, closing his door behind him and flipping the manual lock.

"Out your window," said Syd, feeling around the edges, trying to open it.

"They've already sealed the house," Knox told him.

Syd rushed around the room, hitting at the corners of the window, pulling on the frame. He paced like a caged panther.

"Knox!" his father shouted. "Are you all right?"

"We need to get out of here," Knox told Syd, as if he needed telling.

"We?" Syd pulled on his beat-up shoes without looking up.

The shoes did not match the clothes Knox had given him. It seemed a crazy thing to notice, but Syd felt like all his senses were heightened, a rush of awareness right on the edge of panic. His life as he knew it was unraveling, but still, he noticed the shoes.

"You heard me," Knox said.

"There is no *we*," Syd answered. "There's you and your big house, your not-dead girl and your father, who's worried about you—and there's me, a piece of Valve trash who he wants to kill," Syd said.

"That sounded like my dad was worried about me? He set up the accident just to teach me a lesson."

"Yeah," said Syd. "I noticed."

"Don't you want to know what they found in your blood after the accident? Don't you want to know why he wants you dead? I mean, my father could have killed you a hundred times before now, but he never did. Suddenly, I get a blood transfusion, and now, you're some kind of threat to him? That doesn't make you curious? Why should you matter so much?"

Syd had wondered the same thing, but he wasn't about to admit it to Knox. They never would have run any blood tests on him if it weren't for that stupid accident. This was all Knox's fault.

"*Why* is a patron problem," Syd told him. "I'm more worried about *how*. Like, how do I get out of this house?"

Syd grabbed Knox's chair. He swung it at the window, tried to smash it. The chair bounced off with a loud gong.

"Reinforced plexi," Knox told him. "A fracture cannon couldn't get through that."

"Can you open it?" Syd whirled on him.

"What do you think?" Knox said. A holo appeared over his shoulder, his father's glowering face.

"Knox, are you—" his father began, but Knox swiped it away without even looking.

A few more waves through another datastream holo and the window slid open.

Syd rushed to it.

"Where will you even go?" Knox asked as he climbed out onto the ledge.

"Out, beyond. The wastelands. Maybe I *will* join up with the Rebooters."

"You don't seem like the terrorist type," said Knox.

"I don't know what type I am anymore," Syd answered. "But I'm not your problem. Thanks for the new ID. But I need to be on my own. You've done enough."

He stepped outside. A moment later, Knox was right behind him. If his father wanted Syd dead, then Knox wanted the opposite. If his father didn't want Syd to get to the Rebooters, then that was exactly where they would go. If his father refused to negotiate, Knox would teach him to negotiate. It was time for Knox to show his father exactly what his son was capable of. He was coming with Syd whether his proxy wanted him to or not.

He handed Syd the antique plastic pen.

"Grabbed it from your old pants," he said. "You're gonna

need it." Then Knox slapped a fake ID patch of his own on, watching it dissolve into his skin.

"What are you doing?" Syd couldn't believe his patron was following him.

Knox threw on a new pair of datastream glasses. A wave of his hands and the window shut. He looked through his glasses at the city's blinking warnings, the labels on the trees and buildings in the distance, projections of logos rising above their corporate headquarters. The night sky flickered with advos for his new identity, bras and fashion implants, women's shampoos. Oops. Must have grabbed the wrong patch. Well, it wouldn't last long anyway.

He looked down and got a height reading. It was a dizzying number. He took off the glasses. "You are taking me hostage," he said.

"I'm *not* taking you hostage," Syd replied.

He looked away, started to inch along the ledge with his back pressed up against the house. He had never stood this high up before. The ground seemed to rise and fall with every breath he took. The city shimmered across the horizon. Its heat bent the air. He realized that he had no idea how he was going to get away from this silent neighborhood, let alone out of the city.

He hated to admit it, but he needed Knox. If he ran without Knox, he'd be easy to destroy. Having Knox with him gave Syd leverage.

Through the window beside them, they saw a flash as the bedroom door exploded open. Knox couldn't believe they'd gone in, even though, as far as they knew, he was Syd's hostage. Blasting in like that was what you did to end a standoff if you didn't care whether the hostage lived. Was Knox's father willing to trade his son's life for Syd's? How could Syd possibly matter so much to a man like his dad?

Syd was thinking the same thing.

"Fine," said Syd. "You're my hostage. Now, how do we get out of here? I don't think the Guardians are going to fall for an antique pen."

"They don't have to." Knox didn't elaborate. "Follow me."

And then, without warning, Knox leapt from the ledge and windmilled his arms through the air. He hit the sloping landfill below and rolled.

Syd swallowed hard and jumped, certain he was going to break every bone in his body.

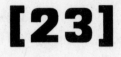

[23]

FOR A MOMENT SYD felt weightless, free, and light. He was flying. The house fell away and the hill raced up toward him. He braced for impact, bent his knees as he hit, and rolled. The grass was soft. He tucked his head to his chest so he didn't snap his neck. The grass smelled like he'd always imagined the color green would smell, fresh and bright.

It tasted, however, like pesticide. He spat out sticky blades of it.

Syd came to a stop at the line of shrubs that marked the edge of the property and Knox yanked him up.

Knox looked back and saw the Guardian at the window to his room. The plexi slid open and without hesitation, the Guardian jumped.

"This way," he said, pulling Syd by the wrist until they were running side by side as fast as they could toward the other side of the house.

"We'll never outrun her!" Syd dared a look back as the Guardian hit the ground. She moved with the easy grace of practiced violence. She was built to catch them. This was her nature. She was gaining ground with every stride.

As they rounded the house, Syd saw five more Guardians coming up the long driveway on foot, all of them holding EMD sticks by their sides. With a high enough setting, an EMD stick could stop your heart with one hit.

Knox skidded to a stop and Syd slammed into him.

"I need that antique pen now," Knox told him.

"I told you," Syd panted. "I don't think the Guardians are going to fall for it."

"They don't have to," Knox said. "Just give it to me."

Syd pulled it out and set in Knox's palm. The moment the plastic touched his skin, Knox squeezed it tight. He gave Syd a wink and then rushed to the transport parked in front of the house. He pulled the door open and beckoned to Syd.

"What are you—?" Syd moved toward him, when he felt a punch in the back, like a dozen rusty salvage nails slammed into his spine. He saw the Guardians running at him, one from the direction of the house, the others from the driveway.

Syd tried to move toward the vehicle, but he stumbled. He told his legs to go but the message never reached them. The ground smacked his cheek. All his muscles tightened. He felt himself writhing on the blacktop driveway, the taste of tar flooding his mouth. He couldn't control his limbs.

They flailed. All he saw was light, painfully bright. He heard Knox shouting, but he couldn't do anything about it.

It was not an unfamiliar pain, but familiarity didn't change how his body responded to it. A high-power hit from an EMD device didn't care what you thought about it; it fried your nerves without asking your brain for permission first.

As he curled and shook on the ground, he felt himself lifted up, dragged across the driveway and heaved, still shaking, onto the soft floor of the transport.

"Hang on," Knox whispered to him as the door slammed shut and the outside sounds were silent. The floor of the transport was soft and cool on his cheeks.

Knox hit the manual door lock panel. He threw on the glasses again and hacked the transport's system as quickly as he could. The engine started. The wheels screeched on the drive as the vehicle took off. The Guardians fired after it, but these executive transports were more secure than most people's homes. As long as they were inside it and Knox's hacks held, they were safe.

"Don't move," Knox ordered, but he wasn't talking to Syd.

Syd forced his eyes to focus and it looked like Knox was holding the antique pen and pointing to the opposite seat. Syd tilted his head farther back with an agonizing burn that shot from deep in his belly button to the tip of his tongue.

And he saw Marie, purple eyes shining, jaw hanging open in surprise.

"Meet your newest hostage, Syd," said Knox. "I think you already know her name."

"Knox, are you glitched?" Marie yelled. Her eyes were fixed on Syd. His hands shook. He couldn't push himself off the floor.

The EMD hit had been far too hard for a mere stunning shot. They were trying to stop his heart. He knew spittle was flying from his lips and his tongue felt like a live wire in his mouth, but he had to tell them. "Baram . . . ," he said, the word hardly coming out. "Warn Baram . . . Valve . . ."

"What is he saying?" Marie leaned forward.

"The Valve," Knox said. "He wants us to go the Valve."

"Return immediately!" Knox's father appeared on a holo. "Surrender now and you will be—"

Knox swiped it away.

"Knox?" Marie's voice again. "We can't go to the Valve."

"You're our hostage." Knox waved the pen at her. "You go where we say."

Marie leaned back and crossed her arms.

"Have to warn Baram . . . ," Syd groaned, but he didn't have enough control over his tongue to say any more. His head fell against the floor. His vision turned red and he knew he was about to pass out. He hoped the patrons understood him. He hoped they would take him to the Valve. He hoped they wouldn't just turn him in. He hoped he'd wake and this had all been a dream. He just hoped.

[24]

KNOX LEANED BACK ON the soft seats of the transport and let out a long, slow breath.

His proxy was on the floor at his feet, half awake, twitching every few seconds. Watching Syd's eyeballs wriggling under his eyelids, sweat beading on his dark forehead, and muscles straining against stray pulses of frying nerves, he realized he'd never seen anyone hit by an EMD burst in person before. He'd seen it happen to Syd in a holo more times than he could count, but in the flesh, no lighting effects, no production values, just a body in pain, was totally different. He couldn't tear his eyes away.

"Knox," Marie said to him, her eyes also fixed on Syd. "Do you have any idea what you're doing?"

Knox looked up at her and clenched his teeth. He thought he'd killed this girl. His skin tingled. He wanted to put his fist through the car window. He wanted to put his fist through her face. He'd never been a violent guy before. He exhaled and tried to relax. He needed to get control of his thoughts.

He tried to project an image of unimpressed confidence, and ignored her question. In truth, he was far from confident. He'd had his share of crazy nights before. He and Chey and Nine and Simi had a damages bill that would have bankrupted lesser parents than theirs—and Syd had the scars to prove it—but tonight was beyond any trouble he'd ever been in.

He wasn't worried about breaking the rules. If you could pay, the rules were yours to break. He was worried that he'd crossed some line where the rules he lived by no longer applied, past where his status, his father's money, or his charm would do any good. And it was Marie's fault.

"You look good for a dead girl," he said.

She shrugged but didn't deign to answer. She didn't feel the need to explain or justify herself to him. She was nothing like the girl he remembered from before the accident. Her saucy laugh, her mischievous winks. This new Marie was cold.

"I mean, seriously?" Knox exploded at her, his face flushing red. "What is going on? How are you alive? Why?"

"Disappointed?" she sneered.

"You just want to yank me around?"

"You haven't even apologized."

"Apologized?" Knox couldn't believe what she was saying. "For what?"

"For killing me."

"Oh, come on!"

"Seriously," said Marie. "I had to die because you wanted to get laid and you were careless and you can't even admit you were wrong and apologize."

Knox shook his head. "It was an accident." The words caught in his throat. "I didn't mean to—"

"You really are an idiot."

"You knockoff slag!" he snapped. "You wanted an apology and then you spit it back in my face."

"This is you apologizing?"

"Screw you." They stared at each other in angry silence as the city raced by outside.

"So what's the plan, now, Knox?" Marie said. "You're taking me hostage? For what?"

"To help Syd get away from my father."

"So . . . that's him?" she said, her eyes fixed on Syd on the floor. "That's your proxy?"

"Syd," Knox repeated.

"Syd," Marie repeated to herself, like she was storing it away. She didn't look afraid. She looked . . . awed. This was not the reaction Knox had expected. Finally, she looked up at Knox. "You realize you're kidnapping me with an antique plastic writing pen?"

Knox looked down at the pen. He squeezed it in his hand. She knew. He tossed it aside.

"I'm still stronger than you." Knox leaned forward. "I can still hurt you."

"No, you can't," Marie said and slid a slim silver EMD stick out from beside her on the seat. She rolled it gently between her hands. "If you're going to take hostages, this is much better protection than a plastic pen."

Knox leaned back. He'd screwed up. He'd underestimated Marie. Again. "Don't do anything crazy, Marie," he said.

"Like what? Kill you?"

Knox nodded. He'd never had a real weapon pointed at him before. He didn't like the feeling. His clothes felt suddenly thin, his skin too, like all his fragile organs were exposed. The slightest move and she'd fry him.

"Relax," she told him. "I'm not going to hurt you. You need my help."

"Wait, what?" Knox wiped his palms on his pants legs. "You want to help me?"

"Not you," Marie tilted her head toward Syd on the floor. "Him."

Knox didn't have a lot of experience kidnapping girls, but he imagined that they didn't usually volunteer to help once they realized that your weapon was a bluff. Marie should be screaming and fighting him now, trying to get away. Or at least ordering the transport to go directly to the nearest Guardian control point.

"I don't want them to hurt your proxy," she said. "That was never what I wanted."

"He's *my* proxy. What do you care?"

"The problem *is* that he's your proxy," Marie finally said. "Don't you see how messed up that is?"

"So you want to set him free or something?" Knox groaned. "You're doing all this for the Cause?"

Knox had dated Causegirls before. They were always

going on about debt reform and refugee forgiveness and all that Rebooter nonsense. Mostly, they wore political T-shirts. He'd actually dated two of them at once, because he thought it'd be hot the way they matched and the way they made his father angry, but their speeches got very dull very fast. Also they argued with each other all the time; one supported the Reboot agenda—violent overthrow of the system—and one supported an adjustment of interest rates. Knox just wanted to make out.

"Look at him," Marie said, pointing. Syd's breathing was shallow, his chest heaving up and down. It looked painful. "You think it's right for someone to go through all this because of you?"

"Because of me?" Knox threw his hands up in the air. "You were in on the accident. He wouldn't even be here if *you* hadn't set me up."

"I had no choice," she said. "Your father threatened *my* proxy, if I didn't help him teach you a lesson. I didn't think things would go this far."

"Some excuse. You knew what would happen to Syd."

Marie shook her head. "I thought it'd benefit Syd in the long run too, if you learned your lesson. We both know the accident wasn't your first offense, so don't act like you care about Syd all of a sudden."

"Hey," Knox objected. "I didn't put him into debt. That's just the way it is. I didn't invent the system."

"That doesn't make it right."

"Debts have to be paid somehow."

"Do they?"

"Oh man." Knox sighed. "You're a believer? Bring on the Jubilee! All is forgiven! Really? Want to hold my hand and sing too?"

"Wouldn't the world be better if the slate was wiped clean? We could start over. Build something more . . . fair." She frowned. "I don't expect you to care."

"I don't get why *you* care," Knox replied. "I mean, your dad's company controls most of the proxy system."

"And yours enforces it," she said. "But here you are."

"I'm here *because* my dad enforces it," said Knox. "My dad used me and he used you, and I'm not going to let him get away with it. If that means getting Syd to the Rebooters, then that's what I'll do."

"Getting back at your dad is the wrong reason to do this."

"Who cares what my reasons are?"

"Reasons matter." She turned away from him.

Behind her, the lights of the restricted speedway zipped past. Knox watched the road, remembering their last drive together. The memory stung, but why should it? He hadn't killed anyone on this road. It was just a road. The girl was right in front of him. She wasn't flirting anymore. She wasn't really flirting back then either.

Marie glanced out the rear window and Knox followed her gaze. The advos along the road were all for the fake IDs. It didn't look like they were being followed, but they were definitely being watched. His father would have a tracker on the transpo already. He was probably sitting in the living room watching them from his datastream.

Syd had better wake up soon. He needed to tell them

where to go in the Valve. They couldn't just cruise on in without him and start asking around for some old man, especially not if his father's enforcers were already after him.

"Listen." Marie turned back to Knox. "For my part in what's going on here, I'm sorry. I want to help. I owe that to Syd. He got hurt so my proxy wouldn't."

Knox took a deep breath. "Fine," he said.

"But they still have to think I'm your hostage," Marie said. "Or else your father will take it out on Beatrice."

"Beatrice?"

"My proxy."

"She's not really my problem," said Knox.

"You really are a heartless bastard." Marie glared at him.

Knox shrugged. After everything he'd been through tonight, what did insults matter? Let her think what she wanted. She didn't know his life. She didn't know what he'd been through, what caring about someone else could cost. Everyone gets hurt in the end. Better to be the one doing the hurting than the one getting hurt. She'd know that if she'd ever really had to suffer, but she was a spoiled rich girl with pretty ideals, whose mommy and daddy let her get away with murder. Murdering herself, sure, but still . . .

"You know, I was actually jealous of you when they told me you'd been kidnapped by your proxy," Marie said. "I was jealous that you got to meet him in person. I imagined that if I could meet mine, we'd be friends."

"Friends?" Knox laughed. "You can't be friends with your proxy."

"Beatrice is her name," Marie said. "I haven't seen her

in years. The only way to see her was to get in trouble and then . . . well, I'd like to see her in person one day. As equals."

"You think she feels the same way about you?" Knox grumbled.

"I'd like the chance to find out."

"That's great," said Knox. "But we're not here to help you with your personal journey toward self-actualization. Syd's running for his life."

"And what are you doing?"

Knox ignored her question. He was helping. Wasn't it obvious?

"Whatever. You're in over your head here," Marie said. "You need my help."

"You're the one with the EMD stick," Knox replied. "I guess *I* don't have a choice."

"I guess you don't," said Marie. "Now, why does Syd want us to go to the Valve?"

"To save some old guy from my father," Knox explained. "I guess everyone's trying to save someone tonight. It's like a charity ball."

"You're not funny," Marie said.

"Oh, you know I am." Knox winked at her, but not to flirt. He hoped it would annoy her.

It did. She was about to let a stream of curses fly his way when the car lurched to stop.

"You have reached your destination," the transport announced, then it powered down around them, dead still in the middle of the road.

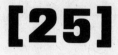

[25]

KNOX GLANCED OUT the window, certain the Guardians were right behind them.

"Why won't it take us in?" Knox asked, tapping at a holo of the transport's systems. On the other side of the fence sat the Valve.

"It's not programmed to go off the patron roads," said Marie. "There's no transpo network on the Valve roads. You'd know that if you ever bothered to read anything."

"Sorry, my dad doesn't subscribe to the terrorist news-letters," Knox said. "He's too busy protecting your daddy's fortune."

Marie rolled her eyes at him. "So what do we do? We can't stay here."

"I don't know if you noticed the fence in our way," Knox told her. "We have to find a way around. Like a gate or something."

"All the gates are guarded and monitored," Syd said

from the floor, his voice cracking as he pushed himself up. He looked up at Marie.

"Hi, I'm—" she started to introduce herself, extending her hand.

Syd's hand went to his forearm and rested over the spot where they'd branded him. "I know who you are."

"I want to help you," Marie said.

Syd looked to Knox.

"She's a Causegirl," Knox explained. "She wants to fight injustice and thinks setting you free will make up for her living the lux life. I'm sure she'd move down to the Valve if she could." He raised a fist. "Solidarity. It's a thing up here."

"A thing?" said Syd. He sighed and pulled himself on the seats.

Knox figured they didn't have Causegirls down in the Valve. Down in the Valve, seeming to care probably wasn't cool. Everyone must have that same detached anger that Syd had. It was all in the eyes. Even just sitting there on the floor of the car, half zonked from the EMD blast, Syd's eyes looked angry. Maybe the Valve wouldn't be such a bad place to live if everyone just chilled out a bit.

"Does it hurt?" Marie asked.

"What do you think?" Syd answered. His eyes went to the EMD stick in her hand. He didn't like being that close to one. She noticed his glance and slid it under her jacket.

"It's not on," she told him.

Knox grunted and shook his head. "Of course not."

"We gotta get down there before your fathers get to Mr. Baram," said Syd. "Whatever's going on here has nothing to do with him."

"My father would never hurt an innocent person," Marie said.

"She actually believes that," Knox scoffed.

"It's true," she said. "Not everyone is a soulless corporate automaton like your dad."

"True enough," said Knox. "Some men are just cowards."

"My father is not a coward." She reached back into her jacket.

Knox held up his hands. "I surrender."

Marie knew he was mocking her, but let it go. He wasn't worth it. This wasn't about the sneering, sarcastic pretty boy. It was about Syd, who was looking out the car windows and ignoring their squabble.

Syd studied the fence and the blast barriers along the side of the road. The hill just beyond them sloped down into the Valve, but not much was visible through the soupy smog that settled over it, thick as tar and just as black. He glanced up toward the sky. He couldn't see any drones above, but at night they were almost impossible to spot.

"The fence is fortified graphene," Syd told them. "We can't cut through it, and it's electrified so we can't climb over it."

Syd looked at Knox. Marie did too.

"What? You think I know how?" Knox pointed at himself. He'd snuck into a lot of places in his life. Concerts, girls' houses, the zoo . . . he never imagined he'd be trying to sneak into a slum with his proxy and some Causegirl.

"You're the only one here with a criminal past," Marie said.

"That's not entirely true," Syd said. "I used to help rob construction sites . . . you still want to help, now you know I'm not just a poor innocent proxy?"

"Don't be cruel," Marie replied. "I do want to help you. As long as I'm your hostage, they aren't going to hurt you. Without me . . ." She let the thought trail off.

Funny that she really believed in her own value so highly, thought Syd. It must be a patron thing. In the Valve, you learned fast and you learned young that no one's life was worth all that much to anyone else.

"They killed you once already," he reminded Marie. "And for dumber reasons than a delinquent proxy on the run."

"That was different," she said, though her voice was quiet. "I wasn't really dead. Medical teams were standing by. We just told Knox I'd died."

Knox looked at her with his mouth hanging open. She described what she'd done to him like she'd snubbed him at a party or spread a nasty rumor, not like she'd torn open his life.

"I was doing it for a good reason," Marie added. "That counts for something."

Knox seethed and Syd worried he was about to punch the girl. If she didn't have the EMD stick, Knox might have.

"I know what to do," Syd told them. "And it's something you two are good at."

Knox and Marie looked at each other, neither of them certain what Syd meant.

Syd hopped out of the car to try to get the engine started again. "We're going to have a crash."

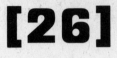

[26]

THE LUXURY TRANSPO WASN'T like the vehicles Syd was used to fixing and its system had completely shut down. Everything in its engine was computer regulated and the battery cells were more complex than any he'd ever seen before. They had to be solar powered, but their distribution was controlled by a processor that he couldn't access.

After ten minutes, the only thing he'd actually accomplished was opening the engine compartment and staring at it.

With every minute that passed, he imagined Guardians closing in on Mr. Baram. Trashing his shop. Terrifying all those children. "Neutralizing" him before their eyes.

All because of Syd.

"It's just a machine," he told himself. "Fix it."

He looked around. The road was wide and smooth. Lights

as bright as day shone down from the fence. It wasn't safe to be stopped like this on the restricted speedway. There were all kinds of security to make sure that none of the Lower City people got up here. It was a patrons-only road.

He wondered if he was the first citizen of the Valve ever to set foot on this road. He wondered if he'd ever get off it alive.

He tapped his finger on the birthmark behind his ear, trying to figure out a way around all the complicated programming.

"So you're saying you can't fix it?" Knox appeared beside him, looking down into the mess of wires and motors and pistons that drove the fancy machine across the fancy roads.

Syd thought back to Tom in school the morning before, standing in the hallway, asking Syd the same question. He couldn't fix Tom's projector and he couldn't fix this car. He couldn't fix anything lately. All he seemed capable of doing was breaking things.

"No one can fix these things," Marie said. "They're designed to be secure."

Knox smirked at her, a braggy smile that wasn't nearly as cute as Knox probably thought it was. "And I'm designed to break security," he said.

He pulled out the AR glasses that he'd brought along, congratulating himself for his foresight. While the other two watched his hands dance in the air, he brought up the schematics for an engine just like the one in front of Syd.

For a moment, he thought he should have used a holo projection instead of doing this in his lenses. What good was performing a brilliant hack, if only he could see it?

"I just unlocked the security on the power source." Knox smiled. "That help?"

Syd leaned back into the engine case and saw that he could now change the circuit running from the batteries. A few wires moved and the car had power to its driveshaft again. It roared to life.

Knox patted Syd on the back. "We're a pretty good team."

Syd didn't answer. He didn't appreciate the smugness when it was Knox's stupidity that got him into all this. If Knox had just left his father's car alone, Syd would be lying down in the back of the shop right now, listening to the Chang family's arguments and daydreaming about Atticus Finch. Well, maybe not *him* anymore. But someone.

No more daydreaming now.

"Stand back," he said. He leaned in to the engine, flipped a switch, and jumped backward as the transpo lurched away with a screech, directly into the fence. A shower of sparks shot up as it crashed itself into the blast barrier. Metal tore, glass shattered, and Syd noticed Knox and Marie flinch. The sound must have been a painful reminder for them. The thought made Syd happy.

He shouldn't be the only one suffering here.

"Won't the crash tell them we're here?" Marie asked.

"Yeah," said Syd. "But they already know."

He pointed up the road. A low-flying drone dropped beneath the smog line and circled. A heavy transport wound its way down the mountain road from above, its lights blazing. Another rumbled up from below. Both of them filled with Guardians.

"We won't be staying long." Syd grabbed Marie's upper arm, yanking her over the ruined fence so hard that she stumbled. "You're the hostage, right? We have to give them a show."

"You could always knock her out," Knox suggested.

Marie mouthed a curse at him. Syd ignored both of them. He really didn't care about their argument. He needed to make sure Mr. Baram was okay and he needed to escape. The patron kids' issues didn't matter to him at all. The patron kids didn't matter to him at all either, except that keeping them close kept the drone above from killing him from the sky.

Syd climbed over the broken barrier and picked his way down the garbage-strewn hill, hauling Marie beside him. Knox followed. He didn't even act like he was a hostage. He could picture his father on the living room couch, watching a holo of the three of them and seething. He wanted his father to know that he'd picked sides.

When Syd reached the first alley between a row of shacks, he heard Marie breathing in his ear. Knox stood on the other side of him. The heat from both their bodies radiated against his back.

"You don't need to stand so close to me," he said.

There were advos on the side of every building, even the shacks made of discarded plastic and tin. They moved and changed, chanted, sang, changed volume, competing for attention. There were too many people down here, with too many marketing profiles, no private streams, no privacy controls. Everyone's wants were on loud display. Knox's head turned at every noise. He'd never heard such chaos of data. Beneath it all, there was the murmur of other voices, human, spoken in shouts and in whispers.

"Is it, like . . . safe for us down here?" Knox asked.

"Nope," said Syd and started off again, jumping over a nasty-looking puddle of green wastewater. He heard a splash behind him and Knox cursed.

Eyes watched them from behind tin doors and plastic curtains. It wouldn't take long before the entire Valve knew that Syd, who'd been hauled off by the Guardians, was back and had two patrons with him. The security firms would be drooling over a reward that couldn't possibly be as big as they were imagining. Still, they'd be getting their kill teams ready.

"People *live* like this?" Knox said as they turned down another alley, passed some open-pit latrines, and skirted a syntholene flophouse, where dead-eyed addicts groaned in the shadows and some Maes goons whispered to one another and pointed at Syd. He heard bird whistles back and forth across the low rooftops.

In the Valve, there were no birds.

Three men were coming toward them down the narrow

alley from the opposite direction. They were large, with long, braided hair and patchwork clothes. They weren't part of any organized unit, but a lynch mob could be just as deadly as an army if you were their target. Even the advos on the walls around them were threatening: snuff holos, weapon sales, cut-rate scar removal. The advos surged forward with them, like an oncoming tsunami.

"Hey, *bwana*, big *gota*," one of them called, holding up his fist as he approached. The dialect wasn't one Syd knew. The man wanted more than a friendly fist-bump, though. In his other hand, he held a large rusted pipe. The other two were similarly armed. Two other guys had moved into the narrow alley behind them, coming up fast.

"I don't like this," Knox whispered.

Although they saw only the three men in front and the two behind, there were at least a hundred eyes on them. If they stopped moving, they'd be mobbed in seconds. Of course, to collect the reward, whoever killed Syd would need to collect his body. With all the competition, that wouldn't be easy. Syd needed to be off the street before someone came up with an idea on how to do that.

The three men rushed forward. Syd turned at the first intersecting alley, yanking Knox and Marie behind him by their shirts. He turned again, doubled back. They started running. The Valve was a maze, even for the people who lived there, but Syd knew the way home well enough.

"Stay close," he warned. As if Knox or Marie needed to be told.

"Where you running, little swampcat?" someone called out. Syd didn't look back, didn't even slow down.

As they turned another corner, a tiny leg shot out of the shadows, tripping Syd. Knox and Marie stumbled over him and they all fell into a brackish pink puddle.

An arrow sliced overhead and a hard-looking woman in a maroon SafeCo uniform stood at the other end of the alley with a crossbow raised. She cursed at her miss and took aim again, when four children jumped her, tackling her into the mud. Marie winced as the woman received a savage beating from a mob of children. She looked away. The sun was just beginning to rise.

The little one who'd tripped them waved for Syd to follow. He led them through a shack where a family was huddled in a corner, eating some kind of boiled leafy thing. The family didn't even look up as they ran through. They followed through several more shacks, each darker and smokier and stinkier than the last. Just when Knox didn't think he could take anymore, they reached the back of a low concrete building.

Before Syd reached the door to his old workroom, it cracked open and he saw the white puff of his boss's beard and the shine of light off his glasses.

"Ah, boychik, you've got yourself in a pickle now, eh? Come inside."

Syd and Knox and Marie slipped inside and Mr. Baram shut the door, snapping heavy bolts into place. The children didn't follow. They'd already dissolved back into the impossible chaos of the Valve at dawn.

"You're in danger," Syd blurted immediately. "You have to get out of here. They're coming for you."

"Please, Sydney, we don't forget our manners," Mr. Baram answered him, with an exasperating calm. "Introduce your friends."

"There's no time, Mr. Baram," Syd cried. "Didn't you hear me? They're coming for you and it's my fault. I'm so sorry."

Mr. Baram rested his hand on Syd's shoulder and looked into his eyes. "They've been coming for me for a long time," he said. "And it's no one's fault but mine. I should have told you sooner."

"Told me what?" Syd felt like a little boy again, like the boy in the orphanage who didn't understand why he had to be punished and who couldn't stop crying, who just wanted the hurting to stop. Now, he just wanted Mr. Baram to tell him what was going on now and, somehow, to make it stop.

"About who you really are," Mr. Baram said. "And why you have to die."

[27]

THE OLD MAN SERVED them some flavored soda to calm their nerves. It tasted like dirt to Knox.

"Fresh berries," Mr. Baram explained.

"Like, organic?" Knox shuddered to think of it. He set the mug down.

Organic.

The word conjured up disease and poverty, the riot of jungles and the desolation of deserts. City life was designed, organized, clean, and controlled. Knox loved that about it. It was completely human. Nature produced nothing but death, disease, and destruction. He didn't like the idea of putting it inside his body.

Marie watched Knox set his cup down and grunted. She took a loud sip, Knox was sure, just to make him mad.

Mr. Baram eased himself back onto a stool across from

the three of them and looked at Syd sadly. Knox wondered why his father would want a man like this dead. The old man couldn't be any kind of threat to the SecuriTech empire. His shop was filled with junk. It was a nasty, squat little building in a stinking street in the slums.

"I really don't understand," said Syd. He sounded so much more fragile than he had before, so much younger. "Why do they want me dead? I didn't do anything."

"No, you didn't." Mr. Baram sucked his teeth and turned to look Knox up and down. "So, this is your patron? He doesn't look like much."

"He's not," said Syd, without looking at Knox.

"I am actually a—" Knox started to object, but he glanced at one of the holos on the wall that showed a crowd gathered in front of the building. Men, woman, children, many of them armed, some of them desperate, and all of them poor, loitered about, watching the building. Knox figured he should stay on Mr. Baram's good side. The old man was his only protection. Patrons did not belong down here. He shut his mouth.

"It is an amazing thing that you've brought him here," Mr. Baram told Syd. "Enough to restore an old man's faith. I see the hand of destiny in it."

"Not this mystical stuff again," Syd objected.

"Oh no," said Mr. Baram. "Nothing mystical about destiny. Destiny is just the inevitable result of choice, from the choices that came before us to the choices we make. They are a river that can only flow in one direction."

"You're talking some deep craziness now," said Syd. "And we don't have time for it. Knox's father wants both of us dead."

"I wasn't honest with you this afternoon, Sydney." Mr. Baram took his glasses off and cleaned them on his shirt. "I suspected something like this was coming. I did my best to make arrangements quickly, but I fear I wasn't quick enough."

"What? What did you suspect? What kind of arrangements?" Syd thought back to the previous afternoon, to Mr. Baram's worried cigarette in the alley, his blathering on about the Holy Land and goat herders and whatever.

"To get you to the Rebooters," Mr. Baram said. "Where you belong."

"I'm not a revolutionary," Syd said.

"I suppose not," Mr. Baram said. "But your father was."

Syd shook his head. "I don't have a father."

"If only that were true." Mr. Baram opened his palms. "But you did have a father and he put a terrible burden on you before he died. He gave you something he should not have and that is why *their* fathers believe you have to die."

Syd glanced at the holo showing the bloodthirsty crowd gathered outside. "You're the closest I've got to a father and we need to get you out of here," he said.

Mr. Baram dismissed Syd's worry. "Those knockoff thugs can jump off the dam. They don't scare me."

"The Guardians are coming for you." Syd stood up and threw his hands in the air. "They'll be here any minute! Does that scare you, huh?"

"The only thing that scares me is if you do not get away," Mr. Baram said. "My life's work erased in a flash. You have a destiny, here, Sydney, and you need to accept it. You must get to the Rebooters."

"No." Syd crossed his arms. "Not without you."

"I do not matter at all." Mr. Baram stood to meet Syd's eyes. Knox and Marie just watched them, unsure what they were supposed to do in this situation. "Only you matter here."

"I'm the one who doesn't matter," Syd said. He needed it to be true. He wanted only to disappear. He didn't want to matter.

Knox shifted in his seat. He didn't like all this sitting around any more than Syd did. He wanted to get out this place as soon as possible. He hadn't signed up for all this conspiracy. He just wanted to run away.

Mr. Baram raised his index finger in the air in front of Syd. He pointed forward as if he were going to poke Syd in the face, but he moved past his eyes, pointed to Syd's ear. He bent his finger and tapped three times on the lump of bone just behind the ear, right on the strange birthmark.

"I know you wondered about this," Mr. Baram said. "I know you noticed it changing."

Syd didn't say anything. He clenched his jaw and waited.

"That is your inheritance," said Mr. Baram.

"That is just some weird skin cancer," Syd blurted. "From living in this dump."

Even as he said it, he knew it wasn't true.

"It is writing," said Mr. Baram. "Old writing, the kind

my people used. Sacred writing. It has almost vanished time and time again, but it survives . . . always survives from one generation to the next, through calamity like you would not imagine."

"Writing?" Syd said. "That grew on my skin?"

Mr. Baram nodded.

"So what's it say?" Knox grunted. "An advo for skin cream?"

Mr. Baram glared at him. Guess he didn't appreciate sarcasm either. No one knew how to lighten the mood down here in the Valve.

"Yovel," Mr. Baram said.

Syd shuddered. The image from his dream came to him, the infant falling, the man with the needles, the whispered word.

"Yovel," repeated Mr. Baram. "In English that means—"

"Jubilee," said Marie. "The day when all debts are forgiven."

Mr. Baram raised his eyebrows at her, impressed.

"She's a Causegirl," Knox explained.

"Yes," said Mr. Baram. "In the old holy books, there was a commandment that every fifty years, all debts were to be forgiven, all slaves were to be freed and all property returned. You are marked with a word of that commandment."

"Marked." Syd snorted.

"It is just a little bit of code buried in the program in your blood."

"My biofeed?" Syd didn't believe it. "I got that after I

was pulled out of the swamps. It was installed by Xelon, here, in the city, just like everyone else."

"Not *that* program," said Mr. Baram. "This was installed before. Your father put this code into your bloodstream when they came to get him. He didn't have anywhere else to hide it, so he hid it in you."

"In me?"

"Like the biotech we all carry," Mr. Baram said. "The same biotech that lets the corporations track you for advertising, that treats the patrons' skin diseases or gets them high"—he gave Knox a disapproving look—"or that gives the Guardians their orders and their strength. Your father was a designer. Just like these high-priced corporate designers, but he didn't build his programs to serve the market. He built them to undermine the market. And the last one he built to infect all the others, to erase them—all the records. All the debts. The entire network severed and destroyed."

"Destroyed? How?" The idea got Knox's attention. "How could a program in some swampcat's blood"—he glanced at Syd—"no offense, change anything?"

Syd looked back to Mr. Baram. He couldn't imagine it either.

Mr. Baram touched Syd's shoulder; Syd yanked it away. He was not in the mood to be touched.

"It's a virus," Mr. Baram said. "A combination of code and biology. It's grown over the years; beneath the skin, invisible, dormant, but I knew it was growing. The only symptom, this mark, this word, was meant to tell me when the virus was mature. That was your father's little clue. He hid it in your cells the way game designers hide surprises in their holos—Easter eggs: a secret level, a bonus point, an inside joke. It won't hurt you. It's inactive, just a little extra data in a bloodstream already swimming with data. But it is the same symptom Knox's father must have seen. It is the reason you have to get to the Rebooters and it is the reason the Guardians will want to stop you at all costs."

"A virus," said Syd. "My father gave me a virus."

"When the Guardians came for him, he had to think quickly. He had to put the virus somewhere safe to mature. It wasn't ready to be uploaded. You were the only viable option, just a baby, easy to hide. So I took you away, hid you in the city, watched you grow. I did my best to protect you, but now, you must go back. There's no hiding anymore. The Rebooters need you. You have to upload this virus. They have the technology. You must get to them."

"You had no right . . ." Syd slumped. "You had no right to lie to me all this time."

"It was for your own good," said Mr. Baram. "You should not have to grow up under the burden your father gave you. *He* had no right. I was simply trying to help."

"*We* can help now," Marie said. "We'll get Syd to the Rebooters."

"What if I don't want to go to them?" Syd said. "Does that matter to anyone?"

"This is bigger than you," said Mr. Baram. "You can bring down this whole system. Erase the data that enslaves so many. Jubilee. Freedom. Forgiveness. Is that not enough?"

"I already said I'm not a revolutionary." Syd spat on the floor. "I just want to get you out of here."

"I don't go anywhere until you are safe." Mr. Baram leaned back in his chair. "You're the one we've all been waiting for, Syd."

"We?" Syd looked around the dim room.

Mr. Baram nodded. Marie, the strange purple-eyed girl, nodded. Only Knox didn't nod. It was the first moment Syd was glad to have his patron around. At least Knox wasn't insane.

"No," said Syd. "You have to come with me."

"If it is God's will, we'll meet again, but you must go now." Mr. Baram pointed at the holo on the wall.

Outside, the crowd was gone. No thugs with metal pipes. No private security guards or curious children or hungry syntholene fiends hoping to score off the chaos of a captured fugitive.

Instead, the building was surrounded by Guardians.

"They have a program in their blood too," Mr. Baram said. "And right now it is telling them to destroy you."

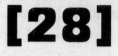

[28]

"SURRENDER IMMEDIATELY AND YOU will not be harmed," a Guardian announced, her voice amplified loud enough to rattle the walls.

The holos on Mr. Baram's wall blurred and reappeared with Knox's father's face taking up the whole image.

"Ari Baram, you are under arrest for harboring a debt fugitive and for conspiracy in the abduction of two patron minors," he said. "Surrender immediately."

His face moved and he saw Marie, holding her soda. He made a motion and a small holo appeared within his holo: a teenage girl with a ponytail, hanging from a strap by her wrists. Her chin rested on her chest in a pose that was all too familiar to Knox. Syd flinched on seeing it.

"Beatrice." Marie gasped. Her proxy.

"Marie, we had an understanding," said Knox's father.

"No," she pleaded. "I'm a hostage here—"

"You aren't fooling anyone," Knox's father said. "Open the door and your proxy will not come to further harm."

"Don't," said Knox.

"Sydney Carton is a fugitive from the law and he will be brought to justice one way or another. Knox, do as I say. Open the door."

Syd clenched his jaw, waited to see which of the patrons would betray him. Knox didn't move. Nor did Marie. In the small picture on the projection, the girl's body jolted and quivered.

Marie gasped.

It jolted again.

"Please," said Marie. "Let her go. I'll surrender. But—"

"I do not negotiate with teenagers," Knox's father said. The body jolted again. "Sydney Carton must surrender."

Syd started to move toward the door. He knew the signs. The girl was going to die if she took any more shocks.

"I'll surrender," he said. "But let her go."

"Stop, Sydney," Mr. Baram commanded him. "You will not leave."

"But they'll kill her," Syd pleaded.

"Step outside, Sydney," said Knox's father.

Syd couldn't let some girl die in his place. That wasn't who he was. What made his life worth more than hers? He moved to the door.

"No." Marie put herself in his way. "You can't."

"They'll kill your proxy," said Syd.

Marie shut her eyes. "I know," she said.

"You would let that happen?" Syd couldn't believe it. "You faked your own death to protect her and now you'd just . . ."

"I believe what Mr. Baram said about you," Marie said.

"You just met me," Syd said back.

"I believe."

"What about Beatrice? You think she believes?" Syd pointed at the holo. "Does she want to die for me?"

Marie didn't answer. She couldn't bear to. Mr. Baram answered for her.

"This is bigger than Beatrice," he said.

Syd hesitated. He didn't want to believe it. He also didn't want to die. His feet felt stuck to the floor.

Knox's father cleared his throat. He had been quietly watching the scene, hovering in midair. He was through watching. "Time's up," he said.

The body on the holo jolted again and quivered for a long moment, an endless, breathless moment. Then the girl fell still. She hung limp on the strap. The front door of Mr. Baram's shop shuddered.

"They're coming in," said Syd. His voice caught in his throat. If he had just surrendered, he might have saved that girl on the screen. If he had just stayed put instead of running, he might have saved Mr. Baram. Now, because he'd run and then because he'd hesitated to do the right thing, some girl he didn't even know had died and he'd accomplished nothing. He and Mr. Baram were next.

"You can't do this!" Knox stepped up to the projection,

his face directly in front of his father's face. The door shuddered. It was built to withstand an assault, but it wouldn't hold forever.

"You can't . . . ," Knox pleaded.

His father looked down at him. "Knox, keep quiet. I will deal with you at home."

"I'm not coming home!" Knox shouted back.

"Many more people will die if your proxy is allowed to live, Knox." His father peeled off his dark glasses. His eyes, so like Knox's, pierced the dim room. "It is time for you to think about someone other than yourself. I know you feel guilty, but there is more to life than feelings."

"At least I have feelings," Knox told him. "And if Mom were still—"

"Do not speak to me about your mother." Knox's father cut him off. "Not in front of these people." He looked at Syd and Mr. Baram with contempt.

"I am not going to let you murder my proxy!" Knox shouted. He was embarrassed to notice he'd even stomped his foot. He was like a little child having a tantrum.

His father's mouth opened to reply, when Mr. Baram shut off the holos. The shop went dark.

"No time for father-son drama." Mr. Baram turned to Marie. "You will go to the zoo. I have arranged for a contact to meet you there to take Syd out of the city."

Marie nodded. "I won't let you down." She almost saluted but stopped herself. Her eyes were wet with tears, but the rest of her face had turned hard as steel.

The old man grabbed his fracture cannon from beneath

the counter and led them into the back of the store where they'd first entered, the same room where Knox had seen Syd arrested. He opened the hatch in the floor and they climbed down it into the storeroom.

"There's no way out of here," said Syd. Mr. Baram's eyes flickered behind his glasses and a small panel in the wall opened, revealing a tunnel.

"I don't tell you all my secrets, Syd," he said.

"I—"

"I promise, Syd, there will come a time when you get to choose your path," he said. "But this is not that time. Now you have to run." He turned to Knox and Marie.

"Follow this tunnel," Mr. Baram instructed. "It will take you out to a safe distance. Then you can make your way on foot due east. You should get to the zoo by mid-morning. Stop for no one. You must protect Syd. I cannot stress this enough. You must keep him safe."

"With my life," said Marie.

Knox didn't say anything.

"What about you?" Marie asked the old man.

Mr. Baram smirked beneath his beard. "I have a trick or two up my sleeve yet. But it is time for you to go."

"But—" Syd said, and Mr. Baram touched his shoulder once more, looked him in the eyes and then gave him a strong one-armed hug. Knox felt strange, standing near them in this intimate moment. Mr. Baram nodded at Marie, who shoved Syd into the tunnel. Knox climbed in behind. Syd didn't resist. His face had taken on a distant quality, vacant. He felt as if he'd stepped into a dream.

Once they were inside, the panel in the wall shut behind them.

"Let's go." Marie crawled to the front and started leading them. Knox nudged Syd forward. The proxy moved like a robot.

"Syd, listen," Knox told him. "Put all this stuff out of your head. We've just got to go. Once you're away, where my father can't get you, then we can figure all this out. Until then, we just have to keep going, okay?"

Syd nodded. His patron was right, of course. A few hours ago, he'd been an orphan. Now he'd gained a dead father and lost the closest thing he'd ever had to a living one. He kept thinking he'd wake up hanging by a strap, waiting for the next EMD hit while Knox watched from a room somewhere, all of this a crazy pain-induced hallucination. He wished for nerve damage instead of this reality.

When they climbed out of the tunnel through a broken sewage grate at the edge of the Valve, Syd knew he was not dreaming. Dreams did not smell this rank.

"Oh, disgusting!" Knox grunted.

Marie covered her face with her jacket.

A giant rat, with patches of glossy gray fur and scabby skin, hissed at them. It had three eyes, but one of them hung loose from the socket. A second mouth flapped open from its side, a snake's tongue darting in and out. The creature snapped its teeth, slashing its long pink tail from side to side like a whip.

Marie pulled the EMD stick on it and fired a pulse, missing by a mile, but the charge in the air was enough to send the creature scurrying away into an empty tin shack half buried underneath a mudslide of dirt, garbage, and human waste, some poor soul's home lost in a flood of filth.

"Which way is east?" Knox groaned. "We gotta get out of this place."

Suddenly, the muck-drenched tin wall sprang to life with sound and a full-color image of the sky. A rocket raced across the pressed tin grooves of the shack and a jumper leapt out, thrill diving from the edge of space. He had a silver Drinkpack in his hand and he chugged it as he plummeted from the wall in lifelike 3-D. A heavy drumbeat blasted all around them.

"Crave Energizer Blast!" a male voice shouted. "Hey, Knox Brindle! When you crave perfection, why don't you blast off with Crave! Energizer! Blast!"

"How is it reading you?" Marie spun on him. "I thought you had fake ID installed?"

"It must have worn off!" Knox cursed and pulled his glasses from his pocket. He raced through his datastream, his hands waving through lines of settings and privacy codes glowing in the air in front of him.

"You glitch-brained idiot!" Marie shouted at him. "Shut it off. The whole city is going to know where we are."

"I got it, okay," he grumbled, embarrassed at his own stupidity. Marie was "dead"; Syd's ID would scan as Frobisher Wick, but, as far as the system knew, Knox was still Knox. Targeted advertising had just put a target on their heads.

He worked as fast as he could, waving his arms frantically

through line after line of code. Marie kept the EMD stick raised, spinning in circles, unsure from which direction an attack would come. Her mind conjured an army of phantoms, but when the advo vanished, they were still alone. The tin wall was just a tin wall. Knox tossed away the projections and pulled his glasses off.

All three of them listened, side by side, breathing heavily, and when Knox was satisfied they hadn't alerted anyone, he dropped the glasses back into his pocket.

"No," said Marie, holding her palm out.

"What?"

"Give her the glasses," Syd ordered.

Knox didn't like to be ordered around by his proxy. He didn't move.

Marie thrust her palm into his face. He sneered at her. He was a hacker. You don't take a hacker's tools.

She raised her EMD stick.

Knox grunted and pulled out the glasses. He looked at Marie and handed them to Syd, giving Marie his widest grin.

Syd dropped the glasses onto the ground and stomped them under his foot, grinding them into muck.

"Do you—do you realize how lux those were?" Knox couldn't believe this swampcat, his total disregard for personal property. Probably never owned anything in his life he'd care about breaking.

"I guess you can add that to my debt," said Syd.

"Look, I didn't mean—" Knox shook his head. "I just think they might have been useful."

"At getting us caught," Marie said.

"Never mind," said Knox. "So where to now?"

"We do like Mr. Baram said." Marie pointed. "Cross out of the Valve and get to the zoo."

"How will we even get inside?" Syd wondered. "They know Frobisher Wick is me."

"Well, if I had my transmitters, I could make some new ID." Knox glared at both of them. "Luckily, I come prepared." Knox pulled another biopatch out of his pocket. "I made a backup while you were napping in my bedroom. It's not as strong, but it'll hold for a little while. Just don't pee too much."

"Pee?" asked Syd.

"It's in the fluids." He extended the patch to Syd. "You are now Vandal Singh, second son of the scion of the GenoFruit Corporation. You're sixteen years old, you're in remission from mild melanoma, and you got back early from a private paracruise across the SoCal Ring of Fire. It is lovely this time of year."

"Uh-huh," Syd grunted, taking the patch and putting it on.

Knox crossed his arms and rocked on his heels while they waited for the patch to dissolve.

"Don't be too proud of yourself," Marie said.

"Oh, but I am," Knox said, smirking. "Vandal here has never been in trouble and his parents are not Xelon customers."

"So?" Syd said.

"So he's got no proxy." Knox smiled. "I thought you might appreciate that."

Syd studied Knox for a moment. Marie's eyes darted back and forth between the boys.

"Yeah," Syd said. "Thanks."

"For my oldest friend, anything." Knox winked. If it came to it, Syd was the one who mattered here and Knox did not want Syd siding with Marie. His proxy might hate him right now, but no one could hate Knox for long. He knew his assets. Why wouldn't they work on a guy like Syd? Without his datastream, he only had one other talent. Might as well use it.

"Now, let's go to the zoo." He turned to Marie. "You think you can stay alive this time?"

Marie glared at him and they turned to the east, heading toward the sunrise.

#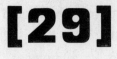

SYD TOOK A DEEP breath and peered across the road-
way outside the zoo, looking for signs of trouble. The sun
was up and it was blazing. Syd couldn't see any Guardians,
but he still didn't feel safe. It wasn't just the Guardians or
the patrons at his side. His own skin was betraying him.
His own blood. A virus.

Knox kept glancing at him, looking at the letters behind
his ear. Yovel.

To Syd, it sounded like a name. It didn't sound like a
word that could end the world as they knew it. Why should
Syd have to carry it? Why should he be responsible? All he
ever wanted was to be left alone. He scratched at the branding on his arm, the metal letters of Marie's name. They
itched. His whole body felt like a wound.

Just in front of the zoo entrance there was a small

wading pool, an artificial swamp filled with a flock of these bright pink birds. The birds each stood on one skinny leg. The other leg was lifted, bent at the knee. It seemed like you could knock them over just by breathing on them. No wonder they didn't survive in the wild. If you wanted to get by, you needed both your feet planted below you. Someone was always going to try to knock you down.

"Relax." Marie leaned forward and put her hand on Syd's. Her skin was soft and smooth and practically glowed white. "No one is going to hurt you. Let's get in there. We'll all stay close."

She tapped Knox on the shoulder with the EMD stick and he flinched, but it wasn't turned on. Then she slipped it back under her jacket, tucked into her waistband like a Maes gang thug. Funny what the rich kids know about the Valve, thought Syd. And what they don't.

Syd would feel better if he was the one with the EMD stick. Whatever happened here, he needed to be able to defend himself. And a person with a weapon and a cause made him just as nervous as the Guardians. You never knew what a believer was capable of.

"Marie?" Syd began when he felt Knox's hand on his back.

"I'm looking out for you, pal," Knox whispered in his ear, apropos of nothing.

"Uh," Syd responded, but he felt Knox's finger slide up and down, just a little movement. He wrinkled his eyebrows and Knox smirked.

It was obvious what Knox was trying to do, but Syd didn't mind. Flirting right now was ridiculous, but it made sense to Syd. Knox was looking for an ally. He was a flirt and now that he knew about Syd, he thought flirting would help keep them united. Knox didn't need to try so hard, really. Because he was so obvious, so incapable of real deception, Syd trusted him. He couldn't keep his own secrets, and for Syd, right now, simplicity was the greatest virtue.

Marie, on the other hand, was inscrutable. She was a patron, but also a Causegirl; she wanted to save the proxies so much she had been willing to die to protect her proxy, then let her proxy die to save Syd, even though he didn't want her to. She wasn't giving him a choice. He wondered what she saw when she looked at him. Did she see a person or just an ideal? Did it matter, so long as she got him where he needed to go?

In front of the zoo, small children raced around on the pavement, shouting and shoving, rushing into the climate-controlled atrium. Some were followed by programmed nannies, little fuzzy bots with grasper arms and cooing voices. A scattering of adults, all of them zoo employees, walked about purposefully, but not one paid any attention to the kids. In a way, all these Upper City kids were orphans too.

Marie pointed to the entrance and nodded. She stood and Syd followed. Knox stayed by his side. Their eyes darted from left to right, looking for threats.

The bots scurried around, keeping the kids in check,

scolding and guiding, working hard to stay in control, following their program.

Syd felt a little like a bot himself, following a program he didn't understand, going on auto, obedient and uncomprehending. No one looked twice at him. With Knox's clothes on, he looked like a patron. He looked like he belonged. Of course, if anyone looked closely, they'd see the blotches on his skin, the nicks and scars from working in the shop, from bug bites and cut-rate food and sleeping in a toxic dump. The sunken eyes, the word behind his ear. He had to remind himself it wasn't visible. Just knowing it was there, however, felt like he had a holo hovering above his head.

He avoided making eye contact with the little kids.

"Vandal Singh, do you miss Murmly?" A projection appeared over the great glass wall behind the flock of bright pink birds. A kindly older woman in soft focus looked right at Syd, her head massive above the birds.

He didn't respond, but the woman in the holo held her smile, patient.

"You're Vandal Singh," Knox whispered.

"I know who I am," Syd whispered back. "But what the hell is a Murmly?"

"I know your dog misses you," the advo woman answered.

"Uh," Syd said. "Yeah."

"For a one-year RePet subscription, we can reproduce Murmly with almost ninety-six percent accuracy. That's the highest percentage in the industry. Sign up right now and you can receive a second resurrection free! Can I tell Murmly you'll see him again soon?" The advo woman flashed her teeth.

"Follow me," Marie said, grabbing Syd by the wrist to make sure he did.

The advo watched them head for the entrance, the smile fading as the double doors swooshed open. Syd glanced back over his shoulder, but Marie pulled him forward. Up here not even the pets die when it's their time, he thought.

By the time the doors closed a new advo was aimed at the next passerby: "Got ideas? Get credit! We'll buy your ideas same day. Open twenty-four hours. When you need credit now, just ping Idea Mine! from your datastream."

Inside the zoo, the air was cool and clean. The sound of children running echoed off the tiled floor and great wide windows ringed the atrium, opening into preview tanks and cages. In one, a black bear slept a sedated sleep while little kids banged on the glass. In another, a bright green eel's long body undulated in the water, a meter above registering its electric output. It didn't swim around, and kids ran right past it without even looking

Marie led the boys to the entrance scanners.

"You took care of this, right?" She glanced back at Knox.

"Just walk with confidence," he said. "I've faked out tougher scanners than these."

Marie went under the entrance scanners first and they followed her into the zoo without being stopped.

As soon as they were inside, Syd's jaw dropped. He must

have looked like every one of those little kids with their fuzzy bots, overwhelmed with wonder.

The polar bear exhibit rose before them. A group of giant white bears rolled around together on top of it, playing as if they weren't the last of their kind on earth. Syd jumped backward.

"Don't worry," said Knox. "There's an invisible fence keeping them in. Particle fields or something. That's the largest amount of ice on public view in the world. Not even the Nigerians have anything like it."

In another display, a flock of penguins squawked and hooted. Right next to them a night-black panther slept in the branches of some jungle tree.

"Pretty lux, right?" said Knox.

Syd nodded. "I've never seen anything like this . . . only animals we have in the Valve are feral cats and dogs."

"And rats," said Marie. They shuddered at the memory of the giant hissing thing.

Knox made a face.

"Don't be an idiot, Knox." Marie looked sympathetically at Syd. "He's never had to go hungry."

"Oh, like you have?" said Knox.

Syd shook his head at both of them. "We don't eat the rats," he said.

"That's not what I meant." Marie blushed. "It's just I . . . I didn't know. I've never met a proxy in person before."

"You!" Syd heard a mechanized yell and spun in its direction, fearing he'd been discovered. The others turned with him and both of them grabbed his arms, protectively. Knox had a grip like a vise. Marie's grip wasn't much gentler.

Syd relaxed and pulled himself free when he saw it was one of the Carebots, with blue-and-green-striped fur, low to the ground so it was at the same height as the children in its care, with a holo display of a cartoon face.

The face did not look pleased and its voice was not the usual kindly burble of the Carebot model.

It zipped past them with a whirr and stopped in front of two children, a boy and girl, siblings it looked like, who had somehow tossed a toy of theirs into the polar bear exhibit. The bears were chewing up the toy, its processors and batteries and all. One of them had a piece of it stuck on its nose. Its giant paws wiped at its snout, but the bear couldn't tear the piece off and the kids laughed hysterically.

They stopped laughing when the bot reached them.

"Oliver! Celia! What did we discuss at home? You two know better," the bot scolded. The children stood rigid before it. "Now we'll see what your misbehavior has cost. Follow me."

The bot moved off and the children followed glumly behind. Syd watched them line up by a wall where there were other misbehaving children. Each stood with his or her bot, or even, Syd noticed, a few actual humans—Upper City teens who wanted to earn some extra cred as nannies—and projections popped up in front of them as the proxies arrived and the punishments were administered.

Syd swallowed hard as the two children received a lecture

about responsibility for the rare wildlife and the destruction of expensive toys. He grimaced as projections appeared in front of the children, revealing two sickly Valve kids, looking frightened with anticipation.

Marie nudged Syd to turn away before the punishments started.

"Don't look," Knox whispered. "It's considered rude."

"Just shut up," Marie hissed. "Can't you see this is hard on him?"

"Don't treat him like a baby." Knox rolled his eyes at her.

"I'm treating him like a person." She clenched her fists. "More than you ever did."

"Syd can stick up for himself," Knox said. "He makes his own choices."

"Is that what you think?" said Marie. "You don't have any idea how the system works, do you? You don't know anything about people like Syd. You don't even care."

"And you do?" said Knox. "I'm the one helping him get away. I don't even know what you're trying to do. You started all this to begin with. If you hadn't set me up, Syd would still be in that little shop, I'd be with some chick who wasn't a psycho and your friend Beatrice would still be alive!"

Marie tried to form a response. "I'm trying to change things," she said. "I'm trying to make the world better . . . for everyone."

Knox crossed his arms. "Don't act like you're better than me because you feel guilty for being born rich."

"Both of you, quiet." Syd cut off their argument. "We've got an audience."

He nodded his head back toward the entrance at a woman in a fashionable green jumpsuit, expertly tailored, with expensive red hair falling in curls over her shoulders. She could have just been a normal patron visiting the zoo, except that the woman was walking straight for them.

"Guardian?" Syd asked, ready to run.

"Guardians don't look like that," Knox told Syd. "They're perfect."

"Everyone up here looks perfect," Syd answered.

"I'll take that as a compliment." Knox squeezed Syd's shoulder and Marie glared at him.

"Knock it off," she grunted.

The woman walked right up to them. As she passed by, she whispered and moved on toward the café.

"Yovel," she said, without slowing down. "Café."

"She's our contact," said Syd. He took a deep breath. On the ceiling, a giant RePet advo appeared, happy children running to greet their animal friends with smiles and tears.

"Animals brought to you by RePet and Xelon Corporation," a cheerful voice announced for all to hear. "Financing available."

Syd turned to face Marie. "You should go home."

"I should . . . what?" She looked startled, pained even.

"This isn't your problem," Syd told her. "Mr. Baram's people will take care of me now and I've got Knox for a hostage. Too many people have already gotten hurt because of me."

Knox nodded. He'd be glad to see Marie go.

"I'm not going anywhere," said Marie. "The only way for Beatrice's death to matter is to tear the system down. If you can do that, then I am sticking with you."

"I can't change the system," said Syd. "I don't want to."

"I think you can," said Marie. "I heard the old man say it."

"And just like that, you believe it?" Knox groaned. "That's all it takes?"

"I believe we have to try," she said.

"No matter what?" Knox said. "Even though your proxy died? Even if you have to die . . . again?"

"Some things are more important than any one person," said Marie.

"You're insane," said Knox.

"And you're a shallow piece of—"

"Quiet!" Syd said. "Something's wrong."

"What?" said Knox.

"What?" said Marie.

Syd pointed up to the holo for RePet on the ceiling. It was gone. His eyes darted to the kiosks throughout the zoo plaza. Their projections had vanished too. No advertisements.

He'd once been to a NeoBuddhist center in the Valve where you could pay by the minute for the advos in the meditation room to disappear. You'd get your quiet, but only if you could afford it. But that wasn't it, not here.

Living in a place like the Valve you learned quickly when something was about to step off. The air crackled with the electricity of impending violence. Everyone growing up there had some ability to feel it and the better your feeling for it, the safer you were. The Slum Sixth Sense, they called it. Syd's sixth sense was firing.

"Where are the advos?" Marie wondered.

"What are you—" Knox said, but his question was cut off.

"Ahhhh!"

A boy's scream.

Syd looked toward the polar bear exhibit as one of the great white beasts leapt into the main plaza and reared up to attack the kid. The invisible fence was down. The polar bears were free. And a little boy was about to die.

[30]

SYD RAN STRAIGHT TOWARD the polar bear exhibit.

It took Knox a moment to realize what was happening. A bear had stepped off the ice and reared up over a little boy. Syd dove at the boy, tackling him out of the way and covering him with his body.

Marie moved next, rushing to them as the bear prepared to come down on both Syd and the boy. Knox stood dumbfounded.

Marie pulled out her EMD stick and shot a pulse into the bear, who recoiled and charged away into the plaza to find easier prey.

Panic ran through the crowd at the zoo like a flash flood in the wastelands. There were far too many children and far too few adults. The robotic nannies tried to lead the children in their care to safety, but their programming was woefully inadequate to face dangers the programmers hadn't imagined. They fired off EMD pulses at the escaped animals, but just as often were kicked aside by other children running scared. Children screamed and cried as the rest of the animals broke from their invisible cages.

Knox was mesmerized by the madness. The zoo had unraveled like everything else in his life. He started to wonder whether he had died in the accident after all and this was the afterlife all those religious nuts were on about all the time. No rules. No fences. No control. This was his hell.

A bot had reached Syd and was zapping him on the ankle to free the boy beneath him. Syd's muscles spasmed with each zap.

"Release him!" the bot commanded, and Syd couldn't even get control of himself to obey. The pulses were as hard as any he'd felt before. The nannies packed a punch.

Knox rushed over. The big vein on the side of Syd's dark neck bulged and his head smacked back against the floor. Knox wondered if all the pulses Syd had been hit with in the last twenty-four hours would do permanent damage to him. His brain might just burst right there on the floor of the zoo.

Knox wondered what the punishment for getting your proxy killed while trying to set him free would be? And who would be punished for it? Knox could picture his father's face. He imagined the scolding: "You can't even defy me successfully! You're no son of mine!"

While Knox stood there thinking about his father, Marie

smashed her foot into the side of the fuzzy pink bot and sent it sailing onto the polar ice.

One of the zookeepers rushed toward a howling monkey, trying to scoop it into his arms, when a jet-black panther leapt down on his back, sinking long fangs into the man's neck. He never even had the chance to scream. Knox turned away, gasping.

Marie reached down to help Syd up onto shaky legs and they both nearly collapsed under him. Knox knocked her out of the way and grabbed Syd under the shoulders and held him up.

"I got him," he told her. He felt a little foolish that he'd stood there doing nothing while Marie saved Syd's life.

"Let me down," Syd grunted, and Knox let him down onto his feet. On the ground, the little boy sobbed. Marie helped the boy up with an angry glance in Knox's direction.

"See those other bots?" Marie pointed. The boy nodded. "You have to follow them. Stay close to them and you won't get hurt, understand?"

"But . . . but . . ." The boy wiped his nose. "They aren't mine."

"It doesn't matter," she said. "Just run."

Marie shoved him toward the little bot that was leading the mischievous brother and sister they'd seen getting in trouble through the chaos. The boy ran after them, his little legs pumping as fast they could.

A lion charged across the plaza behind him, chasing a column of frightened penguins that were waddling toward the exit. The lion caught the slowest one, which let out a bloodcurdling screech.

Knox looked away as the penguin was ripped to pieces, just in time to see the brown bear from the lobby bounding straight at Marie's back. He swung out his arm and grabbed her by the waist, spinning her out of the way, as he snatched her EMD stick and jammed it into the brown bear's chest.

The bear yelped and turned, its paws sliding on the tile floor as it collapsed in a heap of fur.

Marie wiggled free of Knox's grip.

"You're welcome," he said and her eyes shot right to the weapon, now in his hands.

"What is going on here?" Syd asked. "Is this your father's doing?"

"I don't think so." Knox shook his head.

"Let's get to the café," Syd said.

"This isn't right," said Marie. "Something is very wrong." She looked around. There was blood on the floor, birds flying overhead beneath the enclosed glass dome, and everywhere, frightened children.

"You think?" Knox shook his head at her.

"Enough, both of you!" Syd's temper flared. "I'm sick of hearing you two."

"She's the one who—" Knox started, but Syd stepped right up to his face. Their noses were almost touching. Knox could feel Syd's breath on his lips.

Syd looked him in the eye, reached out, wrapping his

dark hand around Knox's. Knox tensed as Syd slid the EMD stick from his grip.

"You guys are my hostages, after all," Syd said with a nod. Then he ran in the direction that their contact had gone, holding the stick up, ready for anything that sprang his way. Knox and Marie ran after him.

Service doors opened and armed security guards rushed in to contain the animals. The zoo café had a wide glass door and beyond it, a scattering of shining steel tables and sleek multicolored chairs. Exotic plants wrapped around columns throughout the room and a large waterfall flowed down a sheet of shining marble against the back wall. Children hid underneath tables and behind the columns, casting frightened glances toward the entrance.

Syd stood still in the middle the room, panting, and Knox ran to his side. He followed Syd's gaze to the slender red-haired woman. She lay facedown in the corner of the café, her coils of copper hair splayed out all around her. A pool of blood blossomed on the tile below, soaking into the cloth of her shirt.

She was dead.

[31]

SYD COULDN'T TAKE HIS eyes off the body on the floor. It struck him as odd to see a patron's blood, to see a patron's body lying just as dead as anyone else's.

It occurred to him that he'd never really thought of them as human before.

He knew they were human, of course, just like him. That was the idea of the entire system. In theory, everyone was equal.

In primitive times, back in the Holy Land, as Mr. Baram called it, they'd used a goat to pay for all their sins. The high priests would confess all the sins of the community to a goat and then send it off into the wilderness to die, freeing the people of their burdens.

Of course, it made no sense.

The goat couldn't object or agree. The goat couldn't forgive. The goat didn't even know what was happening.

Only humans could accept responsibility, and only humans could take on a debt. Only humans could stand in for one another. We all begin as equals, but a contract, like a confession, changes our relationship. One becomes a debtor, one becomes a creditor. One a proxy, the other a patron. The contract defines us until its terms are met. A goat would always be a goat, but humans can change how they define one another and how they define themselves. That was civilization.

But beneath it all, everyone bleeds.

Syd played the thought around in his mind.

Everyone bleeds.

Behind the talk of debts and contracts and obligations, it was all held together by brute force. By blood. And there was something in *his* blood that could unravel it all.

"Well, she was a big help," said Knox. His sarcasm, even in the face of death, astonished Syd. Sarcasm was the easy expression of an empty mind. It carried no information, nothing he could learn except that Knox was an ass, which he knew already. The knowledge wasn't useful.

Suddenly, there was a scream and all their heads turned to the café entrance. A panther stalked into the room and landed without a sound on top of a table. Its sleek black head scanned from side to side, its tail swished just in front of the terrified children crouched beneath the tabletop. Its mouth shone wet with blood.

Syd's grip tightened around the EMD stick, but he didn't raise it at the giant cat. He watched it prowl.

The polar bears had impressed him with their size, but

this animal simply captivated him. All its muscles rippled; its eyes glimmered with graceful danger. The man-made perfection of the Guardians was nothing compared with the panther, returned from a long-gone world. The imagination that had conceived this creature was bigger than any Syd could comprehend.

The cat met his eyes and Syd felt it looking at him as he'd never been looked at before, considering him without envy or hatred or pity or need. It was a look from the wild, as out of place in the patrons' zoo café as Syd was. He never wanted to look away.

But the panther turned and jumped from the table, again without a sound, and left the café, its tail swishing behind it as it went.

"You just stared that panther down," Knox whispered into his ear, resting his hand delicately on the small of Syd's back.

"No," said Syd, wishing Knox hadn't just ruined the moment and stepping away from his patron's touch. He couldn't explain what he'd just felt even if he wanted to. And glancing back at Knox, he was certain that he didn't want to.

"Listen." Knox leaned in conspiratorially. Marie had gone over to the dead woman, leaned down to check her pulse and her breathing, hoping against hope that they hadn't just lost their way out. "Let's just ditch Marie and get out of here. We'll find another way for you to get to the Rebooters. We don't need her. She's crazy. She'll get us all killed."

"I don't even know if I want to go to the Rebooters," he said. "I don't want anyone owning me, your father or them."

"But what if what that old guy said is true? What if you are, like, the savior of the proxies or something?"

Syd shrugged. "Do you think I am?"

Knox didn't answer. He only wanted Syd to go so he could hurt his father and they both knew it. The rest of it didn't matter to Knox. He didn't care about a cause. He hadn't thought this through all that well. If Syd did have some kind of power in him, that'd be it for the world Knox knew. Aside from the last few days, he quite liked the world he knew. It worked for him.

"I'll take that as a no," said Syd.

"Let's just say I'm a skeptic," Knox replied. "But you're safer with me than with her."

"Why are you so committed to helping me?" asked Syd. "Last night you tried to beat my face in. You can't hate your father that much."

"Yes, I can." Knox didn't elaborate. Syd didn't press him. He didn't need to know Knox any better than he did already. He wasn't trying to make a friend.

Syd looked over at Marie, the true believer who put her cause before everything, and then at Knox, the pretty boy who believed in nothing but himself. Syd had the EMD stick. He had the choice. Stay with them. Ditch them. It was up to him.

With the murdered woman in front of him and the chaos of the patrons' zoo all around him, Syd smiled. It was the first time in his life that he ever had a real choice in anything.

He stepped over to Marie and stood over the patron's body. He squatted down in front of her. Knox scuttled over to be in earshot. He didn't want the two of them having secrets from him.

"You think I can change the world," he said.

She nodded with her hand still resting on the dead woman's cheek. "Someone has to."

"If we're going to make it to Old Detroit, I need to know that you and Knox aren't going to kill each other," Syd said.

She nodded again.

Syd rested his hand over hers, pulled it away from the dead woman's cheek, and looked her in the eyes. Her purple irises contracted.

"I can't change the world," he told her, trying to be as clear as possible. He needed her to know he wasn't a hero. He couldn't carry the weight of her faith in him out of the city, across the desert, all the way to the ruins of Old Detroit. If they were going together, they needed to go as people, not as ideas. "I can't take away your guilt. Beatrice is dead and I can't make that right."

She reached up and put her finger, still cold from the dead body, against the bone behind his ear. She touched the four letters of his mark. "You don't have to believe it," she said. "But I know it's true. I just know it."

"You have a serious glitch! You know that?" Knox interrupted. He threw his hands up in the air, exasperated.

"Listen to Syd! He. Is. Telling. You. He isn't a revolution-ary. He's just some—again no offense here, Syd—some swampcat running for his life. He just told me. That's all he wants to be."

"He's not 'just some swampcat'—" Marie started, when she was cut off by the sudden blast of an EMD pulse and sent reeling backward over her heels, twitching on the floor. Syd whirled around, his own EMD stick raised.

"Right-o," said Egan, strolling across the café floor as if he didn't have a care in the world. He gripped a dinged-up old EMD stick in one hand and his beloved antique knife in the other. The blade was wet with bright-red blood. Fresh. "He's *my* swampcat."

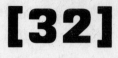

[32]

EGAN WAS IN THE same clothes he'd worn to Arcadia, trying to look lux. Knox could tell there was nothing lux about him. He didn't belong at the patrons' zoo. Even his EMD stick was old.

It took Knox a moment to see the wet blade in his other hand.

"Egan," said Syd, so shocked to see his friend that he didn't check if Marie was okay.

"Girl was trying to strangle you." Egan pointed at Marie with the stick.

"No." Syd shook his head. "She wasn't."

"Oops." Egan shrugged and giggled, his pupils wide as the sky.

Syd started to wonder if he were back in a nightmare. The bloody knife, the body on the floor, the impossibility of Egan . . . he wished it were all in his head. He saw the rise and fall of Marie's chest and felt a little better about the reality he was trapped in. She was breathing. Egan hadn't killed her. One lucky break for the day.

Syd rushed over to his friend.

Knox seethed. Egan had done this, all this. He was the one who had approached Nine about the fake ID. He was the one who brought Syd to Arcadia. If it weren't for Egan, Knox never would have met his proxy. He never would have found out that Marie was still alive. He'd have dealt with his guilt and his father's disappointment and moved on. His life would be . . . well, not *this* anyway.

"What are you doing here?" Syd asked.

"Looking out for my best friend," Egan answered. "Like I always said I would. Now let's get out of here. Extinct animals freak me out."

Knox had to strain to listen to Syd and Egan talking. His alliance with Syd, fragile as it had been, was now in danger of shattering completely. He had to know what Egan was up to.

"You killed that woman." Syd pointed at the dead patron on the floor.

"She was going to send you straight to Sterling," Egan told him. "You can't trust these Upper City people."

"Mr. Baram sent her!" Syd objected.

"Trust me, brother. She was going to sell you out. I know things."

"Did you let the animals go?" Syd asked.

"You think I could do that?"

"That's not an answer," Knox interjected. Egan looked him up and down, then turned back to Syd.

"Can't believe you ran off with . . . *him*," said Egan.

"How did you even find me here?" Syd demanded.

"I had some help. I can't explain now." Egan wiped the blade of his knife on his pants leg and tucked it into his belt. He tapped Syd on the shoulder with the EMD stick—it wasn't turned on anymore—and nodded at Knox. "Want me to fry this knockoff loser?"

Knox stepped back. He spread his hands with open palms, in a gesture he thought looked open and trusting without looking too much like surrender. It was, however, surrender.

For some reason, his mother's face passed through his mind. It was hazy, like a bad transmission. He hardly remembered what she looked like, she'd been gone so long. If Egan killed him right now, maybe he'd get to see her again.

He held his breath, braced for the pain. He didn't know what an EMD pulse felt like, but it looked agonizing. He hoped he could handle it without embarrassing himself. He felt an anxious pressure on his bladder.

"No." Syd pushed Egan's EMD stick down. He was not going to let anyone else die because of him. Not even Knox.

Egan grunted. "Fine. If you want to take your patron, I get it. A little revenge? Maybe something else . . ." Egan smirked and Knox cringed. "But the girl? What possible use could *you* have for *her*?"

Syd rolled his eyes. "It's not that. At all."

"Well, let me know if you change your mind." He smiled widely at Knox and waved the EMD stick in his direction. "I can play matchmaker . . ."

"Don't even joke," said Syd.

"You used to be more fun," said Egan.

"I didn't used to have the whole city trying to kill me," said Syd. "Anyway, Knox stays with me. They both do."

"Fine," Egan grumbled. "But he tries anything, I get to fry him, okay?"

Syd nodded and Knox realized he'd gone from accomplice pretending to be a hostage to an actual hostage. He was unarmed and at Egan's mercy.

Knox had heard about the kids who lived in the Valve since he was little. The ones who survived into adulthood were mostly criminals, unrepentant debtors or worse. They didn't respect contracts or property; they all took knockoff syntholene and expired biode patches. They'd all quite happily watch the Upper City burn if they were allowed to. Egan was about as typical a Valve kid as Knox could imagine, even in his knockoff Upper City clubbing outfit.

"The Valve is going crazy." Egan leaned in to Syd. "Tearing itself apart looking for you. There's a reward—dead or alive—it's insane. Enough to pay off five lifetimes of debt. They even came for Baram."

"Yeah," said Syd. "I know."

"Old bastard fought off a dozen Guardians." Egan laughed. "Gave 'em all the slip."

Syd felt a weight lift off his chest. Mr. Baram was okay. For now.

"Speaking of giving them the slip," Egan added. "It's time to go."

"We've got to wake Marie," Syd told him.

"Better do it fast." Knox pointed out through the glass doors of the café. Just on the other side, a security guard led a line of weary penguins back toward their exhibit. Past the penguins, a half-dozen Guardians were walking in a V formation through the zoo, straight for the café. Behind them, three Arak9 bots clattered across the floor.

Egan cursed.

The boys rushed to rouse Marie.

"Sorry I zapped you, sweetheart." Egan smiled down at her. "I was looking after my boy here. But now, we gotta go."

Marie rubbed her eyes and shook herself awake. Now she knew what the proxies went through with every EMD hit. It wasn't the most pleasant knowledge in the world. She pushed herself off the floor. Her left leg kept vibrating and Knox watched her try—and fail—to put weight on it.

"I guess I could find a use for that one." Egan winked.

"Knock it off." Syd cuffed Egan on the ear. Marie looked up at him with hellfire in her bright purple eyes. Pure hate.

Syd wanted to let her know that Egan talked big, but he was really harmless. Then he glanced at the dead body on the floor, the chaos of the zoo, and it struck him that that wasn't true anymore. Egan was far from harmless.

"Follow me, kiddies," Egan said and guided Syd to the

far corner of the room. They stood beside a plexi wall with a commanding view of the canyon land beyond the city. It stretched on, desolate and lifeless, all the way to the horizon. It was the land of drought and earthquakes, volcanic surges and flash floods. It was a land that humans had long ago abandoned.

It was where they were going.

"You'll never get out this way," Marie said, but Egan tapped his hand on the wall and a projection popped up. A few taps and a service door in the wall slid open without a sound. Egan gave Marie a cocky smile and pulled Syd through.

"We can't go with this guy," Marie whispered. "I don't trust him."

"I don't trust you either," Knox whispered back from the corner of his mouth.

"He's a murderer," she said.

"He's Syd's friend," answered Knox, as if that explained anything at all.

A sudden crash as the glass entrance to the café exploded. The Guardians rushed in, the bots blocked the exits.

"Stop," one of the Guardians commanded and Knox met her eyes. He felt a tug in his stomach. He wanted to obey, wanted to surrender to her authority and put all this behind him.

"Snap out of it!" Marie pulled him back through the service door, which slid shut in his face. He gave her a meek nod of thanks and they turned to sprint after Egan and Syd.

Knox had never seen the working areas behind the zoo exhibits before. This was for staff, security, and their bots only. There was no reason a patron would ever need to know what went on behind the scenes. Now they were racing through the inner workings and it wasn't quite what Knox had imagined.

The walls were brown concrete, dripping with moisture from the tangle of pipes and conduits that ran along the ceiling. Raw LED lighting made the hallways shine like day. And the light revealed all the grime and dirt on the floor.

They caught up to Egan and Syd at an intersection of tunnels. Egan looked down at his feet and then turned left.

Knox realized that Egan had augmented-reality lenses in. He was getting the layout of these tunnels from a datastream that only he could see. How would some slum rat get access to a plan of the tunnels at the zoo? Knox wanted to signal Syd somehow.

At the next junction, Egan turned around. "Hurry up!" he said. "We're not waiting for these patrons if they fall behind."

"You two," Syd told Knox and Marie. "Go in front of me. Now."

Marie nodded and stepped past him. Knox stepped up too, making sure to brush against Syd as he went past.

"Be careful," he whispered into Syd's ear. He wanted Syd to remember who warned him first if things went wrong.

Then they were running again.

They ran past embryonic tanks where new animals were

grown. Half-formed penguins and lions and shapeless blobs that hadn't been given their stem cells yet. Life without a program. It was kind of how Knox felt right now too.

They ran past transformers and solar batteries, network servers blinking and humming, a row of huge cooling fans that blasted hot air away from the exhibits and down the corridor. Knox was soaked with sweat. He was in good shape, but felt like he could barely breathe. There was no climate control back here, just heat and damp.

They reached a heavy steel door, pocked with rust. The pipes and conduits turned away from it, bent back into the rest of the building. There was no handle, no sign.

"What now?" Syd panted, catching his breath behind Knox. They heard noise in the tunnel behind them, the thump of feet coming their way.

"Under control," said Egan.

Knox saw the twitch of his eyes as he accessed something on his lenses, maybe sent a message.

Knox gave Syd a look to make sure he noticed. Syd nodded. Secrets had a way of driving wedges between friends, and Egan was definitely keeping secrets from Syd.

Someone on the other side of the door knocked three times. Egan knocked back four and the door slid open.

Marie gasped and Knox stumbled backward. Syd caught him from falling.

"What the hell are those things?" Knox cried out.

"What?" Egan sneered at him. "You rich kids don't know what horses are?"

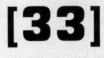

[33]

THE LONG-FACED CREATURE SNORTED and kicked one of its legs. There was a man holding it by some kind of strap and he whispered into its furry ear. It snorted again and made a strange kind of grunting, whining sound.

"I know what a horse is," Knox told Egan. "I've seen the old holos."

"I guess you don't know how to ride one, though, huh?" Egan stepped outside into the bright midday sun.

The others followed, squeezing around the horse at the doorway. Knox pressed himself against the door frame as flat as he could, keeping his distance. Syd tried to move with confidence. He figured that wild animals could sense fear. Then he wondered whether horses were wild. He had a sense that they weren't, but he'd never seen one in person before. He was pretty sure, in spite of his attitude, Egan hadn't either.

There were four horses and three riders with them, rough-looking people with skin cracked and weathered like the landscape of a nightmare. Bandits, for certain. They could probably sense fear too. They were definitely wild.

Syd had to wonder what Egan was doing with this crew.

Only one of them stood on the ground; the other two sat on the backs of their horses, straddling them and holding primitive weapons in their hands. One held a broad sword of rusted and pitted metal. It still looked sharp enough to cut through flesh and bone. Another held some kind of tube weapon that Knox tried to recall the name of from history class. Rocket-propelled something or other.

The one on the ground wore a black scarf around his head so that only his cloudy eyes and wind-burned nose were visible. He held two horses by leather straps.

"How about you?" Egan turned to Marie. "You know how to ride?"

"I'll manage," she said back. Syd had to respect her confidence, even if it was faked. This was a girl who didn't know how to be a victim.

They stood on a slope of rough rock on the edge of a canyon. The zoo was behind them, two hundred feet up on a cliff. They'd run a long way downhill in the tunnels. They still had a long way down to go. A narrow path in front of them led into the canyon lands and the lifeless nothing beyond. Somewhere on the other side was Old Detroit, where Syd's blood was supposed to change the world.

No turning back now.

Marie grabbed the reins attached to the horse nearest

her and pulled herself up onto its back with a deft movement. The big creature bucked and resisted, but Marie held on tight. The rider on the ground laughed, pulling down the black scarf. She was a woman.

"Feisty," she said. "We'd get a good price from the slavers for this one. Don't see a lot of patron flesh in the harvester camps."

Syd saw a ghost of fear glide across Marie's face.

"We're not here on slavers' business," one of the riders grumbled from the back of his mount. "Which one's our swampcat?"

It was Syd's turn to tense, but Egan nodded at him that it was okay.

"I am," Syd said, stepping forward. "And whatever happens to me, happens to these two." He glanced at Marie up on her horse and then back at Knox, standing wide-eyed before the animals. "Think of them as my proxies."

The woman laughed.

"Check him," ordered the guy on the horse.

"I'm telling you, we're tight," said Egan, but his friends didn't seem to care.

"Keep your horse steady or we'll be picking your guts off the canyon floor," the woman told Marie. She nodded down the slope to where the canyon dropped away, then she spat on the ground and stepped away, leaving Marie to hold her horse alone. Marie gripped the reins tightly. The horse shuffled its feet, but it didn't bolt or buck.

The bandit grabbed Syd and pushed his head down; she

wrenched his neck to the side. He had the urge to raise the EMD stick in his hand and knock her straight onto her back. But he fought the urge. She bent his ear and touched the spot where his birthmark was.

"It's him," she said.

"I told you," said Egan. "You guys have some serious trust issues."

Syd wondered if they knew what his birthmark meant. Were they Rebooters?

The woman let his ear go. "We don't have enough horses for everyone."

Syd went to the other empty horse, grabbed the leather reins and climbed up, just like Marie had. If she could do it, why couldn't he? The horse moved around under him, started to turn in a circle, but he pulled it back and straightened it out.

"I'll ride with Syd," Knox volunteered immediately, stepping to Syd's side. He needed to stay close.

In a scramble of grunts and curses, Knox hauled himself up onto the horse behind Syd.

Egan raised an eyebrow at Syd, to make sure he was okay with this, like Knox needed Egan's permission. Syd said it was okay, so Egan climbed onto the horse behind the bandit with the rocket weapon.

"Stay on our tail," said Egan. "I don't want to lose you and that patron of yours. And you!" he called back toward Marie. "Don't fall off . . . we're not waiting for you."

"You made that clear," Marie called back and Syd had

to admit, he liked her. She was calculating and tough and though she was clearly out of her element here, she held her own.

Egan raised his hand toward the zoo and the Upper City behind it, pressed his forefinger to his thumb and flicked. "Bye-bye, you knockoff town!" he shouted, then called back to Syd, "Just a few days to freedom, brother!"

Suddenly, the steel door beside them burst open and two Guardians rushed out, their gray jumpsuits shining in the sun, their perfection a jarring contrast to the jagged landscape.

"Stop!" the Guardians shouted, their voices identical.

The woman next to Marie's horse simply raised her weapon, two rusty tubes stuck side by side on some kind of wooden base. She pointed it at the Guardians the way you'd point an EMD stick and she squeezed a little metal trigger with her finger.

A deafening blast and a puff of smoke from the tubes sent both the Guardians sprawling backward through the door. A splatter of bright-red blood painted the walls beside them, and without hesitating, the woman rushed to the door and slammed it closed on the Guardians.

She leaned her back against it as she split her weapon open and dropped two round cartridges into the tubes and snapped it shut again. She was whistling as she did it. Then she turned and squeezed the trigger again, with another explosion, the metal of the door bent and twisted.

The woman strolled back over to the horse and climbed up behind Marie.

"She just . . . ," Knox whispered in Syd's ear. "She just killed those two . . ."

"I know," said Syd, staring at the flecks of blood on the walls around the mangled door.

"Let's move," the woman called ahead from the back of her horse. "Pull your reins and give a nice loud heyup!"

"Heyup!" Syd said, pulling the reins, and the horse started off with a jolt.

The horse sped under Syd and he felt a tingle up his spine, a thrill. He'd never sat on anything alive before, never felt this much power beneath him, knowing the animal was only just barely under his command. He squeezed his heels into its sides and found he could steer the horse that way, or at least make suggestions to it. As long as his suggestions were respectful, the horse obeyed with tremendous force.

All this death, he thought, and I'm just starting to feel alive.

The horse ran along the edge of the canyon, its hoofs stamping into the dust, as it made its way through the cut in the rocks and started down. High shadows rose above them. The trail wound and twisted and the temperature dropped quickly. Syd caught a glimpse of the horse ahead of them, the horse with Egan, as it rounded a corner.

"Heyup!" he said again and jostled the reins. His horse moved faster.

"You're pretty good at this," Knox said. Syd felt Knox's arms wrap around his waist. It didn't feel like flirting this time, more like the desperate fear of a guy holding on for his life. In that sense, they weren't so different right now. It was the first time Syd didn't actually mind Knox touching him. He sped the horse up.

He heard the snorts and grunts of Marie's horse right behind them. It couldn't be easy for a patron, one minute sitting at home in luxury, the next racing off on horseback through the wilderness.

All for Syd, all because she believed some story about him.

Then there was Egan, who showed up with such convenient timing, who was running with this gang, who'd killed a woman. Again, all for Syd.

He didn't like all this unprovoked generosity.

The only person he felt he could actually trust right now was Knox. Knox's reasons for helping were all about Knox and Knox's hatred of his father. Self-interest made sense to Syd. Everyone else was playing some other game.

They heard a crash behind them. Knox looked back over his shoulder and saw three Arak9 combat robots kicking up dust as they pursued. The horses were fast, but the robots were faster and they were closing the distance between them rapidly.

"Trouble!' Knox shouted.

The lead bandit turned his horse around and waved for the others to pass him. As they galloped by, he swung his weapon off his shoulder and took aim.

A projectile shot from the front of the weapon and zipped through the air straight into the first of the bots. It hit with an explosion of flame and smoke. The bandit was already reloading as the next two bots leapt through the flames. Syd goaded the horse forward, faster. Behind them, they heard two more explosions in quick succession.

Whooping and cheering, the bandit galloped back into the lead and they resumed their course behind him. In the clear blue sky above, a drone circled.

"Why isn't it firing?" Knox asked as they galloped toward the cover of the canyon.

Syd glanced up at it, a black winged shadow overhead. He felt the comforting pressure of Knox's arms around him. Having the patron on his horse was the only reason that the drone hadn't blown Syd into dust. Yet.

"Because it would kill you too," Syd told him. Knox stared up at the drone, wondering how long his father would let them go before he wrote Knox off as collateral damage and let the drone fire. He wondered if his father would even mourn him.

[34]

THE HORSE MOVED STEADILY beneath Syd and he got used to guiding it with a nudge of his heels and a tug on the reins. Knox bounced behind him. He'd gotten more comfortable after a few hours of riding and he didn't need to hang on so tightly to Syd anymore, but he leaned forward to whisper into Syd's ear.

"You know your friend isn't telling you about his datastream," he said. Knox probably didn't need to whisper, but the overhanging rocks and strange turns of the canyon channeled winds and noises in crazy ways. He didn't want to take any chance of being overheard. "Egan is hiding something from you. No way a swampcat and some bandits could rig the zoo to go glitched like that. He's got partners here, powerful ones. We gotta watch out."

"We?" said Syd. "You throw that word around a lot."

"We," Knox repeated firmly. He didn't want Syd to doubt it. They were on the same side here. They had to be. Otherwise, Knox had no one.

"You should know, Egan's not a swampcat," Syd said. "Egan was born in the Valve. He's not a refugee from outside the Mountain City. He was just unwanted. I met him at the orphanage."

Syd thought about Egan at the orphanage, protecting him. Or at school, sticking up for him, sticking by his side no matter what, consoling him when he needed it and goading him when he could handle it. Making him laugh whenever possible. And now Egan had killed a woman.

Syd looked at Egan on the horse in front of him, moving along the sweltering landscape on the narrow lip of the cliff, high red rocks on one side, scorched bone dry, and a steep drop to the other, nothing but air. One wrong step and the horses would plummet off the edge with their riders on their backs.

Egan had a river of sweat soaking his fancy club clothes. Syd realized that his friend hadn't even changed since the night before at Arcadia. That explained why he had data lenses in—Egan always had the nicest stuff—but who was he talking to? Who could hack the zoo and let the animals out? Who would?

"Stay close to the cliff," Egan called back to them.

"He didn't exactly need to tell us that," Knox snorted.

Overhead they heard the buzz of the drone tracking them. Syd wondered how far those things could fly from the city. How far would they fly, looking for him? He was just a Chapter 11 orphan from the Valve, a kid whose name wasn't even his own. He was not some debtor messiah.

Knox must have been having a similar thought, because he flat out asked Syd, "So in all the years you had those birthmarks, you never thought of having them checked out by a doctor? You'd never had a blood test before my . . . accident?"

Syd grunted. He guessed Knox really knew nothing about life in the Valve. It wasn't really his fault. Syd didn't know much about life in the Upper City, after all, except what he saw in pirated holos. "I couldn't afford to."

"What are you talking about?" Knox shook his head, even though Syd couldn't see him. "You could have gotten tons of credit. I had the best policy Xelon offered."

"And I would have been tied to you forever," Syd grumbled. "MediConsult bills add years of debt. There are men in the Valve in their seventies who are still in the system because they had their tonsils out when they were five. Even if all this never happened, you were making my life a hell."

"A hell? Really?" Knox scoffed. "It wasn't that bad. Paid for you to go school, right? And it's not like I got in trouble *all* the time. Hell, I only got caught for half the stuff I pulled. You got off easy."

"Easy?" Syd spurred the horse a little faster. "You call this easy?"

"Well, not this," said Knox. "But before . . . I mean, you just didn't take advantage of the arrangement. Some people know how to use debt, make it work for them. That's, like, the first rule of business."

"This the kind of stuff they teach in patron school?" Syd wondered, trying a bit of sarcasm for himself.

"Yes, it is, actually," Knox answered. "We learn it before we can walk. The market's in our blood. Survival of the fittest. Wield your resources like a knife."

"The Valve's the same way," said Syd. "Except our knives aren't metaphors."

Knox pictured Egan with his bloody knife, the dead woman on the floor. No more metaphors. No more markets. He was a long way from the Upper City.

Out here, without datastreams or credit swaps, he wasn't much more than a bag of blood and bones. What did he really have to offer? He didn't even know how they were going to eat.

The thought of food made his stomach rumble.

"Your friend Egan knows more than he's saying," Knox announced, and Syd got the sense he was talking just to fill the silence. "I don't trust him."

"Uh-huh," Syd grunted. He wasn't going to let Knox in to his thoughts. Whatever Egan was up to was between him and Egan. He didn't like Knox inserting himself into their friendship. He felt strangely possessive of his crazy, murderous friend. What was the old rule of economics? Scarcity creates value. Egan might be a killer and a drug addict, but he was Syd's only friend.

"Listen, Syd, I can help you," Knox said. "But you have to let me in. You have to trust me."

"Trust you?" Syd scoffed at him. "Why should I do that?"

"I told you. We're on the same side," Knox said. "I want you to get to the Rebooters as much as anyone."

"Marie seems to want it pretty bad," said Syd. "And Egan killed a woman to do it."

"Yeah, but . . ." Knox let his voice trail off. He'd overestimated his charm.

"Relax," Syd told him. "You don't need to convince me. They're both dangerous in their own ways. You should be careful. I don't think either of them likes you much."

"I can be dangerous." Knox felt the sting to his pride. "Anyway, Marie's just playing hard to get. She'll come around. Although I think it might be you she'll come around to. You see the way she looks at you? And we know she's a total Causegirl. I bet she'd love to get with a proxy. You might want to give it a try."

"I'm not looking for romance out here," said Syd.

"You ever tried it with a girl?" Knox asked.

Syd ignored him.

"All right, you know what you like; that's fine." Knox let it go.

Syd spurred the horse faster and nearly bounced Knox off the back. Knox caught himself, but he had to smile. Syd was laughing. Maybe Knox had an ally after all.

Far off, Syd saw the stunning display of plateaus and buttes peeling off the desert floor, making purple silhouettes against the horizon. In the Valve, you couldn't see much past the nearest shack or concrete slab of a building. Blast barriers and heaps of trash cut across any line of sight, making their own unnatural landscape. The great towers of the cruciplexes sometimes caught the light and glimmered purple, red, and gold for an instant, but the choking smog that made the Valve sunsets so spectacular burned the eyes and gave a daily reminder of the slow death in which you lived. The lack of life out here made the world seem so much bigger.

They wound their way along narrow trails all the way down into the canyon. The walls were great painted stripes of browns and yellows and reds. The river below had long ago dried up and taken all the life with it too, any trace of green. It left behind a long, barren gorge. No life could thrive out here. After the ice melted and the waters rose, after the wars and the fires and the plagues that collapsed the old civilizations, some people had tried to live out here. They couldn't find food or water and they either died out or gave up and came as refugees to the city, begging for rescue. The corporations were glad to oblige, for a price. And that price was the debt that built the city, restored some kind of order to a corner of the world. The lifeless canyon had, in its way, given life to the city they'd left behind.

Knox wondered if he'd ever see it again.

Once they reached the bottom of the canyon and the cover of the high walls surrounded them, they stopped and hopped off their horses. The bandits passed around a skin pouch filled with water.

"Stay hydrated out here," the woman said. "Dry air will kill you faster than you can say ransom."

"Nice choice of words," said Knox, taking the pouch from her. Syd watched him put it to his lips and tilt his head back.

"Ugh, this is disgusting." Knox spat his out in a sizzling puddle on the hot canyon floor.

"Don't waste water, kid!" the guy with the rocket launcher yelled. "We've got a hell of a long way through this desert before we're through. You'll dry out faster than your mother's tit out here."

Knox glared at the bandit, his nostrils flared, but he lifted the pouch to his lips again and took another hesitant sip, swallowing it this time, even as he gagged. What would his mother have thought about the company he was keeping now?

Syd guessed that Knox had never tasted unfiltered water before. He noticed Marie drinking hers greedily. Egan made eye contact with Syd and rolled his eyes. That was his cue. Maybe now he could find out what Egan was up to. He stepped over to his friend.

"What's going on?" he whispered. "Who are these guys? And how'd you find me? I need some answers, brother."

Egan scratched the back of his neck and leaned closer to Syd.

"They're with the Maes crew," said Egan. "Smugglers. They bring in half the syntholene in the city. They've got labs out here in the desert canyons where no one can find them. They know these canyons better than anybody."

"But how do they know *you*?" Syd asked. Egan had been small-time back in the Valve. He wouldn't run with a gang like Maes. Syd pictured Egan with the bloody knife; pictured the dead patron. Maybe the rumors were true. Maybe that woman's blood was the price of Egan's initiation to the gang.

"When you disappeared from Arcadia last night," Egan explained, "those Guardians came after me. They don't miss a trick, so I knew I couldn't go home, especially after I heard you'd kidnapped your patron. I mean, what are the chances? First time you go partying in ages and boom! You find your patron! And kidnap him? Who *does* that?"

Egan laughed, but Syd didn't laugh with him.

"Right, anyway," Egan continued. "I had to hide somewhere different, somewhere I'd never been before. Needed some lux cover and the only kind like that in Valve—"

"—is Maes," Syd finished.

Egan nodded.

"That doesn't explain finding me," said Syd.

"That was all Maes," said Egan. "He's got contacts, big-time, executive types. A few texts, a little runaround, and he knew. Arranged the whole thing—the animal escape, the getaway, all of it, in, like, an hour." He pulled the lenses out of his eyes, showed them to Syd. "Impressive, right? Guess these won't do much out here. No receivers. A shame. They are lux!"

"Executive types?" Syd's heartbeat raced. He thought of Knox's father with his monsoon-green eyes peering from behind those dark glasses, the casual way he watched Marie's proxy die. He was as brutal as any Valve crime lord; he just wore an expensive suit.

"The big shots fixed it all up for us," Egan bragged.

"And they're taking us to Old Detroit?"

"Wherever you want to go, friend." Egan patted him on the back. "Although, I'm telling you, this thing with the Rebooters is crazy. They're just a bunch of lunatics living in ruined factories, preaching some apocalyptic religion, praying for a debtor messiah who doesn't exist."

"The girl thinks they're waiting for me. Mr. Baram too. They think I'm the—" Syd was embarrassed to say it out loud.

Egan shook his head. "I've known you since forever. I don't get it. I mean, like, what's so special about you? To anyone other than me. I mean."

"I don't know." Syd looked at his feet. His friend was right, of course. It made no sense. He was just some slum kid with a virus in his blood. But what if that virus really could change the world? What if all he had to do was upload it? What if he had a destiny?

"I don't mean to break your heart, pal, but think about it." Egan put his hand on Syd's shoulder. "It doesn't make any sense. Baram's just a religious nut and this girl . . . well, what the hell does some patron chick know?" Egan looked over at Marie. "Trust me. I'm looking out for you. Like always."

"I understand, E, but I have to go to the Rebooters," Syd explained. "No one else can keep me safe. These patrons' parents want me dead at all costs."

"You really think a bunch of terrorists will protect you?"

"I have to try." Syd smirked, trying to cheer Egan up. "Anyway, maybe you'll like it with them. Try a whole new kind of crime?"

"Oh, Syd, you gotta understand, no matter where you go, I can't stay with you."

"What?" Syd couldn't believe it. Against all odds, he was back with his best friend and now he was hearing they'd be splitting up again, probably for good.

"I have a life back in the city," Egan said. "I've got debts that need to be paid."

"You mean, to Maes?" Syd asked. But he knew the answer already.

"This didn't come cheap. I'm with them now," said Egan.

"For me?"

"For you." Egan smirked. "It's almost like I'm your proxy now, huh? Suffering for your sins . . ."

Syd nodded. It was almost like that, but somehow, proxy just didn't seem like the right word, not for this kind of debt. Egan was giving Syd back his life; he even seemed glad to do it. In times like these, you had to find somebody to trust. But looking at the Maes bandits with their executive connections and their practiced brutality, Syd had a sinking feeling that Egan had put his trust in the wrong people.

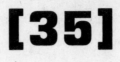

[35]

WHEN NIGHT FELL, THEY sat around a campfire tucked into a giant cave at the base of the canyon. Outside, the horses grunted and stomped and drank water from old stone troughs that smugglers had used for decades, centuries maybe. The smugglers' trails were as ancient as they were secret.

It'd been a hard day's ride, harder than any day Knox had ever known. His whole body ached; his skin stung from exposure to the raw desert sun and his lips were chapped and cracked. He felt like he hadn't slept in days. He actually envied Syd the few hours he'd been unconscious on the floor of the transport on their way to the Valve.

If Nine and Simi could see me now, he thought. Raw and sore and stinking. Running with swampcats and bandits and murderers.

And Marie, the girl he'd killed.

He looked at her on the other side of the fire. She was chatting with one of the bandits, the woman. Maybe chatting was the wrong word. Girls in his school chatted. Marie and this criminal were having a discussion about the Cause.

"The system itself needs to change," Marie told the woman. "It's not enough just to do well for yourself; the whole thing needs to be torn down."

"You noticed where you are, darling?" The bandit laughed. "There's no *system* out here."

"That's not what I mean." Marie was too earnest to notice the bandit was messing with her. Or maybe, she noticed but didn't care. You had to admire her for her commitment. She was lecturing a murderer about social justice. "The system is everywhere. The nomads, the refugees, everyone exists to serve the few, even if they don't know it. Even you."

"Watch yourself," the woman warned.

"Your existence gives the entire security apparatus a reason to exist," she continued. "Without criminals, there'd be no need for violent enforcers to protect the property of a relatively few rich patrons."

The woman laughed. "She's got a point! Hey, I think we should pack it in. Turns out we're working for relatively few rich patrons!"

One of the other Maes bandits laughed and poked his old sword into the embers of the fire. "I still haven't gotten my paycheck from them!"

All three bandits cackled with laughter. Marie gritted

her teeth, waited for the hilarity to pass. Knox figured it must be hard to take oneself so seriously. He wouldn't really know, though. He'd never taken anything seriously.

"So why do you care so much, rich girl like you?" The woman tossed a ChemiFlame into the fire. It flared up briefly, blocking Knox's view. "I mean, the things that happen in places like the Valve don't touch you at all."

"I have my reasons," said Marie.

"Enlighten us," the woman said.

"She saw her proxy die yesterday," said Syd. "Leave her alone."

"That it?" the woman smirked. "You ever meet this proxy of yours?"

"I never did," said Marie.

"So you just feel bad a stranger died?" The woman grunted. "You feel bad for all the strangers out there dying? Out in the wastelands? Or even here? My friends there die in a flash flood in the canyons tomorrow, you gonna cry for them? If I get caught up by organ harvesters, you gonna grieve for me too?"

Marie looked around, saw that everyone was waiting for her to answer. She sat up straighter.

"Beatrice was my fault," she said.

"That the dead proxy?"

Marie nodded.

"Leave her alone," Syd repeated.

"Then it'd also be your fault if we died out here, wouldn't it?" said the woman. "I mean, you want to go Old Detroit, right? You want us to take this kid"—she pointed at Syd—"because you think he's your debtor messiah. Somebody dies along the way, that's your fault too, no?"

"I guess so," said Marie.

"So you want to take on all the pain in the world." The woman ran her hand through her hair and shook it out. "We got a word for that, girls who go looking for pain that don't belong to them."

"What's that?" Marie asked.

"Glitched."

The rest of the gang laughed at her. She just frowned until they were done. She had patience.

"Do you know the story of the Frog Prince?" she asked when they had quieted down.

"The fairy story?" The woman laughed. "What's that got to do with anything?"

"Do you know it?"

"Everyone knows it," the woman said.

"I don't," Knox said quietly. Marie's eyes snapped to him. His father had canceled all the "childish" datastream subscriptions after his mother died. His dad thought it'd help him grow up. The sooner he left childish things behind, the sooner he'd leave childhood pain behind. Too bad the past didn't work like that. Knox had the pain, just not the childhood.

For a moment, Marie's expression softened. She looked at Knox without all the scorn she'd been throwing his way with every glance since he'd tried—and failed—to kidnap her.

"I don't know it either," added Syd. That might have been the first thing he and Knox had in common.

"I don't need to," Egan grumbled, but Syd kicked him in the ankle.

"Let her tell it," he said.

Marie nodded and exhaled. "It's about a beautiful princess who wanted for nothing and had not a care in the world," Marie told them.

"Sounds familiar," Knox grunted. He felt bad about saying it as soon as he saw Egan laugh. He did not want to entertain that knockoff.

Marie continued and they all listened around the campfire.

"The princess had everything she could ever want, but she couldn't sleep at night. The croaking of the frogs from the swamp beside her castle kept her awake. As the swamp grew larger and larger, the frogs grew louder and louder. Night after night, she lay awake in agony, her beauty shriveling into exhaustion. The princess's father worried as the dark circles under his daughter's eyes grew as fast as the swamp. Worry stole his sleep as well. So he ordered the frogs exterminated, every last one, and there was a great murdering of frogs and the swamps were drained and then, there was quiet."

Knox rested his head in his hands. He closed his eyes and listened to the crackle of the fire and sound of Marie telling the story.

"But the quiet did not last long," Marie continued. "The

night after the great emptying of the swamps, the princess heard the croaking of a solitary frog. She called out for her father, who called out for his soldiers, who called out for every man in the kingdom to search the swamp for the one surviving frog.

"While all the men searched for the frog that got away, the princess lay in bed tossing and turning with the sound of its croaking echoing off the walls and shattering her dreams, until suddenly, she felt movement beneath her.

"She hopped from her bed and jumped off her mattress, so thick and soft it was a wonder she could feel anything move beneath it at all, and yet there, below the mattress, croaking loudly, was a pea-green frog. It was big and warty and bug-eyed and loud as a missile. She screamed, but no one was left to hear her. They were all out in the swamp, searching.

"The princess knew that she was all alone, so she took a deep breath and dove at the frog, grabbing it as hard as she could with her delicate hands. It felt slimy and sticky and she looked at it and she hated it for its ugliness as much as for ruining her sleep.

"So she squeezed and squeezed to kill the frog, but as she squeezed, she caught its eye and the eyes, those ugly bulging eyes looked so profoundly sad that she was filled with pity. She stopped squeezing and, instead, she kissed the frog.

"And there was light, like a nuclear blast, and the frog transformed before her into a prince, the prince of the swamps, and he was angry at the murder of all his frogs and the draining of his swamp. He demanded that she seek redemption.

"'It wasn't my idea!' she objected.

"'But it was done in your name,' he said. 'And the guilt is yours to bear.'

"The princess could not undo what had been done and so, racked with guilt, she offered all her riches, and the frog prince took them, but he said, 'It is not enough.'

"She offered her father's kingdom and all its power, and the frog prince accepted, but said again, 'It is not enough.'"

"Greedy frog," muttered Egan.

Marie didn't let the interruption stop her: "The princess offered herself to the frog prince in marriage and the frog prince accepted, but after the wedding, as she offered her body to him as well, he said once more, 'It is not enough.'

"She offered her love to him too, her desires and her cares, all the compassion and truth she had, every part of herself she knew and those parts she had yet to discover, her past and her future, she offered to him, and he accepted and they grew old together, and she made him happy and he too, in a way, made her happy and they had many children, but as he lay upon his deathbed, his breath coming out like the croaks of a long-forgotten frog, he said again, 'It was never enough,' and he died and her debts would never be forgiven, and for her curse, she would live on alone until all the swamps in the world were silent."

Knox opened his eyes and saw that Marie was done.

That was the end of her story. Everyone in the cave was watching her.

Marie wasn't the girl he'd gone out with in the borrowed car, and maybe she never had been. She was painted red and yellow with dirt from their desert ride. Her eyes were ringed with dark circles, like he'd seen on syntholene addicts and holos of refugees at Benevolent Society fundraisers. Tired eyes.

Knox must look the same. He'd never thought he'd be someone with tired eyes. Never thought he'd stare across a fire at a girl who had them, a girl who'd lied to him and insulted him and, really, when it came down to it, ruined his life. He never thought he'd want to keep staring at her.

"So you're in love with Syd," Egan said. "You want to marry him because he's poor? I hate to break it to you, but he's not buying what you're selling."

"You don't understand at all," she said.

"Oh yes, I do," said Egan. "Your mommy played too many stories for you when you were little and now you feel bad for all the proxies in the world and you've turned into a revolutionary because of some crazy story about Syd's blood that you are desperate to believe because it gives meaning to your cushy little life to be part of a cause . . . sound about right?"

Marie looked away from him. Her purple eyes were wet in the firelight. As stupid as it sounded, she'd revealed part of herself with that story and Egan had thrown it back in her face. Maybe Knox would have done the same a few days ago. Even a few hours ago, but he didn't want to now. He looked at Syd. Syd didn't look so amused by Egan either.

"Syd's no frog prince," said Egan. "He's just a guy you screwed over."

"Leave her alone," said Knox. His throat felt dry, and not just because of the desert air. Marie's eyes drifted over the fire toward him. She met his gaze; her purple irises locked with his green ones.

"Or what?" Egan spat at Knox.

Knox looked away, picked at invisible fuzz on his shirt, then found a real bit of fuzz and picked it off. He tried to project some of that old Knox swagger. Indifference.

Egan stood and moved toward him, towered above him by the fire.

"Something bothering you, pretty boy?" Egan snarled. The flickering fire made shadows dance all around them. Knox remembered one of the advos for Cheyenne's parents' NeoBuddhist centers. *Let go of anger and achieve your desire.*

He exhaled slowly, turned to the fire, and felt the uneven heat on his face. He watched an ember ignite in a ferocious red blaze and float up on the heat, twirling and darkening as it rose until it was cool and black and dead. It fell away as ash.

"You want to defend your girlfriend?" Egan mocked him. "Patron solidarity? Can't have us wretched debtors insulting you and your lux life."

"It's not all lux," said Knox. "We've got our own problems."

"Yeah?" Egan kicked at the dirt beside him, showering his pants with dust. "You got malaria? Syd had it. Twice. You got stab wounds? Syd does. You got nerve damage from those EMD pulses, or broken fingers from hauling concrete? You got nightmares? Huh?"

"E!" Syd stopped his friend's rant. "Relax."

"I'm sorry about all that." Knox looked past Egan, spoke straight to Syd. "You have to believe that I am sorry."

"You'll be sorry, that's for su—" Egan said, but Syd cut him off again.

"I believe you, Knox," said Syd, his voice so soft that Knox had to lean toward him to hear. "And I don't care," Syd whispered. "Got it? I believe you're sorry. I. Don't. Care. I don't want your sorry. Live with your guilt. It's the one debt you owe me and I don't ever, ever want it repaid."

Knox didn't have a charming response. He swallowed and searched Syd's dark face for some hint of kindness. He never meant to hurt anyone. He got in trouble, but that was just him being Knox. When Syd got punished that was just how things worked. It wasn't personal.

But it was to Syd.

Knox looked around the campfire. Everyone was watching him. The bandits looked amused. Marie's expression he couldn't read.

The fire crackled. Knox had never felt so alone in all his life, at least, not since the day his mother died.

He was born a patron; he didn't choose it. He didn't choose for his mother to die. He didn't choose Syd as his proxy or the car crash or the virus in Syd's blood. Everything that had ever happened had happened *to* him. He wasn't responsible. He wasn't the princess and he wasn't the frog. He was just a guy getting by the only way he knew how.

"Got no comeback, pretty boy?" Egan chuckled. "Not so brave without Daddy's company around, huh? You need to run back home to your mommy?"

Before Knox could even decide to do it, his muscles uncoiled, and he sprang onto Egan, slamming into his chest with as much force as his legs could give him, knocking the sneering rat onto his back in the dirt.

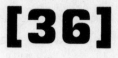

[36]

KNOX PUNCHED HIM IN the chin before Egan got an arm up to block. Then Egan hit Knox in the side with his other hand, a quick strike that Knox felt through his whole body. Egan knew how to aim for the vital organs, that was obvious.

Knox returned the favor, jammed his knee into Egan's crotch—no honor in a brawl, anyway—and tried to land another punch on his face, but Egan had gripped him by the back, trying to spin him over, and he couldn't throw a punch.

"You got nothing," Egan grunted, trying to roll Knox into the fire.

"More than you," Knox grunted back, trying to twist out of Egan's grip.

Knox couldn't get an advantage, couldn't break free, but

Egan couldn't break free from him either. They cast monstrous shadows on the wall, a two-headed beast thrashing in its death throes. No one stepped in to stop the fighting.

Knox expected Syd to dive in to kick him in the ribs or grab him by the neck to defend Egan, but he didn't. He heard Syd's voice, calling them both to stop, but as he turned his head to look over in Syd's direction, Egan smashed into his left eye with a head butt.

"E, no!" Syd shouted.

Knox saw flashing lights, sparkles, and he stumbled. Egan wriggled out from beneath him and wound up for a full-force kick to Knox's face.

Knox saw it coming like it was in slow motion, but he couldn't get his arms up in time.

His shoulders tensed and his face curdled in expectation of Egan's foot smashing into his jaw.

The explosion that came next was not in his jaw.

He didn't realize he'd closed his eyes until he opened them again and saw Egan standing on one foot in front of him, just like one of those pink zoo birds. Still dazed from the head butt, he thought Egan was transforming into one, a pink stain spreading across his chest, splatters of pink on his neck and face. His eyes were wide and black in the firelight. A loud gasp wheezed out of him and he fell into the dirt.

It was a trick of the eyes in the dim cave. The stains weren't pink.

They were red.

Knox looked up at Syd, staring to the other side of the fire. He followed Syd's shocked expression to the woman next to Marie, holding that rusty museum-piece weapon, two metal tubes, smoking in her hands, the same thing she'd used to kill the Guardians.

Marie stood beside her, alert but not afraid.

The other bandits were on their feet now, all of their weapons pointed at Syd.

"Why'd you do that?" Syd yelled. He knelt beside his friend, wrapped Egan in his arms. The boy wheezed and tried to gulp in air. His lux clothes from the club were soaked in blood.

"I'm sorry," Syd said to him, cradling his head. "Don't die. Just don't die."

Egan died.

Just like that.

Syd looked at his friend for a long time. The only sound was the fire crackling, the *pop* and *hiss* of the burning scrap wood, charred fragments from the desert floor. Syd's world had just shrunk to the space in front of him; he couldn't look beyond it, couldn't take his eyes from Egan's face. The mischievous light behind the eyes was gone.

"Can't hurt the rich ones," the woman with the weapon said, like it was nothing that she'd just killed Egan. "We're supposed to get them home safe and sound."

Knox couldn't reconcile his feelings; there were too many jostling for space. Relief and terror churned in his stomach, the bitter taste of adrenaline and the metallic taste of blood, earthy with dust. His back to the fire was hot, while his face was cold.

The rich ones, Knox thought. That's all he was to her.

But Knox had a whole life. He saw pieces of it then, not like people said, not the whole thing, like a holo, but like a dream, flashes of a memory, disjointed and rearranged. His mother playing with him on the floor of their living room, her lips made up zoo-bird pink, kissing him and laughing; his father smiling and dancing with her while old music played, the temper tantrum he threw because he wanted the new—what was it? He couldn't even remember now. She took him out to get it. That's when the men in masks stopped them. They'd come from the Lower City or they were Nigerian agents or they were ghosts. No one ever found out. They grabbed Knox and they grabbed his mother, but Knox slipped away. He was tiny, barely able to walk, but he ran.

"Run," his mother told him, or maybe she just screamed, but he ran and he hid. While he hid, they took her away. Guardians found Knox in his hiding place, brought him home. There was a ransom call, but his father wouldn't pay.

"We don't negotiate," his father said. "You can never negotiate with these people or they'll take everything."

And then her body, dumped on the road. A message for his father, who wouldn't negotiate. His mother's body mutilated by criminals. Knox didn't know what "negotiate" meant, but he knew it was bad, bad enough his mother would never come home because of it.

Even so, Knox kept asking when she would be home.

Then the funeral under a blue sky in a part of the old city, the part they saved for the dead. They said his mother was in the long box on the stand, but that didn't make sense. It was just a box. Why would his mom be in a box?

His father tapped at a projection. He didn't cry. He tapped at a projection and the box burned.

Knox yelled, ran out to stop him. "My mommy's in the box!" he yelled, but the box still burned.

He knew now, of course, that she was already dead, dead as Beatrice, dead as Egan, dead as anyone who'd ever died and there were billions of them. But then, back then, he also knew that only one death mattered and it happened in front of his eyes. He was sure he saw his father kill his mother. He was sure his father blamed him for hiding when the masked men came and blamed him for looking like his mother, for having her smile and her laugh. Her joy.

He cursed his father. A tiny child, barely able to form a sentence on his own, and he cursed his father. Maybe he didn't. Maybe that only happened now, in the instant flash of dreaming in the firelit cave. Knox saw his own face in his father's glasses and behind his face, the flicker of flames.

Knox looked up. Syd had closed his eyes. He was crying. He'd told Knox back in the alley that he never cried anymore, not since he'd first taken Knox's punishments. Then, he'd cried. As little boys, they both had cried together.

And now, in the cave, Knox couldn't help it. He felt a tear roll down his cheek and then another and another. He couldn't stop it, couldn't control it. He wanted to throw up. His body shook; his nose ran. He sobbed, right there in the dirt, with the bandits and Marie watching him, he wept and he didn't know why he wept and he hated himself for weeping. He saw his mother's coffin burning, heard the echo of his own childhood cries. His first memories were of grieving.

"Enough of the histrionics," the woman who'd killed Egan said. "Egan was a low-rent punk and a fool. He should have known better and he got what he deserved."

Knox looked to Syd to see what he would do. Neither of them moved.

"No," said Syd. He held his friend's body on his lap. "No."

The woman sighed.

"He was a bad kid, believe me," she said. "Not worth your tears."

"He was my friend," said Syd, which wasn't the opposite of being a bad kid. He was a liar and a crook, tweaked out half the time and sarcastic all of the time, but how many guys had a friend as good as he'd been? He'd done some bad, maybe would have done more if he'd lived, but he wasn't all bad, not all the time. He was better than the bad he did, but he died just the same.

He died for Syd. Or least, because of.

"He messed up," the woman said. "Mistakes have consequences." She made a clicking sound with her tongue on the back of her teeth. "We needed him because you'd cooperate if he was here and he thought that meant we were on your side."

Syd let his friend's head rest on the ground and he stood. "You aren't taking me to the Rebooters, I guess."

"You guess right," said the woman.

Syd looked down at Egan's body and shook his head a tiny bit, side to side. It was a look of disappointment, not anger. "Figured."

"He did say you were clever."

"So, what now?" Syd looked back at the woman with that same bored look he had on the projection when the Guardians first came for him, like nothing could disappoint him anymore. Something had broken that he did not know how to fix.

The woman dropped two new little cartridges into her weapon, snapped it shut, and pointed it at Syd.

"This is it," the woman said. "Just this and then we're done. The reward for killing you where no one will find your body, and some more for bringing these two home. That's all this is. Nothing personal, Sydney. Maybe your next life will be easier than this one."

Syd glanced to the wall of the cave where he'd left the EMD stick lying. Knox looked at it too. The silver pole shimmered in the firelight, too far out of reach to save him.

Knox pressed his fists into the rocky ground, trying to find the strength to stand. He didn't want to be the little boy who hid when the criminals came. He would always be the little boy who hid.

[37]

SYD SAW KNOX TENSE. If Knox dove for the weapon against the wall, the bandit might hesitate to shoot him. It might buy them enough time. He tried to signal Knox with his eyes, but Knox didn't pick up on it. He had a faraway stare. Tear tracks streaked the dust on his cheeks. What did Knox have to cry for? When this was over, he'd get to go home.

Not Egan. Egan would never go back to that stuffy little room of his. The thought punched Syd in the throat. Egan was dead.

"You kids might want to close your eyes," the woman suggested to Knox and Marie. "Your parents aren't paying us to give you nightmares."

"Father," Knox said, hunched on the ground, starting straight into the fire. Everyone looked his way.

"What?" the woman grunted.

"Not parents," Knox answered her. "It's just my dad and me."

Why did that matter now? Why did Knox feel like that mattered?

"Whatever, kid." The woman shrugged.

"You can't do this," said Marie. "Syd could change the world. He can't die in a cave. He can't die like this."

"Shut that girl up," the bandit with the sword sneered.

"Please, don't do this," Marie begged the woman. She knelt at the woman's feet. "Think of all the people he could help."

"Get off your knees," the woman said. "It's just a fairy tale. That kid can't do anything."

"If you don't believe it, then why kill him? Why do you need to kill him if he's no threat?" Marie stood, still in the woman's face.

"I don't have to believe it as long as your daddies do," she said. "They have a lot of money riding on Syd here never making it to the Rebooters."

"You'd kill him just for money?" Marie spat out the word "money" as if it were a curse, but Syd understood perfectly. The only people who couldn't understand the brutal lengths others would go to for money were the people who'd never been without it.

Syd could see it dawning on Marie that it was over, that hope was lost. She had that look people get when they know they've bet it all on a losing proposition. In the Valve, moments like that drove people to religion or to madness or to suicide. Syd wondered what it'd do to the rich girl as she realized that a fortune would always beat a dream.

"Marie," Syd told her. "Let it go. I'm not worth it."

"You are," she said. "I know you are."

She put her body between the weapon and Syd. Her bravery mocked Knox's cowardice. He was still on the ground in the dirt, like a worm. He hated himself for it, but he couldn't make himself stand.

"Out of the way," the woman commanded, but Marie didn't move, her stillness so different from Knox's.

"Just move her." The bandit with the sword grabbed Marie by the hair, yanking her head to the side with a painful snap.

What hadn't occurred to him, to any of them, was that Marie, like Knox, like all Upper City executives' children, had had self-defense training. And unlike Knox, she had paid very close attention. She had practiced.

Her hands reached out in front of her and she grabbed the hot barrels of the woman's weapon, jerking it down and to the side. Before Syd or Knox knew what was happening, Marie had pulled the weapon free and slammed the back of it into the bandit's groin. Then she brought the weapon down on his head, spun the weapon around and pointed the side-by-side tubes into the woman's face.

The injured man was doubled over in pain on the ground, cursing Marie in a gurgled torrent of profanity.

"No one move," Marie said. She brushed her dark hair from her face and her eyes caught the firelight, flickered.

"Don't be stupid," the woman told her. "You're not a killer and this is not some fairy story. Maybe you're a princess who can't sleep at night, but like your pals said, there's no frog prince here. You're in over your head with the wrong kind of people. Put the gun down, let me do my job, and we'll get you home. You can work all this out with your daddy. Maybe he'll buy you a horsey of your own to apologize."

"No," said Marie. "We're leaving. The three of us. We're going to the Rebooters. Knox! Tie those two guys up."

Knox didn't move. He was lost in his head, his eyes fixed on Egan's body. The shadow of the dancing flames, like when his mother's coffin burned. He couldn't recall her face. At the moment, that seemed somehow important. The gritty earth below his knuckles crunched, cut him. The pain, that too seemed somehow important. He heard his name as if it were shouted through water.

"Knox? Are you hurt? Knox!"

"What?" He snapped to. "I'm okay. What?" He brushed his hands on his pants, looked around the cave at the aftermath of the violence. He felt like he'd been watching a holo and only now was he realizing he was in it too.

"Tie those two up," Marie repeated.

"Tie them with what?" he asked.

"Take the reins off one of the horses outside."

Knox pushed himself off the ground and made his way out of the cave. As he passed, the guy on the ground reached for his own weapon. Syd dove for his EMD stick and fired off a shot that left the bandit sprawled out face-down, twitching.

"Thanks," Knox said, his voice flat, his face a total blank. He turned and walked outside to get the reins off one of the horses.

Syd stepped forward, right over the fire, sparks wicking off his shoes. He stood beside Marie and held the gleaming silver rod pointed right at the bandit who had killed his friend.

The woman's eyes scanned him up and down. He wondered if she could read him the way he could read her. She wasn't afraid.

She could see quite clearly that he was.

"I can stop your heart with this thing if I want," he said, trying to sound confident. He turned up the output. "I have a lot of experience with these."

The woman didn't answer. Syd felt like a coward. This woman had killed Egan. She'd killed two Guardians. No doubt she'd put Egan up to killing that woman in the zoo. She was a Maes gang thug. She deserved to die. She'd earned it. It took all the strength Syd had to keep his hand from shaking. He stared at her and she pursed her lips. All he could see on her face was impatience.

Knox came back in clutching a mess of leather straps. He bent down to tie the bandits up but stopped before he got to them. He froze.

"You don't know how to tie a knot?" Marie groaned.

"I never had to before," he said

Syd kept his eyes locked on the woman's.

"Well?" the woman asked. "You pulled it out, you know how to use it, big boy?"

Syd exhaled. He steadied his hand. A small smirk formed on the woman's lips.

"Go help Knox," Syd told Marie.

"I—" Marie hesitated.

"If you don't help him, they'll never get tied up and they'll take us all hostage and kill me."

"Fine." Marie stepped away to help Knox tie up the men. She handed Knox the gun as she bent down to tie the knots herself. "Keep this pointed at them."

"I'm gonna cut your pretty face off, you spit-shined slag," the bandit who was still conscious snarled at her. Syd heard them grunt as she cinched the leather straps tight, probably cutting off blood flow to important parts of their bodies.

"I like her," the woman said to Syd. "Your girlfriend?"

Syd didn't answer her.

"Oh, right," said the woman. "You don't go for that. Maybe *you* can be *her* girlfriend."

Syd raised the EMD stick to the level of the woman's head.

"Stop kidding yourself, boy." She cleared her throat and spat to the side. "You aren't the type. Why don't you just run out of here so we can get on to the next part."

"What part's that?"

"The part where we hunt you down, torture you to death, and sell your friends back to their parents piece by piece."

Syd swallowed hard. His throat was dry.

The woman leaned forward and smiled. She whispered

in his ear. "Your friend Egan didn't want to kill that woman at the zoo, you know? We told him it was the only way to save you. So he did it. He killed for you." She raised her eyebrows. "And you? Little Chapter Eleven coward, can't even take your revenge. I guess we know who was the man in your relationship. Guess you'll never bend over for Egan again."

She laughed in his ear and the moment he flinched, she grabbed for the EMD stick in his hand.

Syd was faster.

He hardly seemed to move, but the pulse he sent through the woman made her crumble where she stood. She fell straight down in a mass of firing synapses and blasted nerves. She clawed at the dirt and vomited and Syd stood over her until she stopped moving.

He knew what he'd done. He'd stopped her heart. Dead.

A life for a life.

All debts have to be repaid.

"We're going," Syd said and he walked out of the cave into the cool desert air.

[38]

SYD WAS SURPRISED BY how little remorse he felt for what he'd done to that woman, lying dead in the dust. He'd always thought killing would change a person, but he didn't feel changed. He'd just flicked his wrist. It didn't take much to make him a killer. Just a flick of the wrist.

He heard a snuffling beside him, the loud breathing of the horses tied up by the entrance to the cave. They were just dark outlines against the starry sky. He approached one, whispering, urging it to hush.

The horse backed a few steps away but Syd raised his hand and let the horse smell him, and then he rested his palm on the horse's long nose. It was hard and the fur was short and bristly. The horse's giant black eyes darted from side to side. Animals know when something is wrong.

Syd rested his forehead against the horse's snout, holding it still with a hand on either side.

"Shh." He stroked the horse's snout. "Shhh. It'll be okay. It'll all be okay. You're not alone."

When he closed his eyes, he saw that bandit's face when the EMD pulse hit her. She didn't even have time to be surprised. She crumpled into the dust, her last expression caught between a sneer and spasm. Her face was quickly replaced by Egan's, sweat just above his upper lip, his hair tussled, his chest heaving, torn open. He'd looked up at Syd, but he had no clever last words. He didn't go out in a blaze of glory. He just went out.

Syd lifted his head from the horse's. He felt its hot breath on his face.

"They're tied up." Marie came outside. Knox followed her.

Syd knew he owed her his life, but still, she made him uncomfortable. He found her faith in him unnerving. He didn't want to be its object. Why'd she have to believe in him?

"So . . . what do we do now?" asked Knox. His clothes were dusty, his face was bloody, and he'd just witnessed two murders. He wanted nothing more than to be told what to do. He wanted to obey. Knox had crossed some kind of line back there in the cave. He'd started the fight that left Egan dead, and though he knew the bandits would have probably killed the kid anyway, he couldn't shake the feeling that he'd brought it about. From the moment he'd gone out for that joyride in the CX-30, he'd become responsible for all this death. One dumb decision, that's all it took. It was his fault.

"We take the horses and ride to Old Detroit," said Marie, brushing a stray strand of hair from her face. "We have to get Syd to the Rebooters. Nothing's changed."

"Nothing's changed?" Knox said. "People are dead!"

She looked away from him. "If we don't get Syd to the Rebooters, they died for nothing."

Knox shook his head. He looked to Syd. "Should we, like, bury your friend?"

"What for?" said Syd. "That's not Egan in there. That's just a body. Egan's not in it anymore."

Knox wouldn't argue the point. If Syd wasn't the sentimental type, that was fine with him. Syd had his own reasons. Knox couldn't bear to go back inside the cave either. He didn't want to see what he'd done and what had been done because of him.

"Do we even know where Old Detroit is?" Knox asked.

Marie didn't answer. Knox didn't need to be skilled at reading body language to know she had no idea.

"People say there's an old road on the other side of the canyon," Syd said. "They call it the Interstate. Say it runs right across the desert to Old Detroit. If we can get to it, we can follow it all the way."

Marie nodded, ready to go into the great unknown.

Knox, however, looked hesitant, which seemed to Syd like a more sane reaction.

"Do you know the way to this Interstate?" Knox asked. "I mean, are we going to hop onto these things—"

"Horses," said Marie.

"Yes, I know that," Knox grumbled at her. "Onto these horses and just ride out into the wastelands on some rumor of a road? I mean, you heard those thugs. What about flash floods? Earthquakes? Organ harvesters roaming the sand?"

Syd shrugged. "You don't have to come," he said. "You did your part. You got me out of the city, just like you promised. You can go home to your house and your father now. You don't owe me anything."

Knox shook his head and kicked at the dirt with his toe. "I'm not going back there."

"You don't even know how to ride a horse," said Marie.

"I'm not going back to my father," he said. It was that simple. On this point, there would be no negotiation.

"I'm not here to help you work out your issues with your father," Syd told him. "This isn't some patron enrichment program. I'm running for my life and the only person I've ever trusted is dead."

"So trust us." Marie stepped beside Knox. "We can help you."

"I thought you hated him," said Syd.

"I don't have to like him to understand him," said Marie. "We're not so different."

"We aren't?" Knox asked.

"We both have a reason to help Syd," she said, and then she changed the subject to cut off any chance of an argument. "There are four horses and we only need three."

"Two," Knox corrected her.

Syd nodded. "Fine, two . . . but we can't just leave the other horses here."

"We could let them run," Marie suggested. "Maybe they'll find their own way."

It seemed like as good an idea as any. Syd untied two of the horses.

They didn't run. They just stood and stared with their big dumb horse eyes. They didn't know a good thing when they got it.

"Go on!" Syd said. "Run! *Heyup!*"

The horses didn't move.

"Why won't they run?" Syd asked. "They're animals. They should run."

Knox and Marie shrugged.

"Heyup!" Syd smacked one of the horse's haunches. It looked down at him and snorted.

"Go!" he ordered it. "You'll die if you stay! Just go!" He smacked the horse again, harder. "Go! Go!" He held up the EMD stick.

"Syd." Marie grabbed his hand, stopped him from frying the horse's nerves. "You can't make them want to run. That's not how it works."

Syd lowered the stick to his side again, clutching it tight. He bit the inside of his cheeks and looked the horse in the eye.

It worked on me, he thought. I ran.

"I'm riding alone," he told the others and climbed onto the back of the horse he'd been trying to set free. "You take Knox on your horse."

"Okay," Marie agreed, although she didn't seem too excited about it.

Knox turned to Marie and smirked, a little trace of the old smart-ass coming back. "I guess you get to drive this time."

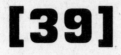

[39]

MARIE CLIMBED ONTO THE large piebald horse and Knox heaved himself up behind her. He wobbled unsteadily as the horse shifted and grunted its objections to the new weight. The other two horses whinnied, as if they were gloating. Their horse tossed its head from side to side and circled, nearly tipping Knox off.

"Whoa!" he said, but the horse kept bucking. For a moment, he feared this would be Marie's revenge for the car accident, but she leaned forward and whispered something in its ear. The horse calmed down.

"What are you saying to it?" Knox asked.

"I gave it a name," said Marie.

Knox was glad that Marie couldn't see his face.

He steadied himself, letting his hands fall to his sides. It felt weird, but he was so close to Marie's back that if he lifted his hands he'd have to hold them all crumpled against himself. He couldn't get comfortable. He stretched them forward and let them wrap around Marie's waist as gently as he could. Why was that so much harder to do than when he rode with Syd?

"You have got to be kidding me," Marie said.

"I just need somewhere to put my hands. It doesn't mean anything. I rode the same way with Syd."

"I noticed," Marie answered, and there was more humor in her voice than he'd heard before. Maybe she was warming up to him. Or maybe she was just tired of being angry. There'd been enough misery in the past few days to last a lifetime. Knox figured it was time they both started acting human to each other. He resisted the urge to make a sarcastic comment back.

Once his hands settled, he had to admit that it felt much nicer holding the curve of her waist than it had Syd's. He suddenly felt very aware of his hands. He focused on keeping them as still as possible so that she didn't make him let go. The horse breathed beneath them.

Syd turned his horse toward the cave and looked into the gaping mouth of stone. Behind him, the stars burned their billion pixels. A golden glow started up on the horizon. A new day was coming and with it the heat and the long ride.

Syd spat onto the ground and then turned his horse at a quick trot in the direction of the sunrise.

"Here we go," said Marie and she nudged her horse forward after him.

Knox felt the full weight of the previous two days hitting him. He'd stayed awake this long before, of course, but usually for a party and usually he had a little chemical help to make it happen. Now, he was running on nothing but willpower, adrenaline, and fear, like an animal.

There were other animal feelings too. His skin burned with a desire to squeeze Marie tighter against his chest.

At the same time, he wished he were riding with Syd again. He had the urge to explain himself, to tell Syd about his mother and his father, like that would justify why he didn't move to help back there in the cave, why he froze up. Maybe he wanted Syd to forgive him.

Guilt.

That might have been the only purely human feeling Knox had left.

They had to ride single file through the narrow cuts in the canyon. If Knox had access to a datastream he could try to bring up a map to the Interstate. It wouldn't be on any of the authorized streams, but someone would have posted it somewhere. Knox felt useless without a network connection.

The sound of the horses clomping kept a steady rhythm in his head. The bounce of their steps jostled his body and he had to keep his legs flexed to hold on to the wide flank of the animal. Each movement rocked him forward into Marie's back and then back away from it so he had to hold on to her to keep from sliding off. It was a pulsing kind of touch, but it was enough to keep him awake as they rode.

Their path twisted and turned. Syd kept stopping and

looking up, as if there were a datastream just over his head telling him where to go. Knox worried for a second that Syd was secretly wearing Egan's old lenses and leading them into some prearranged trap. He beat himself up for not searching the dead kid to get the lenses himself. He hadn't been thinking clearly. Corpse robbery wasn't his first instinct. He guessed it probably wasn't Syd's either. The lenses were still back in the cave.

"He's looking for the sun, I think," said Marie. "Navigating by it. I've read about people doing that."

"You think he knows how?" asked Knox.

"It's not hard," she said, pointing. "The sun's right there. It rises in the east."

"So what are we gonna do when it's right above us at noon?"

The question stumped Marie. Up ahead, Syd was wondering the same thing.

The air in the deep canyon was cool and the high walls cut off the sun. Occasional breaks in the rock sent rays of light down to the trail and there was a pleasant warmth when they rode through them, followed by a deep chill when they trotted out.

They heard the buzz of drones flying over the canyons, but they were safe in the narrow cuts and channels below. Knox took a sip of the water they'd taken from the bandits. They'd taken most of the supplies, leaving only the horses with a bit of water. It was the closest thing those Maes goons would get to mercy and even that was more than they deserved.

The smugglers would know these canyons well, and if they escaped from their ropes, would find it easy to follow three teenagers. Syd doubled back a few times. No sense making it easy on them.

They reached a low arch in the rock in front of them, and had to dismount and lead the horses through on foot. Knox noticed that the dust on Syd's face was streaked, as if he'd been crying. He climbed off the horse and let Marie lead it through the low opening. He rushed up to Syd's side.

"Syd, I'm—" He wanted to say something to him, although once his mouth was moving, he realized he didn't know what to say.

Syd looked back at him, waiting.

The way Syd had held Egan's body and whispered to it made Knox wonder if the two of them had been more than friends, or if Syd maybe had wanted them to be. Or maybe that's just how it felt to lose a friend. If Knox had seen Simi, Chey, or Nine executed in front him, he'd be pretty messed up himself. He tried to picture cradling one of their heads in his own hands as the life drained out of it, but Nine kept making faces and Chey just looked like she was sleeping. Knox never did have much control over his imagination. Or much connection to his friends.

"I don't think anyone can follow us this way," Syd said, his voice scratchy from the dry air and the long silence of the ride. Then he turned his back on Knox and led his horse ahead.

"Come on, Justice, come on," Marie urged her horse.

"Justice?" Knox raised an eyebrow.

"I told you I named her."

"Yeah, but Justice? They're just tools, you know."

"They're beautiful."

"Okay, beautiful tools."

"Sounds like someone else I know." She smirked at him and he remembered their car ride, the snappy responses, the mischievous grin. This girl contained that girl. Whoever she was was also whoever she had been. The same was true for him, he guessed. He wondered if anyone really ever changed, or if stuff just piled on and on, covering up, but never erasing all the different parts. How deep would you have to dig to find who you started out as?

"So . . . Justice?" He patted the horse on the side as they walked.

"It seemed like a good name for her," she said.

"Her?"

Marie nodded. "I don't know a lot about anatomy, but I think this one's pretty obvious."

"I thought she was checking me out," Knox joked. He was trying to capture some of that sparkle, the flirting, the banter. He needed it. Otherwise, he had no idea who he was anymore.

Marie rolled her eyes.

"Did you always hate me?" Knox asked her. "Even before the accident?"

Marie stopped walking with the horse. She looked him over. He brushed a strand of hair out of his eyes. He knew it was a lame move, but old habits died hard.

Marie took a deep breath. "Yes," she said. "I did."

Then she walked the horse around a tight turn and disappeared. He followed and caught up with her in a great bowl-shaped cavern, with just a patch of sky in the center, two hundred feet up. The beam of light that pierced into it lit a perfect circle on the ground. Marie waited inside the circle for Knox to catch up.

"You aren't so terrible when you keep your mouth shut," Marie added as she helped him back onto the horse. Before he could open his mouth again, she smacked the horse's side and gave a loud "Heyup!" They rode on.

When the sun was at its highest, they stopped to rest.

"We need to eat something," said Marie. "And feed the horses."

Syd hadn't even thought about feeding the horses. Or himself.

Marie found some EpiCure pills in the bandits' supplies and handed each of the boys one of them, then took a handful over to the horses.

Syd studied his pill, a bright blue lozenge the size of a knuckle, shining in his palm. It was stamped with a logo from EpiCure Incorporated and a flavor below it. Syd had heard of these pills, but never actually swallowed one. They were too expensive for most Valve kids, who ate food that came from the local grower gardens and the runoff from the EpiCure factory, protein pastes and gristly bone fragments boiled into soup.

The pills were designed to create the mental sensation of taste, while delivering balanced nutrition at preset levels. They were why there was no such thing as a patron who was too fat or too skinny. Their food was the best that science had to offer. Their bodies were designed.

Syd had a pill for something called "Lasagna." He tossed it back and took a slug of water, wincing at the strange sensation of a solid object going down this throat.

After a few seconds, he felt an astonishing warmth in his stomach, a fullness, as if he'd just eaten the New Year's meal at Mr. Baram's and then a flood of flavor in his mouth, hot and bubbly, with a taste of some kind of herb and meat and then a sweetness and a creaminess. He'd never had anything like it and it gave him the urge to burp, which he did, loudly.

"Mmm," said Knox, swallowing his own pill. "Pepper steak. Love that stuff." He laughed to himself. "You know, one time I hacked the EpiCure pill database and made an entire batch of pepper steak taste like armpit. It was a riot."

"A week hauling their factory runoff to the river for dumping, and another selling recalled pills in the Valve," said Syd. "I got punched in the face by a lot of unhappy customers who found the taste of armpit less than appetizing."

Knox cringed. "I thought they had bots for that kind of work."

"They have bots for everything," Syd said. "But they use proxies. It keeps us busy. Keeps us from, you know, joining the Rebooter cause."

The irony was lost on none of them.

When the sun started its descent to the west, they mounted up again and kept riding. They rode all day, twisting and turning and saying very little to one another. As the sun got lower and lower, the canyon floor got colder. Syd stopped under a high overhang in the rock, like a shelf, and tied up his horse on a jagged boulder. Marie did the same and Knox jumped off, his legs sore and bowed.

"I can't tell which way to go at night," Syd explained. "So we'll camp here, get some sleep."

"Can we make a fire?" Knox asked. The bandits had ChemiFlame packs in their supplies, so it'd be easy to light one. The desert cold had already set his teeth chattering and Syd looked even worse. His lips had a light bluish tint to them. He had less meat on his bones than either of the patron kids. Syd liked the idea of a fire, but Marie disagreed.

"The drones would catch that heat signature, even down here," she said.

"We'll freeze to death without it," said Knox.

"There are heat blankets in the supplies we took," Marie said. "The shiny things. We'll wrap up in those and huddle together for the night."

Knox raised an eyebrow at her. He wasn't going to actually say anything.

She rolled her eyes, but she didn't insult him.

Progress.

[40]

ONCE THEY'D LAID THE blankets out beneath the over-hang, they stood side by side considering their bed. Marie turned to Knox.

"I am so not sleeping next to you," she declared.

"Huddling together was your idea," Knox objected. He couldn't help a slight grin from lighting up his dusty face.

"You're a dog," she told him and Knox laughed. He didn't deny it. Hadn't she said she liked him better when he kept his mouth shut?

Syd stepped away from the two of them. He didn't feel like arguing about sleeping arrangements. He stood and shivered near the red rocks of the canyon wall, looking up at a discolored patch high above. It was a painting of some kind, a splotch of black and red and brown sprayed on the wall by an artist who'd been dead for centuries. Anyone it meant anything to was dead.

He stepped back a little to get a better look, and a trick of sound bouncing off the walls made everything Knox and Marie were saying perfectly clear to him where he stood, as if they were whispering right into his ear. He listened, like he used to listen to the Changs arguing in the shack across the alley. The thought that he'd had a virus growing in his blood the whole time, something dangerous and powerful, discolored the memories. Mr. Baram had known it and kept it from him and he couldn't think about his past without the present distorting the memory. Instead, he listened.

"That means Syd's in the middle," Knox whispered to Marie.

"You're a genius," Marie replied.

"But what if he—" Knox lowered his voice, but it didn't change the clarity where Syd stood. "What if he gets . . . you know? Ideas?"

"Ideas?"

"You know . . ." Knox didn't feel he needed to elaborate.

"Oh." Marie nodded. "Like the ideas you're having about me?"

Knox didn't exactly deny it. Syd smirked and kept his back to them. It felt good to smile. He remembered there was more to life than his own misery and regret.

"Grow up, Knox," Marie grunted. "Not everyone thinks about sex all the time."

Clearly Marie didn't know a lot about guys.

"Syd lost his best friend today," she said. "He killed a woman and he's running for his life with two people that he seems to hate. I don't think he's looking to jump you in your sleep. Hard as that must be for you to imagine."

"He kissed me," said Knox.

Syd remembered the feeling of Knox's lips against his, the pulse beating in his neck where his hand gripped it to keep Knox from pulling away, to keep the Guardians from seeing. They say you never forget your first kiss.

"He did not." Marie crossed her arms.

"In Arcadia, after Syd found me, he grabbed me and he kissed me, like, with feeling . . . I was too tweaked to resist."

"You're lying," Marie said.

Nope, thought Syd. He's not. Except the "feeling" Syd had at the time was not the one that Knox was thinking of.

"I am not lying," said Knox. "There were these Guardians after him and he, like, used my face to hide."

"So he didn't really kiss you," Marie said. "He used you."

"He used me *by* kissing me," said Knox. "He could have done something else, but he went right to kissing. What does that say?"

"That you're full of yourself."

Knox grumbled some kind of remark Syd couldn't discern.

"Anyway, what are you afraid of?" Marie teased him. "That he'll make a pass and you'll enjoy it?"

"No . . . ," Knox said. He was pretty sure that wasn't the case.

"Or is this an act?" Marie goaded him. "Do you secretly

want my approval to snuggle with your proxy? They say that everyone gets feelings for their proxy sometime. It's a phase."

"Oh, just shut up," Knox grunted. "Let him sleep in the middle. I'll curl up with him. I don't care."

"Don't worry, Knox." Syd turned around and strolled up to them, grinning. "If anyone asks, I'll say you put up more of a fight."

Knox blushed rust red. He tried to change the subject. "What were you looking at up there on the rocks?" he asked.

"Some painting," said Syd. He didn't know a lot about art. It was not a subject they covered at Vocation High School IV. He wondered if the Upper City kids would think he was dumb. Did they learn about ancient art in their lux schools? If he had a projector, he could look it up in the datastream, but out here, the only data were what you could see with your own two eyes.

Knox and Marie squinted up where Syd pointed. The painting showed a collection of figures, a group of men with sticks around some kind of big animal with horns.

"What do you see?" Syd asked.

"People? Dancing around an animal?" Knox suggested. "Maybe they're worshipping the animal? Like in one of the old religions?"

"I think they're hunting it," said Syd.

"It's a sacrifice," said Marie. "The ancient religions used to sacrifice animals. The blood of the animals was like payment to the gods."

"Payment for what?" Knox wondered.

None of them knew.

"Who do you think painted it?" Syd asked. They didn't know that either. He guessed patrons didn't study this stuff in school either.

"Collectors in the Upper City judge art by price," said Marie. "They have consultants who buy it for them."

"I think my father owns art he's never even seen," said Knox.

They all looked back at the painting. The style looked so basic, so old, the colors organic, almost as if the painting itself were part of the desert, put there by the wind and the heat and time itself. Syd wondered how long it had been since anyone had laid eyes on it.

"We should get to sleep," Marie said. "We'll need to rest for the ride tomorrow."

"Do you know how much farther it is to the, uh, Interstate?" asked Knox.

"No idea," said Syd. "We just have to keep riding east and hope."

A gust of wind tore through the canyon and Syd hugged himself from the cold.

Marie smiled and put her arm around his shoulders. He flinched, but then relaxed. He let himself be guided.

They huddled up where the walls blocked the wind, and wrapped themselves in their emergency blankets, Syd in between Knox and Marie, with the bundle of stolen supplies for pillows. They watched their breath frost in the air in front of them. It was hard to believe how hot the day had been, now that the night was so cold. No wonder humans abandoned the desert regions. Nature clearly did not want them there.

When he closed his eyes, Syd saw Egan's face, looking back at him with unseeing eyes. Dead. He kept his eyes open. He wasn't ready for sleep. The thought terrified him.

"Knox?" Syd asked, sensing that the others were just as awake as he was.

"Yeah?" Knox answered.

Syd dropped his voice to a whisper and rolled onto his side to look Knox in the eyes. He spoke loud enough for Marie to hear: "Will you kiss me good night?"

"I . . . I . . ." Knox stuttered.

Syd rolled onto his back and looked at Marie. A wide grin broke across his face. He burst out laughing, real full-on belly laughs.

"He was totally going to do it," Marie cried.

"You two are glitched." Knox shook his head.

Syd and Marie fell into convulsions of laughter. Syd hadn't laughed like this in ages. He'd never laughed like this with anyone but Egan, in fact, but now, he couldn't stop. It rolled over him in waves.

Knox sat up. "Seriously? Seriously?"

Marie gasped and Syd covered his eyes with one forearm, his whole body shaking. He could hardly breathe.

"Beyond glitched." Knox dropped his head back onto the makeshift pillow.

Syd cackled. "The expression on your face . . ."

"Go on, make jokes," Knox grumbled.

"Look, he's pouting." Marie made a sad face, but she could hardly hold it. Laughter broke it open again. She laughed carelessly, maniacally. Syd wondered if he'd gone too far. The pretty ones could be so fragile. In the sky, lightning flashed.

"Whatever," said Knox. "I only kiss guys when Guardians are watching. I'm an exhibitionist." He exhaled loudly and let a heavy moment pass before he exploded in laughter himself, which set off a new round of laughing in the other two.

"Marie, on the other hand . . . ," Knox added.

"Not on your life!" she said, cackling.

"Well"—Knox pointed toward the horses—"I saw Justice eyeing me earlier, maybe . . ."

Thunder from a distant storm replied and that too seemed funny.

"Quiet down!" Knox yelled at the thunder. "I'm trying kiss a horse!"

The three of them rolled on the ground laughing. The horses whinnied and grunted. In time, the laughter faded. They went back to listening to the wind and the storm. Syd's memories prowled at the edge of his mind like a panther. It was hard to remember what he'd just thought was so funny.

After a while, Knox broke the silence. "I've never slept outside before."

"Me neither," said Marie.

"You get used to it," said Syd.

The silence settled again. Knox filled it with a worry that had been on his mind.

"If we find the Rebooters, do you think they'll let us go?" Knox wondered aloud. "I mean Marie and me. We're patrons. And my father's . . . well . . . you know."

"I'll tell them you're with me," said Syd. He startled himself by saying it. He had to think for a second, to decide if he meant it.

He guessed he did.

"Do you know what you'll do when we get there?" Knox wondered.

Syd shook his head. "I don't know what I'm supposed to do."

"You will," said Marie.

"I don't get why you're so sure of it," Syd told her.

"Because I have to be," she said.

Syd put his head back on his hands and looked up at the sky. It was a funny thing. Marie was running to something while Syd was just running away. He was afraid neither of them would ever really get where they were going.

Syd listened as Knox's breathing changed, slower and deeper, letting out tiny snores. He felt the rise and fall of Knox's chest next to him and soon after, Marie's. He kept his eyes open. He didn't want to see the holos his memory was conjuring, the dead he'd left in his trail.

He didn't meant to sleep, but suddenly, he was on the steel table in the middle of the factory, strapped down, but watching himself on the table from above and there were the men in white suits and blue latex gloves. There were the screams and the explosions.

The nightmare unfolded like always, but this time, when the needles came, he knew. The blood. They were infecting his blood.

"One more," the man said, as always, before he tossed the baby Syd over the railing and jabbed the grown Syd in the birthmark.

But this time, when the man said, "Yovel," Syd knew he meant forgiveness, and this time, when the baby fell, someone else was there to catch it.

It was Knox, staring up, his green eyes glistening as the baby cried in his arms. The man's body lay crumpled on the floor beside him, dead, and Syd also knew who this man was.

His father.

Syd's eyes snapped open and he was lying on the canyon floor, looking up at the underside of the rocky outcropping. The opposite wall of red stone glowed gold with the first light of another day.

Syd felt a heaviness on his chest and saw that beneath the blanket Marie and Knox both had their arms around him, resting across his chest. He fought the urge to reach behind his ear to touch the birthmark. He kept still and listened to the morning.

The only sound was the breathing sleepers and the occasional snort of the horses. He'd never heard such a quiet.

He tried to stay as still as possible, not wanting to wake the other two. He liked the warmth of their bodies beside his, liked the weight of their arms across him, as if they were holding him down to the earth to keep him from floating away. Knox's heavy forearm twitched slightly and Syd's heart pounded against his rib cage so hard that he wondered how it didn't wake him.

He knew once they were up, the ride would begin, the fear and the pressure and the looming unknown. But lying down in that half sleep, the nightmare fading and the day not yet begun, he could feel at peace.

Of course it didn't last.

Memory burned away what was left of sleep. No sense lying there any longer.

He pushed himself onto his elbows, letting the sleepers' arms slip. Knox opened his eyes and quickly retracted his arm, wiping his mouth with the back of his hand. His hair stuck up on one side and his eyes were puffy. He noticed Syd looking at him and he cleared his throat.

"No breakfast in bed?" Knox said.

Nobody laughed. The humor was gone and might as well have never been there. They stood and began to pack for another day's ride. Syd wondered how far the canyon lands went. He hoped close to the Interstate. If they had to cross open plains, the drones would be able to target them easily.

"Hey, Knox, I think you'd better ride with me today," Syd said.

Knox turned around and the glisten of his eyes startled Syd, made him think of the dream.

"Sure, that'd be—" Knox started, when a low rumbling cut him off. He looked in its direction in time to see a torrent of brown water, frothy and churning, smash through the canyon walls.

In a scream of water and rock, the flash flood tore the horses from the ground, engulfed Marie where she stood. Syd had just enough time to catch a look of surprise cross Knox's face before the water sucked him under. A heavy object smashed Syd in the head and the world went brown and red and black.

[41]

KNOX COULDN'T BREATHE OR see, and the only sound was the roar of water in his ears. One moment he'd been talking to Syd, the next he was underwater, spinning wildly, legs over his head, bent backward, slammed hard against the rocks, smashed down and thrust up, turned around, gagging, choking. He clawed desperately for the surface only to smash into rocks and realize he'd been swimming sideways.

The feeling was like a hundred car crashes, a thousand punches in the face, a stampede of horses running him over. Knox knew he was about to die and the irony of drowning in the desert was not lost on him.

He gave up fighting.

That's when the flood spat him up to the surface, half dead, and he grasped and clawed at the air to stay on top of the raging water. Broken branches sank when he grabbed them, debris smashed into his legs, and he felt the sting of drawn blood. A great sucking pulled him below again, his mouth filled with water, but he swam furiously up and vomited it out, reaching, striving, stretching for anything to keep him up.

He caught an object, large and bristly, and he hauled himself onto it, half in the water, his chest resting across it and he knew, then, in the bright, living sunlight, that he was rafting down the canyon on the dead body of Marie's horse, Justice.

He clung to it. Water splashed over him; the horse's body pounded into the cliff sides and cushioned the blows. He looked around the churning chasm for the others, but saw only angry foam and roiling mud. He sank his head down against the damp fur of the dead horse and coughed. The water was thick and oddly sweet and it left a gristly coating of sand in his mouth and his nose.

The flood snaked through the canyon and disgorged itself and its moribund passenger across the sizzling hardpan of the desert floor in a jumble of broken trees and rocks and scattered supplies.

Knox dove off the horse's body just before it rolled on top of him. Its hoof smashed into his shin so hard that he yelled, but he'd gotten free in time. He'd be bruised, but nothing worse.

He crouched, spluttering on his hands knees, studying the cracked ground in front of him. He caught his breath. In, out, in, out. He was alive.

He looked up.

The flood had spat him onto a plain at the edge of the canyon lands. The earth was pink and yellow, run through with dark cracks, and flat all the way to the horizon. The heat shimmered off it, creating strange patches of dancing air, and far-off cloud banks pointed gray fingers down from the sky, jabbing them into the earth. It took him a moment to realize they were tornadoes, half a dozen of them, twisting and turning around one another and lifting huge clouds of dust into the air.

Where he crouched, the sky was clear and blue and empty. Not a cloud above. Not a drone either.

Knox scrambled to his feet and stood, his clothes sagging off him, their pockets weighted with mud.

Along the ground, the flood had dumped all the scattered ruins of the canyon—odd bits of garbage, broken rocks, scrubby trees uprooted and smashed, all the supplies that they had pilfered from the bandits, the mangled corpse of Marie's horse, the writhing, screaming whining body of the other horse, nameless, not yet dead, but clearly on its way.

And there was Marie, her face bloodied, as soaked and half drowned as Knox, sitting up in the dust. Steam rose off her as the desert air sucked the water from her clothes. She appeared shimmering, vaporous.

Knox looked for Syd, and saw him, lying flat on his face, one arm pinned beneath his chest, the other pointed forward like an accusation. He wasn't moving. He too steamed as he dried, and the vapors made it look like a ghost was rising from him, a heap of mud and ash.

Knox ran to Syd, threw himself down beside him, and rolled him over. Syd's clothes were shredded and tattered, all of them brown with dried mud. The only way to tell what was cloth and what was his proxy's skin was that the skin was seeping blood through the grime that coated it. Syd had a gash on his forehead and another on his thigh. Knox listened for breathing, but heard none.

He felt for a pulse—his executive family emergency crisis training finding a use.

He felt no pulse.

"Stay with me, Syd," he muttered. "Not like this. Don't let him kill you like this."

Knox knew the flash flood wasn't his father's doing, but still, the malevolence of nature seemed somehow connected to the vast accumulation of brutality they'd suffered at his command.

Knox tilted Syd's head back and reached into his mouth. Syd's teeth tickled the back of his hand. His fingers found a clump of mud, and he scooped it out, digging Syd's airway free.

He felt Marie standing behind him now; her worry palpable on the back of his neck. He didn't turn to look at her and she didn't question him. She'd had EFECT training too.

He rested one of his hands over the other, linked his fingers, and set his palm onto the center of Syd's chest. Then he leaned forward, straightened his arms and pulsed, up and down, compressing Syd's chest as hard as he could.

He held one of his favorite Tragic Harpie Bingo songs in his head and crunched up and down to the beat, manually pulsing Syd's heart. He knew he'd crack a rib or two in the process, but he'd done worse to Syd in the past. At least this time, the pain might save his proxy's life.

No.

Not his proxy.

His friend.

"Come on!" he yelled at Syd. "You knockoff! Breathe!"

Knox worked to a quick sweat in the desert sun and the sweat dried to a salty paste almost instantly. His arms ached from the chest compressions. The mud that caked Syd's body hardened and cracked around him like a shell.

Knox set his head down on Syd's chest and listened.

"Nothing," he said.

"Do you want me to—?"

"No," Knox cut her off. "I'll do this."

He sat up and hit Syd, pounding his chest with a full fist. Then he interlocked his fingers once more and hummed the same song once more and once more began crunching and crushing and becoming Syd's heartbeat. Every downward thrust of his arms moved the blood through Syd's body and kept him alive.

A few feet away, the dying horse let out a choking shriek, and Marie left Knox and walked over to it. She picked up the double-barreled weapon, snapped it open to check if it had any of the explosive cylinders in it and snapped it shut again. Knox knew what was coming next. He closed his eyes and kept pumping Syd's chest. He grunted with the effort and keeping his eyes shut tight.

There was a too familiar bang and then the horse was silent. Knox didn't open his eyes.

He had no idea how much time had passed. It was a lifetime if it was a minute. Under the scorching desert sun, Knox could not imagine a time when he was not pumping his proxy's blood through his body; he could not imagine a time before or after. All he had was this moment and the vow that Syd would not die on the desert floor.

He stopped and pressed his head to Syd's chest again.

He listened. He counted. He listened some more.

"He has a heartbeat!" he announced. He'd never been more proud of anything he had done in his life. It was amazing how fragile the human body could be, and how so many people walked through their lives not knowing how it worked or how to fix it when it stopped. If Syd had been out here with a patron who didn't remember his training, he'd have died. Maybe there was some destiny at play, Knox figured. Maybe he wasn't a useless, spoiled rich boy after all. He was a lifesaver. He liked the feeling.

Circulation recovered, Knox rushed to the next step of the training. He checked for breathing again.

Still nothing.

His heart sank. He hoped Syd's brain hadn't already died from lack of oxygen.

He tipped Syd's head back, squeezed his nose, and pressed his mouth over Syd's and blew air into his lungs.

Once.

Twice.

Three times.

He pulled away, looked up at Marie and shook his head.

"He can't die like this," she said. "He's not supposed to die like this. Don't stop. Breathe for him. Do it. Just breathe for him."

Knox leaned over Syd again, squeezed his nose, and filled his lungs with air again.

Once.

Twice.

Syd coughed.

His body heaved beneath Knox and he gagged; he strained. His fist pounded the earth and he rolled to the side, vomited a pool of muddy water, coughed, and rested onto his back, gulping air. His eyes were open wide to the cloudless sky.

"Syd!" Knox cried out. "Syd, can you hear me?"

Syd didn't answer and Knox was sure he'd been too slow to bring him back, that Syd's brain had given out, that he was alive but completely brain-dead. Knox had failed Syd again, just as he'd failed him their whole lives. He let him die.

Marie knelt on the opposite side. Her purple eyes shone behind her muddy mask. She put her hands on Syd's head. "Please, Syd, tell us you can hear us. Blink if you understand."

Syd blinked and he tilted his head toward Knox. He

spoke, his voice scratched and strained. "I guess . . . that was . . . our second kiss."

His lips cracked a smile, the teeth blinding white in the sun.

Knox leaned back onto his calves and rested his hands on his knees. He exhaled, relieved.

"Marie?" Syd looked at her.

"I'm here," she said, an urgent kindness in her voice, like that nurse Knox remembered from the hospital. Another side of Marie that Knox had never seen before. He looked at her looking at Syd. Covered in blood and mud and dust, she had never looked more beautiful to him.

"Did your resurrection hurt this bad?" Syd asked.

Marie smiled. "I didn't have Knox breaking my ribs," she said. "Next time I suggest a private hospital. The sheets are softer."

Syd smiled and leaned back against the ground to steady his heartbeat and catch his breath. His side ached, his head throbbed, and his throat stung as if he'd swallowed half a ton of scrap metal, but he was alive and he savored the feeling. He got to spend another day on the earth; messed up, cruel, and dangerous as it was, it was the only place he wanted to be.

He could have lain on the desert floor for hours, just breathing, had his eyes not found the black shape buzzing over the canyon, black wings against the deep blue sky.

A drone.

It dropped down the cliff face and passed over them on

the flat desert, low enough for Syd to see the round casing of its weapon systems. It circled for a second pass. Knox, Marie, and Syd looked up at it. The patrons leaned over Syd, covering him with their bodies, and he hoped that the protection they afforded him would hold. The drone banked hard left and disappeared at high speed over the horizon.

"They're coming," said Knox.

Marie looked up and saw a massive vehicle racing over the desert floor, heading right in their direction. It raised a huge cloud of dust and heat rippled the air around its body.

"Guardians?" Knox wondered.

"Better not find out," Syd suggested. Knox helped him up and they scurried to the edge of the canyon that had spat them out in the flood. Marie stopped halfway and ran back to the scattered debris in the desert.

"What are you doing? Are you glitched? Get back here!" Knox called.

Marie squatted down and rummaged in the debris for more of those cylinders for the antique weapon. Once she'd found them, she sprinted back to the crook of rock where Syd and Knox had hidden themselves. They watched the approaching machine.

It had cut the distance between them in half already, hovering just above the desert floor. Its body was heavy steel, pocked with rust and patched with other discolored metal, topped with a weapons turret. A mishmash of solar panels and wind turbines surrounded the turret, and in the front, where windshields should have been, the hovercraft had only metal slits. Its engines shrieked and rattled, crying out, to Syd's ears, for repair. It bore no corporate logo.

"That's not a SecuriTech vehicle," Knox said.

"Freelancers," said Syd. "Scavengers. Maybe bandits."

"Like the ones we left in the cave?" Knox chewed his lower lip.

"Maes gang," said Syd. "I'd prefer not to find out." He knew that if they had to run, his broken ribs wouldn't let him get far. Hopefully, they hadn't been spotted.

Marie aimed her weapon at the approaching hovercraft, as if it could do anything to a machine that size. It was more for the comfort of something to do, than for the utility of doing it. There was value of going through the motions.

They lay side by side in silence, just like when they'd slept huddled together, Syd in the middle. They waited for the hovercraft to pass.

Except the hovercraft didn't pass.

[42]

WHEN THE MACHINE REACHED the bodies of the horses and the scattered debris from the flash flood, it looped around and settled down onto its landing gear in a cloud of dust. Its engines cut out with a loud rumble and the rear hatch opened with a hiss.

Knox, Marie, and Syd tensed.

Through the dust, they could only see the silhouettes of figures emerging from the hovercraft. A tall figure with an EMD stick stepped down first. It looked like he wore a wig of snakes on his head.

Behind him came a flock of small figures, children spilling from the hatch and scurrying through the hot dust to rummage in the debris.

"Just kids," Marie whispered and lowered her weapon.

"Keep it raised," Syd hissed at her. "You've never seen what scavenge mobs can do."

"Yeah, but little kids?" Knox was as puzzled as Marie. After everything they'd endured, it didn't seem possible Syd would be afraid of some sickly kids in a raggedy hovercraft.

"Kids can sell your organs just as well as adults can," said Syd. "It's a free market."

Marie raised the gun.

The dust began to settle and they made out the children. Their clothes were assembled like the hovercraft itself, from a patchwork of spare parts and mismatched pieces. The man with the weapon did not have on a wig of snakes; he had long dreadlocks, tied back with a bandana so that they cascaded over his shoulders and down his back. His skin was darker than Syd's and he had a thick scar that ran from his eye straight down his face to his neck and disappeared beneath his shirt. He watched over the band of scavenging children, taking an occasional glance at the morning sun rising higher in the sky.

One kid found a sealed bag of EpiCure pills and shoved it into her pocket. Another boy saw her and rushed over. Without warning, he smacked her across the face. In seconds, they were brawling, kicking up a whole new cloud of sand and dust in a riot of screaming and kicking and hair pulling. The other kids had circled around, goading them on.

The man with the dreadlocks waded out into the middle of the fracas, and the children scattered like hissing cockroaches when the lights went on. He tucked his EMD stick into his studded belt and lifted the boy and the girl off the ground by their collars.

"She took foodstuff!" whined the boy in some sort of accent Knox had never heard before.

"Nah me din't!" the girl objected, but the man just tilted his head at her and she melted into tears and confessed, presenting him with the bag from her pocket. The man set the kids down on the ground and knelt in front of the girl, looking her firmly in the eyes, holding the baggie out for her to see, her shame dangling in front of her face.

"Foodstuff gets shared," he said firmly but not cruelly. "Nobody go it alone out here, savvy? We share alike."

The girl nodded. The man gave her shoulder an affectionate squeeze and stood. She and the boy ran off together to keep scavenging, their fight already a distant memory.

Groups of kids gathered around the dead horses with bits of broken glass and metal. Knox cringed and looked away as they started carving up the animals, peeling the skin back and cutting the meat from the bone. He kept swallowing to keep from throwing up.

Syd tried to ignore the throb in his side and the ache in his throat. He focused on the annoying spot where a rock dug into his thigh. A minor discomfort replacing a major one. Just a question of focus. You could endure anything if you could figure out how to distract yourself. He tried not to breathe too deeply. Every breath felt like another rib cracking.

The man with the dreadlocks studied the scene around

his feet. He picked up the tattered emergency blanket and a ruined ChemiFlame package, looked them over, then he turned to look at the canyon. He shielded his eyes with his hand and looked right at the bend in the rock where Syd, Knox, and Marie were crouched.

Syd yanked Knox down and they lay there, staring at the dust, waiting. Listening. Syd's heartbeat pounded in his ears. Knox imagined the ransom call to his father, when these nomads figured out who he was. His father might reward them if they killed Syd, but as for his own son . . . his father didn't negotiate.

Marie peeked up. "He's gone," she whispered.

"What?" Knox lifted his head. The man no longer stood with the children. He wasn't around the hovercraft at all.

"Did you see him go back in?" Syd asked.

"We better pull back into the canyon," said Marie.

"If we leave all the stuff, we'll die out here," said Syd.

"They've already got all our stuff," Marie answered. "There's nothing we can do about it."

"We can't just retreat," Syd told her. "It's suicide."

"There's too many kids to fight off," Knox said. He agreed with Marie. They had to retreat and wait for the scavengers to leave.

"You could surrender, no?" a voice from above them shouted.

The man with the dreadlocks stood on a boulder, his EMD stick pointed down at them. Knox glanced back to the hovercraft. The kids had formed a wall, shoulder to shoulder, each of them holding something heavy or something sharp, and the weapons turret on top of the hovercraft had turned, a fracture cannon aimed straight at them. There was no escape.

Marie looked at Syd.

Knox looked at Syd.

Syd looked back at them. He didn't know what to do either.

"Well." Marie sighed. "We do need a ride." She set her weapon down on the rocks in front of her then stood and raised her arms over her head.

Syd shook his head and exhaled, then he heaved himself up, raising his arms above his head. He grunted as he did it, and Knox wondered how long Syd could keep going with broken ribs and how good either of his companions would be in a fight against a dozen starving children, if it came to it. He stood last, close enough for Syd to lean his raised arm on Knox's shoulder so he could take some of the strain off his ribs. Syd got the hint and leaned on Knox.

"Thanks," Syd whispered.

"You'd do the same for me," Knox answered and Syd wondered if that were true.

"We mean no harm!" Marie pleaded. "We're stranded."

"Who you?"

"We're . . . uh—" Marie started.

"Refugees!" Syd declared. His voice cracked with the strain of speaking. "Come from the Mountain City."

"You runnin'?"

"Bad debt," said Syd.

"No patron cover you, eh?" The man understood the system, it seemed. If the guy knew Knox and Marie were patron kids from the Upper City, he might get curious. If he didn't know about the reward for Syd's death, they might just have a chance of hitching a safe ride in the hovercraft. Or at least, of being left in peace to die of thirst on their own.

"No patron," said Syd. "Just swampcats, all three of us."

"Swampcats? All three?"

Syd nodded. Marie nodded. Knox nodded. The man looked them over. Filthy, bloody, alone . . . they sure looked poor enough. Nothing lux about them. Lux was a distant memory for Knox.

"More like citycats." The man snorted. "This you stuff?" He nodded toward the wreckage spilled over the ground.

"It was," Marie said. Knox worried she'd given them away. Three swampcats wouldn't have EpiCure pills and ChemiFlames and horses, even if they had come from the city.

"Was?" the man considered what she said. "You steal it, eh?"

Marie nodded.

"Who you steal from?"

"Smugglers," said Syd. "From Maes." He wondered how far the criminal networks from the city spread.

"Maes," the man repeated, and for a moment Syd thought the word hadn't meant anything to him, but then, he turned and shouted at the children: "Maes!"

Suddenly, they all scurried, grabbing what they could grab from the road, tossing what they'd found and what horsemeat they'd already cut into sacks and bundles and loading them into the hovercraft. It seemed even in the wilderness beyond all trace of civilization, Maes's smugglers had a reputation.

The man slid down from his boulder, keeping the EMD stick pointed their way the whole time.

"You got big trouble," he said when he hit the ground in front of them. He bent down and picked up Marie's weapon. He looked her up and down and then held it out to her.

She hesitated.

"You'll need this," the man said and Marie took it from him. He looked at Knox. "Where you runnin'?"

"Uh . . ." Knox wasn't sure how much to tell the man.

"He dumb-dumb?" the man asked Syd. "Brain glitch?"

"Brain glitch," Syd confirmed. "Dropped baby. He don't know much, but he's my brother, so . . ."

Knox had the urge to break another of Syd's ribs. Not only wasn't he brain-dead, but Syd had also just called him his brother. No way the guy would fall for that. They didn't look anything alike. Wrong skin color, wrong bone structure, wrong hair.

The man raised his eyebrows. "Your brother?"

"I promised his mama," said Syd. "Debt brothers."

The man nodded, no more explanation needed.

Syd figured the best lies were the closest to the truth. What were he and Knox, if not brothers in debt? A proxy was just a replacement, a substitute, but a brother was something else, a debt that ran in two directions.

Knox looked over at Syd. He'd never had a brother. He didn't know what was expected of brothers. He kept his expression blank. Pretending to be brain-dead wasn't so hard at the moment. He didn't know what to make of this new turn of events.

"Where you come from?" Syd asked him, trying to see if they could form some kind of bond.

"Mercy Camp," the man said and gestured at the other passengers. "Up in smoke."

"Mercy Camp burned?" Syd asked.

"Burned." The man nodded.

Mercy Camp was one of the biggest Benevolent Society displacement camps, somewhere down on the edge of the swamps near the coast. Refugees had been coming to the Valve from it for years, and with them they brought stories of famine and sickness, giant snakes and rotten housing. It made the Valve look like a paradise. They also brought rumors that the Society planned to burn the whole place down to clear it out. Mercy Camp hadn't been profitable for a long time and shareholders were getting restless. Guess they finally did it.

"You're not heading to the Mountain City," said Syd. "You going to Old Detroit?"

The man rubbed his chin. Then he nodded.

"We're headed that way too," said Syd. "Any chance we can ride along?"

The man sighed. "You bring Maes, you bring trouble," he said.

Syd didn't respond. He let the man think.

"You ride with us, eh? You fight, if we need?" the man said.

Syd, Marie, and Knox nodded eagerly.

"Good, we take you." The man jogged over to the hovercraft and motioned for them to follow.

"Hey," Marie called out to him. He stopped in the hatch and turned around. "What's your name?"

"Gordis," he said.

"Gordis," Marie repeated, like she was taking possession of it, storing it someplace safe. Knox hadn't even thought to ask the man's name.

Gordis did not ask their names. Scavenger survival didn't require such niceties.

"Thank you for rescuing us, Gordis," Marie told him, just the same.

Knox was amazed with this girl, crazy enough to fake her own death and ruin Knox's life, but thoughtful enough to say thank you to some filthy desert scavenger. Knox wanted to know her better.

"Looks like we got a ride," said Syd. "Three swampcats on the run to Old Detroit, got it?"

"I got it," said Knox. "And I've got brain damage, huh?"

"Shouldn't be too much of a stretch." Marie smirked and rested her weapon on her shoulder, strolling to the hovercraft like an old-time outlaw.

"Don't worry," said Syd, "I'll watch your back, brother."

Knox found he liked the sound of that.

He followed Syd and Marie toward the hovercraft.

That's when an explosion blew the weapons turret off in a ball of fire.

[43]

THE TWO BANDITS TROTTED their horses from the mouth of the canyon. The bandit with the rocket launcher slung it back onto his shoulder and the other slid his sword into the sheath on his belt. Then he pulled out a small black ball, no bigger than a fist, and tossed it from hand to hand. A combat-certified meltdown grenade—a SecuriTech bestseller.

"Why'd we leave them water?" Knox wondered aloud.

"Because we're better than they are," Marie said. Knox was glad to know her idea of "we" included him, but he would have preferred if they'd let the bandits die in the cave. Or if they'd remembered to take away their weapons. Oops.

"You've got something that don't belong to you!" the bandit with the grenade announced, cocking his arm back to throw.

The other bandit reloaded his rocket launcher. "Turn it over or we'll blow all of you to hell."

Gordis turned slowly toward the riders on horseback. Without a word of instruction, the children scattered in a wide arc around him, armed with sharp objects still wet with the blood of horses.

Knox looked around and knew that this was madness. A bunch of children with broken glass and rusted metal were no match for mercenaries with high explosives. They'd all be dead before they could even raise their arms.

The scavengers stood in the glaring sun, about fifteen yards from the riders. The tips of Knox's ears and the back of his neck ached with what he assumed was sunburn. He'd never felt it before. Syd could barely keep himself on his feet. He leaned more and more weight onto Knox. Marie noticed. Worry for Syd etched lines into her face. Knox figured it didn't occur to her to worry for herself. That's what faith could do. He didn't have faith and he was very worried for himself. And for Syd. He found that worry was a completely renewable resource. The more he had, the more he got.

"I don't see nothing belong to you," Gordis told the men.

"We just want the proxy," one bandit said. "The rest of you can go in peace." He paused and scratched his chin. Then he nodded, like a new idea had struck him. "We'll even buy the patron kids off you, if you want. A good price too."

Gordis cocked his head to look over at Knox, Syd, and

Marie. He pursed his lips, considering this new piece of information he'd been given. His eye lingered on Syd a moment longer, then he turned back to the bandits. "I don't see any patrons here. Proxies neither."

The bandits laughed. The surface of the grenade flashed with blinking lights, armed. "Whatever you say," the bandit said, smiling. "But living or dead, the dark one there in the middle is ours. Payment for an outstanding debt."

Gordis slapped his EMD stick on his palm and looked Syd up and down. Syd stiffened. His cover story hadn't lasted ten minutes. Gordis turned back toward the bandits.

"No debts out here but what you can collect," he said.

Knox liked the sound of that. It was something a scripted badass would say. He filed it away to reuse if he ever got in another fight, if he lived to.

"You make us collect, we'll do it." The bandit kept tossing his grenade from hand to hand. "We can blow this hovercraft and these kiddies of yours to vapor before you can fire off the EMD stick you got there. And as for the girl . . ." He winked at Marie. It made her skin crawl. "Her gun ain't good for much from this distance. And she won't shoot it anyway. You took on some bad passengers, friend. Just turn 'em over and go on your way."

"Maes gang won't let you live. They don't negotiate," Syd whispered to Gordis, his voice jangling with nerves. Knox flinched. He knew what happened to people who didn't negotiate. Syd couldn't read Gordis's face, didn't know if he was tempted by their offer.

"Listen, friend," said the other one. The sun glared off his rocket launcher, forcing Knox to squint. "It's hot out here on this road and we've been riding hard. I know you've seen those drones flying over and trouble's coming with 'em close behind. So why don't we make this easy? You kill that boy there, right now. You just turn your little stick on him and make him dead, and then we'll take the body on our horses and ride away. It ain't much to do. One dead swamp-cat to save all these lives. You won't find a better deal."

"So they *do* negotiate," Gordis said.

"Hey, kid!" The one with the grenade spoke to Syd. "You really gonna let all your friends die for you? All these little kids? Egan wasn't enough? You gonna kill everyone just to hang on to that precious life of yours? What's so great you gotta live for?"

"Maybe he ain't got laid yet," the other bandit suggested and laughed a wheezy laugh.

Syd looked to Gordis and to the line of children braced for a hopeless fight. He looked to Knox and Marie. They were ready to fight for him too, each for their own reasons, but the reasons didn't matter. The willingness was all.

Syd had never been willing to die for anyone. He'd spent his whole life up to now being punished for other people—well, one other person—and he spent the whole time wanting to be free of it. No more connections, no more debts. But here he was, free as he'd ever been, and he had more debts than ever: Beatrice, Baram, Egan . . . he owed them all. They deserved better than this.

He knew he should do the noble thing here and step up, let them kill him so the kids didn't have to die, so Marie and Knox could survive, get back to their lives, maybe use their wealth and power to make the system a little better from within. His life wasn't worth more than theirs; it couldn't be, no matter what Marie believed about him. If he didn't want their blood on his hands, he had to give himself up. One life for all these other lives. Such an obvious deal to make.

But his feet stayed firmly planted on the pavement.

It's not easy to throw your life away, even for a good reason, even when it's the right thing to do. It was simple enough. Debt or no: Syd did not want to die.

Nobody moved.

Marie held her weapon and Gordis his EMD stick. Syd's stick had been lost in the flash flood, and he stood beside Knox with his fists clenched. Knox did the same. He felt stupid, but he did it anyway. He'd imagined being in a battle before, of course. All boys did at some point, right? But he hadn't imagined it would be like this, surrounded by kids, standing beside his proxy and worrying about looking stupid.

The man with the grenade shrugged. He turned to the other one. "Looks like they're the ones that don't negotiate."

The other one spat on the ground. It hit the dust with a splat and a sizzle. "Then we gotta kill 'em all."

"We still get paid if the rich ones die?"

"Guess we'll find out."

[44]

BEFORE ANOTHER WORD COULD be spoken, the bandit threw his grenade straight at Syd.

It landed on the dirt in front of him and rolled at his feet.

At the same time, the other bandit fired his rocket launcher at the hovercraft. It whistled across the short distance in a flash.

Knox and Marie both turned, without hesitation, and dove on top of Syd, knocking him down. The impact tore the breath out of him and sent a stabbing pain through his ribs. The weight of two bodies pressed over him, blotting out the sky.

Knox and Marie slammed their eyes shut tight, and wrapped their arms around each other, just in time to go together into oblivion.

Except they didn't.

No explosions followed.

The rocket hit the hovercraft with a metallic clunk and bounced harmlessly off the hull. Knox and Marie opened their eyes. Syd looked up at Gordis, who stood exactly where he'd been, feet planted firmly on the cracked hardpan of the desert, the explosive ball touching the tip of his toe. Knox was surprised to see that Gordis wore sandals. It was a strange detail to capture his attention, but he couldn't tear his eyes away from the metal ball and the man's big toe.

Gordis kicked the grenade lightly to the side.

"What the—?" the bandit began.

Gordis smirked. "Variable-frequency signal jammer," he said, and with a wave of his hand, he fired off an EMD pulse at the men on horseback.

Actually, Syd, realized, at their horses.

The animals flailed and shrieked, bucking their riders as they fell to the ground in convulsions.

Gordis strolled up to them, casual as could be, and he gave them each a fatal tap with his EMD stick, frying every nerve in their bodies and watching calmly until the shaking stopped. He bent down and snapped each of their necks for good measure, then he nodded at the kids, who rushed to slice the meat from the horses.

And, to Syd's horror, from the men.

"No wasting foodstuff out here," Gordis said.

Marie looked over to Knox. She had one hand clutching her weapon. The other was wrapped around his shoulder.

He had an arm around her waist. Knox looked back at her with just a little twitch of the lips. Her head tilted slightly. Knox's moved forward.

"I hate to interrupt." Syd winced beneath them. "But can you get off me, please?"

They looked down at him, as if they were startled to see him there. Marie blushed and rolled off him. Knox watched her stand, using the weapon to help herself up.

He smirked at Syd and gave him a mischievous wink. "Progress," he whispered and heaved himself off the ground.

It was undeniable, Knox had confidence. A twisted mind, laser focused on one totally inappropriate thing, but still, it was impressive. Even in the face of death, Knox had making out on the brain. He bent down and helped Syd off the ground, letting him lean his weight on him once more.

"They didn't even get a shot off," Knox announced, excitement and pride buoying his voice, like the brief but conclusive battle was something from a holo game. Adrenaline coursed through him; his whole body tingled in a way that petty vandalism or high-speed driving could never create. He was frightened and horrified and yet, somehow, thrilled. He felt more alive than he ever had before. "A signal jammer! Did you see that?"

"I saw," said Syd, watching Gordis oversee the picking apart of the bandits. He wondered who the man really was. No simple scavenger should be so cool in the face of battle, not without training. And what scavenger fleeing Mercy

Camp just happens to have a variable-frequency signal jammer? Syd had been fixing stuff for security contractors since puberty and he'd only ever seen one in Mr. Baram's shop in all that time. They were rare and expensive technology.

Gordis was more than he seemed.

Of course, thought Syd, so are we.

Gordis came over to Syd and Knox and Marie. He rested his EMD stick over his shoulder.

"You two." He looked Knox and Marie up and down. "Patrons? Upper City?"

They nodded.

"And you?" He turned to Syd.

"Just what I look like I am."

The man smiled. "Then you the only man on earth that's true for."

"You okay?" Knox asked Syd. "You're kinda gray."

"Yeah, I'm fine," said Syd, but he knew he wasn't. The adrenaline of the fight was gone, the urgent focus of being chased had vanished, and what was left was only pain. His ribs ached, his head throbbed, and he felt light on his feet. He listed to one side and Knox barely caught him, his strong grip squeezing out a bolt of agony, even as he kept Syd from collapsing on the road.

"Take this." Gordis held out a biopatch. It didn't look like a scavenger's hacked meds, but like something from the Upper City, something lux. Gordis didn't wait for Syd to answer, just slapped it onto his skin, where it lit up gold and silver and green, then faded and dissolved. It seemed to take the pain with it. A wave of peace rolled up from Syd's toes to the tip of his head. He wanted to sleep. More than anything, he wanted to sleep, but first, he had to find out about Gordis. He had to know.

"What about you?" he asked. "Who are you?"

"Just rest," urged Gordis. "Bring him on board," he told Knox.

"No!" Syd objected. He held himself up. He studied Gordis. His arms were thick and strong and he looked well fed. To be well fed as a scavenger was no easy task, and nobody living out in the wastelands pulled it off. They usually arrived in the Mountain City half dead, thin as reeds, and host to a thousand parasitic diseases. Other than the scar on his face, Gordis looked healthy.

"You're a recruiter," Syd suggested. Gordis had to lean in to hear him. Syd could feel the patch taking over. He was fading. "For the Rebooters . . ."

Gordis sucked his teeth; he didn't deny it.

"We need to get to the Rebooters," Marie added eagerly. Gordis nodded.

"These kids," Syd added. "Your recruits?"

"Very impressive, Sydney," Gordis replied.

"I . . ." Syd's vision blurred. He tried to make eye contact with Gordis. "I never told you my name."

"You didn't have to." Gordis reached into his shirt and pulled out a chain. There was a small metal plate on the end of it. He held it up to show Syd. Knox and Marie leaned in to see it too.

The plate was stamped with symbols. Although his vision had begun to blur and his thoughts become foggy, Syd recognized them immediately.

They were the same ones behind his ear.

"I always knew you'd come back," said Gordis. "I always believed."

"Yovel," said Syd, before his legs gave out. Knox scooped him up and carried him into the hovercraft.

"Sydney gonna be okay," Gordis told him as they set him inside on top of some crates.

"Syd," Knox corrected him. "He goes by Syd."

Gordis nodded. "They'll fix Syd up in Old Detroit, all better. You'll see."

All better, thought Knox. That didn't seem possible.

When he closed his eyes, he saw Gordis touching each of those riders with his EMD stick, dropping them dead on the road. He saw the woman in the cave, the moment Syd killed her. He saw Egan's chest exploding and he saw the Guardians in the doorway from the zoo and the woman bleeding out on the floor. He saw Beatrice, hanging like unprocessed meat on a hook. The branding on Syd's arm, the scars. He doubted anything would ever be all better for Syd. The most he could hope for was survival. It was the most anyone could hope for out here and even for that, the chances seemed slim.

[45]

THE HOVERCRAFT WHINED AND rattled as it tore through the evening and into the night.

Syd slept fitfully, wrapped in a silver emergency blanket on some crates behind the pilot's seat. Gordis drove with four holo projections in front of him, showing engine readouts, ground topography, power levels, and the drones prowling in the sky above.

The interior was lit with only dim red running lights, to avoid detection, but given the speed and focus Gordis brought to bear, Knox sensed they'd been spotted and were in a race to Old Detroit. He tried to picture his father in his office, looking down at the hovercraft, debating whether or not to blow up his son to make sure Syd was killed. The hovercraft wasn't trying to outrun the drones. It was trying to outrun Knox's history and his father's calculus—how much was his son worth, when did the bad of Knox's life outweigh the good? Had it ever?

The wind howled through the hole in the roof of the vehicle where the bandits had blasted off the turret. Cold air frosted the metal and the children huddled together, crammed into every open space inside. The ones who'd stayed awake watched Knox and Marie intently, curious how patrons sat and talked and moved and coughed. They'd never seen the rich before.

Knox and Marie shared a stinking patchwork quilt that the children had given them. Knox marveled at how many different kinds of itchy fabric could exist in the world and how they had all come to be a part of this one quilt. He was pretty sure it was giving him a rash. He wished Gordis had offered him a patch like he'd given Syd. He had pain too. He needed sleep.

"You asleep?" Marie asked.

"Nope," said Knox.

Marie shifted, tried to get comfortable, but a metal rivet was digging into her back. There was no getting comfortable in this hovercraft. It was not how she was accustomed to travel. She admired how peacefully the little kids could sleep, in spite of the discomfort. In spite of the danger and the horrors of the day. No one sleeps like little kids, she figured. The thought made her miss her father, made her think about what she was giving up to follow her cause to the end.

It wasn't that her father was a bad man. He'd done bad

things, but he meant well. He meant to keep her safe and the only way to be safe in the Mountain City was to be rich. So he'd made the choices he made. For her. But there were more important things than safety. She hoped he understood that, or that he would one day.

She looked over at Knox, wondering what he must be thinking.

"Do you believe now?" Marie asked him. "Do you believe about Syd?"

Knox had always believed in whatever was most convenient, whatever worked for whatever he wanted at the moment. He hadn't known until a few days ago how fragile that kind of believing could be.

He wanted to tell her yes, now he believed. He wanted to tell her he believed what she believed because maybe then she'd hold his hand, maybe then she'd smile back and remind him who he used to be. But he didn't believe and he didn't say yes. He just couldn't fake it. Instead, he shrugged. "I guess it doesn't matter either way."

"How can you say that?" Marie straightened up, letting the blanket fall from her shoulders.

"Look around." Knox waved his hand toward the kids huddled around the cargo hold, clutching sacks seeping with the blood from raw horse meat and worse, and to Syd lying broken and unconscious. "Is this better than what we've got? Civilization costs something, you know? Some people win and some people lose, but civilization survives because the winners and losers make a deal to keep it working. You tear it down, you break that deal apart, and what do you have? Just death in the desert. I don't want to live in that world."

"But we could build a better system," she objected.

"I don't see how," said Knox. He felt bad about it. Marie believed so strongly in her cause that she couldn't imagine anyone believing something different. She was an optimist. She thought people were better than they were. She thought Knox was better than he was.

"Syd," she said, as if that explained anything. "It has to be him. It's destiny."

Knox rubbed the back of his neck. He tried to form a response.

"Destiny didn't make me take that car or get in that accident," he told her. "Like the old man said, it was just choices. And everything since then too, just choices I made and you made, others we didn't make. There's no meaning to it. I could have just as easily slipped away from Syd at that club, left him to escape on his own."

"But you didn't."

"Because I wanted to get back at my father."

"No." Marie looked up at the blur of stars racing by. "Because you were meant to be part of this."

"I wish I believed like you do," said Knox. He looked down at his lap. He'd disappointed her like he disappointed everybody. "You know, I hoped you might convince me."

"That's not my job. I'm not your mother," Marie said.

When Knox flushed, she knew she'd gone too far.

"Sorry." She pulled back. "I didn't mean to . . . you know . . ."

"It's fine," Knox told her, even though it was far from fine. He didn't like anyone bringing up his mother. She was a private thing. He'd built an airtight container around her memory and only he could slip inside it. Talking about her let the world in and the memory began to decay. But he didn't want the conversation to end with Marie hating him again. He'd come too far. He didn't want to be alone again.

"My father wasn't much for heart-to-heart talks," he told her. "I'm not so good at it."

"You don't have to talk," she said. "I already told you, I like you better when you don't." She smiled at him, put her hand on his. They didn't need words. They didn't need to agree, even. They just needed each other. Her touch sent a shudder through Knox's body.

"Pretty amazing," Marie said, pointing up at the stars through the hole in the roof.

"It's just like looking at a holo," Knox said.

"A lot better than any holo I've ever seen." Marie pulled the quilt back up over her shoulders, leaned against him.

"I think I prefer the digital version," Knox joked. "Smells better."

Marie wrapped an arm around his back. He tucked a stray hair behind her ear. He saw his reflection on a dark panel behind her. It was the first time he'd seen himself in days. His hair was a tangled mess of muddy knots, pressed down and poking up in all the wrong places. His forehead was swollen where Egan had head butted him; he had a cut on his cheek and a nasty yellow-and-purple bruise around his left eye. His lip was cut and caked with dried blood. There were welts and burns all over. The only part of himself that looked familiar were his eyes. They looked so much like they always had that, somehow, they were the most unsettling part of his appearance. He didn't know them at all. They were a stranger's eyes. He looked back at Marie. Hers somehow were not.

He wanted to kiss her.

She shivered and rested her head on his shoulder. Maybe, he thought, when this was over . . .

He breathed quietly in time to her breaths. The air in front of their mouths frosted.

"My father killed my mother," Knox said.

Marie sat up.

"I mean, not, like, literally," Knox said. "But it was his fault. She was kidnapped and he wouldn't negotiate. I saw it happen. I hid when they took her. I wonder, if they had taken me, would he have negotiated then?"

Marie didn't respond. She nodded, letting Knox say what he needed to say.

"I always thought if I could hurt my father, it would make me feel better. Like we'd be even. I'd tried it all those years with everything from stealing to getting tweaked out of my head, but it never really helped. I figured maybe sneaking Syd away would do it. Like if I could save Syd, it would make up for my mom. A life for a life or something. I don't know . . ." Knox wiped his nose on his sleeve. He looked at Syd behind them. "Now I want Syd to get to safety because he's earned it. It's got nothing to do with my father anymore."

Marie grunted. "Earned it?"

"Yeah," said Knox.

"You still don't understand." She frowned at him. "Why should he have to earn it? If people only got what they earned, where would that leave you?"

Knox wanted to reach out and grab her hand again, go back to the almost kiss. He should have kept his mouth shut, should have told her what she wanted to hear, like he used to do with girls. But he didn't. He told the truth.

"I guess it would leave me right where I am," he said. "*This* is what I earned."

"Well, you got that right, anyway." There was no anger in her voice. She leaned against him again. Her hair warmed his neck. They didn't have to agree. Honesty was its own kind of peace.

Knox wondered how many other people had ever known him so well. None that he could think of. Well, Syd perhaps. Syd, who'd known him less than a week, knew him better than anyone. He *had* earned better than this life he'd been living. Even if he hadn't, he *deserved* better now. Knox was afraid of tearing down the system that had served him so well his whole life, but if that's what it took for Syd to be free, maybe it would be worth it. Not for some ideal world. For Syd.

He felt himself dozing off some time in the night, when the land had started to show signs of life. Tiny scrub brush poked from the hardpan earth. A cactus here and there or a strange-leaning type of tree. Fragments of rusted metal signs lay by the side of the road, back from the days before augmented reality, when information was planted in the dirt.

He dreamed about his mother. He saw her on a holo, hovering in the air before him. He was in his living room.

"You haven't changed a bit," she told him.

He wanted to tell her he had changed, that he had grown, that his world was bigger now, but he couldn't speak. It was one of those dreams.

"You only think of yourself." Her voice was his father's voice. His mother didn't know him at all. She'd been gone for so long, she couldn't know him. He wasn't a selfish little boy anymore. Or at least, he wasn't *only* a selfish little boy. When he opened his mouth to tell her that, the sound that came out was his own name.

"Knox."

He trembled.

"Knox."

He opened his eyes. Marie shook him.

"Knox," she said. "Wake up. We're here."

He sat up and looked through the porthole on the side of the hovercraft. They were on a narrow road running through a crumbling jungle city. They sped down a wide avenue, a man-made canyon of steel and concrete that had long ago surrendered to nature.

Moss carpeted the facades of the buildings and dark holes that once were windows gaped black like the gouged eye sockets of a corpse. Vines broke through the sidewalks, and trees tore through the roofs of low rises, strangling one another for sunlight. Branches had grown so long on either side of the street, they met in the middle, crossing and tangling, and formed a covered canopy that muzzled the sun and cast spiderweb shadows over the street below.

They landed beside the loading dock of an old factory and almost immediately, figures rushed out to greet them, armed men in mismatched uniforms from different companies, armies, and eras. A tall medical bot just like the ones in the Upper City rolled with them, a stretcher extended from its midsection.

Gordis opened the rear hatch and the men swarmed in, grabbing supplies and directing the children out of the way. They ignored Knox and Marie, and lifted Syd right onto the stretcher. The bot turned and began to roll away.

Marie jumped out of the hovercraft after him. Knox followed her and they were quickly blocked by one of the armed men with a fracture cannon mounted on his shoulder.

"Gordis!" Marie shouted. "Where are they taking him?"

The bot flashed projections of Syd's vital signs to a man running alongside it. Must have been a doctor. Syd and the doctor and the robot disappeared up a ramp into the factory and vanished through a dark doorway.

Marie tried to push past the soldier.

"We go wherever Syd goes!" Knox yelled. "Whatever happens to him, happens to us!"

The soldier didn't move. He aimed his cannon straight into Knox's face.

"Let them pass," a man called from above.

Knox looked up the ramp to see the old man from the Valve, Mr. Baram, hobble outside, leaning heavily on a crutch, but otherwise unscathed.

"He'll want to see some friendly faces when he wakes up," Mr. Baram said and the soldier swung open like a door. Knox and Marie ran forward after Syd. Mr. Baram followed behind on his crutch and the factory door slid shut.

[46]

WHEN SYD WOKE FROM a dreamless sleep, he was in a bed with clean white sheets and a firm mattress below him. He wore white shorts and a white shirt. Projections floated in the dim light of the room, showing his vital signs, his biodata, and various other information he couldn't decipher.

The walls of the room were paneled in wood, with discolored patches here and there. Above these strange patches were the faded outlines of stenciled letters. He could only make out a few:

RD OTO C MP Y

Syd felt a strange sensation on his arm and pulled it out from under the sheet. He saw the spot where he'd been branded, except the branding was gone. There was scarring and discoloration, but no more metal. No more Marie. He could just make out the *R* and the number *1*. He looked back at the letters on the wall.

Anything man can make can be unmade, he thought. Everything fades.

He kicked the sheets off and felt the cool air on his skin. Climate control. He was in civilization, or some approximation of it. It had to be the Rebooters. If he'd fallen into anyone else's hands, they wouldn't have fixed his wounds or repaired his body. They'd have killed him for the reward. So he was in Old Detroit.

Must be in an old office. He smiled, because he had made it, but still, he didn't know into whose hands he had fallen, or where Knox and Marie had gone, or if he was truly safe, or if he ever could be again.

His bed lay next to a large casement window, but the window was boarded up with mushy-looking wood. Shoots of green broke through the wood and crept along the outside of the glass. He watched a large slug crawl along one of the green shoots. A trail of tiny ants followed it, feeding off the goo it left behind. A tiny patch of boarded window in an abandoned city contained more life than he'd seen in days. He could have watched that slug for hours. He wondered how long he'd been unconscious.

The door swung open and Knox and Marie came in, both of them clean and dressed in new clothes. Marie ran to his bedside and hugged him, and Knox, without hesitation, did the same.

"We thought you might not make it," Knox told him.

"*He* thought," Marie corrected. "I always knew."

Marie still held her weapon, although it looked like it too had been cleaned.

Knox noticed Syd's eyes drift to it. "She hasn't put that thing down except to let Gordis show her how to clean the barrels. Said she's vowed to protect you with her life and she's not about to stop now."

Marie blushed. Syd smiled. "Thanks," he said.

"You're looking much better, by the way," Knox told him.

"You too," Syd said and his voice came out smooth and clear. They'd even fixed his throat. He couldn't recall ever having medical care like this in his life. He found himself wondering what it would cost him—an old habit—when he remembered why they'd treat him this way. He had something the Rebooters wanted. The weight of the memory settled down on him. Everything costs.

"There's someone else here to see you," Marie said. She didn't want to overwhelm Syd just when he'd woken up. She wasn't sure how fragile he would be, but he looked well and he looked eager, so she went to the door and opened it.

Mr. Baram came in on a crutch, his face cracked in a smile so wide that his beard almost parted.

"Ah, boychik!" the old man cried. "You've ridden a rough road, but you made it here at last. I knew Gordis would find you. He's a good man, that one."

"You're—here?" Syd muttered.

"I am here, Sydney, yes," Mr. Baram said, nodding. "Your powers of observation are as sharp as ever."

"No," said Syd. "I mean, what are you doing here? Are we—?"

"We're with the Rebooters," Marie confirmed. "And they've done blood tests. They know it's you. They know you've got this biodata in your blood. You're the—"

"Don't say it." Mr. Baram held his finger in the air. "Please. We don't throw that word around lightly and I would just as rather not. But it is true, Sydney. If you're feeling up to getting dressed, I can show you."

Marie practically bounced on her feet. She looked almost giddy. Knox studied Syd carefully, looking for a change in the boy he'd known as his proxy that would suggest the historic role he was about to play, but he saw the same boy as ever, if a little cleaner and more rested.

Syd dressed and Mr. Baram led him out into the hall, with Marie and Knox at his side. Soldiers flanked the door to his room. They looked no older than he was. As he passed them, he noticed their eyes searching the spot just behind his ear.

Gordis rushed forward to escort them. He saluted when he saw Syd, which seemed a bit over the top.

As they strode down the empty corridors, Syd felt the discomfiting gaze of everyone they passed in the halls. Soldiers and nurses, doctors and even little children. Their looks were eager, expectant, loaded with want. Syd didn't like the attention. He felt oddly nostalgic for living in Knox's shadow, even though he'd hated every moment of it.

"How long have we been here?" Syd wondered.

"Two days," Knox said. "You were pretty banged up. We've been sleeping down the hall in another office. The whole place used to make cars. It's crazy. They've turned it into, like, a fortress. They've got some of their own networks and datastreams, weapons systems, transports, bots. They make their own biopatches and their hackers seem pretty slick."

"You joining the cause now, Knox?" Syd asked him.

Knox shrugged. "It's just some lux stuff is all."

"I guess it's time you see the most 'lux' part of all," Mr. Baram said when they reached a large double door, flanked again by two guards. Gordis pushed the door open and the guards looked at Syd wide-eyed as he passed through. One of them, a ferocious-looking teen with a shaved head and one metal hand, even let out a sigh.

Knox and Syd made eye contact over that one. Knox raised his eyebrows and Syd shook his head.

They stepped onto a metal walkway above a factory floor and Syd gasped. Below him, the space bustled with activity. Men in white suits with white hoods and goggles moved tubes and adjusted dials attached to a wheeled metal table. They all wore blue latex gloves and, when he entered, they all looked up. In his head, Syd heard the distinct whine of a baby crying. He'd been here before, and not just in his dream.

[47]

"ARE YOU OKAY?" MARIE saw Syd's face turn ashen and he gripped the metal railing as if he were about to fall.

"Yeah . . . I'm fine." Syd looked to Mr. Baram. "I know this place."

"Infants do store memories," Mr. Baram said. "This is where your father installed the program."

Syd winced. His hand went to his birthmark. The needles from his dream were real too.

"This is also where your father was killed." Mr. Baram sighed and put his arm around Syd. He led him down to the factory floor.

"So," said Syd. "What happens now? How do we, uh, upload this thing in my blood?"

The medical staff made way for Syd as Mr. Baram led him past the steel table to a large machine in the center of the room. It had a door leading into a small chamber where wires hung from the walls. On the end of each wire was a patch, just like the ones Knox used to hack Syd a new ID. On top of the machine was a large antenna coiled with wires, an old transmitter.

"This machine will capture the code entwined in your DNA structure," explained Mr. Baram. "It works just like any other data transmitter. The code in the cells of this virus will be extracted and relayed through the network's own transmitters throughout the Mountain City, Upper and Lower. It will infect every datastream and every bit of biotech between here and there. It will then erase the data, destroy the records, and sever the connections. It will fry the servers themselves."

Knox exhaled. That was some impressive hacking. He had to admire it.

"Without the data, the system collapses," Marie observed.

Mr. Baram nodded. "No records of wealth or credit and debt. No personal marketing profiles, no security information. No patrons. No proxies. A total reboot of the system. It starts over."

"Jubilee," said Syd.

"Jubilee," said Mr. Baram. "When all is forgiven."

"What about medical programs?" Knox asked. "People use the networked biotech to manage cancers and birth defects. If that goes offline, you'd condemn a lot of sick people. Can't you just target the debt records?"

Mr. Baram shook his head. "Nature cannot be reprogrammed forever. Humans are not meant to run like software. You cannot hack the human condition."

Knox looked to Syd. "Is this what you want? The system's not perfect, but this . . . a lot of innocent people will die."

"Be quiet, Knox," said Marie. "This is the only way. It's Syd's only chance to stop your father."

"Your father's a part of this too," Knox objected.

"And until we destroy this system, he is just as trapped in it as you or me or Syd," she said.

"There is another thing you should know, Sydney," Mr. Baram interrupted their argument. "As I explained, the virus works through the city's existing networks. In order to achieve the necessary signal strength to overwrite the biofeeds of several million networked people, we have to overpower the background radiation it uses. Only that way can the virus be fully effective."

"What's that mean?" Syd asked.

"Our radiation levels have to be . . . substantial." Mr. Baram cleared his throat. "You would not survive the process."

"What?" said Syd.

"What?" said Knox.

"To create a system meltdown of this magnitude . . . ," Mr. Baram said. It appeared that speaking was painful to him. He couldn't finish his sentences.

Syd remembered the Arak9 he'd detonated to escape the Guardians. For a big enough reaction, the robot had to self-destruct.

"To do this, to make this change, demands a sacrifice—" Mr. Baram's voice cracked.

Everything costs, thought Syd.

"You dirty liar!" Knox yelled. He stepped up to Mr. Baram's face, but Gordis shoved him back. "You knew! All this time, you knew that Syd was marked for death if he got here, but you let him go! You knew he wouldn't come here, so you lied to us!"

"I did not lie," said Mr. Baram. "I said that Sydney would have to die."

Knox moved to hit the old man, but Gordis pushed him back.

"Knox, calm down," Marie said, reaching out to comfort him, her own voice cracking with emotion. He slapped her hand away.

"No!" Knox threw his hands in the air. "Do you know what we went through to get here? Do you know what I gave up to save his life? I did not do all this so he could die!"

"This isn't about you, Knox!" Marie yelled. "This is bigger than any of us!"

"It's not!" Knox grabbed Syd's hand, turned to him. "It's not," he repeated quietly, just for Syd. "Your life doesn't belong to me and it doesn't belong to them either. It's yours." He held Syd's gaze. "What do you want?"

Syd looked back into Knox's emerald-green eyes. His sharp jaw tensed. He bit his lower lip.

For the first time, Syd didn't know what Knox was thinking, didn't understand what he wanted. For the first time,

Knox looked at Syd without expectation. He was the only one in the room looking at Syd that way.

Knox's eyes flashed quickly once to the side, just over Syd's shoulder. Then they met his again and Syd read something else in them.

Mischief.

He saw in the reflection of Knox's eyes, a doorway open as a doctor came into the room, a flash of daylight behind him. A way out. The choice was Syd's. He could give himself up for the cause, set all the proxies free, and extract the most destructive revenge imaginable on the wealthy of the Upper City.

Or he could run and change nothing and live.

Knox squeezed his hand. There was no expectation in it. Just a question. Just a choice for Syd to make.

He ran.

[48]

BEFORE ANYONE KNEW WHAT had happened, Knox and Syd were out the door. The soldiers didn't dare shoot, lest they harm Syd. He was only allowed one way to die today.

"Stop!" Mr. Baram pleaded. "Please!"

Syd and Knox came out onto a loading dock and jumped down into an alley beside the factory in what had once been an industrial part of town. It looked remarkably like the alley outside Arcadia, where they'd had their fistfight after they'd first met. The patrons had a done a lux job duplicating Old Detroit in the Upper City, except here, the buildings were overgrown with vines and moss, the air cloying and damp. The city had a greenish tint, and even though the sun blazed in the midday sky, the streets had the dimness of twilight. Insects buzzed through the air, and the shed skin of giant snakes, thin as rice paper, crunched underfoot as the boys ran.

They could hear footsteps behind them, the Rebooters giving chase, but they turned down side streets, dodged hanging vines, and crawled through thick mangrove roots. The overgrown city provided countless opportunities to hide, which was certainly why the Rebooters chose it for their headquarters.

They ran without purpose or direction. They ran only to escape, but they didn't know what escape could mean. There was a world of difference between running to and running from. Even as they sprinted and ducked and turned, they had not let go of each other's hands.

They ducked around a corner and hid behind a curtain of vines that hung over a shattered storefront, crouching to catch their breath. They saw the shadows of a dozen Rebooters run by, the unmistakable silhouette of Gordis's serpentine dreadlocks bouncing as he led the charge.

Knox looked at Syd. Syd looked back at him. Neither knew what to say. Syd was marked for death. Long before he'd ever been Knox's proxy, his life had been on loan, a debt to be called in before he ever had a chance to live it. A fatal inheritance. What words could offer solace for that?

They sat listening to the city on the other side of the curtain of vines. Buildings creaked in the wind. Men shouted. Birds whistled.

Knox shook his head. "I'm sorry. If I'd known, we could have gone . . . somewhere else."

"We never would have made it," Syd said. "Your father's bounty or the Rebooter fanatics would have tracked me anywhere."

"Now I get why my dad was so afraid of you," said Knox. "Not that it makes what he did right . . . but I get it."

Syd nodded. He got it too. Knox's father made a calculation. One poor proxy's life to save countless others, to save all of civilization as he knew it. It was the same calculation Mr. Baram had made, just for a different result. Syd's life was a means to an end.

"It's a funny thing," said Syd. "I could have been anyone. All that matters about me is that I was given this virus. Otherwise, I'm nothing special. If it weren't for my father, no one would care if I lived or died."

"I would," said Knox. "I would now."

Syd nodded. He knew Knox meant it and he knew it hurt Knox to say it. Caring costs.

"Thank you." Syd smiled. He leaned his back against the wall of the store and stared at the opposite wall. A broken display case ran along the back and led to what was probably a storeroom. There'd be a doorway to another alley behind it. Another way out. The chase could go on forever. Syd could just keep running. Maybe Knox would even come with him.

For some reason, a lone shoe sat moldering in the far corner. The store had been looted centuries ago. Whoever had left the shoe was long dead and so was everyone they'd ever known. History erased itself all the time. It didn't need a computer virus. Whatever happened to Syd, he'd eventually be forgotten too. So would Knox and Marie. So would Mr. Baram. The whole Mountain City. On a long enough timeline, all debts are settled, all lives are balanced back to zero.

But if Syd had to die, he didn't want to do it the way he'd lived, with his head down, avoiding connection. He wanted the blaze of glory that Egan didn't get. He wanted it to matter to someone besides himself. He stood.

"I'm going back," he said.

Knox looked up at him. He chewed his lip. "You don't have to. We can run. I can protect you from my father and we can just . . . run."

Syd shook his head.

Knox rose and looked at him for a long time. He put his hand on Syd's shoulder. They turned and stepped together back through the vines and onto the street side by side.

"Get down!" someone shouted.

They looked in his direction and saw a group of Rebooters pointing their weapons. Gordis had his EMD stick raised. The boys raised their hands.

"Get down! Now!" Gordis yelled again, charging at them and firing. The boys dove to the cracked pavement and the pulse Gordis had fired caused a commotion behind them. Syd looked over his shoulder and saw a platoon of Guardians rushing up the street. Three of them had collapsed on the ground in a quivering lump and the others streamed over the bodies.

Gordis sprinted forward while the other Rebooters put down a wall of covering blasts. He grabbed Syd and pulled him off the ground, dragging him away from the fight.

Knox sprinted behind as they ran at full speed back toward the factory.

Turning a corner, they found Marie, running in the opposite direction with three more Rebooters.

"Can't go this way," she said. "Guardians."

"There's too many," said one of the soldiers with her. "They've got the city completely surrounded and they're closing in. We don't have the firepower to hold them off."

They heard a drone circling above and though they couldn't see it through the jungle canopy, it was equipped to see them. A tall building down the block exploded into flame and rubble.

"We have to get off the streets," Gordis commanded.

"Let me go." Syd yanked his arm away. "I've decided to cooperate. I won't run."

Gordis hesitated.

Syd looked at Marie. "I just freaked out there a bit."

"I understand." She put her hand on his face, gently. She smiled sadly at him. He mattered to her too. It hurt her to let him do this, the pain was scrawled across her face, but she believed and such was the price of belief. It gave no discounts to friendship. Gordis let Syd's arm go.

They ran. Guardians closed in and Knox knew his father would be among them, nearby, commanding the battle personally. He realized what they had done by coming here. They'd led his father right to the heart of the Rebooters' operation. If they didn't get back to the machine in time, the entire movement would be wiped out. Knox's father had intended that all along. That's why the drones hadn't vaporized them from the sky as they crossed the desert. It had nothing to do with Knox's safety. It had everything to do with his father's work—destroying the resistance and protecting the system.

A combat robot rolled to the street in front of them. Gordis hit it with a pulse that knocked it over, but it fired off one fracturing blast as it fell. A rusted metal letter *U* from a factory sign exploded with sparks and crashed into the canopy above them. Gordis knocked Syd out of the way as the sign smashed onto the street. Knox, to his own surprise, tackled Marie. He landed on top of her against the pavement.

"Is that your gun in my side, or are you just happy to see me?" he joked.

"At a time like this?" She rolled her eyes at him.

"Especially at a time like this," Knox answered as he helped her up.

They kept running, but the sign had smashed one of Gordis's legs. He couldn't keep up. Another platoon of Guardians had come around a corner.

"Go," Gordis told the others. "I'll delay them. You're going two hundred yards, third door on the right."

They ran. Syd knew it was suicide for Gordis to stay behind, but it was suicide for Syd to keep going, so he didn't even try to convince him otherwise.

They pounded on the door. "It's me!" Syd shouted. "I'm here!"

The door opened and they ran inside. They heard the

Guardians running after them. They didn't need to look back to know that Gordis was already dead.

When the soldiers slammed it shut again, the echo made Knox flinch. Never had he heard a door slam so completely. The locks snapped shut.

"I'm ready," Syd said, swallowing hard. He felt a sudden wave of exhaustion come over him. Strange how tired fear could make you feel. He'd imagined the end would make his adrenaline rush, that he'd shake or cry, but no. All he wanted was a nap. It seemed he'd get one. He wondered if the dead dreamed.

"Boychik." Mr. Baram hugged Syd. Then he held him at arm's length and looked at him. Behind Mr. Baram, the medical personnel in white suits readied the machine.

"There is no man living more proud of a son than I am of you." Mr. Baram clenched his jaw. "You live up to the name you were given."

Syd nodded. "Do I have a real one? One my parents gave me?"

"You haven't guessed it?" said Mr. Baram.

"Yovel," Syd answered, touching his birthmark one more time.

Mr. Baram nodded.

"I guess I like Syd better," Syd told him. "I've grown used to it."

"The names will forever be connected, Syd. You and the Jubilee will be honored in the same breath for generations to come."

Syd shrugged. In death, his memory would belong to the living, but he didn't die for them. This was no payment. The living would owe him nothing nor he them. He gave his life willingly. He gave it as a gift. His knees felt weak.

Mr. Baram steadied Syd and guided him forward toward the machine. Knox and Marie stayed at his side.

"How's . . . uh . . ." Syd pointed. "How's this work?"

"You just step inside," Mr. Baram said. "Put the patches on and we'll close the chamber. We'll do the rest."

Syd nodded. He took a deep breath.

"I promise it won't hurt," said Mr. Baram.

Syd stepped up to the door of the machine.

Outside, they heard an explosion. Then another. Shouts from above.

"They're in the building," one of the soldiers studying a holo announced.

"This is it," said Mr. Baram.

Syd touched the metal of the machine, then opened the chamber door slowly.

Knox turned to Marie and locked his green eyes with the mournful gleam of her purple ones.

"I'm so sorry," he said. She nodded. She understood. She too was sorry. For all of it.

But Knox had something else in mind.

He kicked Marie in the shin. When she bent with grunt, more from shock than pain, Knox snatched her weapon from her and raised it at Syd.

"No one move!" he shouted.

"Knox, no." Marie stepped toward him, but he swung the weapon in her face.

"Knox, what are you doing?" Syd demanded. Knox swung the weapon frantically at anyone who moved. Throughout the building they heard explosions and shouts as the battle drew closer and closer. The Rebooters fought with all they had to slow down the Guardian advance, but it was inevitable. They were coming. The battle was lost. Only the virus could shut the Guardians down now, delete their program, sever their network, sever all the networks.

Knox stepped up beside Syd in front of the chamber and he pointed the weapon at his friend.

"I can't let you go in there," he whispered. "I can't let you do this."

"You have to," said Syd.

"No. I don't." Knox tilted his head and with his free hand, brushed the hair from over his ear and showed Syd his brand-new birthmark, four letters, just like Syd's:

"Yovel," said Syd.

A smirk broke across Knox's face.

The blood transfusion.

Knox had been infected with Syd's blood.

"Knox, you can't." Syd shook his head. "It's my father's virus. It's my destiny."

Syd had spent sixteen years cultivating the virus. Knox had only had it a week. It wasn't his to take.

Another explosion shook the building. The soldiers glanced nervously to the doors.

"No such thing as destiny," Knox said. He lowered his weapon, leaned forward, and wrapped his arm around Syd's waist, pulling his proxy against him and holding him tightly. He grabbed Syd's face in his free hand.

Syd looked back into his eyes.

"I can't let you do this," Syd pleaded. "Not for me."

"I have to," said Knox. "For you."

"I don't want you to die," Syd whispered.

Knox shook his head. "Someone has to. It's my turn."

"What am I supposed to do?"

"Like I know?" Knox shrugged. "It's your future. Choose."

The door above burst open. The Guardians streamed in and the soldiers around the machine opened fire with everything they had—EMD sticks and fracture cannons, antique guns and hand grenades. The Guardians returned fire just as brutally, ignoring one another as they fell.

"The Guardians are here," Knox said. He grinned and then he pulled Syd's face to him, pressing their lips together.

At first, Syd flinched, then he relaxed and let his hands fall to Knox's side. The battle vanished around them, the violence, the debts owed and unredeemable, the world that was and the world that was to come, all disappeared for one instant as their lips held on to each other.

For the tiniest of moments, they were alone.

Knox let go of Syd's face. "Just like our first kiss."

"I—" Syd started.

"Don't get the wrong idea. That was just something to remember me by."

"Hold your fire!" They heard a shout, Knox's father's voice resounding across the factory. Knox released Syd and looked up to the walkway where his father stood, flanked by Guardians.

"He owes you a life," Knox told Syd. "And so do I." He let his weapon clatter to the floor, took one step backward into the chamber, and slammed the machine door shut, sealing himself in alone.

Marie rushed forward. "Someone stop him!" she shouted. "He'll ruin everything!"

"No." Syd pulled her back. "He won't."

He held Marie's arms, let her weight fall into him.

Knox fumbled to attach the biopatches to his skin. He was enough of a hacker to know where to put them. He peeled off his shirt and attached two on one side of his rib cage, one on the other. The last went right behind his ear.

"Stop him!" Knox's father yelled from above. "That's my son!"

The technicians had already begun, their hands dancing in holos floating in front of them, waving and sliding just like the man leading the music in the holo back in Knox's room. In his head, Knox imagined the music, the silent song sent out from his blood that would erase all the data and sever every network on the continent. He felt the urge to dance.

A strange tingling filled his body. Behind Syd and Marie, the soldiers continued to hold off the Guardians with steady fire. Some of them fell.

Knox's father rushed down the stairs and broke through the ring of soldiers, sacrificing two more Guardians to shield himself. He lunged for the machine, but the soldier with the metal hand held him back with an unbreakable mechanical grasp. He reached out for Knox, screaming, tears running down from behind the dark glasses that now sat askew on his face.

All will be forgiven, Knox thought, watching him through the glass. Even you. Even me.

Right in front of Knox, Syd and Marie held hands and watched as he started to squirm. The charge in his body increased. His limbs tingled. Mr. Baram was right. He didn't feel any pain. In fact, it felt kind of cool. Like one of the patches Cheyenne used to give him. He wondered what she was up to. And Simi. And Nine. Knox was about to change their world and they didn't even know it.

The tingle under his skin grew bigger and bigger, like ants crawling all over him. He started to itch. The chamber felt hot. He tried to keep from squirming. He had an audience, after all. He wanted to look his best at the end.

Funny the things that go through your head, he thought.

Syd ignored the sound of Knox's father screaming, the

soldiers fighting, the Guardians beginning to stop, to disengage, to lose their program as the virus spread. He kept his eyes locked with Knox's.

Some of the Guardians fell to the floor, vomiting, or they passed out. Others just sat down, dazed, caught somewhere between what they had been and what they were becoming.

Syd didn't feel any different. Knox started laughing. As the machine hummed louder and louder, sparks began to fly all around Knox. The technicians shouted numbers back and forth to one another, celebrating their status reports, the success of their virus.

Syd's virus.

Knox's.

"Forty-two percent! Forty-nine percent! Fifty-four percent!"

Marie put her hand to the glass where Knox could see it. Syd placed his up too, so close their pinkies touched. Knox's eyes locked on their hands and quivering, he raised his own. It only held a moment.

His body jolted. His skin reddened. It burned. There was pain. But there wasn't only pain. He felt . . . something else.

As the radiation levels rose, the chamber glowed. Syd looked through the glow. His friend's green eyes sparkled, bright as emeralds.

Knox kept them open for as long as he could. He saw his friends and his father, weeping, and behind his father, he saw his mother's face, smiling, and she too raised her hand toward him.

He knew what was happening. He was out of time. He'd

given it to Syd. He hoped his friend would make the most of it. He looked at his old proxy through the glass, glad they could see each other clearly now.

Syd and Marie looked so worried. Knox wanted to tell them it was all okay, it would all be okay.

He winked.

"Did he just—?" Marie wondered.

"Yeah," said Syd, as Knox's body vanished in the vaporizing heat of the machine. "He did."

The action, adventure,
and shocking twists continue
in this sequel to *Proxy*—

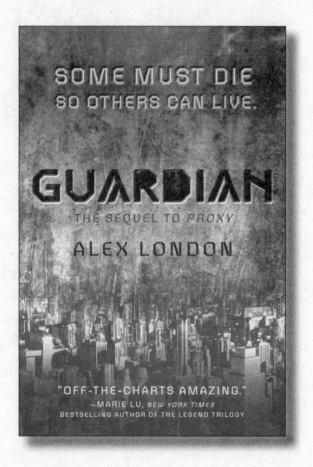

SOME MUST DIE
SO OTHERS CAN LIVE.

GUARDIAN
THE SEQUEL TO *PROXY*

ALEX LONDON

"OFF-THE-CHARTS AMAZING."
—MARIE LU, *NEW YORK TIMES*
BESTSELLING AUTHOR OF THE LEGEND TRILOGY

LIAM WAS ALWAYS THERE, just out of the light, standing in doorways, hovering at the edge of conversations, watching Syd even as he slept.

These were the orders of the Reconciliation: Syd was not to be alone.

Liam tried to give Syd his space, but every inch of air between them amplified the danger. He couldn't do his job if Syd was too far away when an assassin struck. And he certainly couldn't protect Syd if he couldn't find him.

Again.

That was why Liam cursed as he sprinted through the overgrown streets of the jungle city, slashing vines from his face, tearing through thorns, and leaping the gnarly mangrove roots webbed between rusted skyscrapers.

Morning mist shrouded everything, and if Liam hadn't

lived in this jungle city his entire life, he would easily have gotten lost. In overgrown plots, people on clearing details hacked away at the brush; others heaped it in piles for burning. Young Purifiers patrolled in pairs. Clad in their green uniforms, their faces were concealed beneath white balaclavas that let only their eyes and mouths show through. While on duty in service of the Reconciliation, all Purifiers were the same Purifier. The individual was negated by the mask.

Anonymity made it easier to beat their fellow citizens into compliance. Anonymity made it easier for the citizens to submit, made it less obvious that most of the Purifiers weren't even old enough to shave.

Only Liam showed his face, his close-cropped red hair bright as torchlight. He wanted to be visible, known to all. A reputation for violence made violence unnecessary. Mostly unnecessary.

All the Purifiers kept their distance. Liam's orders outweighed theirs: Syd was to be protected at all costs.

Liam reached an intersection and stopped. He rested his hands on the fallen pole across the road, tapped his fingers against it. The metal fingers of his right hand clanged on the hollowness; one of them cracked the surface. Metal and meat, everything rotted; it was just a question of timing.

He wondered, when he died, if his mechanical hand would be recycled before burial or if it would slowly rust beside his corpse, no more enduring than this old lamppost. If anything happened to Syd, he'd soon find out.

The Reconciliation had made it clear to him when he volunteered to be Syd's bodyguard: Syd's death would be answered with his own.

It seemed fair enough at the time.

A few months ago, when the Reconciliation was new, when they still called themselves the Rebooters, Liam had no idea how difficult guarding Syd would be. Syd gave Liam the slip at least once a week. No amount of yelling, scolding, or pleading could convince Syd that the danger to him was real.

Everyone knew who Syd was and what he'd done. Everyone knew it was Syd who sparked the Jubilee, Syd who erased the records of the past, Syd who severed the networks and destroyed the old systems of control. Syd who was the people's savior.

Not everyone was happy about it.

No explaining that it wasn't really Syd at all. His friend Knox had done it, had given his life doing it, in fact.

Syd lived on in the aftermath, just like everyone else.

How long Syd lived on in the aftermath was for Liam to worry about, and he was at the moment quite worried about it.

He bent down and checked the moss on a stretch of sidewalk. Indentations where feet had crushed it, morning dew pressed into the footprints. Recent. On the corner of a building a few yards on, he saw crumbs of concrete on the ground, green and rotted, and he found the spot at shoulder height where they'd broken off. He'd have to teach Syd to be more careful. Rotted concrete breaks easy as dirt and leaves a trail even a novice tracker could follow.

Higher up on the wall someone had carved some scratchiti into the mushy stone:

THE MACHINE WILL

They must have run off before they could finish carving their treason. Purifiers stamped out talk of the Machine wherever they found it. They left the scratchiti—too much effort to erase—but if they caught the scratcher . . . well, Liam had once seen a pile of white Purifier masks delivered to a laundry detail and there was dried blood on every one of them.

He swung around the corner and crept low through an overgrown alley. Plant tendrils and branches tugged at his green uniform and scratched his face. He shifted the brush carefully with his metal hand and followed the path where Syd had passed before.

When he came out on the other side, Liam had gone through a break in a wall into the ruins of a monumental building. A canopy of branches and leaves filtered sunlight through the gaping roof. Patches of marble showed through great curtains of ivy. Daggers of light cut through a high arched window and fell in slashes across two parallel marble staircases, rising to a landing that cut the space in two.

At the top of the landing, there was a figure with his back to Liam, a green uniform, a white mask. The figure was leaning forward, looking down over the railing. He held something in his hand. It caught a glint of light. A weapon?

Liam could hear his own pulse in his ears. He exhaled half a breath and crept up the stairs. Even the change of air temperature from his exhalation could give him away. He didn't want to spook his quarry. If he failed now, when it mattered most, when Syd was in the greatest danger, the best Liam could hope for from the Reconciliation would be a lifetime of hard labor. The more likely outcome would be his own public humiliation followed by his execution.

If he failed now, he would deserve it.

His whole life he had been trained to be a ghost, to slip in and out of secure areas unseen, to attack from the shadows and melt into beams of sunlight. He'd been born a guerrilla, serving the revolution of the Rebooters for every conscious moment of his seventeen years. Now he served the new order, which was the same as the old order, but with a new name: the Reconciliation. He was no longer a destroyer, but a protector.

Step by step, he approached the figure. He fought the urge to shout a warning. Instead, he grabbed the figure's neck with his metal hand and wrapped his other hand around the forehead, quick as heat lightning. He jerked his hands in opposite directions and snapped the thin neck, then shoved the body forward over the railing, where it tumbled end over end and hit the hard earth with a crunch. The metal tube of a blowgun clattered across the floor as it rolled from the lifeless hand.

Liam looked down, where Syd stood just beside the body, staring in shock. Syd's dark eyes, wide as moons, darted up to Liam's.

"You—"

"I've told you it's not safe to go off alone," Liam declared. "If I'd been ten seconds later, you'd be dead."

He didn't add *and so would I*.

PUNISHMENT
A Proxy Story

More heart-stopping thrills in this never-before-seen prequel to *Proxy*. Find out where the adventure began for Syd and Knox—and meet Liam!

[1]

"NO WAY," SYD WHISPERED to Egan. He crouched be-
hind a broken concrete barrier, peering across a putrid lot, to the
fenced-in warehouse beyond. "If we get caught . . ."

"We won't get caught!" Egan didn't even bother to whisper,
standing and resting his elbows on the barrier. "It's perfect. All
that stuff just in there for the taking. You realize how much we
could get for that amount of wiring if we rolled it to the scrap
yard?"

"I *realize* we'll get jumped if we show our faces in the scrap
yard," Syd answered. He pulled Egan down beside him. "Thanks
to your last *perfect* scheme."

"Hey, I didn't think Toussaint would check the processors."
Egan shrugged. Syd's best friend had a unique talent for forget-
ting his own mistakes as soon as the bruises healed.

Syd never forgot a mistake of Egan's, maybe because he
bruised more easily than his friend did.

"Anyway," Egan added, "I never actually *told* the man that
they worked."

Syd shook his head. Egan thought he was quite the criminal
mastermind, but half his plans fizzled out before they started,
and the other half usually cost more in beatings than they
earned in credit. Egan did, however, share everything with Syd,
the beatings and the cred.

"You could pay for a whole year of school with this score."
Egan continued to make his argument for the proposed heist.
He lowered his hood, revealing the shock of white hair he'd
styled—last week it was green, blue the week before. He liked
to coordinate with his outfits, no matter how much it cost him.
He'd just borrow more. His patron never got in trouble, so it
didn't bother him. Unlike Syd's.

Syd's patron hardly went a week without one crime or another for which Syd took the punishment as his proxy. It seemed
to Syd that between his patron and his best friend, he was always paying for someone else's mistakes. It was, however, good
motivation to avoid making any of his own.

"No new debt," Egan told him. "You've only got what? Three
years left stuck with that knockoff patron of yours? We pull off
this job, and you won't need to take another minute of punishment after you turn eighteen. Not a second."

That got Syd's attention. Eighteen was only three years away.

Egan grinned. Syd didn't like taking stupid risks, but he
liked taking on new debt even less. School was expensive, and if
the system expected slumrats like him to pay for it, they had to
expect a robbery here and there. It was a free market after all.
There was always a buyer.

Some of the Upper City businesses used warehouses in
the Valve for storage because space was cheap. They could
simply pay some local thugs to clear out a building, dump their
material inside, and protect the place. The bigger corporations
paid for Guardians to watch over their warehouses. No one
could sneak past them. Guardians were genetically modified
with patches and biodata and all kinds of programming that
made them the perfect enforcers of corporate order. A warehouse under their protection was impenetrable.

But this place? It didn't look like anyone with any connections, legitimate or otherwise, was looking after it.

"*Somebody* is going to rob that place," Egan assured Syd. "It might as well be us."

Syd tapped nervously at the birthmark behind his ear. The tapping calmed him down, helped him think. It was a habit he'd had for as long as he could remember. As far as he knew, he'd never sucked his thumb as a baby, just tapped his fingers on his birthmark.

"I don't know why I always agree to this stuff," he said.

"Because we're partners in crime," Egan said. "For now and forever."

"Forever?" Syd raised an eyebrow. "If I'm still pulling these heists with you when I'm seventy, I think I'll jump off the dam."

"Come on," Egan scoffed. "When we're seventy we'll be in our Upper City mansions hooking up with lux chicks. Girls love criminal masterminds."

"Then what will they think of *you*?" Syd smiled.

Egan punched him in the arm. "Knockoff!"

"Ow!" Syd punched him back, catching Egan in the gut.

Syd laughed at his doubled-over friend, but Egan charged him, tackling Syd into the dirt, holding him down with all his weight, his forearm across Syd's chest. He made a throat-clearing sound, building up a wad of phlegm.

"Don't you dare . . . ," Syd told him. "Don't you even think . . ."

Egan pursed his lips, then he rolled off Syd and helped him up. They leaned back against the blast barrier.

"So what's your plan, mastermind?" Syd asked.

Egan waved his hand and brought up a holo projection hovering in the air between them. It showed the blast barrier where they were crouched and, on the other side, an open heap of trash, which young pickers scoured for useful salvage. And just on the other side of that, behind a flimsy wire fence, was the warehouse.

"There's only one guy on the perimeter, walking a loop," Egan said. "Except he spends most of his time sitting under the light right there." He jabbed his finger into the holo. "Playing some nudey game on his datastream."

"Nobody would have just one guy guarding their scrap," said Syd. "Not down here."

"They don't have 'just one guy.' This is the best part." Egan smiled wide, his pale cheeks turning rosy with glee. "The trash pickers. The company's paying them to keep an eye out for intruders."

"Those kids?"

Egan nodded. He reached into his pocket and pulled out a whole stack of biopatches with the staff and snakes etched on them, the MediCleanse Corp logo. "Anti-itch patches," he said. "Those pickers are always scratching at some nasty skin thing. I got two dozen of these patches to fix them right up."

Syd took one from Egan and held it up to the light, looking through it at the lines and squiggles embedded in the material. It was some lux treatment. Putting one of these on your skin would rewrite your biodata to clear up any rashes, pimples, or mild irritations for weeks. You could swim in raw sewage with an open wound and come away sparkling clean if you put one of those patches on.

Except the patches Egan had were fake and not even great ones at that. The logo's color wasn't even right.

"You're going to bribe those kids with knock-off patches?" Syd shook his head.

"My guy tells me they still work," Egan said. "It's only the logo that's fake. They're still good. Brand names are for suckers, anyway."

Syd knew better than to believe Egan or Egan's "guy," whoever that was. "What happens when the kids figure out you traded them knock-offs?" Syd asked.

"We'll be long gone with the wire," said Egan. "And all your financial worries will be over."

Syd sighed. Not much of a plan, but he didn't have another one. Crime wasn't really his strong suit. He was a sidekick at best and only because, without him, Egan would probably have gotten himself killed by one of his "guys" by now.

Syd stayed around to protect his friend from himself as much for the proceeds from any score his friend proposed. Friends, even sketchy friends with harebrained schemes, were the most valuable thing in the world and not easy to come by in the Valve. Syd only had the one, after all."

And if Egan's scheme worked, Syd might just get himself out of debt. No more punishments on behalf of that Upper City brat. No more being a proxy to the worst patron in Mountain City. Maybe Syd would even have credit left over to go to the game center, play a few levels of something, run into some guys from school. Finch was there just about every night.

Syd could buy Finch a few minutes of play . . . maybe start up a conversation. He'd have to explain it to Egan somehow . . . why he was more interested in gaming with a goon like Finch than hanging out with whatever lux girls Egan had in mind.

Not that Egan would judge Syd for his preferences—it was a free market after all—just that Egan wouldn't understand. Not that Finch was a guy, but that Finch was a jerk.

It was a lot to explain. Syd preferred to keep his private thoughts private and he knew the moment he told Egan, he'd never have a moment of peace. Egan was always trying to get him a girl and once he knew what Syd really wanted, he wouldn't rest until he'd gotten Syd a date, no matter how mortifying that process was for Syd.

Better not to date at all.

Ever.

He'd spend his cut of their credit from the take another way. Riches came and went, but humiliation was nonrefundable.

He shook away the whole line of thought. Not worth worrying about the spoils of a crime before the crime was even committed. First the robbery, then the reward.

"Let's do this," said Syd.

Egan patted him on the back and stood up with the handful of patches. He whistled for the trash-picker kids, who all turned to him at once, eyes narrowing as they crept forward. Most of them held jagged pieces of glass or metal spikes or even a real forged blade or two for protection, and when Syd saw how many of them there were, his heart beat a little faster.

"I sure hope they don't spot those knock-offs while we're around," Syd whispered.

"If they do," Egan whispered back, "I have another plan."

"What's that?"

"Run fast."

Syd looked at his friend. "You really are a criminal genius."

Egan smirked. "Don't I know it."

[2]

LIAM HAD TO ADMIT, for a brutal man, the CEO of SecuriTech knew how to throw a party. For his son Knox's fifteenth birthday, Eeron Brindle had rented out Xelon Park and spared no expense in its transformation. The manicured lawns and engineered weeping willows became the lux backdrop for the elites of the Upper City to sip intoxicant-infused electrolytics and down customized EpiCure pills with flavor profiles no one had before experienced. Cocoa and Chili Beef, or Brandy-poached Nigerian Akara with rose petal and rhino stuffing.

How anyone knew what a rhino was meant to taste like, Liam couldn't imagine. They'd been extinct for centuries. The patrons' zoo didn't even have a rhino.

Maybe that was how the designers knew.

The music was tailored to every guest's personal data profiles and broadcast with targeted harmonics so everyone heard their own soundtrack at their preferred volume. At dramatic moments throughout the party, the music would sync across all the guests, based on a complicated algorithm SecuriTech had first developed to predict market fluctuations after Rebooter terrorist attacks.

Good thing they have the program, thought Liam. *Because they are about to have just such an attack.*

He crouched in the crook of a weeping willow, the lights

and holos below casting him in darkness. The party's decor itself blinded the revelers to the danger they were in.

Fitting, Liam thought. *Their excess will be their downfall.*

There were at least a dozen Guardians patrolling the perimeter of the park, as well as a few combat robots. The place was impenetrable, so it was good thing that Liam had entered the park days ago, knowing he'd never make it in on the day itself.

He'd been hiding out in the trees and in holes he'd dug beneath hedgerows. He ate ration pellets from his pockets, moved only at night, avoided the patrol bots, the Guardians, and even the work crews setting up the party.

Finally, it was the night when he would make his move. He'd come from Old Detroit to Mountain City on the most important mission of his young career.

He was going to kill Eeron Brindle, CEO of SecuriTech, and he was going to do it in front of all the top executives of the city.

The Senior Rebooters didn't believe Liam could do it, didn't believe it could be done, but Liam knew. He felt it. He had a role to play in history. Maybe even *the* role to play. Someone had to be the one . . . why not him?

"Youthful foolishness," Commander Pei had called it. But she did not forbid him. These sorts of lone wolf operations cost the Rebooters nothing. If Liam was captured, he knew well enough to kill himself before they could torture answers out of him, and if he was killed—either by the Guardians or at his own hand—Rebooter military operations were down one teenage soldier, nothing more. They had plenty of those to spare, even if none were as talented as Liam.

And if his mission succeeded? It would be a crushing blow to the system. It would send a message that no executive was safe from the wrath of the Rebooters, not even the CEO of SecuriTech.

A lone assassin killing a man like Eeron Brindle would

empower every would-be revolutionary in the Valve; every downtrodden, debt-ridden proxy would see that the patrons were not invulnerable. They were human and they could bleed. This assassination would be the signal that could spark a general uprising against the injustice of the corporations. The Jubilee, the day when all debt would be forgiven. Maybe he was the one who could do it; maybe this was the moment it could be done . . .

Liam took a deep breath, getting his grandiose thoughts under control. He couldn't celebrate victory before the foe was vanquished. A good assassin thinks only of the action at hand. Let the consequences sort themselves.

He flexed and unflexed the metal fingers of his artificial hand. He still felt the ache of the phantom fingers sometimes, but they weren't the only thing he'd lost that day. His parents had sacrificed themselves to facilitate his escape. They'd killed four Guardians before a combat bot took them out. Liam had seen it happen as he fled, just a boy, bleeding where his own mother had hacked off his hand at the wrist before the patch install could infiltrate his bloodstream. She'd looked him in the eyes when she'd done it, not even flinching.

"They will not turn you into one of them," she'd said. "Never."

Then she'd told him to run.

Bleeding, he'd obeyed. He'd run. And he never saw her again.

His missing hand wasn't the only wound that ached, but it was the only one that healed.

Vengeance, he thought, as he watched Eeron Brindle of Se-curiTech at his lux party below. *Vengeance is a kind of healing.*

Eeron Brindle laughed at some joke a bald-headed executive told. He pointed to a cluster of teenagers, the same age as Liam, who were whispering to one another on the periphery of the party. Liam recognized one from the holos that were projected all over. He had the same bright green eyes and square jaw as his father. That had to be the birthday boy, Knox Brindle, the CEO's son.

Liam felt a brief moment of hesitation. He had done his research. There was no mother around, just Knox and his father and endless wealth. Knox would never have known a pang of hunger or an ache of want. He had everything a boy could desire. His cheeks were flushed from pilfered drinks, his lips soft and pink as ripe berries. Liam couldn't peel his eyes away.

Knox was whispering to one of his friends, a girl with short hair, and bracelets of fashionable NeoBuddhist prayer beads around her wrists. She rolled her eyes at whatever he'd said and Knox gave her a wink. She shoved the boy, but it was obvious she'd enjoyed whatever he'd whispered. It was also obvious that he'd enjoyed the shove. Was she his girlfriend? Maybe. Maybe that was for the best. Knox would have a shoulder to cry on. He was about to witness the death of his father, after all. The boy had no idea that he was moments away from joining a brotherhood with Liam.

"We all end up orphans someday," Liam said to himself. "This is his day."

Liam shifted on his branch and pulled out the long electro-muscular-disruption stick he'd brought. It could be set at a variety of levels, from minor discomfort to a fatal, heart-stopping pulse that fried every nerve in the human body. It was the tool most commonly used on proxies when they were punished for their patrons' crimes. It would be a fitting way for Eeron Brindle to die.

Except at that moment, something went terribly wrong.

The trees stopped changing color. The holos vanished.

The teenagers spread out and Knox, the birthday boy, opened his arms wide, grinning an impish grin.

"Ladies and gentlemen," Knox shouted. Every executive looked in his direction. "Thank you for coming to my party tonight! I hardly know how to repay you for your generosity. The gifts you've brought honor me and I'm sure my father will remember that when it's time to pay out bonuses."

An uncomfortable murmur rippled through the crowd.

"Knox!" Eeron Brindle called out. A toothy smile did little to hide the sudden rage pasted onto his face. "What are you doing?"

The boy grinned widely at his father across the party. "I'm showing my appreciation for all these nice friends of yours," Knox said, doing little to hide the dripping sarcasm in his voice. Then he called out to all the puzzled guests. "If you'll direct your attention to the nearest holo projection, you'll see the thank-you gift I've gotten each of you."

Projections popped up all over the party, hovering in the air; one by one they appeared at eye level, shimmering and wavering, casting a bluish light on everything. All around, the guests cocked their heads and studied the sudden images.

Liam crouched back, trying to hide deeper in the shadow of his tree branch. He knew this was the moment to make his move, when everyone was distracted, but he stopped himself. He was curious to see what this rich kid had done.

Eeron Brindle studied one of the projections and Liam saw the man's face redden, his jaw ripple.

"Knox!" Eeron Brindle shouted, charging across the grass. He grabbed his son by the collar and dragged him to the edge of the park.

"What is it, Dad?" Knox smirked, calling out loudly as he was dragged away, taking an insouciant sip of an electrolytic cocktail he was too young to be drinking. "Your friends don't want to see the private SecuriTech files you've collected on each and every one of them?"

Liam gasped. The rich kid had just committed a bigger terrorist attack on SecuriTech than the Rebooters had ever dreamed, and it seemed he'd done it for a laugh.

[3]

KNOX'S FATHER PRESSED HIM up against the trunk of some kind of knotty tree and glared into his son's face. Knox felt a lump digging into his back as his father jabbed him in the shoulder with an aggressive finger, which made Knox spill the drink he was holding onto his shoes.

"Whoops." He giggled.

"Wipe that smirk off your face," his father snapped at him, then glanced at the holo floating right beside Knox—Knox's own secret file. "And shut these off, right this instant."

"Oh, come on!" Knox said. "Your friends can take a joke, can't they?"

It really was an ingenious bit of hacking he'd pulled off. Knox was rather proud of it. He'd entered the system through the musical target analysis program, accessing everyone's sonic taste profiles. There wasn't much security around those files, because no one imagined that the consequences of someone's musical preferences being hacked were terribly dire.

From those files, however, Knox could pinpoint the unique code that linked every person's biofeed to their datastream. The data was in their blood, after all, and the datastream tracked them with a set of unique codes that every transmitter could pick up. That way—the ads, the music, and the communications systems—everything could always find you. Those little bits of personal identification made the whole system work. Once Knox had that, he could cross that code with his father's private files—the password was, cruelly, his mother's name, after all—and *BOOM!* With those bits linked, Knox could share everything his father had collected on all his guests.

Knox didn't see it as leaking corporate secrets. He was leaking people's own information back to them, leaking what they already knew about themselves. Knox was leaking all over his father's fancy friends.

He had to chuckle at that turn of phrase. He couldn't believe no one else was laughing.

At the current moment, Dr. Elvarthi was reading about the affair he'd had with one of his lab technicians, and the president of Birla Nanotech was watching a holo of himself eating small handfuls of dirt he kept in a desk drawer in his office. All the kids his age were reading their parents' files, but then, they weren't laughing either. Simi looked so glum reading about his dads' plans for divorce, and Nine didn't seem to appreciate his parents' dwindling wealth being shared with everyone else's parents. But it was funny! Every one of them was a hypocrite in one way or another. Did no one but Knox have a sense of humor?

Knox's own file—every petty theft or clever bit of vandalism—was also shared, so that his father's friends didn't think him withholding or unjust.

Chey and Nine switched to the file of their school's headmaster, who had not been invited to the party, but whose file Knox thought might be of interest to all the gathered parents and students of the high-end institution. The fact that their headmaster had been fired from three *other* lux schools in the past three years was of great interest. At least his friends found *that* amusing. He gave them a smirk and wink, hoped it made up for embarrassing their parents. Simi shook his head. Knox often forgot that not everyone felt about their parents the way he felt about his father.

"You think you're being cute?" Knox's father snapped at him. "You are not only damaging your reputation *and mine*, you are hurting SecuriTech's shareholders right now. My business is secrecy and you are damaging that business. Shut it off this instant."

Knox set his jaw. Stared at his father. He wasn't smirking anymore, but he wasn't backing down. "It's no big deal. Just a bunch of gossip anyway."

"I have responsibilities to my investors, to the security of my clients, and to the safety of this city. You . . ." His father exhaled loudly. "You only think about yourself. Now, shut the system off or it won't just be your proxy feeling the sting of this punishment."

Knox crossed his arms.

"Three," his father said, like Knox was a little child. "Two . . . you don't want me to reach the last number."

Knox rolled his eyes and dropped his hands. "I was just joking around . . ." He brought up his own holo and moved around a few lines of code, deleted a few others, and tossed the whole glowing light show away. All over the park, the holos vanished. All eyes turned to look at Knox and Eeron Brindle.

"Apologies," his father announced to the party. "My son has a . . . unique sense of humor. I assure you, your data is perfectly safe with SecuriTech. If you'd like to make an appointment with my office for next week, I would be happy to address any concerns you may have." He looked back to Knox. "For now, I have to take my son inside and teach him a lesson about manners."

He grabbed Knox by the arm and led him from the park, past two Guardians standing sentry, and across the road into their sprawling home of concrete, glass, and steel. Once they were inside, his father practically tossed Knox onto the couch in the living room.

Knox stared blankly through the transparent wall beside him, which overlooked the park and the city below it. The park was dim now and the skyscrapers twinkled beyond it through the haze. Below them, far away, the lights of the Lower City slums burned a sickly green. Knox wondered if kids in a place like the Valve ever had to endure lectures from their selfish fathers like he did. Sometimes he envied those poor kids, who ran wild and free through the streets, no responsibility or expectations. No one to disappoint.

While his father glared down at him, seething, a Guardian came into the room.

"The guests are being shown to their transports," she explained. She was an older model Guardian, near retirement, but still stunning to look at, like they all were. The theory being it was easier to obey beauty and that power should be easy on the eyes.

And it was.

Knox's eyes flitted over the Guardian's tight-fitting jumpsuit, taking in the perfect curves of her body. The grace of her wrists, the small mark on the back of her hand where the data upgrades went. Uploads and downloads, her body constantly coded to perfection. The thought of it made him wonder what a Guardian would look like outside of her jumpsuit.

"Thank you," his father said to her. "And the proxy?"

"Is being retrieved presently," the Guardian answered.

"Good," said Knox's father. "Bring the holo up in here when it's ready and see that my guests get home safely. And please have Knox's friends escorted home. I am sure their parents would like their proxies summoned as well."

"Yes, sir," said the Guardian.

"But Simi, Chey and Nine didn't have anything to do

with—" Knox started to object but his father silenced him with one finger.

"They are not your concern right now, Knox," he said. "Right now you need to be concerned with yourself and the consequences of your actions."

"You mean *your* actions," Knox said, defiant as ever. "*You* invited all those people. *You* spied on them. They aren't my friends. All I did was tell them the truth about you."

"All you did was make a spectacle of yourself," his father replied. "I can repair the damage you caused to my company, but only *you* can repair the damage you've caused your reputation. I want you to think about that. When people talk about tonight, I assure you, they will not be talking about me. They will talk about what an ungrateful brat Knox Brindle is."

Knox snorted and looked away.

Knox's father seemed to deflate. His voice softened. "Knox, I just don't know what to do with you. I leave you alone, and you act out. I throw you a party, and you act out. I don't understand you at all."

"Why don't you just read my file then?" Knox replied.

His father's face twisted and Knox could see he'd hurt him, and he was glad for it. His mother never would have thrown that kind of party for Knox. She would have known him better. She would have known his friends better. She would have cared what Knox wanted.

He crossed his arms and didn't say another word. He looked out the window, until his father swiped his hand in the air and the plexi clouded, darkened, and turned opaque. He didn't turn away, just stared at the blank wall. He and his father waited in the air-conditioned hum of the living room while Knox's proxy was fetched for the punishment to begin.

[4]

THE TRASH-PICKER KIDS SLAPPED on their patches seconds after agreeing to the deal. Syd had wanted to delay their payment until after the heist, but they wouldn't accept that.

"Pay up front," one of the boys said. "Or we shout out right now that you're trying to rob the place."

"Sweet kids," Egan joked, but gave them their patches. Syd tried not to look nervous. The patches settled on their skin and lit up, just like they were supposed to. Some of the bigger bumps and welts around the patches did seem to vanish. The kids watched their own skin skeptically. "I told you it takes time to work," said Egan. "Now hold up your end of the bargain."

"Why should we?" one boy, who seemed to be the leader, said. "We got your patches already."

Egan's fist clenched, ready to fight, but Syd saw they were surrounded and outnumbered in the dark, and these scavenger types would carve them up and sell them to organ harvesters without a second thought.

Quickly, Syd waved his hand in the air and brought up a holo projection of his own datastream. It glowed bright in the lightless, empty garbage lot. Syd expanded it so that the kids could all see the complex shapes rotating in midair, the lines of code and equations. He jabbed his fingers into the projection, moving it around. The kids eyed him warily, clutching their jagged weapons in their grubby fists.

"If you don't hold up your end," said Syd, "then I'll rewrite the code in those patches to flay you alive."

"Flay?" the boy asked.

"It means burn your skin clean off you where you stand," Syd explained. He tapped some more lines of text into the holo. Some of the kids started to pick at their patches, trying to take them off again. The leader boy looked around, looked at the patch on his own arm.

Syd knew he had him, now he just had to give the boy a way to say yes without losing face in front of the other kids. "No reason you all can't keep your patches and heal just fine. All you have to do is honor your word and distract that guard until we can get away with what we came for. It's a good deal."

"I know it's a good deal," the boy snapped. "You don't need to tell me what's a good deal, swampcat."

Syd let the insult pass. The boy barely came up to his chest and Syd had a policy of ignoring insults from anyone who stood below the level of his chin. He swiped away the holo once more and gave the boy a nod.

"Excellent." Egan threw himself into the conversation, knocking fists with the big boy. "You're a wise man."

"I ain't a man," the boy responded. "I'm a girl."

Syd and Knox looked at each other and then back at the trash picker. She was covered in dirt and wore baggy, tattered clothes, but as they looked closer, they could see some small curves to her, well hidden beneath her outfit, her size, and her general surliness.

"Apologies, ma'am," said Egan, stifling a giggle.

Syd elbowed him in the ribs. He was *not* going to be killed because Egan was immature about gender roles.

The trash-picker kids went off to raise hell and distract the guard, while Syd and Egan crept around to the side door of the warehouse. The heavy smog that settled over the Valve blocked any moonlight, and Syd's dark skin made him practically invisible on the dark side of the building. Egan had to pull up his hoodie again to hide the bright white of his hair.

"Now if we could just cover up that bone-white face of yours, we'd be set," Syd joked.

Egan sneered and gave Syd another punch in the air, which this time, focused on the job, Syd didn't return.

"Hey, what was that with the kids back there?" whispered Egan. "I didn't know you could hack biodata patches."

"I can't," said Syd. "That was my calculus homework."

"Your . . ." Egan's mouth hung open.

"I figured those kids couldn't read."

Egan laughed. "You may be a virgin, my friend, but you have got one big swinging set of ba—"

"Shh," Syd snapped and pulled Egan down behind a pile of stinking refuse, just as a figure rounded the corner of the warehouse.

"The kids crossed us?" Egan clenched his fists.

Syd shook his head, peeked around the corner, and his blood froze in his veins.

There were two Guardians standing just a few yards away, a male and a female, each a perfectly engineered human specimen, as beautiful as they were dangerous. What could they possibly be doing all the way down here in the Valve at some run-down wire storage site?

"Sydney Carton," one of them announced in a voice that

carried easily across the entire lot without the aid of amplification. "On behalf of SecuriTech, per the terms of your proxy agreement with the Xelon Corporation, you are hereby requested to surrender yourself for Administrative Punishment."

Syd didn't move. *Administrative Punishment.*

A fancy way of saying his patron had done something stupid and Syd was about to be hurt for it in his place.

Egan sighed. "Unbelievable," he whispered. "I mean, the timing?"

"Come out now," one of the Guardians commanded. "Or you will be charged with violation of your contractual agreement, given one year of debt for every minute of delay, and your associate will be executed for Interference with Commerce."

"Associate?" Egan was puzzled, then realized they meant him. "Oh, man . . ."

Syd stood up. "I'm here. Relax." He held his hands up and walked slowly toward the Guardians. He glanced back at Egan as he went. "Sorry about the score, pal. Maybe next time."

Egan dropped the hood from his head, his white hair slicing the dark, and he pouted. He was out all those knock-off patches for nothing.

Syd turned to the Guardians, falling in step between them as they led him to a nearby container to be used as a temporary holding cell. It would give them enough privacy for their administrative punishment, and they wouldn't have to waste any more energy than necessary hauling Syd to a SecuriTech depot.

He knew the drill.

When they were done, he'd be dumped out on the street again, with an apology for the inconvenience. He'd taken so many punishments for his patron that he wasn't even afraid anymore. Every punishment he suffered because of his patron pushed Syd to work even harder to get himself out of debt for good. He was almost grateful. He knew it would hurt—it always hurt—but the pain reminded him he would one day be free.

"So, what'd he do *this* time?" Syd asked as they led him into the dimly lit cell.

[5]

THE GUARDIANS SLID INTO the park from all sides. The multicolored trees turned bright white, every leaf illuminated, and the nighttime park glowed like noon on a clear day.

"Ladies and gentlemen," one of the Guardians called out with a firm but polite tone. "Eeron Brindle thanks you for your understanding as he deals with personal matters and urges you to take a gift tote with you as you leave. If you could please make your way to the waiting transports. On behalf of SecuriTech and the entire Brindle family, we thank you for your attendance and apologize for the abrupt end to the festivities."

"Boys will be boys," a tipsy executive called out and few other guests laughed nervously.

Liam looked down from the branch as the Guardians fanned out, ushering the guests to the opposite side where their transports were lined up to take them home. With the trees all turned into white lights, his shadow would be completely visible to anyone who bothered to look up. The brightness would blind them for a moment, but his silhouette would stand out as if he'd been stenciled against the sky.

He tried to stay completely still. People's eyes are drawn to movement, and as long as all the movement was on the ground, no one had any reason to look up. Not even the Guardians. They were genetically engineered, biohacked, and programmed since childhood, but still, in the end, they could be deceived like anyone else.

He clenched the metal fingers of his right fist, touched the back of the hand with his good fingers.

And, if it came to it, like anyone else, they could be killed.

Liam pivoted slowly around the branch, so that he could keep as much of the tree between himself and those below him as possible. He only moved when they moved. He could no longer see through the mirrored plexi windows of the mansion on the other side of the park, but he knew his target had retreated inside with his bratty son and now they would be fetching the boy's proxy. That's how these things went.

Liam didn't know what the punishment for Knox's prank tonight would be or how long it would take to administer. Liam had never been a proxy. Thanks to his parents, he wasn't in the system and didn't even have a biofeed in his blood. That made him invisible to the sensors and the scanners and the transmitters. There were no records of his buying history or personal tastes. No medical histories or tracking software. No credit and no debt. He was a data hole, which made him an ideal assassin.

The problem was, he'd waited too long, hesitated when he should have acted, and now he felt his entire mission slipping away from him. Inside the house, with its reinforced windows and complex security systems, Eeron Brindle was untouchable.

Thanks to Knox's foolishness, Liam had no chance at his target.

He fingered the small orb in his pocket, using the good fingers of his left hand. He felt the coolness of the device on his flesh, imagined the heat contained within.

A detonator.

He could light the air on fire with it, send a blast of hell out twenty feet in every direction.

Did he rush the house and try to take out the Brindle father and son in one flash of brutal glory? Did he dare a suicide mission?

Let it go, he told himself. *Live to fight another day.* He had no desire to die.

His stomach sank. Liam wanted to live to see the new world that would be born when the old system fell. He wanted to see the Jubilee, the day when all debts were forgiven.

That was when he knew he wasn't the one.

He knew it then the way he imagined a person falls in love, a sudden knowing of what you've always known. Were Liam actually Yovel, the one who could bring about the Jubilee, the one whose destiny it was to erase all the wealth and debt and injustice, he'd have charged right into the lux party and blown them all to bits without a moment's hesitation or a moment's doubt.

But he'd hesitated already. He'd had doubts.

He was no savior. He was no hero. He was just Liam, a teenage assassin in the service of the Rebooters, doing what he could until the Jubilee.

After the flash of disappointment passed, he realized it felt amazingly good to give up on the fantasy that he had some vital role to play in history. He didn't have that burden to bear. He had only to do his job. He had to be a good assassin.

And a good assassin adapts.

Liam accepted that his original mission was impossible. Now he had to adapt his mission: Get past a dozen Guardians and out of this park without getting killed. Survive.

The party crowd had thinned. There were now about three

guests left for every one Guardian inside the park. There were about four more Guardians at the far perimeter, and two patrolling combat bots. The bots had infrared sensors and mounted fracture cannons. Even if he made it past the Guardians, he'd never make it past the bots.

The Guardians were programmed, however, in the event of a threat, to protect the wealthy charges in their care. He could use that against them, as long as he used it now.

No more hesitation.

No more stealth either.

He tucked his EMD stick into his belt and slid down the trunk of the tree, hitting the ground with a roll and popping to his feet. He thrust his hand into his pocket and activated the detonator. He counted one, two, three.

"You!" a Guardian called out, seeing him. Her electro-muscular-disruption stick rose up, threatening. She had, no doubt, already scanned the datastream for his identity and found nothing. That would explain her hesitation to fire. If he'd been an identifiable trespasser, he'd already be dead. "Don't move."

Liam smiled. He held up his metal hand and wiggled the metal fingers. The Guardians all looked the same, and a chill ran along his spine. In the memory of the day he'd lost that hand, the Guardian had looked just like this one. Except his parents had killed that one before they were killed. Then there were more just like her. His parents couldn't kill them all.

Maybe he could.

With his other hand, Liam flung the detonator straight for her and dove behind the tree.

With a flash of light, a whoosh of air, and a sudden blast of heat, the park caught fire. The conflagration struck two of the weeping willows, which flared up like torches. Patrons screamed, running for their transports. Guardians hustled them forward, using their own bodies to shield the privileged few from the rain of white-hot ash.

Liam was already on his feet, running for the road.

He felt a tingle in his wrist, a twitching up his elbow.

He glanced back. One Guardian was after him and had fired her EMD stick at him. The pulse lost power being fired from a distance. It was much better to make direct contact, stick to skin, but she'd hit him just the same, and his running felt sloppy. Pain danced behind his eyeballs as his nerves went haywire. He did his best to control his feet, his arms, and his bowels all at the same time. She'd set it only to stun. Perhaps they wanted to interrogate him.

Not a chance.

He pulled out his own EMD stick, charged it while he ran, and dove straight toward the first combat bot he saw.

He didn't know a lot about technology, but jabbing his weapon straight into the thing's leg joint as it discharged its pulse had the desired effect.

The bot exploded six seconds later, just as three Guardians ran by it.

Liam stood up from the pavement he didn't remember hitting. His face was cut, his shirt shredded, and his good hand bloodied. He felt like he'd broken at least two good fingers, and at least two ribs. But he was in better shape than his pursuers. Their ashes were the same color as their jumpsuits, lifeless gray.

He was running again, racing down a steep hill toward the putrid, twisting alleyways of the Valve, for the safe house where he could lay low and let the Rebooter cadres in the city smuggle him out. He had his contact, knew the password. He could let an adult take over for a bit. He'd done enough for one night.

The revolution of the Rebooters could claim credit for an action. Xelon Park was trashed, a few Guardians were dead, and Liam had ruined a perfectly good party. Well, Knox had ruined it, but Liam had no problem taking the credit. Couldn't let the handsome rich boy have all the fun.

He took one last look at the shining mansions on the hill, lit now by the burning trees in the park.

The Brindle family's time would come. The patrons couldn't cling to power forever. Even if Liam wouldn't be the one to do it, he knew someone would come and wipe away their corruption. He was simply glad to play his part.

"Enjoy it while it lasts," he said aloud, and disappeared into the lower city.

[6]

THE HOLO APPEARED IN front of the wall opposite the sofa. It showed a dim room with metal walls pressing in impossibly close on the three figures inside.

There were the Guardians, shimmering in their gray uniforms, perfect features seeming brighter than the projection itself, and then there was the dull brown skin of the proxy, who stood in profile, his arms raised up over his head where they were suspended in restraints. His shirt had been removed, revealing a brown back straight as iron, nicked with scars. Behind his ear he had an odd birthmark that always made Knox wonder why he hadn't had it removed. They had patches that could clear up those sorts of blemishes and remove those scars. He could even have lightened his skin, if he wanted. It's not like the boy lacked for credit. He could borrow and borrow and borrow. Knox's father would keep paying for that proxy contract forever.

He'd have to. What an embarrassment it would be for the CEO of SecuriTech's own son not to have a proxy. What would people say?

The proxy was breathing deeply where he stood, but even as his chest rose and fell, his face stayed firmly fixed on the wall in front of him, his jaw slammed shut and his eyes locked forward, bracing himself against the pain he had no way to prevent.

For a moment Knox wondered why the boy wouldn't look into the holo directly, but he reminded himself that the proxy didn't know where the transmitters were, nor even who was watching him. Patron Confidentiality was essential to the system. The patron needed to see the suffering his actions caused to others, but the proxy needn't know anything about the patron. There'd be no purpose to the proxy knowing much of anything. It was a simple law of nature, taught in every social science class at Knox's school: Information breeds resentment among debtors, while it fosters responsibility among creditors. Put another way, what Knox's proxy didn't know couldn't hurt him.

The boy stood there like a burnt statue. Knox's father looked between the holo and the sofa, where Knox did his best to look bored. He didn't want to give his father the satisfaction of seeing Knox upset by this "lesson." He didn't even really listen as the Guardian laid out the charges against Knox and the penalty that his proxy would pay.

He studied his fingernails while the proxy was given the option to pay off his debt and free himself from the contract that bound him to Knox. It always went this way and his proxy never had any way of paying off his debt. None of the proxies ever did, but the offer made the whole system fair. They all had the right to be free of their debt. No one was forcing them to borrow more than they could repay, right?

"Pay attention," Knox's father snapped at him. "This is your doing and you will see what you have done."

Knox looked up and watched through narrowed eyes as the Guardian raised her silver EMD stick to his proxy's side. The dark-skinned boy bit down on his lip and twitched as the pulse shot through his body. He quivered, but did not fall.

"One," the Guardian said.

Knox watched as the stick touched the boy's side again. This time his whole body jolted; he flailed on the end of his arms, like plastic caught on a fence, flapping in a breeze. Two more jolts came in quick succession. The boy drooled a little and his head slumped. The fifth jolt snapped him upright again, and when his arms and legs stopped twitching, he fixed his eyes on the wall once more, his face as blank as when they'd started. Not even a hint of emotion.

The Guardian stepped up to wipe the spittle from his mouth with a small cloth and the proxy spit in her face. She didn't react, but Knox did, letting out an involuntary laugh. Guess there was some emotion in there after all.

His father's expression wiped the grin off Knox's face. He glared down at his son as the holo went dark again, and the blank wall blazed white where the tiny cell had been a moment before.

His father didn't say a word. Fifteen years of disappointment stuffed into the silence until it was filled to bursting.

"May I be excused now?" Knox said.

His father exhaled loudly through his nose.

"Please, *sir*?" Knox added with exaggerated servility.

"When will you grow up?" his father said. "When will you learn to think of anyone but yourself?"

Knox stood. He turned his back on his father and walked to the stairs. "As soon as you do," he called back on his way up the stairs.

He'd already sent a sly message to Nine, to find out what happened after he left his party and if any of the girls were asking about him.

His friend didn't write back and he heard his father take an urgent call and rush from the house, activating the security system behind him.

Knox laughed to himself. If he wanted to, he could break out of there in less than five minutes, and the night was still young, after all. But as he stood in the hall, halfway to his room, he froze where he stood. He couldn't think of a single place to go.

[7]

THEY LEFT SYD OUTSIDE the metal container, holding his shirt in his hands. The night was humid and his sweat beaded on his skin. He knew he smelled pretty rank. He wiped under his arms with the balled-up shirt and didn't bother putting it back on. He knew he wouldn't be able to lift his arms over his head for at least an hour, and clutching the ball of fabric kept his hand from shaking too obviously. The pain had passed but his nerves were still prickling, like he was balanced on a beam atop a skyscraper, hanging on to the air itself to keep from falling.

"Some knockoff, glitch-brained Chapter Eleven punk of a patron you've got, huh?" Egan's voice called out from the shadow of the container. He'd been squatting in the dirt waiting for Syd all this time. Syd gave a weak smile, took a stumbling step.

In a flash, Egan was at Syd's side, holding him up under the shoulder.

"I got you, pal," Egan said. "Come on."

He helped lead Syd away from the metal container, through a broken alley and in a wide arc back to the far side of the trash pickers' lot.

"Why are we back here?" Syd asked when Egan helped him sit.

"You think I'm just going to let a score like this go?" Egan scoffed. "Never! No Chapter Eleven patron is gonna take this score away from me."

"Would you just stop with the Chapter Eleven stuff?" Syd sighed.

Chapter 11, one of Egan's favorite expressions. It meant a bankrupt, someone with no credit, but also someone who liked a matching pair, like the 1 and 1 . . . a girl who preferred girls, a guy who preferred guys.

"What?" Egan laughed. "You want to defend that Upper City knockoff? He's nothing but misery for you."

"I don't care about him," Syd answered. "Just leave off the Chapter Eleven, okay?"

Egan opened his mouth to crack a joke, then, narrow his eyes, looked at Syd more closely. "Oh," he said. "Oh."

"Yeah," said Syd.

Egan shrugged. "All the same to me, Syd." He looked back at the warehouse. "As long as you can watch my back without, you know . . . *watching* my back."

He burst out laughing and Syd punched him in the arm.

"In your dreams," said Syd.

"The only thing in my dreams is inside that warehouse," Egan said. "Now, you ready for the heist of the century?"

"I would be," said Syd. "If that's what you'd planned, but . . ." Syd jerked his head toward the warehouse door. The trash-picker kids were helping load giant spools of wire into a transport truck to haul it out of the Valve. Even in the dark, Syd could see one of them peel the patch off his arm, wave it in the air, and make a rude gesture in their direction.

"Oh man . . ." Egan sighed.

"Guess we'll get 'em next time, huh?" Syd suggested.

Egan muttered curses to himself, but put his arm around Syd again, to help him make his way back toward the alley where he lived in the back of Mr. Baram's shop. Syd let his friend vent without interrupting him. He was too worn out to talk and Egan was too upset to listen, anyway.

When they arrived, the shop was shuttered, which wasn't unusual for this time of night, but the back door that Syd used to get to his bunk was also locked and his key wouldn't open it. He knocked, but got no answer.

"I'm locked out," he told Egan.

"Hold on," said Egan, helping Syd lean on the wall for support. Then he crouched over the lock, fumbling for a minute while Syd stared at his back and tried to keep from passing out. Those EMD blasts had taken more out of him than he'd thought. Not even sixteen and he already knew he was too old for this.

A tweaked-out syntholene addict came staggering out of a nearby flophouse and walked with the jerky steps of someone whose DNA was coming apart, his eyes changing colors, his hair growing and falling out and growing back. He made a gargling sound as he staggered by, and then leaned against a wall three doors down to nod off, oblivious to the world.

"No lock in this city can stop me," Egan declared, standing up with a flourish. He pushed the door open with two fingers.

"You better keep that to yourself," Syd said. "If Baram knows you can pick his lock, he'll have your fingers broken. It's easier than changing the locks."

"That old coot? What's he got against me?"

"Well," said Syd. "You picked his lock, for one thing."

Egan didn't argue with that.

"Good night, E," said Syd. "I'm really sorry about your heist."

"It's your patron's fault," Egan grunted. "If it weren't for him, we'd be rich right now. I swear, if I ever meet that kid, I am going to teach him a lesson he will never, ever forget."

"Haven't you figured it out by now?" Syd shook his head. "There's no teaching these people lessons. Best we can do is survive them."

"We can do so much better," Egan objected. "We're Syd and Egan! We can do anything we want!"

"I'll believe it when I see it," Syd replied.

"Patience, my Chapter Eleven friend." Egan laughed. "Stick with your pal Egan and you'll see that anything is possible. Anything at all."

"Right."

"I'm gonna get you a date," Egan declared proudly, turning on his heels and whistling through the grimy alley, practically skipping past the syntholene tweaker.

Syd sighed and closed the door. His workshop at the back of the shop was cool and quiet. His mattress had been neatly made—probably by Baram himself—and all his tools were exactly where he'd left them.

His skin still tingled, like roaches crawling over his muscles, moving his arm hairs from below. He was shuffling toward his bed when he heard a noise from the front of the shop. He went to check it out, then paused, wondering about the locked doors. There were no signs of a robbery, but Baram ran all kinds of strange businesses in here with all kinds of strange characters. Maybe he would not want to be interrupted.

Syd flipped on a projector by the door that led to the front of the shop and he saw a holo of Mr. Baram in the dim light, talking to someone at the front door, which was now open. It hadn't been open a moment ago. Syd thought he caught a glimpse of metal, a flash of pale skin, but he couldn't tell. The light was dim, and the figure was already gone. Baram followed him out, locking up the front behind him. Syd was alone again.

He climbed into bed and stared at the ceiling, trying to ignore the ringing in his ears and the itch of his skin. He had school tomorrow. He needed to rest and do his best. No big scheme of Egan's was going to get him out of debt. He was going to have to do it himself, one school day at a time.

He took a breath in and let it out slowly, wondering what Baram was up to, who he'd been talking to, then reminding himself to mind his own business. Everyone is entitled to his own secrets.

Although, Syd thought, *letting them out once in a while felt pretty good*. Maybe Egan really would get him a date and maybe Egan really wouldn't humiliate him in the process. Who knew?

As he drifted off to sleep, Syd smiled. Like Egan said, anything was possible. Anything at all.